THE MODERN LIBRARY

OF THE WORLD'S BEST BOOKS

THE FLAME OF LIFE

The Publishers will be glad to mail a complete list of titles in the Modern Library. The list is representative of the Great Moderns and is one of the most important contributions to publishing that has been made for many years. Every reader of books will find titles he needs at a low price and in an attractive form.

THE
FLAME OF LIFE

By GABRIELE D'ANNUNZIO

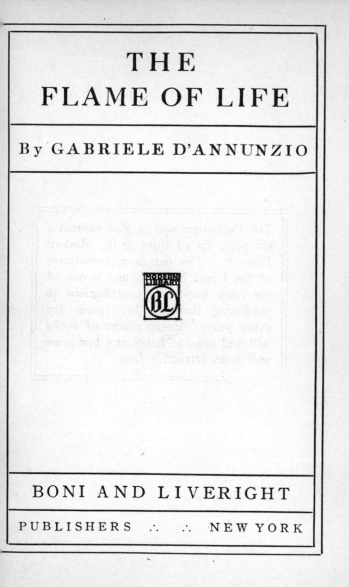

BONI AND LIVERIGHT

PUBLISHERS ∴ ∴ NEW YORK

Fifth Impression, April, 1909
Sixth Impression, September, 1911
Seventh Impression, January, 1914
Eighth Impression, November, 1916
Ninth Impression, May, 1919

THE COLONIAL PRESS
C. H. SIMONDS CO., BOSTON, U. S. A.

TO TIME and TO HOPE

Without Hope it is impossible to find the unhoped for.—*Heraclitus of Ephesus.*

He who sings to the god a song of Hope shall see his wish accomplished. — *Æschylus of Eleusis.*

Time is the Father of Miracles. — *Hariri of Basra.*

CONTENTS

I

THE EPIPHANY OF THE FLAME

The Flame of Life

I

THE EPIPHANY OF THE FLAME

"STELIO, does not your heart fail you for the first time?" La Foscarina asked with a slight smile, touching the hand of the silent friend sitting beside her. "I see you are a little pale, and you seem preoccupied. Yet this is a beautiful night for the triumph of a great poet!"

She gathered into one deeply conscious glance all the beauty scattered so divinely through that last hour of the September twilight. In the dark, living firmament of her eyes the neighbouring garlands of light, created by the oar as it dipped in the water, seemed to encircle the fiery angels that shone from afar on the towers of San Marco and of San Giorgio Maggiore.

"As ever," she added in her sweetest voice, — "as ever, all things are favourable to you. On an evening like this what soul could remain closed to the dreams that it shall please your words to bring forth? Do not you feel already that the crowd is eager to welcome your revelation?"

Thus, delicately, she soothed her friend, wrapping him round with continual praise, exalting him with continual hope.

"No more unusual and no more magnificent festival could have been imagined for the purpose of enticing from his ivory tower a disdainful poet such as you are. This joy, of entering for the first time into communion with a multitude in a sovereign place such as the Hall of the Greater Council, was reserved for you alone. You will speak from the throne whence once the Doges addressed the assembled patricians; their background the *Paradiso* of Tintoretto, and over their heads the *Gloria* of Paolo Veronese."

Stelio Effrena looked her deep in the eyes.

"Do you wish to intoxicate me?" he said, with sudden gaiety. "This that you are offering me is the cup you would place before one going to the scaffold. Well, then, yes, my friend, I confess that my heart does shrink a little."

A sound of applause burst from the Passage of San Gregorio, echoing along the Grand Canal, re-echoing in the precious discs of porphyry and serpentine adorning the house of the Darios, that stooped under their weight like a decrepit courtesan under the pomp of her jewels.

The royal barge was passing.

"Here is the one among your listeners whom the ceremony bids you crown with some flower of your speech in the preamble," said the woman, alluding to the Queen. "In one of your first books, I believe, you confess your taste and your respect for ceremonials. One of your most extraordinary feats of imagination is that which has for its motive the description of a day of Charles II. of Spain."

The two occupants of the gondola saluted the barge as it passed them. The Queen, blonde, rosy, illu-

mined by the freshness of the inexhaustible smile that
was for ever rippling among the pale meshes of her
Buranese laces, looked back, moved by an impulse of
spontaneous curiosity, as she recognized the poet of
Persephone and the great tragic actress.   By her side
was Andriana Duodo, the patroness of Burano, the
industrious little island where she cultivated a dainty
garden of thread for the marvellous renewing of
antique flowers.

"Don't you think, Stelio, that those two women
have twin smiles?" La Foscarina said, watching the
water gurgle in the furrow left by the receding gondola, where the reflection of that double glamour
seemed to prolong itself.

"The Countess is a magnificent and ingenious
spirit, one of those rare Venetian souls that have remained strongly coloured like their ancient canvases," said Stelio, with grateful remembrance.   "I
have a deep devotion for her sensitive hands.   They
are hands that tremble with joy when they touch beautiful lace or velvet, and linger there with a grace that
seems half shy of being so languid.   One day, as I
was taking her through the halls of the Academia,
she stopped before the *Massacre of the Innocents*,
by the first Bonifazio (you certainly remember the
green of the prostrate woman that the soldier of
Herod is about to strike: it is a note you cannot
forget).   She remained standing there a long time,
the joy of full and perfect sensation diffused all over
her.   Then she said, 'Take me away, Effrena, I must
leave my eyes behind on that dress, I want to see
nothing else.'   Ah, dear friend, don't smile, she
was simple and sincere in saying this.   She had in all

truth left her eyes behind on that fragment of canvas which art, with a little colour, has made the centre of an indefinitely joyous mystery. In all truth, it was a blind woman that I was leading. And I was all reverence for that privileged soul, in which the spell of colour had had the power to abolish for a time every vestige of its ordinary life and to stop all other communications from the outside. What would you call this? A filling up of the chalice to the brim, it seems to me. This, for instance, is what I would do to-night, if I were not discouraged."

A fresh clamour, louder and longer, rose from between the two watchful columns of granite, as the barge came to shore by the crowded Piazzetta. A confused roar, like the imaginary rushing that animates the spirals of some sea-shells, filled the open spaces of the ducal balconies at the surging of the dense, dark multitude. Then, suddenly, the shout rose higher in the limpid air, breaking up against the slim forest of the marbles, vaulting over the brow of the taller statues, shooting beyond the pinnacles and the crosses, dispersing in the far distances of twilight. The manifold harmonies of the sacred and pagan architectures all over which the Ionic modulations of the Biblioteca ran like an agile melody, continued unbroken in the pause which again followed, and the summit of the naked tower rose like a mystic cry. And that silent music of motionless lines was so powerful, in its contrast with the spectacle of an anxious multitude, that it created almost visibly the phantom of some richer and more beautiful life. That multitude, too, seemed to feel the divinity of the hour, and in the greeting it sent up to the modern symbol of royalty stepping on its ancient landing-place, the fair Queen beaming with her inextinguishable smile, perhaps it exhaled its obscure aspiration to transcend the narrowness of its daily life and to reap the harvest of eternal poetry growing over its stones and its waters. In those men, oppressed by the tedium and labour of their long mediocrity, the strong covetous souls of their forefathers, who had applauded so many returning conquerors of the sea, seemed to be waking up confusedly, and as they woke they seemed to remember the rush of the air, stirred by the hissing, implacable banners of old that had shamed enemies without number as they dropped to rest, refolding like the great wings of victory.

"Do you know, Perdita," suddenly asked Stelio, — "do you know of any other place in the world like Venice, in its power of stimulating at certain moments all the powers of human life, and of exciting every desire to the point of fever? Do you know of any more terrible temptress?"

The woman he called Perdita did not answer, her head bent as if in greater concentration, but in all her nerves she felt that indefinable quiver that the voice of her friend always called up when it unexpectedly revealed the vehement and passionate soul to which she was drawn by limitless love and terror.

"Peace! oblivion! Do you ever find them down there, at the end of your deserted canal, when you return home parched and exhausted from having breathed the atmosphere of the theatre — of the theatre that any gesture of yours lashes to frenzied enthusiasm? For my part, I can never find myself on these dead waters without feeling that my life is being multiplied at a bewildering speed, and at times my thoughts seem to take fire as if delirium were imminent."

"The flame and the strength are in yourself, Stelio," said the woman, without raising her eyes, almost humbly.

He was silent, intent. Images and impetuous music were being generated within him, as if by the magic of some instantaneous fertilisation. And the unexpected flood of that abundance was filling his spirit with joy.

It was still the hour that in one of his books he had called "Titian's hour," because in it all things seemed, like that painter's nude creations, to shine with a rich glow of their own, and almost to illumine the sky rather than receive light from it. The strange, sumptuous octagonal temple drawn by Baldassare Longhena from the dream of Polifilo was now emerging from its blue green shadow with its cupola, its scrolls, its statues, its columns, its balustrades, like a temple dedicated to Neptune, constructed after the pattern of tortuous marine shapes, and shading off into a haze of mother of pearl. In the hollows of the stone the wet sea-salt had deposited something fresh and silvery and jewel-like, that vaguely suggested pearl shells lying open in their native waters.

"Perdita," said the Poet, a kind of intellectual joy running through him, as he saw the things which his imagination called to life multiplying themselves everywhere, " does it not strike you that we seem to be following the princely retinue of dead Summer?

There she lies, sleeping in her funeral boat, all dressed in gold like the wife of a Doge, like a Loredana, or a Morosina, or a Soranza, of the enlightened centuries. And the procession is taking her to the Island of Murano, where some masterly Lord of Fire will make her a crystal coffin. And the walls of the coffin shall be of opal, so that when once submerged in the Laguna, she may at least see the languid play of the sea-weed through her transparent eyelids, and while awaiting the hour of resurrection give herself the illusion of having still about her person the constant undulation of her voluptuous hair."

A smile poured over La Foscarina's face, springing from eyes that might have well seen the beautiful figure. Indeed that sudden allegory in both its form and rhythm truthfully expressed the feeling that was permeating all things. As the milky blue of the opal is filled with hidden fire, so the pale monotonous water of the harbour held dissimulated splendours that were brought to light by each shock of the oars. Beyond the straight forest of ships motionless on their anchors San Giorgio stood out like a vast rosy galley, its prow turned to the *Fortuna* that attracted it from the height of its golden sphere. A placid estuary opened out in the centre of the Giudecca. The laden boats that came down the rivers flowing into it brought with their weight of splintered trunks what seemed the very spirit of the woods that bend over the running waters of their far-away sources.

And from the *Molo*, from the twofold miracle of the porticoes open to the popular applause, where the red and white wall rose as if to enclose that dominant will, the Riva unfolded its gentle arch towards the

shady gardens and the fertile islands, as if to lead
away the thoughts excited by the arduous symbols
of art to the restfulness of nature. And almost as
if still further to complete the avocation of Autumn
there passed a string of boats laden with fruit, like
great floating baskets that spread over the waters
reflecting the perpetual foliage of the cusps and
capitols, the fragrance of the island fruit gardens.

"Do you know, Perdita," began Stelio, gazing with
visible pleasure at the golden bunches and the purple
figs not inharmoniously heaped in those boats from
poop to prow; "do you know a detail of ducal
chronicles which is quite charming? The wife of the
Doge, to defray the expenses of her state dress,
was given certain rights over the duty on fruit.
Does not this amuse you, Perdita? The fruit of the
islands clothing her in gold and girding her round
with pearls, Pomona giving Arachne her due; an
allegory that Veronese might well have painted for
the ceiling of the *Vestiario*. Whenever I picture to
myself the stately lady standing on her high slippers
with the gemmed heels, I like to think that something
fresh and rural clings to her between the folds of
heavy cloth, the tribute of the fruit. How many new
savours seem thus added to her magnificence. Well,
dear friend, let us now imagine that these figs and
grapes of the new Autumn are to yield the price of
the golden dress in which dead Summer is wrapped."

"What delightful fancies, Stelio!" said La Foscarina, youthfulness springing up in her for a moment,
so that she smiled in the surprised manner of a child
before a picture-book. "Who was it that one day
called you the Image-maker?"

"Ah! those images!" exclaimed the poet, penetrated. "In Venice, in the same way that one cannot feel except in music, one cannot think if not in images. They come to us from all quarters, in countless numbers, in endless variety, and they are more real, more living, than the people that elbow us in the narrow streets. They let us bend down to scrutinize the depths of their lingering eyes, and we can divine the words they are going to say by the curves of their eloquent lips. Some are tyrannical, like imperious mistresses, and hold us long under the yoke of their power. Others come to us wrapped in veils, like virgins; or tightly swaddled, like infants; and only he who can tear away those husks will raise them to perfect life. When I awoke this morning, my soul was already full of them; it was like a great tree with a load of chrysalides."

He stopped and laughed.

"If they all break open to-night," he added, "I am saved. If they remain closed, I am lost."

"Lost?" said La Foscarina, looking at him in the face with eyes so full of confidence that his gratitude to her became immense. "You cannot lose yourself, Stelio. You are always safe, you carry your fate in your own hands. I think your mother can never have feared for you, even in the worst of moments. Is it not true? It is only the excess of your pride that causes your heart to falter."

"Ah, dear friend, how I love you for this, and how grateful I am to you!" Stelio confessed candidly, taking her hand. "You are constantly feeding my pride in myself and letting me half believe that I have already acquired those virtues to which I continually aspire. Sometimes you seem to have the power of conferring I know not what divine quality to the things that are born of my soul, and of placing them at such a distance that they appear adorable in my own eyes. You put in me the religious wonder of the sculptor, who, having taken his idols to the temple at fall of day, still warm from his touch, and I would almost say still clinging to the moulding fingers that shaped them, finds them next morning raised on pedestals and wrapped in a cloud of incense, breathing divinity from every pore of the deaf and dumb matter in which his perishable hands had fashioned them. You never enter my soul without accomplishing a like deed of exaltation, and because of this, every time that my good fortune allows me to be near you, you become necessary to my life. And nevertheless, during our too long separations, I can live on, and so can you, both knowing to what splendours the perfect union of our lives might give birth. Thus while I fully know all you bring me, and further, all you *could* bring, I consider you as lost to me, and I call you by that name I have given you because I want to express this boundless consciousness and infinite regret — "

He interrupted himself, feeling the hand he still held tremble in his own.

"When I call you Perdita," he added in a lower voice, after a pause, " I feel that you ought to see my desire advancing towards you with a deadly weapon thrust in its heaving side. Even if it succeed in touching you, the chill of death will have already reached the points of its rapacious fingers."

A suffering that she knew too well flooded her as

she listened to the beautiful, the perfect words flow-ing from her friend's lips with a readiness that proved their sincerity. It was once again a fear and anxiety that she herself did not know how to define. She seemed to lose the sense of her personal being and to find herself thrown into a kind of fictitious life both intense and hallucinating, that made even breathing difficult. Once drawn into that atmosphere, as fiery as the encircling neighbourhood of a forge, she felt her-self capable of suffering all the transfigurations that it should please the Life-Giver to work in her for the satisfaction of his own constant desire of poetry and of beauty. She felt that in his poetic spirit her own image was not of far different nature to the image, so evident as to be nearly tangible of the dead Sum-mer wrapped in her opalescent shroud. And an almost childish desire assailed her, of seeking in his eyes, as in a mirror, the reflection of her true likeness.

What made her suffering heavier was the fact that she could trace a vague resemblance between this agitated feeling and the anxiety that always possessed her at the moment of entering into a stage fiction in order to incarnate some sublime creation of Art. Was he not drawing her on to live in a similar higher zone of life, and, that she might figure there oblivious of her everyday personality, was he not covering her with a splendid mask? But, while to her it was only given to prolong such a state of intensity by a su-preme effort, she knew that he moved in it, as easily as if it were his natural mode of being, ceaselessly enjoying the miraculous world of his own that he renewed by an act of continual creation.

He had brought about in himself the intimate marriage of art with life, and he thus found in the depths of his own substance a spring of perennial harmonies. His spirit had found the means of uninterruptedly maintaining itself in that mysterious condition which gives birth to the work of beauty and of thus suddenly transforming into ideal species the passing figures of his varied existence. It was precisely to this conquest of his that he alluded when he put the following words in the mouth of one of his personages: "I stood by and watched within myself the continual genesis of a finer life wherein all appearances were transfigured as in a magic mirror." He was gifted with an extraordinary facility of language that enabled him to instantly translate into words even his most complex modes of feeling with a precision so detached and vivid that they seemed at times to belong to him no longer, to have been made objective by the isolating power of style. His limpid and penetrating voice, that seemed to draw a clear outline round the musical figure of each word, still further enhanced this singular quality of his speech; so much so that an ambiguous feeling made of admiration and aversion crept over those who heard him for the first time, because of his manifesting himself in a form so sharply defined that it seemed to be a result of his constant determination to establish between himself and those who were to remain strangers to him a deep and impassable difference. His sensibility, however, equalling his intellect, it was easy for those who came near to him and who loved him to catch the glow of his vehement and passionate soul through the crystal of his words.

These knew how wide were his powers of feeling and of dreaming, and from what combustion he drew the beautiful images into which he was wont to convert the substance of his inner life.

She whom he called Perdita knew it well. As the pious one awaits from her God the supernatural help that is going to work her salvation, she seemed waiting for his guidance to place her at last in the necessary state of grace. Then perhaps she might elevate and maintain herself in that fire to which she was impelled by her mad desire of burning and melting away. The loss of even the last vestige of her youth made her desperate. She was terrified of finding herself alone in a gray desert.

"Now it is you, Stelio," she said, with her slight concealing smile, gently taking her hand away from her friend, — "now it is you who wish to intoxicate me. Look," she exclaimed, to break the spell, pointing to a laden boat that was coming slowly towards them, — "look at your pomegranates."

But her voice was unsteady.

Then in the evening dream they watched the boat pass on the delicate water that was green and silvery like the new leaves of the river-willow, the boat overflowing with the emblematic pomegranates. They suggested the idea of things rich and hidden, they seemed caskets of red leather bearing the crown of the kingly giver, some tightly closed, some half-open over their agglomeration of gems.

In a hushed voice the woman murmured the words Hades addresses to Persephone when in the sacred drama the daughter of Demeter tastes the fatal pomegranate:

" When thou shalt pluck the Colchian herb in flower
Upon the tender meadow-grass of Earth,
Beside thy blue-robed mother, and, one day,
See glimmer on the tender meadow-grass
The white feet of the Oceanides,
Then there shall come to thine immortal eyes
Remembrance, and a sudden weariness,
The weariness of daylight ; and thy soul
Shall tremble in thy heart, Persephone,
Mindful of its deep sleep, and looking back,
Persephone, to its deep kingdom.   Then
Thy blue-robed mother shalt thou see in silence
Weeping apart, and thou shalt say to her :
' O Mother, Hades calls me to his deep
Kingdom ; now Hades calls me far from day
To queen it among shadows ; Hades calls
Me lonely to his insatiable love.' "

" Ah, Perdita, how well you diffuse the shadows
over your voice," interrupted the poet, feeling the
harmony of the night that darkened the syllables of
his verse.   " How well you become nocturnal at the
fall of day !   Do you remember the scene where
Persephone is on the point of sinking into Erebus,
while the chorus of the Oceanides is moaning?   Her
face is like yours when you darken it.   Her crowned
head drops backwards as she stands rigid in her
crocus-dyed peplum ; it seems as if night itself were
flowing into her bloodless body, deepening under
her chin, in the hollow of her eyes, round her nostrils, transforming her into a sombre mask of tragedy.   It is your mask, Perdita.   The memory of you
helped me to bring forth her divine person while I
was composing my ' Mystery.'   That little velvet
ribbon that you nearly always wear round your neck
taught me the colour most fit for the peplum of

Persephone. And one night, in your own house, as
was taking leave of you on the threshold of a room
where the lamps had not yet been lit (an agitated
evening last autumn, if you remember), you succeeded with a mere gesture in bringing the creature
to light in my soul that was still lying there undevel-
ped, then, unconscious of having produced that
sudden nativity, you disappeared into the intimate
shadow of your own Erebus. Ah, I was quite certain I could hear you sob, yet a torrent of ungovern-
able joy was coursing through me. I have never
told you this before, have I? I ought to have consecrated my work to you, as to an ideal Lucina."

She sat there suffering under the gaze of the Life-
giver; suffering because of the mask that he admired
in her face, and of the joy that she felt was for ever
springing up within him as from a source that could
never run dry. The whole of her own self gave her
pain; the mutability of her features; the strange
mimic power possessed by the muscles of her face,
the unconscious Art that regulated the meaning of
her gestures, the expressive shadow that she had so
often known how to wear on the stage like a veil
of sorrow in some moment of expectant silence.
And this was the shadow that now was filling up the
hollows carved by time in her no longer youthful
body. The hand she loved caused her cruel suffering, — the noble, delicate hand whose gift or caress
yet had such power to hurt her.

"Don't you believe, Perdita," Stelio said after
another pause, "in the occult beneficence of signs?"
As a river's meandering forms, encircles, and nour-
ishes the islands of the valley, that clear though tor-

tuous, course of thought to which he gave himself up
left in his spirit dark isolated spaces whence he knew
full well that some new treasure would be forthcom
ing in his own good time. " I am not speaking o
astral science, of the signs of the horoscope. I mear
that as some believe themselves subject to the influ
ence of a certain star, likewise we can create an idea
correspondence between our soul and some earthly
thing, so that the latter, saturating itself little by little
with our own essence, and itself being magnified by
our illusion, at last appears almost representative to
us of some unknown fatality, and becomes something
like the figure of a mystery by appearing at certair
crises of our life. This, Perdita, is the secret by which
we may restore something of a primeval freshness to
our souls that have become a little arid. I know by
experience what wholesome effects are derived from
intense communion with some natural thing. Ou
soul must now and then become like the hamadryad
in order to feel the fresh energy of the tree, the life
of which gives it its own life. You have gathered
already that in saying this I allude to your own word
on the passing of the boat. Briefly and obscurely
you were expressing this same truth when you ex
claimed ' Look at your pomegranates ! ' To yo
and to those who love me they can never be any
thing but *mine*. To you and to them the idea o
my person is indissolubly bound up with the fruit tha
I have chosen for an emblem, and have overchargec
with mysterious significances more numerous than it
own grains. If I had lived in the ages when the me
who excavated the old Greek marbles used to fin
the roots of the ancient fables still moist in the earth

no painter could have represented me without placing the Punic apple in my hand. To sever my person from that symbol would have seemed to his ingenuous soul like cutting off a living part of me, because, to his paganly inclined imagination the fruit would have seemed joined to my arm as to its natural bough. His idea of me would have been no different from that which he would have had of Hyacinthus, of Narcissus, or of Ciparissus, who all three would necessarily appear to him alternately under the aspect of youth and symbolised by a plant. And even in our own times there are a few agile and highly coloured spirits ready to understand all the meaning and enjoy all the savour of my invention. Yourself, Perdita, have you not trained a beautiful pomegranate in your garden that each summer you might see me blossom and bring forth fruit? A letter you once wrote me that was winged like a heavenly message describes the graceful ceremony by which you decked out the ' Effrenic ' shrub with necklaces on the day you received the first copy of *Persephone*. Thus, you see, for you and for those who love me, I have truly renewed an antique myth by thus projecting myself into one of the forms of eternal Nature; so that when I die (and Nature grant that before then I may have manifested myself wholly in my work!) my disciples will honour me under the symbol of the Pomegranate. In the sharpness of the leaf, in the flame-colour of the blossom, in the gem-like pulp of the crowned fruit, they will recognise some of the qualities of my art: by that leaf, by that flower, and by that fruit, as if by a posthumous teaching of their master, their intellects will be led to that same

flame, sharpness, and enclosed opulence. You se
now, Perdita, what the true benefit is. By affinity
myself am led on to develop myself in accordanc
with the magnificent genius of the tree by which
chose to signify my aspirations to rich and arden
life. It seems as if this vegetating effigy of mysel
were sufficient to reassure me that my powers ar
conforming to nature in their development, so as t
obtain in a natural way the effect for which they wer
destined. 'Thus hath nature disposed me,' is Leo
nardo's epigraph that I wrote on the title-page of my
first book; and the pomegranate as it blossoms and
brings forth fruit unceasingly repeats that simpl
motto. We can only obey the laws written in our
own substance and by them we must remain com
plete in a fulness and unity that fill us with joy
amongst so many dissolutions. There is no discord
between my art and my life."

He spoke with complete freedom, and in a flowing
stream, as if he felt the spirit of the listening woman
become concave like a chalice to receive that wave,
and wished to fill it to the brim. An ever clearer
intellectual joy was spreading over him, together
with a vague consciousness of the mysterious process
that was preparing his mind for the effort which
awaited it. Now and then as he bent over his lonely
friend and heard the oar measuring the silence that
rose from the great estuary, he would catch a glimpse,
like a flash, of the crowd with its innumerable faces
that was thickening in the great hall, and a quick
tremor would shake his heart.

"It is very singular, Perdita," he went on, gazing at the pale far waters where the low tide

blackened the shore, — " it is very singular to note how easily chance assists our fancy in giving a mysterious character to the conjunction of certain appearances with the aim we have imagined. I cannot understand why the poets of our day wax indignant at the vulgarity of their age and complain of having come into the world too early or too late. I believe that every man of intellect can, to-day as ever, create his own beautiful fable of life. We should look into life's confused whirl in the same spirit of fancy that the disciples of Leonardo were taught to adopt in gazing at the spots on a wall, at the ashes of fire, at clouds, even mud and other similar objects, in order to find there ' admirable inventions ' and ' infinite things.' The same spirit prompted Leonardo to add : ' In the sound of bells you will find every word and every name that you choose to imagine.' That master well knew — as the sponge of Apelles had already pointed out — that chance always befriends the ingenious artist. To me, for example, the ease and grace with which chance seconds the harmonious unfolding of my invention is a constant source of astonishment. Don't you think that black Hades forced his bride to eat the seven grains on purpose to furnish me with the subject-matter of a masterpiece ? "

He interrupted himself with a burst of the youthful laughter that always so clearly revealed the native joy dwelling within him.

" See, Perdita," he added, laughing, " whether I am right. In the very beginning of last October I was invited to Burano by Donna Andriana Duodo. We spent the morning in her gardens of thread ;

during the afternoon we went to visit Torcello. I had already begun living in the myth of Persephone in those days, and the work was being slowly formed within me, so that I felt as if I were gliding on Stygian waters and passing into the regions that lie beyond them. Never had I known a purer and sweeter foretaste of death, and that feeling had made me so light that I could have walked on the meadow of Asphodel without leaving a footprint. The air was damp, soft, and grayish; the canals meandered between banks overgrown with discoloured herbs. (Perhaps you only know Torcello in the sunshine.) But meanwhile some one was talking and discussing in Charon's boat. The sound of praise awoke me. Alluding to me, Francesco de Lizo was lamenting that a princely artist so magnificently sensual — they are his own words — should be forced to live apart far from an obtuse and hostile crowd, and to celebrate the feast ' of sounds, of colours, and of forms ' in the palace of his lonely dream. Giving way to a lyric impulse he recalled the splendidly festive lives of the Venetian artists, the public consent that lifted them up like a whirlwind to the heights of glory, the beauty, strength, and joy that they multiplied around them and reflected in the numberless figures they painted on high walls and arched ceilings. And Donna Andriana said : ' Well, then, I solemnly promise you that Stelio Effrena shall have his triumphant festival in Venice itself.' It was the Dogaressa who spoke. At that moment I saw a pomegranate laden with fruit break the infinite squalor of the low, greenish bank like a hallucinating apparition. Donna Orsetta Contarini, who was seated next to me, gave a cry of delight, and held out two hands as impatient as her desire. Nothing pleases me so much as the sincere and powerful expression of desire. 'I adore a pomegranate!' she exclaimed, as if already enjoying its pleasant sub-acid flavour. She was as childlike over it as her archaic name. I was stirred, but Andrea Contarini seemed deeply to disapprove of his wife's eagerness. He is an Hades having but little faith, it would seem, in the mnemonic virtue of the seven grains as applied to lawful wedlock. The boatmen, however, had been stirred too, and were making for the shore. I jumped on the bank first and fell to stripping the tree, my blood relation. It was truly a case of repeating with pagan lips the words of the Last Supper: 'Take, eat, this is my body, which is given for you. Do this in remembrance of me.' How does all this strike you, Perdita? You must not think I am inventing. I am quite truthful."

She was being carried away along that free and elegant play of words by which he seemed to exercise the nimbleness of his spirit and the facility of his eloquence. There was something undulating, variable, and powerful about him that conjured up the twofold image of flame and of water.

"Now," he continued, "Donna Andriana has kept her promise. Guided by that taste for antique splendour that so largely survives in her, she has prepared a festival truly worthy of the Doges in the Ducal Palace, in imitation of those that were celebrated towards the close of the sixteenth century. It is she who thought of rescuing the Ariadne of Benedetto Marcello from her oblivion, and of making her sigh

out her lamentation in the very place where Tintoretto has painted the Minoide in the act of receiving the crown of stars from Aphrodite. Does not
the same woman who left her clear eyes behind on
the ineffable green gown shine in the beauty of this
thought? Add to it that there is an ancient counter-
part to this musical performance in the Hall of the
Greater Council. A mythological composition by
Cornelio Frangipani, the music by Claudio Merulo,
was recited in the same hall in the year 1573 in
honour of the most Christian emperor Henry III.
Confess, Perdita, that my learning bewilders you.
Oh, if you knew how much of it I have accumulated
on the subject. I will read you my discourse some
day when you deserve severe punishment."

" But will you not read it at the festival to-night?"
La Foscarina asked, surprised and fearful lest he
should have resolved to disappoint the expectation
of the public, with his well-known careless ignoring
of obligation.

He divined his friend's anxiety and confirmed it.

" This evening," he said, with quiet assurance, " I
am coming to take an ice in your garden and to
enjoy the sight of the begemmed pomegranate,
gleaming under the sky."

" Oh, Stelio! What are you doing?" she exclaimed, starting up.

There was in her words and action so sharp a
regret, and at the same time so strange an evocation
of the expectant crowd, that they troubled him. The
image of that crowd, the formidable monster with the
numberless human faces, stood before him amid the
purple and gold of the great hall, bringing him a

foretaste of its fixed stare and its stifling breath. Suddenly, too, he measured the danger he had decided to face in trusting only to the inspiration of the moment, and he realised what the horror would be of a sudden mental darkening, of some unlooked-for bewilderment.

"Reassure yourself," he said. "I was jesting. I will go *ad bestias*, and I will go unarmed. The sign appeared again a moment ago; did you not see it? Do you think it can have appeared in vain after the miracle of Torcello? It has come to warn me once more that I must only assure those attitudes for which Nature has disposed me. Now you well know, dear friend, that I can only speak of myself. Therefore from the throne of the Doges I must only speak to the audience of my own soul under the veil of some seductive allegory and with the enchantment of some beautiful musical cadence. This I shall do *ex tempore*, if the flaming spirit of Tintoretto will only pour down to me from his *Paradiso* something of his own fervour and daring. The risk tempts me. But what a singular self-deception I was about to fall into, Perdita! When the Dogaressa announced the festival and invited me here to do it honour, I began writing a pompous discourse, a truly ceremonious piece of prose, ample and solemn, like one of the purple state gowns in the glass cases in the Correr Museum; not without a deep genuflection to the Queen in the preamble, not without a leafy garland for the head of the most serene Andriana Duodo. And for some days, with curious complacency I dwelt very near the spirit of a Venetian patrician of the sixteenth century, Cardinal Bembo, for instance,

adorned with all learning, academician of the *Urania*
or the *Adorni*, and assiduous frequenter of the gardens of Murano and the hills of Asolo. I am sure
there was a certain correspondence between the turn
of my periods and the massive gold frames that encircle the paintings in the ceiling of the Council Hall.
But, alas! as I reached Venice yesterday morning, and
in passing by the Grand Canal dipped my weariness
in the moist transparent shadows where the marble
still exhaled the spirituality that night gives it, I felt
that my sheets were worth much less than the dead
sea-weeds rocked by the tide, and seemed strangers
to me no less than the *Trionfi* of Celio Magno or the
Favoli Maritti of Anton Maria Consalvi that I had
quoted and commented on in them. What was I to
do, then?"

He cast an exploring glance round sky and water
as if to discover an invisible presence, or recognise
some newly arrived phantom. A yellowish glare was
stretching to the more solitary shores, that stood out
in it as if drawn there in finely pencilled lines, like the
opaque veining of agates; behind him, towards the
Salute, the sky was scattered over with light-spreading
vapours, violet and rosy, that made it comparable to
a changing sea peopled by sea-anemones. From the
neighbouring gardens there descended an exhaled fragrance of plants saturated with light and warmth, like
floating aromatic oils heavy on the bronze-like water.

"Do you feel the autumn, Perdita?" he asked his
absorbed friend, awakening her with his voice.

The vision returned to her of dead Summer being
lowered among the sea-weeds of the laguna, shrouded
in its opalescent glass.

" It is upon me," she answered, with a melancholy smile.

" Did you not see it yesterday, when it descended on the city? Where were you yesterday at sundown? "

" In a garden of the Giudecca."

" I was here, on the Riva. Does it not seem to you that when human eyes have seen a similar vision of joy and beauty, the lids ought to close over them for ever to keep them sealed? It is of these secret hidden things that I should like to speak to-night, Perdita. I should like to celebrate in myself the marriage of Venice with Autumn, giving it an intonation as little different as possible from that of Tintoretto when he painted the Marriage of Ariadne and Bacchus for the hall of the *Anticollegio*, — azure, purple and gold. Yesterday an old germ of poetry suddenly broke open in my soul. I remembered the fragment of a forgotten poem in *nona rima* that I began writing here when I came to Venice for the first time, one September in my earliest youth that I spent at sea. It was called *The Allegory of Autumn*, and it sang the praises of the god no longer crowned with vine-leaves, but with jewels like one of Veronese's princes, fired with passion, about to migrate to the sea-city with the arms of marble and the thousand girdles of green. At that time the idea had not reached the degree of intensity necessary for it to enter into the life of Art, and instinctively I abandoned the effort of manifesting it as a whole. But, in the active spirit as in the fertile soil, no seed is ever lost : it returns to me now at the right moment urgently demanding expression. What a just but mysterious fate governs the world of the mind! It was essential that I should respect that first germ in order to feel its multiplied virtue expand in me to-day. That Vinci, who has darted a glance into every profound thing, certainly meant to convey this particular truth by his fable of the grain of millet that says to the ant, 'If you will in so far please me as to let me enjoy my desire of new birth, I will restore myself to you an hundredfold.' Admire this touch of grace in those fingers that could bend iron. Ah, he ever remains the incomparable master. How shall I forget him awhile that I may give myself up to the Venetians?"

Of a sudden the gay irony with which he addressed himself in his last words died out, and his whole attention seemed to bend over his thoughts. With bowed head, his body feeling a kind of convulsed contraction that answered to the extreme tension of his spirit, he began to trace some of the secret analogies which should bind together many images appearing to him as if in the rapid intervals between successive lightning flashes, and to determine some of the broader lines upon which those images should be developed. Such was his agitation that the muscles of his face quivered visibly under the skin, and the woman felt, as she watched him, a reflected anguish not unsimilar to what she would have felt had he made before her a spasmodic effort to draw the string of a gigantic bow. And she knew that he was far away, estranged, indifferent to everything that was not his own thought.

"It is already late, the hour is drawing near, we must go back," he said, suddenly pulling himself together as if pressed by anxiety, as if the formidable monster with its innumerable human faces that would occupy the great resounding hall had reappeared. "I must get back to the hotel in time to dress."

And his youthful vanity blossomed again at the thought of the unknown women whose eyes were to fall upon him for the first time that night.

"To the Hôtel Daniele," La Foscarina called to the oarsman.

As the dentellated iron at the prow veered round on the water with a slow swing like a crawling animal, both felt a different but equally acute suffering at leaving behind them the infinite silence of the estuary, already mastered by shadow and death, at turning back towards the magnificent City of Temptation, in whose canals, as in the veins of a voluptuous woman, the fever of night was kindling.

They were silent awhile, absorbed by the internal tempest that belaboured them, penetrating to the roots of their being and forcing them as if to tear them up. The aromas descended from the gardens swimming like oil on the water, that showed a glitter as of burnt bronze here and there in its folds. There was something like the phantom of past pageants in the air, which they perceived in the same way that they had felt a worn note of gold while contemplating the harmony of the durable marbles on the palaces that age had dimmed. That magic evening seemed to renew the breath and reflection of the east clinging as of old to the round, hollow sails and curved flanks of the galleys that brought them home with their beautiful spoil. And all things around seemed to exalt the forces of life in the man who would have drawn the very universe to himself in order not to die, in the woman who would have thrown her burdened soul to the stake if that could have made her die pure. And both sat with their anxiety growing upon them, listening to the flight of time, as if the water on which they glided were flowing through a fearful clepsydra.

Both started at the sudden burst of the salute that hailed the lowering of the flag on board a man-of-war anchored near the gardens. They saw the striped bunting flutter above the black mass and descend along its staff, and its folds drop like some heroic dream suddenly vanishing. The silence seemed deeper for a moment, and the gondola slipped into denser shadow as it grazed the flank of the armed giant.

"Perdita," Stelio Effrena said unexpectedly, "do you know that Donatella Arvale who is going to sing in *Ariadne ?*"

In that deeper shadow his voice echoed with singular resonance against the ironclad.

"She is the daughter of Lorenzo Arvale, the great sculptor," La Foscarina answered after a moment's pause. "She is one of my dearest friends, and she is also my guest. You will meet her, therefore, at my house after the festival."

"Donna Andriana spoke to me about her last night with great warmth as a marvellous being. She told me that the idea of unearthing this *Ariadne* came to her one day on hearing Donatella Arvale sing the air, '*Ah come mai puoi — Vedermi piangere.*' We are going to have some wonderful music at your house, then, Perdita. Ah, how I thirst for it! Down there in my solitude I have had no music for many months but that of the sea, which is too terrible, and my own, which is too confused as yet."

The bells of San Marco gave the signal for the Angelus, and their ponderous roll dilated in long waves along the mirror of the harbour, vibrated through the masts of the ships, spread afar towards the infinite lagoon. From San Giorgio Maggiore, from San Giorgio dei Greci, from San Giorgio degli Schiavoni, from San Giovanni in Bragora, from San Moise, from the churches of the Salute and the Redentore and beyond, over the whole domain of the Evangelist, from the far towers of the Madonna dell' Orto, of San Giobbe, of Sant' Andrea, bronze voices answered, mingling in one great chorus, spreading over the silent company of stones and water one great dome of invisible metal, the vibrations of which seemed to reach the twinkling of the earliest stars. In the purity of evening the sacred voices gave the City of Silence a sort of immensity of grandeur. From the summit of their temples they brought anxious mankind the message sent by the immortal multitudes hidden in the darkness of deep aisles, or mysteriously troubled by the light of votive lamps; they brought to spirits worn out by the day the message of the superhuman creatures figured on the walls of secluded chapels and in the niches of inner altars, who had announced miracles and promised worlds. And all the apparitions of the consoling Beauty invoked by unanimous Prayer, rose on that storm of sound, spoke in that aerial chorus, irradiated the face of the marvellous night.

" Can you still pray?" asked Stelio, in a low voice

on seeing that the woman's lids were lowered and
motionless, her hands clasped on her knees, her whole
person absorbed in some interior act.

She did not answer, only pressing her lips closer
together. And both listened on, feeling that their
distress was about to overtake them, in the fulness of
its tide, like a river no longer interrupted by a cataract. Both had a grave, confused consciousness of
the strange interval, in which a new image had sprung
up unexpectedly between them and a new name had
been uttered. The ghost of the unforeseen sensation
they had felt on entering the shadow of the ironclad
seemed to have remained in them, like an isolated
encumbrance, like an indistinct, and nevertheless persistent, point round which was a kind of unexplored
void. Distress in the fulness of its tide now suddenly seized them, throwing them towards each
other, uniting them with such vehemence that they
dared not look into each other's eyes for fear of
reading there some too brutal desire.

"Shall we not meet again to-night, after the festival?" asked La Foscarina, with a tremble in her faint
voice. "Are you not free?"

She hastened to detain him, to imprison him, as if
he were about to slip from her, as if she hoped that
night to find some philtre that would lastingly attach
him to her. And, while she felt that the gift of herself had at length become a necessity, yet the fearful
lucidity that pierced the flame within her had shown
her the poverty of the gift so long denied. And a
sorrowful modesty, made of fear and of pride, contracted her faded limbs.

"I am free; I am yours." the young man answered

in a lower voice, without looking at her. "You know that nothing is worth to me that which you can give."

He too was trembling to the depths of his heart, with the two aims before him that caused him to strain his energy like a mighty bow,— the city and the woman; both deep and tempting and tired with having lived too much, and languid with too many loves; both over-magnified by his dream, and fated to delude his expectation.

For some seconds a violent wave of regret and desires overcame him. The pride; the intoxication of his hard, dogged labour; his boundless, uncurbed ambition that had been forced into a field too narrow for it; his bitter intolerance of mediocrity in life; his claim to princely privileges; the dissembled craving for action by which he was propelled towards the multitude as to the prey he should prefer; the vision of great and imperious art that should be at the same time a signal of light in his hands and a weapon of subjection; his strangely imperial dreams; his insatiable need of predominance, of glory, of pleasure,— rebelled tumultuously, dazzling and suffocating him in their confusion. And his sadness inclined him to the last love of the lonely, wandering woman who seemed to carry in the folds of her dress the silenced frenzy of those far-off multitudes from whose pent-up brutality her cry of passion or burst of sorrow or enthralling pause had wrenched the sublime pulsation that Art quickens. A troubled desire drew him to the despairing woman in whom the traces of every pleasure were visible — towards that ageing body saturated with endless caresses, yet still unknown to him.

" Is it a promise? " he asked, controlling his agitation. "Ah, at last!"

She did not answer, but gave him a look of almost
insane ardour, which escaped him.

And they remained silent, and the roll of the bells
passing over their heads was so strong that they felt
it at the roots of their hair, like a quiver of their own
flesh.

" Good-bye," she said, near the landing-place.
"On coming into the courtyard let us meet at the
second well on the side of the Molo."

" Good-bye," he said. " Place yourself so that I
may distinguish you among the crowd when I am
about to utter the first word."

An indistinct clamour came from San Marco,
above the sound of the bells, spreading over the
Piazzetta, dwindling away towards the Fortuna.

" May all light be on your forehead, Stelio," said
the woman, holding out her dry hands to him passionately.

Stelio Effrena entered the court by the south
door. On seeing the Giant's Staircase invaded by
the black and white multitude that swarmed up
under the reddish light of the torches fixed in the
iron candelabra, he felt a sudden movement of
repugnance, and stopped in the long covered gallery.
There was a contrast that jarred on him too acutely
between the meaner intruding crowd and the sight
of those architectural forms, magnified still more by
the unusual illumination in which the strength and
the beauty of their former life were expressed in
such varied harmonies.

" Oh, how wretched ! " he exclaimed, turning to the friends who accompanied him. " In the Hall of the Greater Council, from the throne of the Doges, how can one find a metaphor that will bring emotion to a thousand starched shirt-fronts ! Let us go back; let us go and drink in the odour of the other crowd outside, the real crowd. The Queen has not yet left the palace ! We have plenty of time."

" Until I see you on the platform," Francesco de Lizo said, laughing, " I shall not be sure that you are really going to speak."

" I think Stelio would prefer the balcony between the two blood-like columns to the platform in the hall, would prefer haranguing a rebellious populace that had threatened to set fire to the new *Procuratie* and the old *Libreria*," said Piero Martello, wishing to flatter the master's taste for sedition and the factious spirit that he himself imitated in his affectation.

" Yes, certainly," said Stelio, " if the harangue were sufficient to stop or hasten an irreparable act. I grant you that the words we write should be used to create a pure form of beauty contained and shut in by a book as by a tabernacle that is only approached by election, and by an act of that same deliberate will necessary for the breaking of a seal; but it seems to me that the words we address directly to a multitude should have no other aim but action, even violent action, if need be. Only on this condition can a spirit that is a trifle haughty communicate with the crowd by means of voice and gesture without lowering itself. In any other case his game can only be of a histrionic nature. For this reason I bitterly repent having accepted my present office of ornate and pleasure-giving orator. Each of you may grasp how much is humiliating to me in this honour of which I am made the mark, and how much is useless in my coming effort. All these outside, wrested for one night from their mediocre occupations or their favourite pastimes, are coming to hear me with the same futile and stupid curiosity with which they would go and listen to any virtuoso. To the women among my listeners the art with which I have composed the knot of my cravat will be far more appreciated than the art with which I round my periods. And, after all, the effect of my speech will probably be a burst of deadened applause from gloved hands, or a low, discreet murmur which I shall acknowledge with a bow. Don't you think that I am indeed about to touch the highest summit of my ambitions?"

"You are wrong," said Francesco de Lizo. "You must congratulate yourself on having succeeded in impressing the rhythm of art on the life of a forgetful city for a few hours, and in having given us a glimpse of the splendours that might beautify our existence through a renewed marriage of art with life. If the man who built the Festival Theatre at Bayreuth were present, he would applaud this harmony which he himself has announced. But the admirable part of it is that, though you were absent from and ignorant of it, the festival seems to have been disposed by the guidance of your own spirit, by an inspiration, a design of your own. This is the best proof of a possibility of restoring and diffusing taste, even in the midst of present barbarities. Your influence is deeper at the present day

than you think. The lady who has wished to do
you honour, she whom you call the *Dogaressa*, has
asked herself at every new idea rising in her mind,
' Would this please Stelio Effrena? ' You don't know
how many men of the younger generation are now
asking themselves the same question when they
consider the aspects of their inner life ! "

" For whom should you speak, if not for these ? "
said Daniele Glauro, the fervent, sterile ascete of
Beauty, in that spiritual voice of his that seemed
to reflect the inextinguishable white-heat of a soul
cherished by the master as the most faithful. " If
you look round when you stand on the platform
you will easily recognise them by the expression
of their eyes. They are very numerous, some,
too, have come from afar, and they are waiting
with an anxiety that you perhaps cannot understand. Their number is made up of those who
have drunk in your poetry, who have breathed the
fiery ether of your dream, who have felt the clutch
of your own chimera. It is made up of those
to whom you have promised a stronger and more
beautiful life, to whom you have announced the
world's transfiguration by the miracle of a new art.
They are the many, many whom your hope and joy
have carried away. They have heard that you are
going to speak in Venice, in the Ducal Palace, in
one of the most glorious places on earth. They
are going to see and hear you for the first time,
surrounded by the magnificence that seems to them
the only fitting frame to your nature. The old
Palace of the Doges, that has slept in darkness for
so long, is suddenly reillumined and revivified.

In their eyes it is you alone who have had the power of relighting its torches. Do you not understand their expectations? And does it not seem to you that you ought to speak for them alone? You can carry out the condition you just laid down for him who speaks to a multitude, you can stir up a vehement emotion in their souls that shall turn them towards the Ideal and hold them there for ever. For how many of them, Stelio, you might make this Venetian night unforgettable!"

Stelio laid his hand on the prematurely bent shoulders of the mystic doctor and smilingly repeated the words of Petrarch: "*Non ego loquar omnibus sed tibi, sed mihi et his.*" . . .

The eyes of his unknown disciples shone within him; and with perfect clearness he now felt within himself, like a tuneful modulation, the sound of his own exordium.

"Nevertheless," he added merrily, turning to Piero Martello, "to rouse a tempest in this sea would be a much more stirring thing."

They were standing near the corner column of the portico, in contact with the noisy, unanimous crowd gathered in the Piazzetta that prolonged itself towards the Zecca, was engulfed near the Procuratie, barricaded the black tower, occupied every space like a formless wave, communicated its living warmth to the marble of the columns and the walls against which it pressed in its continual overflowing. Now and then a greater outcry would come from the distance, at the further end of the Piazza, growing in volume until it burst quite close to them like a clap of thunder; then it would dwindle until it expired beside them like a murmur. The upper outline of the arches, the loggias, the spires, and the cupolas of the golden Basilica, the attics of the Loggetta, the entablatures of the Biblioteca were shining with numberless little lights, and the high pyramid of the Campanile, twinkling together with the silent constellations in the bosom of night, conjured up for the multitude drunk with its own noise the immensity of the silent heavens, the boatman at the far end of the laguna, to whom this light must seem a new kind of signal, the cadence of a solitary oar disturbing the reflection of the stars in the water, the holy peace closed in by the walls of some island convent.

"To-night I should like to be for the first time with a woman whom I desired on a floating bed somewhere beyond the Gardens, towards the Lido," said Paris Eglano, the erotic poet, a fair, beardless youth who had a handsome and voracious red mouth in contrast to the almost angelic delicacy of his features. "In an hour's time Venice will offer some Nero-like lover hidden in some gondola-cabin the Dionysian spectacle of a city that has been set on fire by its own delirium."

Stelio smiled as he noticed to what extent those who approached him were steeped in his own essence, and how deeply the seal of his own style had stamped itself on those intellects. The image of La Foscarina flashed on his desire, La Foscarina as she was: poisoned by art, laden with voluptuous learning, with the savours of maturity and of corruption in her eloquent mouth, with the dryness of a vain fever in those hands that had pressed out the

substance of all deceitful fruits, with the traces of a
hundred masks on that face that had simulated the
fury of mortal passions. It was thus he pictured
her to his desire, and his pulse quickened at the
thought that before long he would see her emerging
from the crowd as from an element by which she was
enslaved, and would draw from her look the necessary intoxication.

"Let us go," he said to his friends, ready now;
"it is time."

The cannon announced that the Queen had left
the residence. A long quiver ran along the living
human mass, like that which precedes a squall at
sea. From the shore of San Giorgio Maggiore a
rocket darted up with a vehement hiss, rose straight
in the air like a stem of fire, scattered a rose of fire
at its summit, then bent downwards, dwindled, dispersed in trembling sparks, died out on the water
with a dull crackling. And the joyous acclamation
that greeted the beautiful Queen, the united cry of
love echoed by the marbles and repeating her name,
—the name of the white starry flower of the rocket
that had the pure pearl for its meaning, — all this
summoned up in Stelio's mind the pomp of the
ancient *Promissione*, the triumphant procession of the
art that accompanied the new Dogaressa to the ducal
palace; the immense wave of joy on which Morosina
Grimani, resplendent in her gold, soared to her throne,
while all the arts bowed down to her laden with gifts.

"If the Queen loves your books," said Francesco
de Lizo, "she will wear all her pearls to-night. You
will find yourself in a labyrinth of precious stones
all the heirlooms of the patricians of Venice."

"Look, Stelio, at the foot of the staircase," said Daniele Glauro, "there is a group of your devotees awaiting your passage."

Stelio paused at the well indicated by La Foscarina, and bent over its bronze rim, feeling the carved outlines of its cariatides against his knees, and discerning in its deep, dark mirror the vague reflection of the far-off stars. For a few seconds his soul isolated itself, grew deaf to surrounding voices, withdrew into the circle of shadow whence came a slight chill revealing the dumb presence of water. The fatigue brought on by his state of tension made itself felt, and with it a desire to be elsewhere, an indistinct need of going beyond even the ecstasy that the night hours were to bring him, and in the last extreme depth of his being the consciousness of having there a secret soul that, like the mirror of water, remained strange to all things, motionless and intangible.

"What is it you see?" said Piero Martello, he too bending over the edge, worn by the ropes of the pitchers that had been lowered down over it for centuries.

"The face of Truth," answered the master.

In the rooms surrounding the Hall of the Greater Council, once inhabited by the Doges, now by the pagan statues forming part of the booty of ancient wars, Stelio Effrena was awaiting a sign from the master of ceremonies to appear on the platform. He smiled calmly on the friends who were talking to him, but their words reached his ears between one pause and another like the intermittent sounds that wind brings from afar. Now and then he would approach one of the statues with an involuntary movement as if seeking some frail spot where he might break it, or bend intently over a medal as if to read there some sign impossible to decipher. But his eyes were sightless, being turned inwards to that region where the accumulated powers of his will called up the silent forms which his voice would presently raise to perfection of verbal music. His being contracted under the effort of bringing the representation of the singular feeling that possessed him to the highest degree of intensity. Since he was going to speak only of himself and his own world, he would at least gather into one ideal image the more resplendent qualities of his art, thus showing those who followed him what an invincible force it was that hurried him through life. Once more he would prove to them how, in order to obtain victory over man and circumstance, there is no other way but that of constantly feeding one's own exaltation and magnifying one's own dream of beauty or of power.

As he bent over a medal of Pisanello's he felt the pulse of his thought beating with incredible rapidity against his burning temples.

"Do you see, Stelio," said Daniele Glauro, drawing him on one side with that pious reverence that veiled his voice whenever he spoke of those things which made up his religion, — "do you see how the mysterious affinities of art are working upon you, and how your spirit, about to manifest itself, is being led by an infallible instinct in the midst of so many forms towards the one model or footprint of the highest and most accurate expression of style. Through the necessity of coining your own idea, you are brought to bend over a medal of Pisanello's; you come in conjunction with the sign of one who is among the greatest stylists that have appeared in the world; the most frankly Hellenic soul of the whole Renaissance. And your brow at once becomes marked by a ray of light."

On the bronze was the effigy of a young man with fair, waving hair, imperial profile, and Apollo-like neck. His was so perfect a type of elegance and vigour that the imagination could not picture him in life except as entirely exempt from all decadence, changeless for all eternity. *Dux equitum præstans Malatesta Novellus Cesenæ dominus. Opus Pisani pictoris.* And close to it lay another medal by the same hand, bearing the effigy of a virgin with narrow bosom, swan-like neck, and hair drawn back as if it were a heavy bag, with a high receding forehead that seemed already vowed to the halo of the blessed; a vessel of purity for ever sealed, hard, precise, and clear as the diamond, an adamantine pyx enshrining a soul that, like the Host, seemed consecrated to sacrifice. *Cicilia Virgo, Filia Johannis Frencisci primi Marchionis Mantuæ.*

"See," said the subtle expert, pointing out the two rare impressions, — "see how Pisanello has gathered with an equally wonder-working hand the proudest flower of life and the purest flower of death. Here you have the image of profane desire and the image of sacred aspiration in the same metal, both fixed by the same idealism of style. Don't you recognise in them the analogies that unite this form of art to your own art? When your *Persephone* picks the luscious fruit of the infernal pomegranate, there is also something mystic in her fine gesture of desire, because in breaking it to eat the grains she unconsciously determines her fate. The shadow of mystery, therefore, accompanies her sensuous act. This reveals the character of your whole work. No sensuality is more ardent than yours, yet your senses are so sharpened that, while enjoying the appearance, they penetrate to the greater depths until they come upon the great mystery, and shudder. Your vision prolongs itself beyond the veil on which life has painted the voluptuous images that give you pleasure. Thus, conciliating in yourself that which seems irreconcilable, blending without effort the two terms of an antithesis, you are setting the example of a complete and ultra-powerful life. You should make this felt to them that listen to you, because it is this, above all, that should be recognised for the sake of your glory."

He had celebrated the imaginary marriage of the proud Malatesta, leader of knights, and the blessed Mantuan virgin, Cecilia Gonzaga, with the faith of a pious priest at the altar. Stelio loved him for this faith; loved him, too, because in no other man had he ever felt so deep and sincere a belief in the reality of the poetic world, and because his own consciousness often found some revealing expression in him and his comments often threw unforeseen light on his own work.

"Here comes La Foscarina with Donatella Arvale," announced Francesco de Lizo, who was watching the crowd that came up the Censor's Staircase and grew denser in the large hall.

Once more distress took hold of Stelio Effrena. He could hear the murmur of the multitude mingling in his ears with the throb of his arteries as in some indefinite distance, and Perdita's last words came back to him above that roar.

The murmur rose again, then dwindled, and ceased altogether as with a light, sure tread he ascended the steps of the platform. Turning towards the crowd he saw for the first time the formidable monster with the numberless human faces staring in his dazzled eyes from among the gold and sombre purples of the great hall.

A sudden leap of pride helped him to master himself. He bowed to the Queen and to Donna Andriana Duodo; both threw him the same twin smiles as from the gliding barge on the Grand Canal. His glance sought La Foscarina in the glitter of the first rows, travelled to the back of the assembly, where only a dark zone dotted with pale spots appeared. The silent, expectant multitude appeared to him in the image of a gigantic many-eyed chimera, its bosom covered with shining scales, stretching its blackness under the enormous scrolls of the rich, heavy ceiling that hung over it like a suspended treasure.

Splendid indeed was that chimeric bosom on which necklaces glittered, that had certainly flashed before under that same ceiling on the night of some coronation festival. The diadem and ornaments of the Queen and her many pearl necklaces, graduated drops of light that suggested a miraculous falling in grains of a smile just about to break out; the dark emeralds of Andriana Duodo, originally torn from the hilt of a scimitar; the rubies of Giustiniana Memo, set after the manner of carnations by the inimitable

workmanship of Vettor Camelio; the sapphires of
Lucrezia Priuli, taken from the heels of the high san-
dals on which the Most Serene Zilia had stepped to
her throne on the day of her triumph; the beryls of
Orsetta Contarini, so delicately set in opaque gold by
the artist hand of Silvestro Grifo; the turquoises of
Zenobia Corner, turned strangely pale by the mysterious disease that had changed them one night as
they lay on the moist bosom of the Lusignana among
the pleasures of Asolo, the proudest jewels that had
adorned the old-time festivals of the Sea-City,— flashed
with renewed fire on the chimera's bosom, and from
it a tepid exhalation of feminine skin and breath went
up to Stelio. The rest of that shapeless, strangely
spotted body stretched backwards into an appendage
something like a tail, between the two gigantic
spheres that recalled to the memory of the image
maker the two bronze spheres on which the blind-
folded monster presses its leonine claws in the Allegory of Giambellino. And that accumulation of
blind animal life, void of all thought before him who
in that hour was alone to think, gifted with the same
inert fascination possessed by enigmatic idols, covered by its own silence as by a shield capable of
receiving and repulsing any vibration, waited for the
air to palpitate under his first dominating word.

Stelio Effrena measured the silence in which his
first word should fall. As his voice rose to his lips,
an effort of will leading it and strengthening it against
his instinctive emotion, he caught sight of La Foscarina
standing against the iron railing round the celestial
sphere. The head of the tragic actress rose from her
unadorned neck, and the purity of her bare shoulders

above the orbit of the signs of the zodiac. Stelio admired the art of that apparition. Fixing his own on those far-off adoring eyes, he began speaking very slowly, as if the rhythm of the oars was still in his ears.

"One afternoon not long ago, returning from the Gardens along the warm bank of the Schiavoni, that must often have seemed to some wandering poet like I know not what golden magic bridge stretching out over a sea of light and silence to some infinite dream of beauty, I thought, or rather I stood by and watched my own thoughts as I would an intimate spectacle, — I thought of the nuptial alliance of Autumn and Venice under those skies.

"A sense of life was diffused everywhere; a sense of life made up of passionate expectation and restrained ardour, that surprised me by its vehemence, but yet could not seem new to me, because I had already found it gathered in some belt of shadow under the almost deathly immobility of summer, and I had also felt it here vibrating now and then like a mysterious pulsation under the strange, feverish odour of the waters. Thus, I thought, this pure City of Art truly aspires to the supreme condition of that beauty that is an annual return in her as is the giving forth of flowers to the forest. She tends to reveal herself in a full harmony as if she still carried in herself, powerful and conscious, that desire of perfection from which she was born and formed through the ages like some divine creature. Under the motionless fires of a summer sky she seemed pulseless and breathless, dead indeed in her green waters; but my feeling did not deceive me when I divined her secretly labouring under a spirit of life that would prove sufficiently powerful to renew the highest of older miracles.

"This I thought as I stood by and witnessed the splendid spectacle that my eyes were made capable of contemplating by a peculiar gift of love and poetry, seeming to change their faculty of sight into a deep and lasting vision. . . . But how shall I ever communicate to those who hear me my vision of joy and beauty? There can be no dawn and no sunset to equal such an hour of light on the waters and among the stones. And no sudden appearing of a beloved woman in a wood in spring could be intoxicating like the unexpected revelation in full daylight of the heroic and voluptuous city, bringing to my arms, to be crushed there, the richest dream ever dreamed by a Latin soul."

The voice of the speaker, clear, penetrating, almost icy at first, seemed to have been suddenly warmed by the invisible sparks that doubtless were wrung from his brain by the effort of improvisation governed by the acute vigilance of his fastidious ear. As the words flowed without impediment, and the rhythmic line of his periods closed round them like a figure drawn at one stroke by a bold hand, his listeners could feel under that harmonious fluidity the excess of the tension tormenting his spirit, and were held captive by it as by one of those savage Circensian games in which all the energies of the athlete are made manifest, the vibration of his sinews and the swollen tissue of his arteries. They could feel how much was actual, warm, and alive in the thoughts so expressed, and their enjoyment was greater because

so unlooked for, all having expected from that untiring seeker after perfection the studied reading of a
laboriously composed discourse. With deep emotion
his devotees witnessed the audacious test, as if the
mysterious process whence the forms had arisen that
had held out to them so many gifts of joy was being
laid bare before them. And that first emotion diffused
by contagion and indefinitely multiplied by numbers
became unanimous, and flowed back to him who had
produced it, threatening to overcome him.

It was the expected peril. He swayed as if under
the shock of a wave too strong for him. And for
some seconds a thick darkness filled his brain, the
light of his thought went out like a torch at the
breath of some irresistible wind, his eyes clouded as
in the early stage of faintness. He felt how great
the shame of defeat would be if he yielded to that
bewilderment. And in that darkness, with a kind of
sharp percussion, as of steel on flint, his will created
the new spark.

With a look and gesture he lifted the eye of the
crowd up to the masterpiece spreading over the ceiling of the hall, a kind of sun-given radiance.

"Thus I am sure," he exclaimed, — "thus the city
appeared to Veronese while he was seeking within
himself the image of the triumphant Queen. Ah, I
am sure he must have trembled to his remotest fibres
and bent his knee like one stricken and bewildered
by a miracle, prostrating himself in adoration, and
when he tried to manifest his wonder to mankind
and to paint her here, he, the prodigal artist who
seems to have collected in himself all the imagina-
tions of the most unbridled satraps, the magnificent

poet whose soul was like that Lydian river called by
the harmonious Greeks Chrysorroes, from whose gold-
yielding springs a whole dynasty of kings came
forth laden with wealth, — he, Veronese, scattered
in profusion gold, jewels, amaranth, purple, ermine,
all that is sumptuous elsewhere, but he could only
picture the glorious face in a halo of shadow.

"We should unite in exalting Veronese if only
for that veil of shadow! All the mystery and the
fascination of Venice are in that shadow, small yet
infinite, composed of things living but unknowable,
gifted with the portentous virtue of the fabulous cav-
erns where gems had eyes to see, and where men
have found coolness and ardour at the same time in
one inexpressibly ambiguous sensation. We must
praise Veronese for this. The giving a human aspect to his representation of the queenly city has
enabled him to grasp its essential spirit, which is
only symbolically an inextinguishable flame seen
through a veil of water. And I know of one whose
spirit, having been long saturated with these things,
withdrew it enriched by a new power, and henceforth treated his art and his life with a more ardent
touch."

Was he not himself that one? He seemed to recover all his assurance and to feel himself out of
danger after this assertion, master of his thoughts
and words, capable of drawing into the circle of his
dream the giant chimera of the bosom covered with
glittering scales, the elusive and versatile monster
from whose sides emerged the tragic muse, her head
raised above the belt of constellations.

Obeying his gesture, the numberless faces turned

to the apotheosis. The unveiled eyes gazed wonderingly at the marvel, as if they saw it for the first time, or under a hitherto unknown aspect. The wide, bare shoulders of the woman with the golden helmet shone on the cloud with strongly accentuated muscular life that made it as tempting as a palpable body. And from that living nudity, conqueror of time that had obscured beneath her the heroic images of sieges and battles, a voluptuous charm seemed to emanate, made sweeter by the breath of the autumn night floating through the open windows that stirred it as it stirred the wave of perfume hovering round the fragrant rose-bushes, while the princesses from on high, bending over the balustrades between the two spiral columns, inclined their burning faces and their opulent bosoms towards their latest worldly sisters in the hall below.

Under this incantation, the poet began tossing his periods to his audience, harmonising them like lyric stanzas.

"It was indeed some such flame which I felt yesterday rising to extreme vehemence and conferring on the beauty of Venice a power of expression never before seen. The whole city kindled with desire before my eyes, and throbbing with expectation within its thousand girdles of green like a woman in love awaiting her hour of joy. She held her marble arms out to the wild autumn whose perfumed breath reached her from the delicious death of the distant landscape, and watched the light vapours that rose from the confines of the lagoon drawing near her, silent, like furtive messages. Intently she listened to the slightest sounds in the silence she herself had made, and the breath of the wind flying through her rare gardens had a musical continuation that prolonged it outside the enclosures. A kind of stupor gathered round the solitary imprisoned trees that were changing colour, becoming resplendent like some burning things. The dry leaf that had fallen on the worn stone of the bank shone like some precious thing; at the summit of the wall adorned with fair lichens the pomegranate, swollen with maturity, burst suddenly like a beautiful mouth that breaks open by an impulse of cordial laughter. A boat passed, slow and wide, filled with bunches like a wine-press spreading through the air, and above the waters with their tangle of sea-weed, the intoxication of the vintage season, and a vision of solitary vineyards full of young men and women singing. A deep eloquence spoke from all surrounding objects, as if invisible signs adhered to visible aspects and all were living by some divine Hellenic privilege in the higher truth of art.

"Surely, then," I thought, — "surely there must be in the city of stone and water, as in the spirit of the pure artist, a spontaneous and constant aspiration to ideal harmonies. A kind of fictitious rhythmical imagination seems to spaciously elaborate its representations, conforming them to an idea, as it were, and directing them to a premeditated end. Her marvellous hands seem to weave her light and shadows into a continual work of beauty; she dreams over her work, and from her own dream, transfiguring the heritage of centuries, she draws that tissue of inimitable allegories by which she is covered. And, because poetry alone is truth, he who knows how to contemplate it and draw it into himself by the virtue of thought will be near knowing the secret of victory over life."

He had sought the eyes of Daniele Glauro while uttering the last words, and had seen them shine with joy under the vast, thoughtful brow that seemed swollen by the presence of an unborn world. The mystic doctor was there with his whole legion, with some of those unknown disciples whom he had described to Stelio as eager and anxious, full of faith and expectation, panting to break through the narrowness of their daily servitude, and to know some free ecstasy of joy or pain. Stelio saw them there, serried together in a group, like a nucleus of compressed forces, leaning against the great reddish bookcases whose numberless volumes of forgotten and inert science lay buried. He could tell them by their intent, animated faces, their long, thick hair, their mouths that were either opened in child-like stupor or tightened with a sort of violence full of sensitiveness, their light or dark eyes to which the breath of his words seemed to bring alternate lights and shadows like the passing of a breeze over a bed of delicate flowers. He seemed to be holding their united souls in his hands, able to agitate one or the other, and crush it, or tear it and burn it as if it were only some light banner. Whilst his spirit stretched and relaxed in its continual discharge, there still remained to him an extraordinary lucidity of exterior analysis, a kind of separate faculty of material observation, that seemed to become ever more acute and more sharply defined as his eloquence warmed and quickened. Little by little he felt his effort becoming easier and the efficacy of his will being supplemented by an energy free and obscure as an instinct that rose from the depths of his unconsciousness, operating by an occult process impossible to gauge. Association reminded him of the extraordinary moments in which — in the silence and intellectual heat of his remote chamber — his hand had written an immortal verse that had seemed to him not born of his brain, but dictated by an impetuous deity to which his unconscious organ had obeyed like a blind instrument. A not unsimilar miracle was now taking place within him, surprising his ear by the unforeseen cadence of the words that fell from his lips. An almost divine mystery was unfolding through the communion into which his soul had entered with the soul of the crowd. Something greater and stronger was adding itself to the feeling he had about his own person. And at every moment it seemed that his voice was acquiring a higher virtue.

He saw the ideal picture complete and living within himself, and his manifestation of it in the language of poetry was after the manner of the master-colourists who reign in that place. The luxuriance of Veronese, the ardour of Tintoretto, was in his speech.

" And the hour was approaching; the hour of the supreme feast was at hand. There was an unusual light in the heavens coming from the far-away horizon, as if the wild bridegroom were waving his purple banner as he drew nearer in his fiery chariot. The wind roused by his speed was heavy with all the perfumes of the earth, and reminded the expectant one on the water where the vague sea-locks floated of the white, compact rose-bushes that here and there grew against the balustrades of the gardens overlooking the Brenta, melting little by little like masses of snow. The distant country seemed entirely reflected in the crystal of the air as by the fallacious mirage of the desert; and that impression of nature served to magnify the rarity of the dream of art, for no autumnal pageant of woods and meadows was comparable in the memory to the divine life and transfigurations of those ancient stones.

"Is not some god coming to the city who offers herself? I asked of my own spirit, overcome by the anxiety and desire of pleasure expressed around me as if a fever of infinite passion invaded all things. And I called up the most powerful artist to picture that young, expected god with proud form and refulgent colours.

"He was indeed coming! The inverted goblet of the sky poured down a stream of splendour that, at first, seemed incredible to me, for it was of a quality richer even than the richest light of inspired thought or involuntary dream. The water was like some starry matter of an unknown, changeable nature, suggesting in myriads the indistinct images of a fluid world. A perpetual quiver drew from it harmonies for ever new by a series of stupendously easy destructions and creations. Between the wonders of sky and water the stones that were multiform and many-souled, like a forest or like a people, the silent company of marbles from which the genius of art has extracted the occult conceptions of nature, on which time has accumulated its mysteries and glory engraved its signs, along the hidden veins of which the human spirit rises towards the ideal, as the sap ascends to the flower through the fibres of the plant, — the multiform and many-souled stone constantly took on some expression of life so new and intense that law seemed destroyed for it, and its original inertness flooded by a miraculous sensibility.

"Each second after vibrated on these things like an unbearable flash. From the crosses on the tops of the cupolas swollen by prayer to the slight saline crystals hanging under the arch of the bridges, all glittered in a supreme jubilation of light. Like the sentinel on the rampart throwing his sharp cry to Expectation quivering like a storm below him, so the golden angel from the summit of the greater tower at last flashed out the announcement.

"And He appeared. He appeared sitting on a cloud as on a chariot of fire, the long ends of his purple raiment trailing behind him, imperious though gentle, his half-open lips full of sylvan murmurs and silences, his hair floating over his strong neck, his titanic breast, hardened by the breath of the forest quite bare. He turned his youthful countenance to the City Beautiful. An indescribable inhuman fascination emanated from that countenance. I know not what refined yet cruel brutality that contrasted with his deep eyes full of knowledge shining under heavy lids. His blood leapt and pulsated violently throughout his body to the extreme joints of the firm hands and to the toes of the nimble feet; and occult things were about his whole being, concealing joy as the grape still in flower conceals the wine; and all the tawny gold and purple that He brought with him were like the raiment of his senses. . . .

"With what passion, palpitating under her thousand

girdles of green and the weight of her great jewels, the City Beautiful gave herself up to the magnificent God!"

Lifted up in the vortex of those words, the soul of the crowd seemed to reach the sense of Beauty at one bound, at a height never before attained, and to stand surprised there. The poet's eloquence was seconded by the expression of all that surrounded him; it seemed to resume and continue the rhythms obeyed by all that effigied strength and grace; it seemed to sum up the unlimited concordances between the forms created by human art and the qualities of the natural atmosphere that perpetuated themselves. This was why his voice had so much power; why his gesture so easily enlarged the outlines of images; why in every syllable he pronounced there was added to the significance of the letter the suggestive power of sound. And it was not the effect of the usual electric communication established between speaker and audience only, but of the spell that held the wonderful edifice to its foundations and that gathered extraordinary vigour from the unaccustomed contact of that palpitating agglomerated humanity. The pulse of the crowd and the voice of the poet seemed to restore their own life to those ancient walls, and to renew its original spirit in the cold museum with its nucleus of powerful ideas, made concrete and organic in the most durable of substances to bear witness to the nobility of a race.

A splendour of youth almost divine fell on the women, as it might have fallen in a sumptuous alcove; they too had felt the anxiety of expectance and the joy of surrender, like the City Beautiful. They were smiling with vague languor as if exhausted by a sensation that had been too stirring, their bare shoulders emerging like flowers from their corollas of gems. The emeralds of Andriana Duodo, the rubies of Giustiniana Memo, the sapphires of Lucrezia Priuli, the beryls of Orsetta Contarini, the turquoises of Zenobia Corner, all the heirlooms in whose flame there was a little more than the mere value of their substance, just as in the decorations of the great hall there was a little more than even the value of art, seemed to throw on the white faces of the patrician women the reflection of a joyous, shameless anterior life, as if awakening in them and by some secret virtue raising from the abyss the souls of the voluptuous women who had offered men their bodies saturated with myrrh, with musk, and with amber, and to the public their rouged uncovered breasts.

As he watched the bust of the large many-eyed chimera on which the feathers of the women's fans flapped softly, hot intoxication swept over his thoughts, disquieting him, suggesting words of almost carnal essence, some of those living substantial words with which he had often touched women as if with caressing and inviting fingers. The multiplied reverberation in himself of the vibration produced by him shook him so deeply that he was about to lose his usual balance. He felt himself swinging above the crowd like a concave and sonorous body in which the various resonances were generated by the action of an indistinct though infallible will. During the pauses he would anxiously await the unforeseen manifestation of that will, while the interior echoes still remained as of a voice not his own having pronounced words expressive of thoughts that were new to him.   And that sky, and that water, and those marbles, and the autumn as he had described it, seemed to have no connection with his own late sensations, but to belong to a world of dreams of which he had caught sight while he was speaking — in a rapid succession of flashes.

It surprised him, this unknown power that converged in him, abolishing the limits of his own person and conferring the fulness of a chorus on his solitary voice.   This, then, was the mysterious truce that the revelation of beauty could bring to the daily existence of the breathless multitude; this the mysterious will that could possess the Poet about to answer the multiform soul questioning him as to the value of life and yearning to raise itself, if once only, towards the eternal idea.   He was only the means by which beauty held out the divine gift of oblivion to the men gathered in a place consecrated by centuries of human glory.   He was only translating in the rhythm of words the visible language with which the ancient artists had already set forth in that very spot the prayer and aspiration of the race.   Those men would now contemplate the world, for an hour at least, with different eyes; surely they would think and dream with a different soul.

It was the highest benefit of beauty made manifest; it was the victory of art, the liberator, over the misery and anxiety and tedium of ordinary existence; it was one of those happy intervals in which the stabs of necessity and pain seem to cease and the clenched hand of destiny slowly to relax its hold. His thoughts overstepped the walls that closed the palpitating crowd into a sort of heroic cycle, a zone of red triremes and fortified towers and triumphant processions. The place seemed too narrow now for the exaltation of his new feeling, and once again the real crowd attracted him, the great, unanimous crowd he had seen outside and had heard sending up in the starry night a clamour by which it was itself intoxicated as by wine or blood.

And his thoughts went out not only to this but to infinite other multitudes. He conjured them up crowded in a theatre, held by a dominating idea of truth and beauty; silent and intent before the great arch of the stage open on some marvellous transfiguration of human life, or frenzied by the sudden splendour radiating from an immortal phrase. And his dream of higher Art as it rose again showed him mankind once more seized by reverence for the poets as for those who alone can interrupt human anguish for a while, assuage its thirst, and dispense oblivion. And the test he was undergoing, now seemed much too slight: he felt himself capable of creating gigantic fictions. And the still formless work that he was nourishing within him leapt with a great shudder of life as he saw the tragic actress standing out from the sphere of constellations, the Muse with the diffusing voice who seemed to carry the very frenzy of those distant multitudes silenced in the folds of her dress.

Almost as if the intensity of the life he had lived during the pause had exhausted him, there was a more subdued note in his voice when he began speaking again.

"Under this image," he resumed,— "under this image so real and evident to me at the time I saw it that it seemed nearly tangible, do you not see the analogies that make it significant of singular things?

"The mutual passion of Venice and Autumn that exalts the one and the other to the highest degree of their sensuous beauty has its origin in a deep affinity; for the soul of Venice, the soul fashioned for the City Beautiful by its great artists is autumnal.

"The correspondence between the external and the interior spectacle once discovered, my enjoyment found itself unspeakably multiplied. The crowd of imperishable forms that peoples its churches and palaces seemed from these latter to answer the harmony of daylight with a chord so deep and powerful that it soon became dominant. And — because the light of Heaven alternates with shadows, but the light of Art lasts in the human soul and cannot be extinguished — when the miracle of the hour ceased to cover all those things, my spirit felt itself alone and ecstatic among the splendours of an ideal autumn.

"It is under this aspect that the artistic creation hemmed in between the youth of Giorgione and the old age of Tintoretto appears to me. It is purple, golden, rich, and expressive, like a pageant of the earth under the sun's last flame. Whenever I consider the impetuous creators of so much powerful beauty an image presents itself to my mind drawn from a fragment of Pindar, — 'When the centaurs became acquainted with the virtues of wine, which is sweet as honey and conquers men, they at once banished the white milk from their tables and hastened to partake of their wine in silver horns.' None in the world knew and tasted of the wine of life more than they. They drew from it a sort of lucid intoxication that multiplied their power and communicated a fertilising energy to their eloquence. And in the most beautiful of their creations the violent throb of their pulses seems to have persisted through the ages, like the very rhythm of Venetian Art.

"How pure and poetic is the sleep of the Virgin Ursula on her immaculate bed! A gentle silence hovers in the solitary room; the habit of prayer seems sketched on the pious lips of the sleeper. The shy light of dawn pierces through the doors and the half-open windows, pointing to the word written on the corner of her pillow. INFANTIA is the simple word spreading round the maiden's head, something like the freshness of morning: INFANTIA. The maiden, already betrothed to the princely barbarian and destined for martyrdom, sleeps on. As she lies there fervent, ingenuous, and chaste, does she not seem the image of art such as the precursors saw it in the sincerity of their child-like eyes? INFANTIA. The word calls up all the forgotten ones round that pillow, —Lorenzo Veneziano and Simone da Cusighe, and Catarino and Iacobello, and Maestro Paolo and Giambono, and Semitecolo and Antonio, Andrea and Quirizio da Murano, and the whole of the laborious family by which colour, afterwards the rival of fire, was prepared in the burning island of furnaces.

"But would not they themselves have uttered a cry of surprise had they seen the wave of blood that poured from the breast of the Virgin when pierced by the handsome pagan archer? Blood so crimson flowing from a maiden nurtured on 'white milk'! It is a very orgy of slaughter; the archers have brought their finest arms to it, their richest apparel, their most elegant gestures, as to a festival. The golden-haired barbarian aiming his dart at the martyr with so proud an act of grace seems the youth Eros chrysalised and wingless.

"This same agreeable slayer of innocence will presently give himself up to the enchantment of music, and laying aside his bow will dream a dream of infinite pleasure.

"Well may Giorgione be considered as the one to infuse the new soul into him, and to kindle it with an implacable desire. The music that enchants him is not the melody of angelic lutes diffused between the arches that curve over radiant thrones, or dwindling into serene distances in the visions of the third Bellini. It is still at the touch of religious hands that it rises from the harpsichord, but the world it awakens is full of a joy and of a sadness in which sin lies hidden.

"Whoever has looked at the *Concerto* with sagacious eyes has fathomed an extraordinary and irrevocable moment of the Venetian soul. By means of the harmony of colour, the power of significance of which is unlimited as the mystery of sound, the artist shows us the first workings of a yearning soul to whom life suddenly appears under the aspect of a rich inheritance.

"The monk sitting at the harpsichord and his older companion are not monks like those that Vittore Carpaccio painted flying from the wild beast that Jerome had tamed, in San Giorgio degli Schiavoni. They are of nobler and stronger essence, and the air they breathe is finer and richer: it is propitious to the birth of a great joy or a great sorrow or a haughty dream. What notes do the beautiful sensitive hands draw from the keys where they linger? Magic notes they must be, certainly, to succeed in working in the musician so violent a transfiguration. He is half-way through his earthly existence he is already detached from his youth, already on the verge of decay, and life is only now revealing itself adorned with all its good things, like a forest laden with purple fruit, of which his hands that were intent on other work have never known the velvet bloom. He does not fall under the dominion of some solitary tempting image, because his sensuality slumbers, but he undergoes a confused kind of anguish in which regret overcomes desire while on the web of the harmonies that he seeks, the vision of his past — such as it might have been and was not — weaves itself, before his eyes like a design of Chimeræ. His companion, who is calm because already on the threshold of old age, divines this inner tempest; kindly and gravely he touches the shoulder of the passionate musician with a pacifying movement. Emerging from the warm shadow like the expression of desire itself, we see the youth with the plumed hat and the unshorn locks, the fiery flower of adolescence, whom Giorgione seems to have created under the influence of a ray reflected from the stupendous Hellenic myth whence the ideal form of Hermaphrodite arose. He is there, present and yet a stranger, separated from the others as one having no care but for his own good. The music seems to exalt his inexpressible dream and to multiply infinitely his power of enjoy-nent. He knows that he is master of the life that escapes both the others; the harmonies sought after by the player seem only the prelude to his own feast. He glances sideways intently as if turning to I know not what that fascinates him, and that he would fascinate; his closed mouth is a mouth heavy with a yet ungiven kiss; his forehead is so spacious that the leafiest of crowns would not encumber it, but if I consider his hidden hands, I can only imagine them in the act of crumpling the laurel leaves to perfume his fingers."

The hands of the Life-giver moved as if they were imitating the gesture of the covetous youth and truly extracting its essence from the aromatic leaf; the manner of his voice gave to the image thus presented an appearance so strongly detached that all those among his listeners who were young thought their unspeakable desire was at last finding expression, and their inner dream of uninterrupted and unending pleasure being made manifest. A profound emotion seized them, an obscure agitation of controlled impulses; they seemed to divine new possibilities, the prey that was unhoped for and distant seemed henceforth tangible. Stelio recognised them here and there along the whole length of the hall, leaning against the great reddish bookcases where the numberless volumes of inert and forgotten wisdom lay buried. They occupied the space left free all round, making a border for the compact mass that was like a living hem; and as the extreme edges of a flag that waves in the wind have a stronger flutter, thus they too throbbed more than the rest of the audience at the valiant breath of the poet's words.

Stelio recognised them all. Some he could distinguish by the singularity of their attitude, by the excess of emotion betrayed in the curve of their lips, or the throb of their temples, or the fire of their cheeks. On the faces of some that were turned to the open balcony he divined the enchanting effect of the autumn night and their delight in the breezes coming from the weedy lagoon. The eyes of another, in a ray of love, would point out to him some seated woman, looking as if she had given herself up to herself, with an indefinable expression of impure languor, with a soft snow-white face where the mouth seemed the entrance to a hive moist with honey.

A strange lucidity possessed him, which gave unusual evidence to the things he saw, as if they appeared to him in the hallucination of fever. All things in his eyes were living a hyperbolic life; the portraits of the Doges that recurred round the room among the white meandering of the maps breathed as truly as the bald old men at the further end whose monotonous gestures he could discern at intervals as they wiped their pale, heated brows. Nothing escaped him; not the persistent tearfulness of the hanging torches in the bronze baskets that gathered up the wax yellow as amber, nor the extreme fineness of a gemmed hand that would press a handkerchief to sorrowful lips as if to soothe a burn, nor the folds of a light scarf thrown round bare shoulders to which the night breeze breathing through the open balconies had brought a shiver. And, nevertheless, while he noted these thousand transient aspects, there remained in his vision the entire image of the vast thousand-eyed chimera, from whose side the tragic

Muse emerged, her head rising above the belt of constellations.

His eyes constantly returned to the promised woman who was appearing to him there as the living fulcrum of a starry world. He was grateful to her for having chosen such a way of appearing to him in the moment of that first communion. He no longer saw in her now the passing mistress of a night, a body ripened by long ardour, laden with voluptuous knowledge, but as the admirable instrument of a new art, the apostle of the highest poetry. He saw in her the woman who was to incarnate his future fictions of beauty in her manifold person; whose unforgettable voice was to carry the words of enlightenment to distant peoples. It was not by a promise of pleasure that he now bound himself to her, but by a promise of glory, and the work that was still formless within him leapt once more.

"You who are listening to me," he continued, "do you not see some analogies between these three symbols of Giorgione's and those three generations living at the time and illumined by the dawn of a new century? Venice, the triumphant city, reveals herself to their eyes like a great overpleasing banquet where all the wealth gathered by all the centuries of war and commerce is to be spread out without measure. What richer fountain of pleasure could there be to initiate life in insatiable desire? It is a moment of emotion, almost of bewilderment, that, because of its fulness, is worthy an hour of heroic violence. Stirring voices and laughter seem to come from the hills of Asolo, where in the midst of her pleasures reigns the daughter of San Marco,

Domina Aceli, who found the girdle of Aphrodite in the myrtle gardens of Cyprus. The youth of the white feathers comes at last towards the banquet, a leader followed by an unbridled retinue; and at last we see all the strongest appetites burning like torches, the flames of which are ceaselessly quickened by an impetuous wind.

"Thus begins that divine autumn of Art to the splendour of which man will turn with a deep throb of emotion as long as the human soul is capable of aspiring to transcend the narrowness of its daily existence to live a more fervent life or die a nobler death.

"Giorgione is now imminent on that marvellous sphere, but I cannot recognise his mortal person, and I seek him in the mystery of the fiery cloud that girds him round. He appears more like a myth to us than a man. The destiny of no poet on earth is comparable to his. All, or nearly all, concerning him is unknown. Some have gone so far as to deny his existence. His name is written on no work of his, and no work is attributed to him with certainty. Yet the whole of Venetian art seems to have been inflamed by his revelation. The great Cisan appears to have received from him the secret of infusing a stream of luminous blood into the veins of the beings he creates. In all truth Giorgione represents in Art the Epiphany of the Flame. He deserves to be called the Bearer of Fire, like Prometheus.

"When I consider the rapidity with which the sacred gift has passed from artist to artist, glowing ever more gloriously from colour to colour, the image rises spontaneous in my spirit of one of those festivals by which the Greeks attempted to perpetuate the image of the Titan son of Japetus. On the day of the festival a group of young Athenian horsemen would ride, galloping from Ceramicus to Colonos, their leader waving a torch lit at the altar of the temple. Whenever the rapidity of their course extinguished it, the bearer would give it up to his companion, who, still galloping, would relight it, and this one passed it to the third, and the third to the fourth, and so on ever galloping until the last laid it, still burning, on the altar of the Titan. This image, with all that is vehement in it, is in some way significant to me of the feast of the master-colourists of Venice. Each of them, even the least glorious, has had the sacred gift in his hand, at least for a moment. Some even, like that first Bonifacio whom we should glorify, seem to have gathered with their incombustible fingers the inner flower of this flame."

His own fingers moved in the air as if to pick the ideal flower from the invisible summit of the wave that the seething soul of the chimera was propelling towards the poet who had conquered it. And his eyes travelled to the celestial sphere, silently offering the fiery gift of that flower to her who watched over the godlike beasts of the Zodiac. "To you, Perdita."

But the woman was smiling to some one far away, pointing to some one with her smile. And so, by following the thread of her smile, he was led to an unknown person suddenly lit up on a background of shadow.

Was not that the creature of music whose name had resounded against the iron of the ship in the silence and the shadow?

She seemed to him almost an interior image sud-denly sprung up in that part of his soul where the ghost of the sensation that had fallen upon him as he entered the shadow of the ironclad had remained like an obscure and indistinct point. For a second she was beautiful, with the beauty of his own unexpressed thoughts.

"A City to which similar creatures have given so powerful a soul," he added, agile on the rising wave, " is only considered to-day, by the many, as a great inert shrine full of relics, or as a refuge full of peace and oblivion!

"Indeed I know of no other place in the world — unless it be Rome — where an ambitious and robust spirit can spur on the active virtue of his intellect and all the energies of his being towards the supreme degree, better than on these sluggish waters. And I know of no marsh capable of provoking in human pulses a fever more violent than that which at times creeps towards us from the shadow of a silent canal. And those men who spend their noontide buried in the ripe crop during the dog-days feel no wilder wave of blood rise to their temples than that which dims our eyes when we bend too intently over these waters, seeking lest by chance we should discover in the depths below them some ancient sword or old lost diadem.

" Nevertheless, do not all fragile souls come here as to a place of refuge? those who hide some secret wound, those who have accomplished some final renunciation, those whom a morbid love has emascu-lated, and those who only seek silence the better to hear themselves perish? Perhaps Venice is in their eyes a clement city of death, embraced by a sleep-giving pool. Their presence, however, weighs no more than the wandering weeds floating about the steps of the marble palaces. They only serve to increase the singular odour of sickly things, the strange feverish odour on which we have often found it sweet, towards evening, after a laborious day, to nurse the fulness of our own feelings, at times so akin to languor.

"Yet the ambiguous city does not always indulge the illusion of those who worship her as a peace-giver. I know of one who started up from his rest on her bosom as terrified as if he had been lying with the pliant fingers of his beloved on his tired eyelids and had heard snakes suddenly hissing in her hair.

"Ah, if I could only show you the prodigious life that I see throbbing under her vast necklaces and her thousand girdles of green! Day by day she absorbs more of our soul: now giving it back to us intact and fresh, and renewed with a primitive new-ness on which the traces of the morrow's things will impress themselves with ineffable clearness; now giving it back to us infinitely subtle and voracious, like a flame melting all that approaches it, so that at evening, among the dross and ashes of it, we some-times come upon some extraordinary sublimate. She entices each of us into the act that is the very genesis of our species: the effort to surpass our-selves unceasingly. She shows us the possibility of transforming pain into the most efficacious of stimu-lating energies; she teaches us that joy is the most certain means of knowledge offered us by Nature.

and that he who has suffered much is less wise than he who has much enjoyed."

Here and there a vague murmur of dissent rippled through the audience; the Queen denied the assertion with a slight shake of her head; some ladies communicated a sort of graceful horror to each other in an exchange of glances. Then all was lost in the zeal of the youthful applause that on every side went out to him who taught with such truthful daring the art of ascending to superior forms of life by the power of joy.

Stelio smiled as he recognised his own, who were many; smiled on recognising the efficacy of his teaching that had already cleared the mists of inert sadness from more than one spirit, and in more than one had killed cowardice and vain tears, and in more than one had instilled for ever a scorn of complaining sorrows and weak compassions. He was glad of having given utterance once more to that principle of his doctrine which flowed naturally from the soul of the art he was glorifying. And they who had withdrawn into a hermit's cell to adore a sad phantom that only lived in the blurred mirror of their own eyes; and they who had made themselves kings of a windowless palace, from time immemorial awaiting a visitation there; and they who had hoped to dig up the image of Beauty from under some ruin and had only found a worn sphinx that had tormented them with its endless enigmas; and they who sat down evening after evening on their doorsteps, pale, to await the arrival of a mysterious stranger bringing endless gifts under his mantle, and pressed their **ears flat on the** ground to hear the footsteps that now seemed to draw near and now to fade away; all those who were sterilised by a resigned mourning or devoured by a desperate pride; those who were hardened by a useless obstinacy or kept sleepless by some continually disappointed expectation, — he would have bid them all come and recognise their disease under the splendour of that ancient yet ever-resurgent soul.

"If its whole population were to emigrate," he said, in a voice full of exaltation, "forsaking its homes, attracted by other shores, as once its own heroic youth were tempted by the arch of the Bosphorus in the time of the Doge Pietro Ziani, and no prayer were again to strike the sonorous gold of the curved mosaics, no oar were again to perpetuate with its rhythm the meditation of the silent stones, Venice would yet and for ever remain a City of Life. The ideal creatures guarded by its silence live in the whole past and in the whole future. We constantly find in them new concordances with the edifice of the Universe that is about to be, unexpected meetings with the idea that was born only yesterday, clear announcements of that which is only a foreboding in us as yet, and open answers to that which we have not yet dared to ask. They are simple, and yet charged with numberless significances; they are ingenuous, and yet clothed in curious raiment. If we contemplated them for an indefinite length of time, they would never cease from pouring dissimilar truths into our spirits. If we visited them every day, they would appear to us every day under an unforeseen aspect, like the sea, the rivers, the fields, the woods, and the rocks. Sometimes the things

which they say to us do not reach as far as our
intellect, but are revealed to us in a kind of confused
happiness causing our own substance to dilate and
quiver from its very depths. Some clear morning
they will show us the way to the distant forest where
the beautiful one awaits us from time immemorial,
buried in her mystic hair.

"Whence comes their unlimited power?

"From the pure unconsciousness of the artists
who created them.

"Those profound men ignored the immensity of the
things which they expressed. Striking a million roots
into the soil of life, not like single trees, but like the
vastest forests, they have absorbed infinite elements,
which have been transfused and condensed by them
into ideal species whose essences have remained unknown to them, as the taste of the apple remains unknown to the branch that bears it. They have been
the mysterious means continually chosen by Nature
to satisfy her continual aspiration to those types which
she has not succeeded in producing in an integral
manner. Because of this, while continuing the work
of the Divine Mother, their mind has become transformed, as Leonardo says, into a 'likeness of the
divine mind.' And because creative force incessantly rushed to their fingers like sap to the buds
of the trees, they have created with joy."

All the desire of the artist panting to obtain the
Olympic gift, all his envy of those colossal, untiring, and undoubting forgers of beauty, all his thirst
for happiness and glory, stood revealed in the
accent with which he pronounced the last words.
Once more the soul of the multitude was in the

poet's power, strained and vibrating like one only chord made of a thousand chords, that incalculably prolonged every resonance. That resonance awakened in it the sense of a truth that it had contained all along, but that the words of the poet were suddenly revealing in the form of a message never heard before. It no longer felt a stranger in the sacred place, where one of the most splendid of human destinies had left so deep a trace of its splendour; but it could feel the aged mass living round it and beneath it, from its deepest foundations, as if its memories, no longer motionless in the shadow of the past, were circulating through it like the free winds of a deeply-stirred forest. In the magic respite given to it by the virtue of strength and poetry the multitude seemed to perceive in itself the indestructible signs of its primitive generation, almost a vague effigy of its remote ascendency; it seemed to recognise its right to an old heritage of which it had been despoiled, — that heritage which the messenger was telling them was still intact and within their power to recover. It was experiencing the agitation of one about to regain a lost fortune. And over the night that could be seen glittering through the open balconies, with the red glare of the illumination that was to encircle the harbour below beginning to appear, there seemed to be spread the expectation of a foretold home-coming.

In that sonorous silence the solitary voice reached its climax.

"To create with joy!" It is the attribute of Divinity! It is not possible to imagine at the summit of our spirit a more triumphal act. The

very words that express it have about them the
qualities of the dawn's resplendence.

"And these artists created by a means that is in
itself a joyous mystery: by colour which is the
ornament of the world; colour, which seems the
effort of matter to become light.

"And such was their extreme musical sense of
colour that their creation transcends the narrow
limits of the pictured symbols, and takes on the
high revealing power of an infinite harmony.

"Never has the sentence pronounced by that
Vinci on whom Truth flashed one day with its thousand sacred faces appeared so evident as before their
great symphonic canvases. *Music cannot be called
other than the sister of painting*. Their painting
is not only silent poetry, it is also silent music.
For this, the subtlest seekers of rare symbols and
those most anxious to impress the signs of an internal Universe on the purity of a thoughtful brow
seem to us almost barren in comparison to these
great unconscious musicians.

"When we see Bonifacio in his Parable of Dives
intoning with a note of fire the most powerful harmony of colour in which the essence of a haughty
and voluptuous soul has ever stood revealed, we do
not pause with our inquiry at the fair youth listening
to the music, seated between the two magnificent
courtesans, whose faces have the gleam of lamps lit
in pure ether. But piercing through the material
symbol we give ourselves up with anxious emotion
to the power of evocation held by those far-reaching
chords, in which our spirits of to-day seem to find
the foresight of I know not what evening, heavy with

autumnal gold as with beautiful destinies, on a harbour quiet as a basin of perfumed oils where a galley throbbing with oriflames shall enter in the midst of a strange silence, like a twilight butterfly fluttering into the veined chalice of a great flower.

"Shall not our mortal eyes really see it landing under the palace of the Doges some glorious evening?

"Does it not appear to us from a prophetic horizon in that Allegory of Autumn which Tintoretto offers us, like a superior created image of our dream of yesterday?

"Seated on the shore like a deity Venice receives the ring from the young vine-crowned god who has descended into the water, while Beauty soars on her wings with the diadem of stars to crown the wonderful alliance.

"Look at the distant ship! it seems to bring some announcement. Look at the body of the symbolic woman! both seem capable of bearing the germs of a world."

The vast bursting applause was overpowered by the youthful clamour that rose like a whirlwind towards him who had made so great a hope flash before their anxious eyes, towards him who had revealed himself as possessing so lucid a faith in the occult genius of their race, in the growing virtue of the ideals handed down by their fathers, in their sovereign dignity of spirit, in the indestructible power of Beauty, in all the great values held as nothing by modern barbarity. The hearts of his disciples went out to the master with an impulse of love, with all the effusion of gratitude, for his ardent words had brought torch-lights to their souls, and had excited their sense of life to the point of fever. Giorgione's creation lived again in each of them: the youth with the beautiful white feathers, about to grasp the immense accumulated spoil. And to each it seemed as if his power of enjoyment had been infinitely multiplied. Their cry was so expressive of internal tumult, that the Life-giver shivered inwardly, filled by a sudden tide of sadness as he thought of the ashes of that transient fire, of the morrow's cruel awakening. Against what sharp and ignoble hindrances would it not have to break, this, their terrible desire of living, and the violent will to direct all the energies of their being to a sublime end, to shape the wings of victory for their own fate!

But the night was favourable to that youthful delirium. The dreams of domination, of pleasure, and of glory that Venice has first nursed, and then suffocated in her marble arms, seemed to rise again from the foundations of the palaces, entering by the open balconies, throbbing like a people newly restored to life under the enormous scrolls of the ceiling that was rich and heavy like a suspended treasure. The strength that was swelling the muscles of the gods, kings, and heroes effigied round the ample dome and the high walls; the beauty that flowed like visible music through the nudity of the goddesses, the queens, and the courtesans; the human strength and beauty transfigured by centuries of art, — harmonised in one single image, that those intoxicated men seemed to see real and breathing before their eyes, erected there by the new poet.

Their intoxication vented itself in the shout they sent up to him who had offered their parched lips a cup of his own wine. All henceforth would be able to see the inextinguishable flame through the veil of water. Some one among them already imagined himself crumpling laurel leaves to perfume his fingers, and some already dreamt of discovering at the bottom of a silent canal the ancient sword and the old, lost diadem.

Stelio Effrena was alone with the statues in one of the rooms of the neighbouring museum, impatient of any other contact, feeling the necessity of recollecting himself and quieting the unusual vibration by which his whole essence had been dissipated and dispersed over the manifold spirit of the crowd. There was no trace in his memory of his recent words; he could find no sign of his recent images. All that persisted in his mind was that "inner flower of the flame" that he had mentioned when glorifying the first Bonifacio, and had gathered with his own incombustible fingers for the promised woman. It again struck him how at the moment of a spontaneous offer, the woman had withdrawn herself, and how, in the place of her absent eyes, he had found the indicating smile. The cloud of ecstasy that had been on the point of dissolving seemed to again condense above his head; assuming the vague shape of the creature of music, and holding the flaming flower in an attitude of dominion, it seemed that she was emerging above his inward agitation as on the incessant tremble of a summer sea. The first notes of the symphony of Benedetto Marcello reached him from the neighbouring hall as if to celebrate that image,

their fugue-like movement at once revealing its character of great style. A clear, sonorous idea, strong
as a living person, developed itself in the measure of
its power, and in that music he recognised the virtue
of the same principle round which as round a thyrsus
he had entwined the garland of his poetry.

Then the name that had already echoed against the
flank of the ironclad, in the silence and the shadow,
the name that had been scattered like a sibylline leaf
by the immense wave of the evening bells, seemed to
propose its syllables to the orchestra for him, like a
new theme picked up by the bows of the instruments.
The violins, the viols, and the violoncellos sang it in
turn; the sudden blasts of the heroic trumpets exalted it; finally, with a uniform impetus the whole
quartette launched it into that heaven of joy where
the crown of stars offered to Ariadne by the golden
Aphrodite would presently shine.

In the pause which followed, Stelio underwent a
singular bewilderment, almost a religious stupor, as if
he had assisted at an annunciation. He understood
what a precious thing it was to him to be alone among
those pure, silent images in that inestimable lyric
moment.

A shred of the same mystery that he had grazed
under the flank of the ironclad as one touches a floating veil seemed to waver before his eyes in that deserted room that was yet so near to the human crowd.
It was silent, like the sea-shell lying on the shore by
the rushing waves. Again, as before at other extraordinary hours of his journey, he felt that his fate was

present and about to give his being a new impulse, perhaps to call to life in it a marvellous act of will. And as he reflected on the mediocrity of the many obscure destinies hanging over those heads in the crowd, that were eager for the apparitions of ideal life, he rejoiced at being where he was to adore the auspicious demon-figure that had secretly come to visit him and to bring him a shrouded gift in the name of an unknown mistress.

He started at the burst of human voices saluting the unconquered king with a triumphant acclamation.

" Viva il forte, viva il grande." . . .

The deep hall echoed like a vast timbrel, and the reverberation diluted along the staircase of the censors and the Golden Staircase, to the loggias, the passages, the porches, the vestibules, to the wells, to the foundations of the palace, like a thunder of gladness rolling in the serene night.

" Viva il forte, viva il grande
Vincitor dell' Indie dome." [1] . . .

It seemed that the chorus was saluting the apparition of the magnificent god invoked by the poet upon the Sea-City.   It seemed as if the hem of his purple raiment fluttered in those vocal notes like flames in a crystal tube.   The living image hung suspended over the crowd that it was nourishing with its own dream.

" Viva il forte, viva il grande." . . .

In the impetuous *fugue* movement of the bassi, the contralti and the soprani repeated their frenzied acclamation of the Immortal of the thousand names and

[1] " Hail to the strong, hail to the great conqueror of vanquished India."

the thousaud crowns, "born on an ineffable bed, like to a young man in his first youth."

The old Dionysian intoxication seemed to revive and diffuse itself over the divine Chorus. The fulness and freshness of life in the smile of Zeus, who loosed the hearts of men from human sufferings, was expressed there with a luminous burst of joy. The inextinguishable fires of the Bassarides flamed and crackled there. As in the Orphean hymn the light of a conflagration illumined the young brow crowned with azure hair. "When the splendour of fire invaded all the earth, he alone chained up the shrill whirlwinds of flame." As in the Homeric hymn the barren bosom of the sea throbbed there, the measured stroke of the numerous oars that were pushing the well-built vessel to unknown lands echoed there. The Florid, the Fruit-bearer, the visible Remedy of mortals, the sacred Flower, the Friend of pleasure, Dionysius the liberator, suddenly reappeared before the face of man on the wings of song, crowning that nocturnal hour with bliss, incessantly holding out to his senses as in a full chalice all the good things of life.

The strength of the song was increasing, the voices blending in its rush. The hymn now celebrated the tamer of tigers, of panthers, of lions, and of lynxes. The Mænads seemed to scream out here with heads thrown back, and locks scattered, and dresses loosened, striking their cymbals, shaking their citherns. "Evoe!"

A broad pastoral rhythm rose unexpectedly from these heroic sounds, bringing forth the images of the Theban Bacchus of the pure brow circled with gentle thoughts.

"Quel che all' olmo la vite in stretto nodo
  Pronuba accoppia, e i pampini feconda." [1]

Only two voices in a succession of sixths now sang
the leafy nuptials, the green marriage-feast, the flexible ties. The image of the boat on the lagoon, laden
with bunches like a wine-press about to be trodden,
already created by the poet's words, passed again
before the eyes of the multitude. And the song
seemed to repeat the miracle witnessed by the prudent pilot Medeia. "And it came to pass that a
sweet and most fragrant wine ran along the swift,
black boat. . . . And a vine unfolded itself up to
the top of the sail, and from it hung numberless
bunches. And a dark ivy twisted itself about the
mast, and it was covered with flowers, and beautiful
fruits grew on it, and garlands were about the rowlocks."
The spirit of the fugue then passed into the orchestra, disburdened itself there in beautiful volutes while
the voices struck the web of the orchestra with a
simultaneous percussion. And like a light thyrsus
brandished above the Bacchic crowd, a single voice
repeated the impartial melody, smiling with the grace
of that pastoral marriage.

"Viva dell' olmo
  E della vite
  L' almo fecondo
  Sostenitor!" [2]

The single voices seemed to call forth a picture
of erect Tiades gently waving their thyrsi in the

---

[1] " He who tightly clasps the vine to the elm-tree, weds them one
to the other, and fructifies its tendrils."

[2] " Hail to the great, fruitful supporter of the vine and the elm-tree."

fumes of their intoxication, dressed in long crocus-coloured garments, their faces alight, palpitating like the women of Veronese who were bending from aerial balustrades to drink in the song.

The heroic applause came up once more with final vehemence. The face of the conquering God flashed again among the madly waved torches. Voices and orchestra thundered in unison in a supreme impulse of joy at the huge chimera full of eyes under the hanging treasure of the ceiling in the circle of red triremes and armed towers and triumphant processions.

> " Viva dell' Indie,
>   Viva de' mari,
>   Viva de' mostri
>   Il domator ! " [1]

Stelio Effrena had come as far as the threshold; through the throng that gave way as he passed he penetrated into the hall, and remained standing against one of the sides of the platform occupied by the singers and the orchestra. His anxious eyes sought la Foscarina by the heavenly sphere, but did not find her.

The head of the tragic muse no longer rose above the belt of constellations. Where was she? Where had she withdrawn herself? Could she be seeing him without his seeing her? An obscure feeling of agitation perturbed him, and all they had seen that evening on the waters returned to his spirit confusedly accompanied by her parting words of promise. As he looked through the open balconies he thought

[1] " Hail to the conqueror of India, of the seas, and of the monsters."

she had gone out into the night air, and that perhaps she was leaning against the parapet, feeling the waves of music pass over her cold neck, deriving from them a joy as of shivers communicated by long kisses.

The expectation of the revealing voice, however, overpowered every other thought, abolished every other anxiety. He noticed that a deep silence had come over the hall, as in the moment when he had opened his lips for his first syllable. As in that moment the elusive and versatile monster with the thousand human faces seemed to stretch out dumbly, making a void in itself to receive a new soul.

He heard some one round him whisper the name of Donatella Arvale; he turned his eyes towards the platform beyond the dark hedge of the violoncelli. The singer was invisible, concealed by the delicate, quivering forest, whence the sorrowful harmony was about to arise that was to accompany Ariadne's lament.

In the propitious silence the violins unfolded the prelude. The viols and the violoncellos then added a deeper sigh to that imploring moan. After the Phrygian flute and the Berecinthian cithern, after the instruments of revelry the sounds of which trouble the reason and spur on delirium, was not this, grave and sweet, the august Doric lyre, the harmonious fulcrum of song? It was the birth of the Drama from the noisy Dithyramb. The great metamorphosis of the Dionysian rite, the frenzy of the sacred festival converted into the creative enthusiasm of the tragedian, seemed figured by that musical vicissitude. The fiery breath of the Thracian god had given life to a sublime form of art. The crown and the tripod decreed as the prize of the poet's victory had taken the place of the lascivious goat and the Attic basket of figs. Æschilus, keeper of a vineyard, had been visited by the god, and had received the infusion of his spirit of flame. On the slope of the Acropolis, by the sanctuary of Dionysius, a marble theatre had arisen worthy of containing the chosen people.

Thus, suddenly in the inner world of the Life-giver the pathways of the centuries had opened up, and were stretching away into the distance of primitive mysteries. That form of art to which the effort of his genius was tending, attracted by the obscure aspirations of human multitudes, now appeared to him in all the sanctity of its origins. The divine sorrow of Ariadne, coming like a melodious cry out of the furious Thiaros, imparted a throb to the already living, though still formless, work that he was nourishing within him. Again his glance sought the Muse of the propagating voice against the belt of constellations. As he did not see her, he turned to the forest of instruments whence the moan arose.

Then, among the slight bows that rose and fell on the strings with an alternating motion, he saw the singer. She was standing straight as a stem, and like a stem swaying a little to the hushed harmony. The youthfulness of her agile yet robust body seemed resplendent through the tissue of her garments like a flame seen through the thinness of polished ivory. The bows seemed to draw their note from the occult music that was in her as they rose and fell round her white form. When she curved her lips for her first words Stelio felt the strength and purity of the voice before he heard its modulation, as if she were before

him like a crystal vase in which he could trace the
ascension of a living spring.

> " Come mai puoì
> Vedermi piangere ? " [1] . . .

The melody of antique love and sorrow flowed
from those lips with an expression so strong and
pure, that as it passed into the manifold soul of the
audience it immediately changed into mysterious joy.
Was it indeed the divine weeping of the daughter
of Minos as she held out her deluded arms to the
Flavian guest from the deserted shore of Naxos?
The fable vanished, abolishing the deception of time.
The eternal love and eternal sorrow of gods and
men breathed in the sovereign voice. The useless
regret of each lost joy, the last recalling of each
fugitive good, the supreme prayer to every sail vanishing in the sea, to every sun hiding in the mountains, the implacable desire and the promise of death
passed into the great, solitary song, transformed
by the virtue of art into sublime essences that the
soul could receive without suffering. The words
themselves dissolved in it, lost all meaning, changed
into indefinitely revealing notes of love and sorrow.
Like a circle that is closed and yet dilates continually
with the same throb as universal life, the melody had
circumscribed the manifold soul that yet dilated with
it in an immense joy. Through the open balconies,
in the perfect calm of the autumn night, the fascination spread over the torpid waters, rose to the vigilant stars, went beyond the motionless masts of the
ships, beyond the sacred towers inhabited by the

---

[1] " How can you bear to see me weep ? "

now silent bells. In the interludes the singer would bend her young head, apparently lifeless as an image, all white in the forest of instruments, surrounded by the alternate motion of the long bows, perhaps unconscious of the world that her song had in a moment transfigured.

Stelio Effrena reached the courtyard by a secret outlet, so as to be spared the curiosity of the importunate, and took refuge in a fragment of shadow. Thence he watched the throng at the head of the Scala dei Giganti and waited for the two women, the singer and the actress, who had promised to meet him at the well.

At every instant his expectation became more anxious. The immense cry rising round the outer walls of the palace reached him and then lost itself in the heavens that were illumined by a red glare as of a conflagration. An almost terrible joy seemed spreading over the Sea-City. It seemed that a vehement breath had suddenly come to dilate the narrow hearts, and that a superabundance of sensual life was swelling the arteries of man. The repetition of the Bacchic chorus celebrating the crown of stars laid by Aphrodite on the forgetful head of Ariadne, the great hymn of glory followed by the supreme clamours of the revels of Thiaros, had drawn a cry from the throng gathered on the Molo under the open balconies.

At the final elevation, in unison on the word "Viva!" in the chorus of Mænads, Satyrs, and Egipans, the chorus of the populace in the harbour of San Marco had answered like a formidable echo. And at that point it had seemed as if their delirium, remembering the woods burned of old on the sacred nights, had given the signal of the conflagration in which the beauty of Venice was finally to stand resplendent.

The dream of Paris Eglano flashed on Stelio's desire, — the spectacle of the miraculous flames offered to love on the floating bed. The image of Donatella Arvale persisted in his eyes: a nimble, youthful figure, powerful and shapely, standing out of the forest of sound in the midst of the alternating motion of the bows that seemed to draw their note from the hidden music that was in her. And, with a strange pain in which there passed something like a shadow of horror, he saw the image of the other woman, — poisoned by art, overcharged with voluptuous knowledge, her eloquent mouth full of the savours of maturity and corruption, a dryness as of fever in her hands that had pressed the juice from all deceitful fruits, and the traces of a hundred masks on her face that had shammed the fury of mortal passions. To-night at last, after the long intermediate desire, he was to receive the gift of the ageing body, that was saturated with caresses and yet still unknown to him. How he had trembled and vibrated a little while ago, as he sat by the side of the silent woman, gliding towards the City Beautiful on waters that had seemed to both as if rushing through a fearful clepsydra! Ah, why was she now coming towards him with the other temptress? Why was she placing, by the side of her knowledge full of despair, the pure splendour of that young life?

With a deep throb he noticed the figure of la Foscarina standing in the light of the smoking torches at the top of the marble staircase, so tightly pressed by the crowd upon that of Donatella Arvale that they blended into each other in one same whiteness. His eyes followed them down the staircase in the same suspense, as if at every step they were putting their feet on the margin of an abyss. In those brief hours the stranger had already lived within him a life so intense that his emotion on seeing her draw near him was such as he would have felt had he suddenly been met by the living incarnation of one of the ideal creatures born of his art.

She was coming slowly down through the human tide that her song had raised for a moment to the height of joy. Behind her, the Palace of the Doges, crossed by sudden flashes and confused sounds, gave the impression of one of those fabulous awakenings that suddenly transfigure the inaccessible palaces in the midst of a wood where the long hair on some royal head had grown in their solitude through the ages, feeding on their silence like the eternal willows on a lethal river. The two guardian Giants blazed red in the red light of the torches; the cusp of the Golden Gate glittered with little lamps; beyond the north wing, the five cupolas of the basilica reigned in the heavens like vast mitres studded with chrysolites. And still the great clamour rose, rose above the crowd of marbles, bold as the lowing of the sea in a storm against the walls of Malamocco. Stelio saw the two temptresses come to his desire in the midst of this festive tumult, in this contrast of unusual appearances, both emerging from

the crowd as from the clasp of a monster. And
his desire pictured to him extraordinary promiscuities which he believed could be realised with the
facility of dreams and the solemnity of liturgic
ceremonies. He thought Perdita must be leading
that magnificent prey to him for some recondite
aim of beauty, for some great work of love which
she herself would help him accomplish. Perdita's
words that night, he thought, would be wonderful
in their meaning. And the indefinable melancholy
he had felt on leaning over the bronze edge, on
gazing at the reflection of the stars in the dark
inner well, passed over his spirit; he seemed to feel
himself in the expectation of some event about to
stir that secret soul in the last depths of his being
which had remained, like the mirror of water, un-
moved and strange and intangible. By the dizzy
quickening of his thoughts, he understood that he
had attained the state of grace, that he was near
the divine delirium which only the virtues of the
lagoon could give him. And he went forth from the
shadow to meet the two women with an intoxicating
presentiment.

" Oh, Effrena," la Foscarina said, coming up to
the well, " I did not hope to find you here. We
are very late, are we not? But we were hemmed in
by the crowd without escape. . . ."

Turning to her companion, she added, smiling,
" Donatella, here is the Lord of the Flame."

Without speaking, yet smiling, Donatella Arvale
acknowledged Stelio's deep salute.

Drawing her towards her, la Foscarina resumed:

" We must go and look for our gondola. It is wait-

ing for us at the Ponte della Paglia.   Are you coming
with us, Effrena?   We must seize our moment.   The
crowd is rushing towards the Piazzetta.   The Queen
comes out by the Porta della Carta."

A long, united cry greeted the appearance of the
fair pearled Queen at the head of the staircase, whence
at one time, in the presence of the people, the Doge
was wont to receive the ducal ensign.   Once more
the name of the white starry flower and of the pure
pearl was repeated by the crowd and echoed by the
marble.   Flashes of joy sparkled in the sky ; a thousand pigeons of fire flew away from the pinnacles of
San Marco like flaming messengers.

"The Epiphany of the Flame," exclaimed la
Foscarina, as on reaching the Molo she came upon
the hallucinating spectacle.

By her side Donatella Arvale and Stelio Effrena
stopped, struck with wonder, looking at each other
with dazed eyes.   And their faces, lit up by the
reflection, shone as if they were bending over a
furnace or the mouth of a crater.

All the innumerable appearances of volatile and
many-coloured Fire spread over the firmament,
crawled on the water, twined round the masts of the
vessels, garlanded the cupolas and the towers, adorned
the entablatures, wrapped themselves round the
statues, budded on the capitals, enriched every line,
transfigured every aspect of the sacred and profane
architectures in the midst of which the deep harbour
was like an enchanted mirror that multiplied the
marble.   The astonished eye could no longer distin-

guish the quality of the various elements: it was deluded by a mobile and measureless vision, all the forms of which lived a lucid, fluid life suspended in vibrating ether, so that the slim prows curving on the waters and the myriad pigeons of fire in the heavens seemed to vie with each other in a similar flight and to both reach the summit of the immaterial edifices. That which in the twilight had seemed a silvery palace dedicated to Neptune and built after the likeness of tortuous marine forms, had now become a temple built by the willing genii of Fire. It seemed, on a giant scale, one of those labyrinthian dwellings rising on the andirons at the hundred doors of which the two-faced presages with their ambiguous gestures appear to the watching maiden; it seemed, on a giant scale, one of those frail, regal palaces, all vermilion, at the thousand windows of which the salamander princesses look out for an instant, laughing voluptuously at the thoughtful poet. The sphere of the Fortuna, borne on the shoulders of the Atlantides, radiated on the triple loggia near by, rosy as a waning moon, a cycle of satellites springing from its reflection. From the Riva, from San Giorgio, from the Giudecca, fiery bunches of stars sparkled ceaselessly, converged on high and burst there into roses, lilies, palms, into flowers of Paradise forming an aerial garden that continually melted and continually renewed itself with ever richer and stranger blossoms. It was like a rapid succession of supernal springs and autumns; an immense rain of sparks made of leaves and petals fell from the dissolution of the heavens, wrapping all things in its tremulous gold. Through the gap that opened out in that thickness one could see still far off a beflagged flotilla advancing from the lagoon: a flock of galleys similar perhaps to that which might float through the dream of a child of pleasure, sleeping his last sleep on a bed steeped in deadly perfumes; like those dream-vessels, they too perhaps had cables made of the twisted hair of female slaves brought from conquered countries and still dripping with sweet oils; like them, perhaps, their hulls too were full of myrrh, spikenard, benzoin, balsam of Syria, cinnamon, all the aromas; and of sandal, cedar, terebinth, all the odoriferous woods in different layers. The indescribable colours of the flags that adorned them suggested perfumes and spices. Blue and green and greenish blue, crocus-coloured, violet, and of indistinct blendings, those flags seemed to escape from an internal conflagration and to have been coloured by unknown processes. Thus, perhaps, in the fury of ancient sieges fire was set to reservoirs that contained the essences destined to the wives of the Syrian princes; and thus, on the water dotted over by the molten matters gathered in its hulls, the magnificent lost fleet advanced towards the harbour, slowly as if its pilots were ecstatic dreams that would lead it to the foot of the columned Lion, there to consume itself like a gigantic votive pyre, perfuming and stupefying the soul of Venice for all eternity.

"The Epiphany of the Flame! What an unforeseen commentary to your poem, Effrena! The City of Life responds by a miracle to your act of adoration. She is all burning, through her veil of water. Are you not satisfied? Look! Millions of golden pomegranates are hanging everywhere."

The actress was smiling and the festival illumined her face. She seemed under the empire of that singular gaiety of hers that Stelio well knew, and that because of its dull creaking sound gave him the idea of a deep, shut-up house where violent hands suddenly opened all the doors and windows, causing them to turn on their corroded hinges.

"We must praise Ariadne," he said, "for having given this harmony its highest note."

He only said those words that the singer might be induced to speak, only because of his desire to hear what the tone of her voice would be when not lifted up in song. But his praise was lost in the reiterated clamour of the crowd that overflowed on the Molo, making delay impossible. From the shore where he stood he helped the two friends into their gondola, then sat down on the stool at their knee, and the long dentellated prow, throwing out sparks, entered into the enchantment.

"To the Rio Marin, by the Canalazzo," la Foscarina ordered the boatman. "Do you know, Effrena, we are going to have some of your best friends to supper, — Francesco de Lizo, Daniele Glauro, Prince Hoditz, Antimo della Bella, Fabio Molza, Baldassare Stampa — ?"

"It is going to be a banquet, then?"

"Alas! not that of Cana!"

"But will Lady Myrta not be there with her Veronese-like greyhounds?"

"Certainly, Lady Myrta will not fail; did you not see her in the hall? She was sitting in one of the first rows wrapped up in you."

Because they had looked each other in the eyes

as they spoke, a sudden confusion invaded them.
And the remembrance of the full twilight hour they
had lived on that same water cleaved by that same
oar filled their souls like a tide of troubled blood;
they were surprised by a swift return of that same
anguish which both had felt when on the point of
leaving behind them the silence of the estuary already
in the power of shadow and death. And their lips
rebelled against vain, deceitful words, and their souls
withdrew from the effort of inclining themselves for
the sake of prudence towards the passing ornaments
of the life of joy that now seemed worthless, absorbed
as they were in the consideration of the strange figures
that were rising from their own depth with an aspect
of monstrous wealth never before seen, like the heaped
up treasures that shafts of light were discovering in
the night waters.

And because they were silent as they had been
when they approached the vessel with the descending
flag, they felt the presence of the creature of music
weigh the more heavily on their silence, as in the
interval when they had first heard her name; and,
little by little, that weight became intolerable.
Nevertheless, she appeared to be as distant from
Stelio, who was sitting at her knee, as she had been
a moment ago among the forest of instruments: apart
and unconscious, as a moment ago in the joy of her
song. She had not yet spoken.

Almost timidly and only to hear her speak, Stelio
asked her: —

" Are you staying some time longer in Venice? "

He had tried to choose the words he should address
to her: all those that had come as far as his lips had

troubled him, had seemed too full of ambiguous meanings, too much alive, insidious, fit for incalculable transformations of life like the unknown seed from which spring the thousand roots. And it had seemed to him that none of these could be heard by Perdita too without her love being left the sadder for them.

Only after having uttered the simple, usual question he noticed that even in its words an infinity of hope and desire could lie hidden.

"I shall have to leave to-morrow," answered Donatella Arvale; "even now I ought not to be here."

Her voice, that was so clear and powerful in the heights of song, sounded low and sober as if suffused with a slight opaque quality, suggesting the image of a precious metal wrapped in the most delicate velvet. Her brief answer suggested a place of suffering to which she was about to return, where she would submit herself to some well-known torture; a sorrowful strength of will, like iron tempered in tears, sparkled through the veil of her young beauty.

"To-morrow!" exclaimed Stelio, with sincere regret. "Have you heard, Signora?"

"I know," said la Foscarina, gently, taking Donatella's hand. "And it is a great sorrow to me to see her go. But she cannot remain too long away from her father. Perhaps you still ignore . . ."

"What?" Stelio asked quickly. "Is he ill? It is true, then, that Lorenzo Arvale is ill!"

"No, he is tired," la Foscarina answered, touching her forehead with an involuntary gesture that showed Stelio the horrible threat hanging over the genius of the artist who had seemed as fertile and untiring as one of the old masters: a Della Robbia or a Verrocchio. "He is only tired. He needs rest and soothing balsams, and his daughter's song is an unequalled balm to him. Do not you too, Effrena, believe in the healing power of music?"

"Certainly," he said. "Ariadne has a divine gift by which her power transcends all limits."

The name of Ariadne came spontaneously to his lips to indicate the singer such as he saw her. It seemed to him that he could not utter the girl's own name preceded by the ordinary generic epithet imposed by social customs. As he saw her, she was singular and entire, freed from the small ties of custom, living her own secluded life, like a great work on which style should have set its inviolable seal. In his eyes, she was isolated like those figures that stand out because of sharp and deepened outline, a stranger to ordinary life, fixed on some profoundly secret thought; and already, before the intensity of that concentration, he felt a kind of passionate impatience not dissimilar to that of the curious man who should find himself before some hermetically closed thing that tempts him.

"Ariadne had for the healing of her sorrows that gift of oblivion," she said, "which is denied to me."

A perhaps involuntary bitterness coloured her words. In it Stelio perceived the landmarks of an aspiration towards some life that should be less oppressed by useless suffering. His rapid intuition divined her indignation at her state of slavery, her horror of the sacrifice to which she was forcing herself, the vehement desire in her of rising towards joy, and the aptitude in her of being drawn like a beautiful bow by some strong hand that should know how to use it as its weapon for a great conquest. He divined that she had lost all hope of her father's recovery; that it was painful to her to henceforth feel herself no more than the custodian of an extinguished hearth, of ashes that had no sparks; and the image of the great stricken artist appeared to him not such as he was, since he had never seen his perishable mask, but such as he was pictured to him by the ideas of beauty which he had expressed in lasting bronze and marble. And he gazed fixedly at that image in an agony of terror more icy than that which the most awful aspects of death could have inspired. And all his strength and all his pride and all his desire seemed to resound within him like a bundle of arms scattered by a threatening hand, and there was no fibre in him which did not quiver.

La Foscarina raised the funeral pall that in the midst of the splendours of the festival had changed the gondola into a coffin.

"See there, Effrena," she said, pointing to the balcony of Desdemona's house. "See the fair Nineta receiving the homage of the Serenade seated between her monkey and her pet dog."

"Ah, the fair Nineta," exclaimed Stelio, shaking off his sad thoughts, bending towards the smiling balcony and, with cordial vivacity, sending a greeting to the little woman who was listening to the musicians by the light of two silver candelabra. Garlands of the year's last roses hung entwined about the sconces. "I have not seen her again yet. She is the gentlest and most graceful animal I know. What a piece of good fortune it was for our dear Hoditz to have discovered her behind the lid of a harpsichord while rummaging in an old curiosity shop at San Samuele! Two pieces of good fortune in one day: the fair Nineta and a lid painted by Pordenone. From that day the harmony of his life has been complete. How I should like you to penetrate to his nest! You would find there a truly admirable example of what I was saying to-day at sunset. Here is a man who by obeying his native taste for subtlety has composed his own little fable with minute art, and in it he lives as happy as his Moravian ancestor in the arcadia of Rosswald. Ah, how many exquisite things I know of him!"

A wide *peota* adorned with many-coloured lanterns full of singers and musicians was floating under the house of Desdemona. The old song of brief youth and passing beauty rose sweetly to the little woman who listened, smiling her childlike smile, between her monkey and her little dog as in a print by Pietro Longhi.

> " Do beni vu ghave,
>   Beleza e zoventu ;
>   Co i va no i torna piu,
>   Nina, mia cara." [1]

"Don't you think that this is the true soul of Venice and that the other one which you have pic-

---

[1] "Two good things are yours,
      Beauty and youth;
      When they go they will not return
      Nina, my dear."

tured to the crowd is only your own, Effrena?" said
la Foscarina, her head swaying a little to the languid
melody that floated all along the Grand Canal,
repeated far away by the other song-boats.

"No, this is not it," answered Stelio. "There is
within each of us, flitting like a butterfly on the surface of our deep souls, a more trivial soul, an *animula
vagula*, a slight playful spirit that often carries us away
and persuades us to yield to easy, mediocre pleasures,
to puerile pastimes and light melodies. This animula vagula is there, even in the gravest and most
violent natures, like the clown attached to the person of Othello, and often it deceives our judgment.
You are listening now to the child-soul of Venice,
humming on its guitars; but her real soul is only
to be discovered in her silence, and most terribly,
be sure of that, in full summer, in the full noontide, like the great Pan. Nevertheless, there on
the harbour of San Marco I had indeed thought
that you were feeling its vibration in the immense
conflagration. You are forgetting Giorgione for
Rosalba."

Round the *peota* full of song other boats had assembled, full of languid women, who turned towards
the music with gestures of lassitude, as if on the
point of sinking into invisible arms. And round all
that accumulated voluptuousness, the reflections of
the lanterns in the water trembled like a flowering
of luminous multicoloured water-lilies.

"Se lassarè passar
La bela e fresca età,
Un zorno i ve dirà
Vechia maura;

E bramarè, ma invan,
Quel che shavevi in man
Co avè lassà scampar
La congiontura." [1]

It was truly the song of the year's last roses fading
away as they twined round the sconces. In Perdita's
soul it conjured up the pageant of dead summer,
the opalescent veil in which Stelio had wrapped the
gentle corpse dressed in gold. Through the glass
sealed by the Lord of the Flame, she could see her
own image lying at the bottom of the lagoon, on
its field of seaweeds. A sudden chill took hold of
her limbs; again the horror and disgust of her own
ageing body gripped her. And, remembering the
recent promise, thinking how her beloved might that
very night exact the keeping of it, her whole body
contracted in the pulsation of her sorrowful modesty
made of fear and of pride. Her experienced, despairing eyes ran over the woman beside her, sought
her out, penetrated her, felt her occult but certain
strength, her intact freshness, her pure healthiness,
and that indefinable virtue of love emanating like
an aroma from the chaste bodies of virgins once they
have attained the perfection of their blossoming.
She seemed to admit the secret affinity that already
ran between the girl and the Life-giver. She seemed
to divine the words with which he silently addressed
her. The anguish was so fearful that it bit her

[1] " If you let your fine, fresh age pass away,
One day it will call you
A ripened old thing;
And you will desire, but in vain,
All that you had
When you let the occasion slip."

bosom intolerably, and her convulsed fingers clutched the black rope running along the side of the gondola, and the little metal griffin that held it creaked at her involuntary movement.

That movement did not escape Stelio, who was watching her anxiously. He understood her extreme anguish and himself suffered from it acutely for a few moments; but his feeling was mixed with an almost angry impatience, because her anguish, like a cry of destruction, crossed and interrupted a fiction of transcendant life that he had been inwardly composing in order to conciliate the contrast, to conquer the new force presenting itself before him, like a bow ready to be drawn, and at the same time not to lose the savour of that maturity which life had steeped in all its essences, the benefit of that passionate attention and faith by which his intellect was sharpened, as by a kindling drug, and his pride nourished as by a continual act of praise. "Ah, Perdita," he was thinking, "why has not a pure spirit of human love sprung from the fermentation of your numberless human loves? Ah, why have I finally conquered you with my desire, although I know that it is too late; and why do you let me read in your eyes the certainty of your coming gift, in the midst of a flood of doubts that will not be sufficient to revive the abolished prohibition? Both of us, well knowing that all the ability of our long communion was in that prohibition, have not known how to preserve it, and are going to yield blindly, at the last hour, to the command of a turbid, nocturnal voice. Even a little while ago, when your head was standing out from the belt of constellations, I no longer saw in you the carnal mistress, but the muse and the apostle of my poetry. And all the gratitude of my soul went out to you for your promise of glory, not for your promise of pleasure. Have you not understood, as you always do? With marvellous fancy, as ever, have you not led my desire along the ray of your smile towards something resplendent with youth that you yourself had chosen and reserved for me? In descending the staircase and coming towards me together with her, had you not the appearance of one bearing a gift, of one bringing an unexpected announcement? Nor wholly unwaited for, Perdita, not wholly unwaited for, because I knew some extraordinary act must come from your infinite wisdom."

"How happy the fair Nineta is with her monkey and her little dog!" sighed the despairing woman, looking back towards the light song and the laughing balcony.

> "La zoventu xe un fior
> Che apena nato el mor,
> E un zorno gnanco mi
> No saro quela." [1]

Also Donatella Arvale turned and Stelio Effrena with her. The light skiff carried the three faces of that heavy destiny, without sinking, over the water and the music.

> "E vegna quel che vol,
> Lassè che vaga!" [2]

---

[1] "Youth is a flower
No sooner born than dead ;
And I, too, one day,
Will be the same no longer."

[2] "And come what will,
And let it go!"

All along the Grand Canal, repeated in the distance by all the boats, flowed the melody of transient pleasure. Fascinated by its rhythm, the slaves of the oar united their voices to the joyful chorus. That joy, which had seemed terrible to the Life-giver, when he heard it in the first cry of the crowd massed on the Molo, had now become attenuated, more lascivious, had blossomed into grace and playfulness, had become soft and indulgent. The more frivolous soul of Venice repeated the refrain of forgetful life, lightly touching its guitars and dancing among the festoons of lanterns.

> "E vegna quel che vol,
> Lassè che vaga!"

Suddenly, in the curve of the canal, before the red palace of the Foscari, a great galleon flamed like a burning tower. More lightning crackled in the sky. More fiery pigeons flew up from the fortress, surpassed the small light towers, slipped down along the marbles, fluttered, hissed on the water, multiplied themselves in numberless sparks, and floated there, smoking. Along the parapets, from the decks, from the poop, from the prow, a thousand fountains of fire opened up, dilated, blended, illuminating the canal from one part to the other, painting it a violent red as far as San Vitale, as far as the Rialto. The galleon disappeared from sight, transformed by the ceasing of the fireworks into a purplish thunder-cloud.

"Turn down San Polo, turn down San Polo," la Foscarina called to the oarsman, lowering her head as under a storm, and pressing her hands to her ears to defend them from the roar.

And with dazzled eyes Donatella Arvale and

Stelio Effrena again glanced at each other. And their faces were as resplendent, lit up by the reflected glare, as if both had been bending over a furnace or the mouth of a crater.

The gondola entered the canal of San Polo and slipped into its shade. A sudden veil of ice fell on its three silent occupants. Under the arch of the bridge, the cadence of the oar struck upon their souls and the noise of the festival seemed infinitely far away. All the houses were dark; the belfry rose lonely and silent among the stars, the *Campiello del Remer* and the *Campiello del Pistor* were deserted, and the grass breathed there in peace; the trees hanging over the walls of the little gardens seemed to feel their leaves dying on their branches lifted up to the quiet sky.

" The rhythm of art and the pulse of life then have again beaten in Venice with one same throb, at least for a few hours," said Daniele Glauro, lifting from the table a chalice from which only the sacred Host was missing. " Let me express, also, in the name of so many who are absent, the gratitude and fervour that are blending in one single image of beauty the three persons to whom we owe the miracle, — the lady of the banquet, the daughter of Lorenzo Arvale, and the poet of Persephone."

" Why the lady of the banquet, Glauro? " la Foscarina asked, smiling, with astonished grace. " I, like yourself, have not given but have received joy. It is Donatella whom we should crown and Stelio Effrena The glory of it goes to both."

"But your silent presence in the Hall of the Greater Council, near the celestial sphere, a little while ago," answered the mystic doctor, "was not less eloquent than Stelio's words, nor less musical than Ariadne's song. Once more you have divinely carved your own statue in silence, and it shall live in our memory together with the words and the song."

Stelio Effrena, with a deep, inward shiver, again saw the ephemeral, versatile monster from whose side the tragic muse had emerged, with her head lifted to the belt of constellations.

"True, true," exclaimed Francesco de Lizo. "I think so too. Whoever saw you, while listening to the song, the words, and the symphony, could not but recognise in you the visible centre of that ideal world that each one of us — us the faithful, us the near ones — felt was growing out of his own aspirations."

"Each one of us," said Fabio Molza, "felt that there was great and unusual significance in your person as it stood before the poet, dominating the crowd."

"It seemed that you alone were about to assist at the mysterious birth of a new idea," said Antimo della Bella; "everything seemed animating itself to generate that idea which must soon be revealed to us, if having waited for it with so much faith has made us at all worthy."

The Life-giver, with another shudder, felt the work which he was nourishing leap within him, formless still, but already a living thing, and his whole soul stretched out with an impetuous movement, as if carried away by a lyric breath, towards the power of fertilisation and of revelation that emanated from the

Dionysian woman to whom the praise of those fervent spirits was rising.

She had suddenly become very beautiful, a nocturnal creature forged out of dreams and passions on an anvil of gold, a breathing image of immortal fate and eternal enigmas. Although she was motionless, although she was silent, her well-known accents and her memorable gestures seemed to live about her, vibrating indefinitely, like melodies round the chords that repeat them, like its rhymes round the closed book where love and pain go in search of them, to find comfort and intoxication. The heroic fidelity of Antigone, the fury of Cassandra, the devouring fever of Phædra, the fierceness of Medea, the sacrifice of Iphigenia; Mirra before his father, Polissena and Alcestes before the face of death, Cleopatra, changeable like the wind and flame of the world; Lady Macbeth, that dreaming murderess of the little hands and the large lilies pearled over with dew and with fears; Imogen, Juliet, Miranda; and Rosamund and Jessica and Perdita, the sweetest souls and the most terrible and the most magnificent, — were all in her, living in her body, flashing through her pupils, breathing in her mouth that knew of honey and of poison, of the gemmed goblet and the cup of wormwood. Thus, with an unlimited vastness and through endless time, the outlines of human age and substance seemed to widen and perpetuate themselves; and for no other reason than the motion of a muscle, a sign, a gesture, a line of feature, a tremor of the eyelids, a slight change of colour, an almost imperceptible bend of the brows, a changing play of light and shade, a lightning-like virtue of expression radiating from that thin, frail body, infinite worlds of undying beauty were continually generated. The very genii of the places consecrated by poetry breathed over her and girded her round with alternating visions: the dusty plain of Thebe, the parched Argolide, the burnt up myrtles of Trezene, the sacred olives of Colonus, the triumphant Cydnus, the pale landscape of Dunsinane, Prospero's cave, the wood in the Ardennes, regions furrowed with blood, laboured by pain, transfigured by a dream or lighted by an inextinguishable smile, appeared, receded, and melted away behind her head. And other remote regions: regions of mist, northern plains, the immense continents beyond the ocean where she had passed like an unknown force, carrying her voice and her flame with her, melted away behind her head; with the multitudes, their hills and rivers, the gulfs, the impure cities, the ancient forsaken races, the strong peoples panting for the dominion of the world, the new peoples that wrest from nature her most secret energies to make them the slaves of omnipotent labour in edifices of iron and glass, the colonies of bastard races that ferment and grow corrupt on virgin soil, all the barbarous crowds to which she had appeared as a sovereign revelation of Latin genius, all the unconscious masses to which she had spoken the sublime language of Dante, all the innumerable human herds whence the aspiration to beauty, had risen towards her on a wave of confused hopes and anxieties. As she stood there, a creature made of perishable flesh and subject to the sad laws of time, an immeasurable mass of real and ideal life seemed to weigh upon her and widen round her, throbbing with the rhythm of her breath. It was not on the stage only that she had cried out and suffocated her sobs, but she had loved, fought, and suffered violently in her daily life for herself, for her own soul, for her flesh and blood. What loves? What battles? What spasms? From what depths of melancholy had she drawn the sublimate of her tragic power? At what springs of bitterness had she watered her free genius? Certainly she had witnessed the cruelest misery, the darkest ruin; she had known heroic efforts, pity, horror, and the threshold of death. All her thirsts had kindled again in the delirium of Phædra; and in the submission of Imogen all her tenderness had trembled anew. Thus Life and Art, the irrevocable past and the eternally present, had made her profound, many-souled and mysterious, had magnified her ambiguous fate beyond human limits, making her equal to the temples and the forests.

She stood on, breathing under the eyes of the poets, who saw her one and yet different.

"Ah, I will possess you as in a vast orgy; I will shake you like a bundle of thyrsi; I will shake from the knowledge of your body all the divine and monstrous things that weigh upon you; the things you have accomplished, and those still in travail that are growing in you as in a sacred season," spoke the lyric demon of the Life-giver, recognising in the woman's mystery the surviving power of the primitive myth, the renewed initiation of the deity which had fused all the energies of nature in one single ferment, and with the varying of its rhythms and in the enthusiastic worship of himself had raised human senses and the human spirit to the summit of joy and pain.

"It will be good, it will be good, to have waited so long. The passing of years, the tumult of dreams, the agonies of the struggle and the swiftness of triumph, the impurity of many loves, the enchantment of poets, the applause of the crowd, the wonders of earth, the patience and the fury, the footsteps in the mud, the blind flights, all the evil, all the good, what I know and what I ignore, what you know and what you ignore, — all this had to be, to make the fulness of my night that is coming."

He felt himself suffocate and turn pale. Desire seized him by the throat with a wild impulse, to leave him no more; and his heart swelled with that same anxiety that both had felt in the evening when they had glided over the water that had seemed flowing in a frightful clepsydra.

As the exaggerated vision of places and events vanished suddenly, the nocturnal creature reappeared stilll more profoundly knitted to the city of the vast necklaces and the thousand girdles of green. In the city and in the woman he now saw a power of expression that he had never seen before. The one and the other burned in the Autumn night, and the same fever that ran through the canals was running through her veins.

The stars glittered, the trees swayed behind Perdita's head, a garden stretched out beyond the windows open on the balconies. Whiffs from the sky stole into the supper-room, agitating the little flames of the candelabra and the chalices of the flowers; they passed through the doors, giving the curtains a light throb, animating that old house of the Capello where the last great daughter of San

Marco whom the people had covered with glory and with gold had collected her relics of republican magnificence. Galleon lamps, Turkish targets, quivers of leather, bronze helmets, velvet sheaths, adorned the rooms of the last descendant of that marvellous Cesare d'Arbes who had kept the Art of Comedy alive against the goldonian reform, and changed the agony of the Serene Republic into a convulsion of laughter.

"All I ask is to serve that idea humbly," la Foscarina said to Antimo della Bella, with a slight tremor in her voice because she had met Stelio's gaze.

"You alone can make it triumph," said Francesco de Lizo. "The soul of the crowd is subject to you for ever."

"The drama," declared Daniele Glauro, "can only be a rite or a message. The performance should be once more solemn as a ceremony, including as it does the two elements that make up all worship, — the living person on the stage in whom, as before the altar, the word of the revealer is made incarnate, and the presence of the multitude silent as in its temples. . . ."

"Bayreuth!" interrupted Prince Hoditz.

"No, the Janiculum!" cried Stelio Effrena, suddenly emerging from his dizzy silence, "a Roman hill. Not the bricks and the wood of Upper Francony. We will have a marble theatre on our Roman hill."

The sudden opposition of his words seemed to have been almost brought about by a kind of joyful contempt.

"Do you not admire the work of Richard Wagner?"

asked Donatella Arvale, with a slight frown that for an instant made her Hermes-like face seem almost hard.

He looked her straight in the eyes, feeling all that was obscurely hostile in the girl's manner and himself sharing against her that indistinct enmity. He saw her living her own encircled life apart, immovable in some deeply secret thought, a stranger and inviolable.

" The work of Richard Wagner," he answered, " is founded on the German spirit, and its essence is purely northern. His reform has some analogy with that which Luther attempted ; his drama is nothing if not the supreme flower of the genius of a race, the extraordinarily efficacious summing up of the aspirations that have burdened the soul of the symphonists and of the national poets from Bach to Beethoven, from Wieland to Goethe. If you could imagine his work on the shores of the Mediterranean, among our light olive-trees and our slender laurels, under the glory of the Latin sky, you would see it grow pale and dissolve. Since, according to his own words, it is given to the artist to see a still unformed world shining in its future perfection, and to enjoy it prophetically in desire and in hope, I announce the advent of a new or renewed art that by the powerful, sincere simplicity of its lines, by its vigorous grace, by the ardour of its spirit, by the pure force of its harmonies, shall continue and crown the immense ideal edifice of our elect race. I glory myself that I am a Latin, and — forgive me, dreaming Lady Myrta, forgive me, Prince Hoditz, — I see a barbarian in every man of different blood.

" But he, too, Richard Wagner, started from the

Greeks in developing the thread of his theory," said Baldassare Stampa, who, having just returned from Bayreuth, was still full of the ecstasy.

"A confused and unequal thread," answered the master. "Nothing is further from the Orestiades than the tetralogy of the Ring. The Florentines of Casa Bardi have perceived the essence of Greek tragedy far more deeply. All homage to the Camerata del Conte di Vernio."

"I have always thought that the Camerata was an idle gathering of *savants* and rhetoricians," said Baldassare Stampa.

"Do you hear, Daniele?" exclaimed Stelio, turning to the mystic doctor. "When was there in the world a more fervid fire of intelligence? They sought the spirit of life in Greek antiquity; they tried to develop all human energies harmoniously, to manifest man in his integrity by all the means of art. Giulio Caccini taught that not only things in particular, but all things together are needful to the excellence of the musician; the tawny hair of Jacopo Peri and of Zazzerino flamed in their song like that of Apollo. In the discourse that precedes his *Rappresentazione di Anima et di Corpo*, Emilio del Cavaliere gives us the same ideas on the foundation of the new theatre that have since been carried out at Bayreuth, even to the precept of perfect silence, of propitious darkness, of an invisible orchestra. Marco da Gagliano in celebrating a festive performance eulogises all the arts that contributed to it 'in such a manner that every most noble feeling is flattered through the intellect at one same time by the most pleasure-giving arts that human talent has discovered.' Is not that enough?"

"Bernino," said Francesco de Lizo, "gave an opera in Rome for which he himself had constructed the theatre, painted the scenery, carved the ornamental statues, invented the machinery, written the words, composed the music, regulated the dancing, instructed the actors, in which he himself danced, sang, and recited."

"Enough, enough!" cried Prince Hoditz, laughing; "the barbarian is conquered."

"And it is still not enough," said Antimo della Bella; "we should glorify the greatest of these innovators, he who is anointed a Venetian by his passion and death, whose sepulchre in the Church of the Frari is worthy of a pilgrimage, — the divine Claudio Monteverde."

"His was an heroic soul of pure Italian essence," Daniele Glauro confirmed reverently.

"He accomplished his work in the storm, loving, suffering, struggling, alone with his fate, his passion, and his genius," la Foscarina said slowly, as if absorbed in the vision of the brave life full of pain that had fed the creatures of its art with its warmest blood. "Tell us about him, Effrena."

Stelio quivered as if she had suddenly touched him. Again the expressive power of her diffusing voice called up an ideal figure, that rose from some indefinite depths as from a tomb, assuming before the eyes of the poets the colour and the breath of life. The old viola-player, bereaved and ardent and sad like the Orpheus of his own fable, appeared in the supper-room.

It was a fiery apparition, prouder and more dazzling by far than that which had lit up the harbour of

San Marco; an inflamed force of life, expelled from the inner bosom of nature towards the expectancy of the multitudes; a vehement zone of light breaking out from an interior sky to illumine the more secret depths of human will and desire, an unknown Word springing from primitive silences to say that which is eternal and eternally inexpressible in the heart of the world.

"Should we speak of him, if he himself could speak to us?" said the Life-giver, troubled, unable to contain the growing fulness that surged within him like an anguished sea. And he gazed at the singer; and he saw her as when she had first appeared to him in the pauses, among the forest of instruments white and lifeless as a shadow.

But the spirit of beauty which they had invoked was to manifest itself through her.

"Ariadne," Stelio added in a low voice, as if to awaken her.

She rose without speaking, went to the door, entered the neighbouring room. They heard the rustle of her skirts, her light footfall, and the sound of the instrument being opened. All were quiet and intent. A musical silence seemed to occupy the place that had remained empty in the supper-room. Once only a breath of wind slanted the candle flames, disturbing the flowers. Then all became anxious again, and motionless in expectation.

"Lasciatemi morire!" [1]

Suddenly their souls were ravished by a power that seemed the lightning-like eagle by which Dante

[1] "O let me die!"

in his dream was ravished up to the flame. They were burning together in undying truth; they heard the world's melody pass through their luminous ecstasy.

"Lasciatemi morire!"

Was it Ariadne, still Ariadne, who was weeping in some new pain? rising, still rising, to new height in her martyrdom?

> "E che volete
> Che mi conforte
> In cosi dura sorte,
> In cosi gran martire?
> Lasciatemi morire!"[1]

The voice ceased; the singer did not reappear. The aria of Claudio Monteverde composed itself in the memory like a changeless feature.

"Is there any Greek marble that has reached a simpler and securer perfection of style?" said Daniele Glauro, in a low voice, as if he feared to disturb the silence which was still ringing with the music.

"But what sorrow on earth has ever wept like this?" stammered Lady Myrta, her eyes full of tears that ran down the furrows of her poor bloodless face, while her hands, deformed by gout, trembled as they wiped them away.

The austere intellect of the æsthete and that of the sweet sensitive soul in the old infirm body gave witness to the same power. In the same way, nearly three centuries before in Mantua, six thousand spectators had been unable to control their tears, and

[1] "And what can comfort me
In my hard fate,
In my great martyrdom?
O let me die!"

poets had believed in the living presence of Apollo on the new stage of the famous theatre.

" Here, Baldassare is an artist of our own race," said Stelio Effrena, " who, by the simplest means, has succeeded in touching the highest degree of that beauty which the German rarely approached in his confused aspirations towards the fatherland of Sophocles."

" Do you know the lamentation of the ailing King?" asked the young man with the long sunny hair worn by him as an heirloom of the Venetian Sappho, of the " high Gasparra," the unfortunate friend of Collatino.

" All the anguish of Amfortas is in a *mottetto* I know: ' Peccantem me quotidie; ' but with what lyric impulse, what powerful simplicity! All the forces of tragedy are there, I should almost say sublimated like the instincts of a multitude in the heart of a hero. Palestrina's much older expression seems to me also purer and more virile.

" But the struggle of Kundry and of Parsifal in the second act, the Herzeleide motive, the impetuous figure, the figure of pain drawn from the motto of the sacred banquet, the motive of Kundry's aspiration, the prophetic theme of the promise, the mad kiss on the mouth of the youth, all that heartrending and intoxicating contrast of desire and horror. . . . ' The wound, the wound! Now it is burning, it is bleeding in me! ' And above the despairing restlessness of the tempter, the melody of submission. . . . ' Let me weep on your bosom, let me be united to thee for an hour, and even if God repel me I shall be redeemed and saved by thee! ' And Parsifal's answer in which the motive of the madman now transfigured into the promised hero returns with so grand a solemnity: 'Hell is before us for all eternity, if only for one hour I let thee fold me in thy arms.' And the wild ecstasy of Kundry. . . . 'As my kiss has made thee a prophet, the entire caress of my love shall make thee divine. One hour, one hour only with thee, and I shall be saved!' And the last efforts of her demoniac will, the supreme gesture of inducement, the prayer and the furious offer. . . . 'Only thy love can save me! Let me love thee! Mine for one only hour! Thine for one only hour.'"

Madly Perdita and Stelio looked into each other's eyes. For a second they rushed into each other, were united, knew joy, and gasped as on a bed of pleasure and death.

The Marangona, the largest bell of San Marco, rang out in the night, and as once before in the evening hour, they seemed to feel the roll of the bronze in the roots of their hair almost like a quiver of their own flesh. They again felt, passing over their heads, the vortex of sound in which the apparitions of the consoling beauty invoked by unanimous Prayer had suddenly arisen. The phantoms on the water, the infinite waverings of dissimulated desire, the anxiety, the promise, the farewell, the festival, the monster with the innumerable human faces, and the great starry sphere, and the applause and the symphony and the song, and the miracles of Fire, and the passage along the sonorous canal, the song of brief youth, the struggle and mute anguish in the boat, the sudden shadow on their three destinies, the banquet illumined by the beautiful idea, the announcement, the hope, the pride, — all the pulsations of strong life met and renewed themselves within them, quickened, became a thousand, and became one. And it seemed to them that they had lived beyond human limits in that instant, that an unknown immensity was spreading before them which they could absorb as the ocean absorbs, because having lived so much, they yet were empty, having drunk so much, they yet were parched. A violent illusion mastered their souls full of riches. The one seemed to grow immeasurably in the other's wealth. The maiden had disappeared. The eyes of the wandering, despairing woman were repeating: " The full caress of my love shall make thee divine. One hour, one only hour with thee, and I shall be saved! Mine, even if for one only hour! Thine, even if for one only hour! "

And the eloquence of the enthusiast continued building up the sacred tragedy. Kundry, the furious tempter, the slave of desire, the rose of hell, the original perdition, the cursed one, now reappeared in the spring dawn, reappeared humble and pale in the garb of the messenger, her head bent, her gaze dim, her hoarse, broken voice knowing one word only: " Let me serve; let me serve! "

The melodies of solitude, of submission, of purification, prepared round her lowliness the enchantment of Good Friday. And Parsifal reappeared in his black armour, with closed helmet, with lowered spear, absorbed in an infinite dream: " I have come by perilous roads, but perhaps this day shall see me saved because I hear the murmur of the holy forest." Hope, pain, remorse, remembrance, promise, faith panting for salvation, sacred, mysterious, melodies seemed to weave the ideal mantle that was to cover the Simple, the Pure one, the Promised Hero sent to heal the incurable wound. "Will you lead me to Amfortas to-day?" He grew languid, fainting in the arms of the old man. "Let me serve; let me serve!" The melody of submission spread through the orchestra again, destroying the original impetuous figure. "Let me serve!" The faithful woman was bringing water, was kneeling in her lowliness, fervently washing the beloved feet. "Let me serve!" The faithful woman drew from her bosom a vase of ointment to anoint the beloved feet, and then wiped them with her loosened hair. The Pure One bent over the sinner, pouring water on her wild head: "Thus I accomplish my first office; receive this baptism and believe in the Redeemer." The brow of Kundry lay low in the dust as she burst out weeping, freed from desire, freed from the curse. And then, from the profound final harmonies of the prayer to the Redeemer, the melody of the flowery meadow spread and rose with superhuman sweetness. "How beautiful the meadow is to-day! marvellous flowers once drew me to them, but the grass and the flowers were never before so fragrant." Parsifal in his ecstasy gazes at the meadow and the dewy forest, smiling in the morning light.

"Ah, who shall forget the sublime moment," exclaimed the fascinated man, his thin face flashing again with the lightning-stroke of joy. "All, in the darkness of the theatre, were fixed in perfect stillness like one single compact mass. In each of our veins our blood had stopped, seeming to listen. The

music rose like light from the Mystic Gulf; the
notes seemed to transform themselves into rays of
spring sunshine, coming to life with the same joy
as the blade of grass that breaks through the earth,
as the flower that opens, as the branch that buds, as
the insect bringing forth its wings. And all the
innocence of things just born entered into us, and
our souls lived again I know not what dream of far
away infancy. . . . *Infantia*, the device of Vettor
Carpaccio. Ah, Stelio, how well you repeated it to
our old age a little while ago, and how well you
have found the way of making us feel our sorrow
for what we have lost, and our hope of recovering
it by means of an art that shall be indissolubly re-
united to life!"

Stelio Effrena was silent, oppressed by the weight
of the gigantic work of the barbaric creator whom
the enthusiasm of Baldassare Stampa had called up
and placed against the burning figure of the tragedian of Ariadne and Orpheus. A kind of instinctive
rancour, of obscure hostility which was not of the
intellect, raised him up against the tenacious German
who had succeeded in inflaming the world. To
obtain his victory over men and things, he too had
exalted his own image and magnified his own dream
of dominating beauty; he too had been drawn to
the crowd as to the preferable prey, he too had
made his discipline of the effort to surpass himself
without respite. And now he had his temple on the
Bavarian hills.

"Art alone can bring men back to unity," said
Daniele Glauro. "Let us honour the great master
who has always had this for his faith. His theatre.

although of bricks and wood, although small and imperfect, has a sublime significance. In it the work of art is religion brought under the senses in a living form ; the drama there becomes a rite."

"Let us honour Richard Wagner," said Antimo della Bella ; "but if this hour is to be memorable as the hour of an announcement, and a promise from him who a little while ago was pointing the mysterious vessel out to the crowd, let us again invoke as our patron the heroic soul which has spoken to us through the voice of Donatella Arvale. In laying the foundation stone of his theatre, the poet of Siegfried consecrated it to the hopes and the victories of his German people. The theatre of Apollo which is rapidly rising on the Janiculum, where once the eagles descended with their prophecies, must be no other than the monumental revelation of the idea towards which our race is led by its genius. Let us reinforce the privilege by which nature has made our blood so great."

Stelio Effrena was silent, overwhelmed by vortex-like forces that laboured in him with a kind of blind fury similar to the subterranean forces that swell, break up, and transfigure a volcanic territory, creating in it new mountains and new abysses. The elements of his inner life, carried away by that shock, seemed at the same time to dissolve and to multiply themselves. Grand, terrible images passed over the tumult in musical storm-clouds. Rapid concentrations and dispersions of thought succeeded each other like electric discharges in a hurricane. At intervals, he seemed to hear shouts and songs, as if a door continually reclosed were being continually thrown open; as if blasts of wind were bringing him the distant cries of a massacre, alternating with an apotheosis. Suddenly, with the intensity of a feverish vision, he saw the dry, fated land, in which he was going to place the souls of his tragedy; he felt all its thirst in himself. He saw the mythic fount that alone broke in upon its dryness, and on the throb of its springs the whiteness of the virgin who was to die there. He saw the heroine's mask on Perdita's face, in all the beauty of an extraordinarily calm sorrow. The ancient dryness of the plain of Argos then seemed to convert itself into flames, the fount of Perseia flowed like a river. The two primordial elements, fire and water, passed over all things, cancelled every sign, diffused themselves, wandered, struggled, triumphed, spoke, found words and a language with which to reveal their inner essence, to tell the innumerable myths born of their eternity. The symphony expressed the drama of the two elemental Souls on the stage of the Universe, the pathetic struggle of the two great living and mobile Beings, of the two forces of cosmic Will, such as the shepherd Arya on his plateaus imagined it, when his pure eyes first saw the spectacle. Then from the very centre of the musical mystery, from the inner depth of the symphonic ocean, the Ode arose, brought by the human voice, and soared to its greatest height. The miracle of Beethoven renewed itself. The winged Ode, the Hymn, burst up from the depths of the orchestra to tell, in an imperious and absolute manner, the joy and the sorrow of Man. Not the chorus, as in the Ninth Symphony, but the solitary, dominating voice that was the interpreter, the messenger

to the multitude. "Her voice! her voice! She has
disappeared. Her voice seemed to touch the very
heart of the world, and she was beyond the veil,"
said the Life-giver, having once more before his eyes
the crystal statue in which he had seen the ascending
veins of melody. "I will seek you, I will find you
again, I will master your secret. You shall sing my
hymns, raised up on the summit of my music." Freed
from impure desire, he now considered the virgin's
form as the receptacle, as the custodian of a divine
gift. He heard the disembodied voice rise from the
depths of the orchestra to reveal the part of eternal
truth hidden in the passing fact, in the fleeting event.
The Ode was crowning the episode with light. Then,
as if to lead back to the play of images his spirit,
which had been rapt "beyond the veil," a dance
figure designed itself on the rhythm of the dying Ode.
The silent dancer appeared within a parallelogram
traced in the arch of the stage, as within the limits of
a strophe; her body, redeemed for a while from the
sad laws of gravity, imitating fire and water and the
whirlpool and the evolution of stars. "La Tanagra,"
the flower of Syracuse, made of wings, as a flower is
made of petals! Thus he conjured up the image of
the already famous Sicilian who had rediscovered the
ancient art as it was in the times when Frinico could
boast of having as many dance figures in himself as
a stormy winter's night raises up waves upon the sea.
The actress, the singer, and the dancer, the three
Dionysian women, appeared to him as three perfect, almost divine instruments of his creations. By
means of words, gesture, and symphony, and with
incredible rapidity, his work would complete itself

and live its powerful life before the conquered multitude.

He was silent, rapt in an ideal world, intent on measuring the effort necessary to manifest it.

"Richard Wagner affirms that the only creator of a work of art is the people," Baldassare Stampa was saying, "and that all the artist can do is to gather up and express the creation of the unconscious throng. . . ."

The extraordinary feeling that had surprised him while he had been speaking to the crowd from the throne of the Doges returned and occupied him. During that time of communion between his own soul and the soul of the crowd an almost divine mystery had taken place; something greater and stronger had added itself to the feeling he habitually entertained about his own person, an unknown power had seemed to converge within him, abolishing the limits of his particular personality and conferring the harmony of a chorus to his solitary voice. There must, therefore, be in the multitude some hidden beauty from which only the hero and the poet can draw a flash. Whenever that beauty revealed itself by a sudden clamour arising in theatre or entrenchment or public place, a torrent of joy must swell the heart of him who had called it forth with his verse, his harangue, or the action of his sword. The word of the poet, when communicated to the crowd, must, therefore, be an act like the deed of a hero, — an act creating instantaneous beauty in the numberless obscurities of the soul, in the same way as a wonderful sculptor, from a mass of clay and by the mere touch of his plastic thumb brings forth a divine statue. The silence that had been spread like a sacred veil on the completed poem would then cease. The substance of life would no longer be signified by immaterial symbols, but life itself would be manifested in its entirety through the medium of the poet, the Word made flesh, the rhythm quickened in a breathing, living form; the idea would spring forth in the fulness of its strength and freedom.

"But Richard Wagner," said Fabio Molza, "believes that the crowd consists of all those who feel some mutual infirmity. Do you hear, a mutual infirmity? . . ."

"Towards Joy, towards eternal Joy!" thought Stelio Effrena. "The people are all those who feel an obscure necessity of raising themselves by means of Fiction out of the daily prison in which they serve and suffer." The small city theatres disappeared before him, those theatres where in the midst of a suffocating heat that is saturated with every impurity, before a band of debauchees and harlots, the actors take on themselves the office of prostitutes. On the steps of the new theatre he saw the true crowd, the immense, unanimous crowd that he had smelt and heard a moment ago among the marbles under the stars. His art, though imperfectly understood, would bring to those rough unconscious souls, by the mysterious power of rhythm, an emotion deep as that felt by the prisoner on the point of being freed from his chains. The joy of their liberation spread little by little over the most abject, the furrowed brows cleared and lips opened in wonder that were accustomed to violent outcry; lastly the hands — the rough hands enslaved by instruments of toil — stretched out in one unanimous movement towards the heroine who was exhaling her immortal sorrow under the stars.

"In the life of a people like ourselves," said Daniele Glauro, "great manifestations of art weigh much more than a treaty of alliance or a tributary law. That which is undying is worth more than that which passes away. The daring and the cunning of a Malatesta are preserved for all Eternity in a medal of Pisanello's. Of all Machiavelli's politics nothing would survive if it were not for the sinews of his prose. . . ."

"True, true," thought Stelio Effrena; "the fortunes of Italy are inseparable from the fate of Beauty, of whom she is the mother." And that sovereign truth now seemed to him the approaching sun of the divine, far-away ideal fatherland through which Dante wandered. "Italy! Italy!" The name that has intoxicated the world sounded over his soul like a rallying cry. Should not a new art, robust in both roots and branches, rise from ruins steeped in so much heroic blood, and should not this art sum up within itself all the forces latent in the hereditary substance of the nation? Should it not become a constructive and determining power in the third Rome, pointing out to the men who were taking part in its government the primitive truths to be made the basis of new forms? Faithful to the oldest instincts of his race, Richard Wagner had foreseen and forwarded by his effort the aspiration of the German States toward the heroic greatness of empire. He had presented them with the magnificent figure of Henry the Fowler rising up and standing under the ancient tree. . . . "Let the warriors rise up from every German land!" At Sadowa and at Sedan the warriors had won. With one same impulse, with the same doggedness, the people and the artist had accomplished their aim of glory. One same victory had crowned the work of the sword and the work of the lyre. The poet as much as the hero had accomplished an enfranchising act. His musical figures had contributed as much as the will of the Chancellor, as much as the blood of the soldiers, to the work of exalting and perpetuating the soul of his race.

"He has been here a few days; he is staying at the Palazzo Vendramin-Calergi," said Prince Hoditz.

Suddenly the image of the barbaric creator approached him, the lines of the face became visible, the sky-blue eyes shone under the vast forehead, the lips closed tightly above the powerful chin that was armed with sensuality and pride and disdain. The small body bent with old age and glory drew itself up, growing gigantic like its work, the appearance of a god coming over it. Its blood coursed like the streams on a mountain-side; its breath heaved like the wind in a forest. All of a sudden the youth of Siegfried filled it, was like the dawn shining through a cloud. "To follow the impulse of my own heart, to obey my own instinct, to listen to the voice of nature speaking within me. Let this be my supreme and only law." The heroic words rising from the deep vibrated in it, giving expression to the young healthy will that had overcome every obstacle and every evil enchantment, that had always felt itself in harmony with the law of the Universe. And at this, the flames brought forth from the rock at the stroke of Wotan's staff rose up in a circle.

" A way has been opened through the sea of flames. Great is the joy of being steeped in that fire. Oh that in that fire I might find my bride ! " All the phantoms of the myth seemed to flash and then become dark again. The winged helmet of Brunehilde glittered in the sun. " Glory to the sun, glory to the light, glory to the radiant day ! My sleep was long; who has awakened me ? " The phantoms became tumultuous and dispersed. Suddenly Donatella Arvale, the Song-maiden, reappeared on a background of shadow, such as he had first seen her in the crimson and gold of the Great Hall holding the fruit of the flame in an attitude of dominion. " Do you not see me, then? My consuming eyes and my flaming blood, do they give you no fear? Do you too feel this wild ardour?" Her power over his dream seemed to return with her absence. Infinite music welled up from the silence that filled her empty place in the supper-room. Her Hermes-like face seemed to withhold an inviolable secret. " Do not touch me, do not disturb me, and I will reflect your luminous image for ever. Love yourself and give me up." Once more, as on the feverish water, a kind of passionate impatience dogged the Life-giver, and again he saw in the absent one the faculty of being drawn like a beautiful bow by a strong hand that should know how to use it as a weapon for some great conquest. "Awake, virgin, awake ! Laugh and live ! Be mine ! "

Violently his spirit was being drawn into the circle of the imaginary world created by the German god: its visions and harmonies overcame him, the figures of the northern myth built themselves up over the figures of his own art and his own passion obscuring them. His own desire and his own hope were speaking the language of the barbarian. "It is necessary that smiling I should love you, and smiling I should blind myself. It is necessary that still smiling we should unite ourselves and lose ourselves in that union. O radiant Love! O propitious Death!" The exaltation of the warrior maiden standing on the flame-encircled rock touched its steepest height; her cry of freedom and pleasure rose to the heart of the sun. Ah, what had that formidable stirrer of human souls not expressed? what apex and what abyss had he not reached? what effort could ever equal his effort? what eagle could ever hope to soar higher? His gigantic work stood complete in the midst of men, the last chorus of the Grail, the thanksgiving hymn echoed through the earth. "Glory to the miracle, redemption to the Redeemer!"

"He is tired," said Prince Hoditz, "very tired and worn out. This is why we did not see him at the Ducal Palace. His heart is ailing . . ."

The giant became human again, turned into a small body bent with age and glory, worn with passion, dying. And it seemed to Stelio Effrena that he was once more hearing those words, uttered by Perdita, which had made a coffin of their gondola: the words alluding to another great and stricken artist, the father of Donatella Arvale. "The name of the bow is Bios, and its work is Death." The young man saw his way stretching before him, traced out by victory, the long art, the short life. "Forward! Forward! Higher and still higher!" At every hour, at every second, he would have to feel, fight, and strengthen himself against destruction, diminution, violation, and contagion. At every hour, at every second, he would have to keep his eyes fixed on his aim, bringing all his energies to converge towards it without truce and without respite. He felt that victory was as necessary to him as air. A furious desire of battle was awaking in his agile Latin blood at that contact with the barbarian. "To you I now leave the task of willing," the latter had cried out from the stage of the new theatre on the day of inauguration: "In the work of art of the future the fountain head of all inventions shall never run dry." Art was as infinite as the beauty of the world. There are no limits to strength and daring. He must seek further, still further, and find. "Forward! Forward!"

One single, vast, formless wave summed up the anguish and the aspirations of that delirium, contorting itself into a vortex, rising in a tidal wave, seeming to condense itself, to take on the very qualities of plastic matter, to obey the same inexhaustible energy that shapes all things and all beings under the sun. A form of extraordinary purity and beauty was born of that travail, took life and shone with almost unbearable happiness. The poet saw it, gathered it up into his pure eyes, felt its roots striking into the very centres of his spirit. "Ah, only to express it, to manifest it to mankind, to fix it in its perfection for all eternity!" It was one of those sublime instants that have no return. Then everything vanished. Ordinary life flowed on around him, fleeting words sounded, expectation throbbed, all desire fell consumed.

And he looked at the woman. Stars twinkled, trees waved behind Perdita's head, a garden deepened out, and still the eyes of the woman said: "Let me serve! Let me serve!"

In the garden, the guests had dispersed along the walks and under the vine-trellises. The night air was damp and lukewarm; delicate eyelids could feel it on their lashes like the approach of a warm, mobile mouth. The hidden stars of the jessamine shrubs yielded their acute perfume in the shadow; the odour of the fruits too was as strong and even heavier than in the island gardens. A vivid fertilising power emanated from that small space of cultivated earth that was enclosed like an exiled thing by its girdle of water, becoming all the more intense from its banishment, like the soul of the exile.

"Do you wish me to stay? Do you wish me to return after the others have gone? Tell me. It is late."

"No, no, Stelio, I beg of you. It is late. It is too late. You say so yourself."

Mortal dismay was in the woman's voice. Her bare neck and her bare arms shuddered in the darkness; and she longed to deny herself and she longed to be possessed, and she longed to die and longed to be shaken by his man's hands. She trembled; her teeth trembled in her mouth. A stream that seemed to flow from a glacier submerged her, rolled over her, chilled her from the roots of her hair to the tips of her fingers. The joints of each limb ached as if ready to fall asunder, and the jaws stiffened by her terror seemed to change her voice. And she longed to die, and longed to be suddenly taken and overthrown by the violence of his manhood; and over her dismay and over her chill and over her body that was no longer young the same terrible sentence hung suspended that the loved one had pronounced and that she herself had repeated: "It is late; it is too late."

"Your promise, your promise! I will wait no longer. I cannot, Perdita."

The harbour, voluptuous like a proffered bosom, the estuary lost in darkness and death, the City kindled by its twilight fire, the water running in the invisible clepsydra, the vibrating bronze of the bells close to the heavens, the suffocating desire, the tightly drawn lips, the lowered lids, and dry hands, the whole fulness of the tide returned with the memory of the silent promise. He desired, with a savage desire, that flesh full of deep things.

"I will wait no longer." His turbid ardour came to him from far, far away, from the remotest of origins, from the primitive brutality of sudden unions, from the antique mystery of sacred lusts. Like the throng that the god possessed and that descended the mountain-side, tearing up trees, pushing on with a fury ever more and more blind, swelling its numbers with other madmen, spreading insanity along its passage until it became an immense animal and human multitude, spurred on by a monstrous will, the crude instinct in him rushed by, troubling all the figures of his soul and dragging them with it in its rush with one manifold agitation. And what he most desired in that despairing woman full of knowledge, was the creature weighed down by the eternal servitude of her nature, destined to succumb to the sudden convulsions of her sex, the creature who habitually slaked the lucid fever of the stage with obscure, sleep-giving pleasures, the actress full of flame who passed from the frenzy of the crowd to the embrace of manhood, the Dionysian creature who was wont to crown her mysterious rites by the act of life as in the Orgies of old.

His desire lost all proportion and became mad, full of the quiver of conquered multitudes and the intoxication of her unknown lovers and the vision of orgiastic promiscuities; cruelty, rancour, jealousy, poetry, and pride were in his desire. Regret stung him for never having possessed the actress after some theatrical triumph, still warm with the breath of the crowd, covered with sweat, pale and panting, still wearing the traces of the tragic soul that had wept and cried out in her, with the tears of that intruding soul still damp on her convulsed face. For the space of a lightning-flash he saw her outstretched, full of the power that had drawn a howl from the monster, throbbing like a Mænad after the dance, parched and tired, yet needing to be taken, to be shaken, to feel herself contracting in a last spasm, to receive some violent germ, in order to quiet down at last to a lethargy without dreams. How many men had come forth from the crowd to clasp her after having panted for her lost in the unanimous mass? Their desire had been made of the desire of thousands, their vigour multiplied. Something of the drunkenness of the people, something of the fascinated monster, would penetrate into the bosom of the actress with the pleasure of those nights.

"Don't be cruel; don't be cruel!" implored the woman, feeling all that turbulence in his voice and reading it in his eyes. "Oh, do not hurt me!"

Once more, under the voracious gaze of the young man, her body seemed to contract at the resistance of a painful modesty. His desire reached her like a wound that tore her open. She knew how much was pungent and impure in that sudden excitement, how deeply rooted was his opinion of her that considered her a poisoned and corrupt thing laden with many loves, an expert in all that was pleasure, a wandering, implacable temptress. She divined his ill-will, his jealousy, the malignity of the fever that had suddenly been kindled in the dear friend to whom she had consecrated all that, shut up within herself, was precious and sincere, for whom she had preserved the value of that offering by a constant refusal. Henceforward all was lost, all had been devastated at a blow, like a beautiful domain that has become the prey of vindictive rebel slaves. And almost as if she had been on her death-bed and in her last agony, the whole of her sharp, stormy life rose up before her, her life of pain and struggle, of bewilderment, passion, and triumph. She felt all the weight, all the encumbrance of it. She remembered the ineffable feeling of joy, of terror, and of liberation that had possessed her when she gave herself up for the first time in her far-away girlhood to the man who had deluded her. And there passed through her soul with a frightful stab the image of the virgin who had withdrawn herself that day, who had disappeared, who was perhaps

still dreaming in her solitary chamber, or was weeping or promising herself, or prostrate was tasting
already the joy of her promise. "It is late; it is too
late!" The irrevocable word seemed to pass continually over her head like the roll of a bronze bell.
And his desire reached her like a wound that tore
her open.

"Oh, do not hurt me!"

She stood imploring him, white and slight like the
swansdown that ran round her neck and on her restless bosom. She seemed to have separated herself
from her power, to have become light and weak,
clothed with a secret, tender soul that was so easy to
be killed, to be destroyed and offered up as a bloodless sacrifice.

"No, Perdita; I will not hurt you," he stammered,
suddenly unnerved by her voice and countenance,
seized at the entrails by a feeling of human pity
which had arisen from the same depths as his first
savage instinct. "Forgive me; forgive me."

It would have pleased him now to take her in his
arms, to nurse her, comfort her, to feel her weeping
and to drink in her tears. It seemed to him that he
did not recognise her, that it was an unknown person
who stood there before him, one infinitely pained
and lowly and deprived of all strength. And his
pity and remorse were a little like what one would
feel if one had unwillingly offended or hurt a sick
person or a child, some little and inoffensive lonely
being.

"Forgive me!"

It would have pleased him to kneel down before
her, to kiss her feet in the grass or say some little

word to her. He stooped and touched one of her hands. She shuddered from head to foot, turned her widened eyes towards him, then cast them down again and remained motionless. The shadows accumulated under the arch of her eyebrows, marking the undulation of the cheek-bone. Again the icy stream submerged her.

They heard the voices of the guests who were scattered about the garden; then a great silence came. They heard the gravel creak under some footstep; then again a great silence came. An indistinct clamour reached them from the distance of the canals. All at once the perfume of the jessamine seemed to have become stronger, like a heart that has quickened its throbs. The night seemed to be heavy with wonders. The eternal forces were harmoniously at work between the earth and the stars.

"Forgive me! If my desire gives you pain, I will go on suffocating it. I am even capable of giving it up, of obeying you. Perdita, Perdita, I will forget what your eyes said to me up there among the useless words. . . . What clasp, what caress, could have united us more deeply? All the passion of night urged us and threw us towards each other. I received you all into myself like a wave. And now it seems that I can no longer divide you from my own blood, it seems that you too cannot go away from me, and that we should set out together towards I know not what daybreak . . ."

He was speaking in a low voice, putting his whole self into his words, as if he had become some vibrating substance in which at every moment all the changes of that nocturnal creature seemed to impress themselves. It was no longer the heavy human prison, a bodily shape made of opaque and impenetrable flesh that was there before him, but a soul that was revealing itself in a variety of appearances as expressive as melodies, a sensibility delicate and powerful beyond all measure that was creating in her in turns the frailty of flowers, the vigour of marble, the vehemence of the flame, all that is shadow and all that is light

"Stelio!"

She only just said the name, and yet in the dying breath that came from her pale lips there was as great an immensity of wonder and exaltation as in the loudest cry. She had caught the sound of love in the words of the man beside her, — of love, love! She, who had so often listened to beautiful perfect words flowing towards her in that limpid voice and had suffered from them as from a torture and a mockery, now, because of this new accent in it, saw her own life and the life of the world transfigured Her soul seemed to reverse itself, the heavy encumbrances falling to unknown depths, disappearing in endless darkness, while there came to the surface something light and luminous, something free and spotless, that dilated and curved into a glorious dome like a morning sky; and as the wave of light creeps from horizon to zenith in its silent harmony, the illusion of happiness rose upon her lips. An infinite smile diffused itself there, so infinite that the lines of her mouth trembled in it like leaves in the wind, her teeth shone in it like jessamine blossoms in the light of stars, — the slenderest of shapes in a vast element.

"All is abolished; all has vanished. I have not

lived, I have not loved, I have not enjoyed, I have not suffered, I am new again. This is the only love I know. I am pure again. I would that I could die in the joy you will reveal to me. Years and their facts have passed over me without touching that part of my soul that I have been keeping for you, that secret heaven which has opened up suddenly and has conquered shadows, and has remained alone to hold the strength and sweetness of your name. Your love is saving me; the fulness of my clasp will make you divine. . . ."

Words of ecstasy sprang from her enfranchised heart, but her lips dared not speak them, and she went on smiling, smiling that infinite smile of hers, still in silence.

"Is it not true? Tell me! Answer me, Perdita. Do not you too feel this necessity? This necessity that has become stronger with all the strength of our renunciation, with all the constancy we have shown in waiting for the fulness of the hour? Ah, it does indeed seem to me that all my hopes and all my presentiments would be as nothing, Perdita, if this hour were not to come. Tell me that you could not get to that daybreak without me as I could not without you. Answer me."

"Yes, yes!"

In that faint syllable, she gave herself up irreclaimably. The smile went out; the mouth became heavy, appearing in almost hard relief against the pallor of her face, as if thirst were swelling it, strong to attract, to take, to hold, insatiable. And her whole person, that had seemed to shrivel in her pain and terror, drew itself up again as if a new framework had

suddenly grown within it, reconquered its carnal
power, was overswept by an impetuous wave, became once more desirable and impure.

"Let us wait no longer; it is late."

He was trembling with impatience. The fury was
again taking hold of him; frenzy had again seized
him by the throat with its feline claws.

"Yes," repeated the woman, but in a different
tone, her eyes plunged into his as if she were now
certain of possessing the philtre that was to bind him
to her lastingly.

He felt the many joys that must pervade that flesh
full of deep things enter his heart. He looked at her
and turned pale, as if his blood had suddenly been
dispersed over the earth and was sinking into it to
nourish the roots of growing things, as if he were
standing in a dream, outside all time, alone with her
who was alone.

She was standing under the fruit-laden shrub which
she had adorned with necklaces; her whole person
was sharply drawn and curved like her lips, and
ever darted from all her limbs like the breath darts
from between the lips. The unexpected beauty
made up of a thousand ideal forces that had illumined her in the supper-room renewed itself in her
still more intensely, made up now of a flame that
never fades, of a fervour that never languishes. The
magnificent fruits, bearing upon them the crown of
the kingly giver, hung above her head, the myth of
the pomegranate was revivified in the night as it had
been at the passage of the laden boat on the evening water. Who was she? Persephone, Queen of
Shadows? Had she lived there where all human

agitations seem but the wind's sport amid the dust
of an endless road? Had she seen the world where
its springs are, counted in a subterranean world
the roots of flowers immovable like the veins in
a petrified body? Was she tired or drunk with
human tears and laughter and lusts, and with having
touched all mortal things one by one to see them
blossom and to see them perish? Who was she
then? Had she struck upon the cities like a curse?
Had her kiss for ever closed all lips that sang?
Had she stopped the throb of tyrannous souls
and poisoned youths with the sweat of her body
that was salt like the foam of the sea? Who was
she; who was she? What was the past that made
her so pale, so ardent, and so perilous? Had she
already told all her secrets and given away all her
gifts, or could she still accomplish some new work
that would bring wonder to this new lover, to whom
life, desire, and victory, all three, meant one only
thing? All this and still more, still more was offered
to his dream by the thin veins on her temples, the
undulation of her cheeks, the power of her body
the bluish-greenish shadow as of the sea that was the
element in which her face lived as the eye lives in
its own moisture.

"All evil and all good, that which I know and
that which I ignore, that which you know and that
which you ignore, all was reserved for the fulness
of our night." Life and dream had become one
only thing. Thoughts and senses were as wines
poured out in one same cup. Their garments and
their bare faces, their hopes and the sight of their
eyes were like the plants of that garden, like the air

the stars, and the silence. The hidden harmony of Nature became apparent, by which she has mixed together and dissimulated all her differences and diversities.

It was one of those sublime moments that have no return. Before even his soul was conscious of it, his hands went out to her in their desire, touched her body, drew it towards him, found pleasure in feeling that it was cold and sweet.

When she felt his strong hands on her bare arm, the woman threw her head back as if about to fall. Under her dying eyelids, between her dying lips, the white of her eyes and the white of her teeth glittered like things that glitter for the last time. Then quickly she raised her head and revived; her mouth sought the mouth that was seeking it. They stamped themselves on each other. No seal was ever deeper. Love, like the shrub above them, covered both those deluded ones.

They separated; they gazed at each other without seeing. They could see nothing. They were blind. They could hear a terrible roll as if the quiver of bronze bells had re-entered their very forehead. Nevertheless they heard the dull thud of a pomegranate that had fallen on the grass from a branch they had shaken in their violent clasp. They shook themselves as if to throw off a mantle that was burdening them. They saw each other and became lucid again. They heard the voices of their friends who were scattered about the garden and a distant indistinct clamour from the canals where perhaps the antique pageants were repassing.

"Well," asked the young man, eagerly, scorched

to the marrow by that kiss that had been full of flesh and soul.

The woman bent down to the grass to pick up the pomegranate. It was quite ripe and broken by its fall; its blood-like juice was flowing; it moistened her parched hand and stained her light dress. With the remembrance of the laden boat, the pale island, and the meadow of asphodel, the words of the Life-giver came back to her loving spirit. " This is my body. . . . Take and eat."

" Well ? "

" Yes."

She pressed the fruit in her hand with an instinctive movement, as if to crush it. The juice trickled in a streak over her wrist. Then her whole body contracted and vibrated as if round a knot of fire, craving for subjection. Again the icy river submerged her, passing over her, chilling her from the roots of her hair to the points of her fingers without extinguishing that knot of fire.

" How? Tell me ! " the young man urged, almost roughly, as he felt his madness rising again and the odour of the Orgy returning from afar.

" Leave when the others leave, then come back. I will wait for you at the gate of the Gradenigo Garden."

The wretched carnal trembling shook her. She had become the prey of an invincible power. He saw her again for the space of a flash as he had pictured her before, outstretched, moist, and throbbing like a Mænad after the dance. Again they gazed upon each other, but they could not bear the suffering brought by the fierce eyes of their desire. They parted.

She went away towards the voices of the poets who had exalted the idealism of her power.

Lost! lost! Henceforth she was lost! She was still living, yet overthrown, humiliated, wounded as if she had been pitilessly trodden under foot; she was still living, and the dawn was rising, and the days were beginning again, and the fresh tide was flowing again into the City Beautiful, and Donatella was still pure on her pillows. It was already melting into infinite distance, although it was still so near, that hour in which she had waited for her lover at the gate, had heard his steps in the almost funereal silence of the deserted sidepath, had felt her knees give way as under a blow, and the terrible roll as of bronze bells fill her head. That hour was already very far, yet in all her body, together with the tremulousness that pleasure had left there, the sensations of that time of waiting persisted with strange intensity; the chill of the railing against which she had laid her brow, the acrid odour that rose from the grass as from a retting-tank, the warm moist tongue of Myrta's greyhounds that had noiselessly come and licked her hands.

" Good-bye, good-bye! "

She was lost. He had risen from her bed as from the couch of a courtesan, almost a stranger to her, almost impatient, attracted by the freshness of dawn, by the freedom of morning.

" Good-bye! "

From her window she caught sight of him on the shore, drinking in a wide breath of vivid air: then

in the great calm she heard his firm, clear voice
calling the gondolier: —

"Zorzi!"

The man was sleeping in the bottom of his gondola
and his human sleep was like the sleep of the curved
boat that obeyed him. As Stelio touched him with
his foot, he awoke with a start, jumped to the stern,
seized his oar. The man and the boat woke up at
the same time, in perfect harmony with each other,
like a single body, ready to glide on the water.

"Your servant, master," said Zorzi, with a good-
natured smile, glancing at the sky that was growing
lighter. "Do you sit down, and I will row."

Opposite the palace some one threw open the great
door leading to some works. It was a stone-cutting
establishment, where steps were being cut out of
the stone of Val di Sole.

"To ascend," thought Stelio, and his superstitious
heart gladdened at the good omen. The name of
the quarry, too (the Valley of the Sun), seemed
radiant on the door-plate. The image of a staircase
signified his own ascension. He had already seen
it in the abandoned garden on the coat of arms of
the Gradenigo. "Higher, ever higher!" Joy was
again bubbling up from the depths. The morning
seemed to stimulate all the works of man.

"And Perdita? And Ariadne?" He saw them
again at the top of the marble staircase in the light
of the smoking torches, thrown so close to each
other by the throng that they had blended in one
same whiteness, — the two temptresses, both emerging from the crowd as from the clasp of a monster.
"And la Tanagra?" The Syracusan with the long

goat-like eyes then appeared, in a restful pose, knitted
to her mother earth, as the figure of a bas-relief
is attached to the marble in which it is carved.
'The Dionysian Trinity!" He pictured them to
himself as freed from every passion, like the creatures of Art. The surface of his soul was being
covered with splendid, rapid images, like a sea
scattered over with swelling sails. He had ceased
to suffer. The increasing daylight was spreading
a sharp sense of newness over his whole substance. The heat of the night's fever was entirely
dispersing in the breeze; its fumes were being dissipated. What was happening all around, happened
in himself too. He was being born anew with the
morning.

"There is no need for me to light you any more
now!" murmured the oarsman, putting out the gondola lantern.

"By San Giovanni Decollato, to the Grand Canal,"
cried Stelio, sitting down.

And while the dentellated prow turned into the
Canal of San Giacomo dall' Orio, he turned to look at
the palace, which was leaden in the shadow. An illuminated window suddenly grew dark like an eye that
is blinded. "Good-bye, good-bye." His heart gave
a leap, pleasure waved back into his veins, images of
pain and death passed over all the others. The woman no longer young had remained up there alone,
with the expression of a dying thing on her face;
the virgin was preparing to go back to the place of
her torment. He knew not how to pity, he could
only promise. From the abundance of his strength,
he drew the illusion of being able, for his greater joy,

to change those two destinies. He ceased to suffer. All uneasiness yielded before the simple pleasure of the eyes offered him by the sights of the morning. The leaves peeping over the garden walls, behind which the twitter of the sparrows was already awakening, hid from him the pallor of Perdita; the sinuous lips of the singer were lost in the water's undulation. That which was happening around, happened to him too. The arch and the echo of the bridges, the swimming seaweeds, the moan of the pigeons, were like his breathing, his confidence, his hunger.

"Stop in front of the Palazzo Vendramin-Calergi," he ordered the boatman.

As he passed by a garden wall, he tore away a few frail, flowering plants from the interstices of the bricks that had the rich, dark colour of clotted blood. The flowers were violet, of extreme delicacy, almost impalpable. He thought of the myrtles that grow along the Gulf of Ægina, hardy and erect, like bronze bushes. He thought of the little dark cypresses that crown the stony tops of the Tuscan Hills, of the high laurels that protect the statues in the Roman villas. His thoughts increased the value of the autumnal flowers that were too slight an offering for Him who had known how to give his life the great victory He had promised it.

"Go to shore."

The Canal was deserted; it was like an ancient river, full of poetry and silence. The green sky was mirrored in it with its last dying stars. At the first glance the palace had an aerial appearance as of a painted cloud laid on the water; the shade in which it was still wrapped had about it something of the quality of velvet, the beauty of something rich and soft. And in the same manner that the pattern slowly discloses itself in thick velvet, slowly the lines of the architecture became visible in the three Corinthian orders that rose with their rhythm of grace and strength, to the summit where the emblems of noble estate, the eagles, the horses, and the pitchers, were entwined with the roses of the Loredan. NON NOBIS, DOMINE. NON NOBIS.

It was there that the great ailing heart was beating. The image of the barbaric creator reappeared, with its blue eyes shining under the vast brow, its lips closing above the robust chin that was armed with sensuality, pride, and disdain. Was he asleep? Could he sleep, or did he lie sleepless with his glory? The young man recalled strange things that were told of him. Was it true that he could not sleep, except on his wife's heart, closely held by her, and that even in his old age there persisted in him this need of a loving contact? He recalled a story of Lady Myrta's, who, when she was in Palermo, had visited the Villa d'Angri, where the cupboards in the room inhabited by the old man had remained impregnated with so violent an essence of roses that it still turned her faint. He saw the small, tired body adorned with gems, wrapped in sumptuous sheets, perfumed like a corpse prepared for the funeral pyre. And was it not Venice that had given him, as of old it had given Albert Dürer, a taste for things sumptuous and voluptuous? It was in the silence of the canals that he had heard the passing of the most ardent breath of his music, — the deadly passion of Tristan and Isolde.

Now the great ailing heart was throbbing there, and there its formidable impulse was dying out. The patrician palace with the eagles and horses and pitchers and roses was shut up and as dumb as a great sepulchre. The sky above the marbles was reddening at the breath of dawn.

" Hail to the victorious one ! " And Stelio threw the flowers down before the door.

"Go on! Go on!"

The oarsman bent over the oars, spurred by that sudden impatience. The slight boat skipped over the water. The canal was all alight on one side. A tawny sail passed noiselessly. The sea, the bright waves, the laugh of the sea-birds, the wind out in the open, rose up before his desire.

" Row, Zorzi ! To the Veneta Marina by the Canal dell' Olio," cried the young man.

The canal seemed too small for his soul to breathe in. Victory was as necessary to him now as air. He wanted to test the well-tempered quality of his nature, after the night's delirium, in the light of the morning, and in the sharpness of the sea. He was not sleepy ; there was a circle of freshness round his eyes as if he had bathed them with dew. He felt no need of rest, only a horror of his hotel bed as of a resting-place too vile for him. " The deck of a vessel, the smell of salt and pitch, the throb of a red sail . . ."

" Row, Zorzi ! "

The gondolier rowed with increased vigour; the rowlock now and then creaked under his effort. The Fondaco dei Turchi melted away like worn and marvellously discoloured ivory, like the surviving portico of a ruined mosque. The palace of the

Cornaro and the palace of the Pesaro passed them, like two opaque giants blackened by time as by the smoke of a conflagration. The Ca'd'Oro passed them like a divine play of stone and air ; then the Rialto showed its ample back already noisy with popular life, laden with its encumbered shops, filled with the odour of fish and vegetables, like an enormous cornucopia pouring on the shore all round it an abundance of the fruits of the earth and sea with which to feed the dominant city.

"I am hungry, I am hungry, Zorzi," said Stelio, laughing.

"A good sign when the night makes you hungry; only the old are made sleepy by it," said Zorzi.

"Go to shore!"

At a stall he bought some of the grapes of the Vignole, and some of the figs of Malamocco, heaped on a plate of vine-leaves.

"Row!"

The gondola veered under the warehouse of the Tedeschi, slipping along the dark, narrow canals towards the Rio de Palazzo. The bells of San Giovanni Crisostomo, of San Giovanni Elemosinario, of San Cassiano, of Santa Maria dei Miracoli, of Santa Maria Formosa, and of San Lio were joyously ringing in the dawn. The noise of the market, with its odours of fishery, of green stuff and of wine, was drowned in the salutation of the bronzes. The strip of water under the strip of sky, between the still sleeping walls of brick and marble, became ever more resplendent before the metal of the prow, as if the race were lighting it up, and that increase of light gave Stelio the illusion of a flaming swiftness. He thought of a boat that is being launched, raising sparks as it slips into the sea: the waves fume all round, the crowd shouts and applauds.

"To the Ponte della Paglia!"

A thought as spontaneous as an instinct was leading him to the glorious place where it seemed that there must still remain some trace of his own lyrical animations, and some echoes of the great Bacchic Chorus. "*Viva il forte!*" The gondola grazed the powerful flank of the ducal palace, standing compact like a single mass worked by chisels that had been as apt at finding melodies there as the bows of musical instruments. He embraced that mass with the whole of his newly arisen soul; there, once more, he heard the sound of his own voice and the crash of applause, saw the great, many-eyed Chimera, its bust covered with resplendent scales, its length blackening under enormous gilded scrolls, and distinctly saw himself oscillating above the multitude like a hollow, sonorous body inhabited by some mysterious will. He was saying the words: "To create with joy! It is the attribute of Divinity! It is impossible to imagine at the summit of our spirit a more triumphant act. The very words which express it have something of the splendour of dawn. . . ." He went on repeating to himself, to the air, to the water, to the stones, to the ancient city, to the young dawn: "To create with joy, to create with joy." When the prow passed under the bridge, he absorbed in the wider breath he drew, together with all his own hope and courage, all the beauty and all the strength of his anterior life.

"Find me a boat, Zorzi, a boat that will go out to

sea." He seemed to need still more breathing space, to need the wind, the sea salt, the foam, the swollen sail, the bowsprit pointed towards an immense horizon.

"To the Veneta Marina! Find me a fishing boat. Some *braghozzo* from Chioggia."

He caught sight of a great red and black sail that had only just been hoisted, and was flapping as it caught the wind, haughty as an old republican banner, bearing the Lion and the Book.

"There it is! there it is! We must overtake it, Zorzi."

Impatiently he waved his hand to the boat, signing to her to stop.

"Shout out to the boat that they must wait for me!"

The man at the oar, heated and dripping, threw a cry of recall to the man at the sail. The gondola flew like a canoe in a regatta to the panting of the gondolier's mighty breast.

"Bravo, Zorzi!"

But Stelio was panting too, as if he were about to overtake his fortune, or some happy aim, or the certainty of empire.

"We have run in and won the flag," said the oarsman, rubbing his heated hands with a frank laugh that seemed to refresh him. "What folly!"

The gesture, the tone, the popular wit, the astonished faces of the fisherman leaning over the parapet, the reflection of the sail that made the water bloodlike, the cordial odour of bread that came from a neighbouring bakehouse, the odour of boiling tar from a neighbouring dockyard, the noise of the arsenal work-people going to their warlike labour, all the strong emanation of that shore where one could still smell the old rotten galleys of the Serene Republic and hear the resounding under the hammer of the Italian iron-clads,— all those rough and healthy things called up an impulse of gladness that burst forth in a laugh from the young man's heart. He and the oarsman laughed together under the tarred, patched flank of the fishing boat, that had the living aspect of a good patient beast of burden, its skin harsh with wrinkles, excrescences, and scars.

"What is it you want?" asked the elder of the fishermen, bending towards the sonorous laughter his bearded and weather-beaten face in which the only light things were a few grey hairs, and the grey eyes under the eyelids turned up by the salt winds. "What can I do for you, master?"

The mainsail was flapping and hissing like a banner. "The master would like to come on board," answered Zorzi.

The mast creaked like a living thing from head to foot.

"Let him come up, then. Is that all you wish?" said the old man, simply, and he turned to take the stepladder.

He hooked it along the stern. It was made of a few worn pegs, and a single double knotted rope that was also worn. But that too, like every detail of the rough boat, seemed to Stelio a singularly living thing. On putting his foot upon it, his thin glossy shoes embarrassed him. The large hard hand of the sailor, marked with blue emblems, helped him up, pulled him on board with a wrench.

"The grapes and the figs, Zorzi!"

The oarsman from the gondola handed him the plate of vine-leaves.

"May it go into so much new blood for you!"

"And the bread!"

"We have got hot bread," said a sailor, lifting up his fine, fair, round form, "just fresh from the oven."

Hunger certainly would give it a delicious flavour, would find all the goodness of the grain gathered there.

"Your servant, master, and fair wind to you," cried the oarsman, saluting.

"Pull!"

The Latin sail with the Lion and the Book swelled crimson. The boat made for the open, turning its prow towards San Servolo. The shore seemed to arch itself as if to push it off. The veins of water in the ship's track made an opaline whirlpool as they mingled, one rosy, one blue-green, then they changed; all the colours alternated as if the wave at the prow were a fluid rainbow.

"Steer to the right!"

The boat veered with all its might. A miracle caught it; the first rays of the sun pierced the throbbing sail and flashed on the angels above the towers of San Marco and of San Giorgio Maggiore. They kindled the sphere of the Fortuna; their lightning crowned the five mitres of the Basilica. The Sea-City was queen on the water, and all her veils were rent.

"Glory to the miracle!" A superhuman feeling of power and freedom swelled the heart of the young man as the wind swelled the sail that was being transfigured for him. He stood in the crimson splendour of that sail as in the splendour of his own blood. It seemed to him that the mystery of so much beauty demanded of him the triumphal act. The consciousness came to him that he was ready for its accomplishment. "To create with joy!"

And the world was his!

II

THE EMPIRE OF SILENCE

THE EMPIRE OF SILENCE

THE EMPIRE OF SILENCE

"In Time!" La Foscarina had paused for a long time in one of the rooms of the Academia before the old woman of Francesco Torbido, — that wrinkled, toothless, flabby, yellowish old woman, incapable of either weeping or smiling any longer, that kind of human ruin far worse than putrefaction, that kind of earthly *parca* holding between her fingers in place of spindle, thread, or scissors the placard with the warning.

"In time!" she repeated to the open air, interrupting the silence full of thoughts during which, little by little, she had felt her heart grow heavy and descend to its depths like a stone in dull water. "Stelio, do you know the shut-up house in the Calle Gambara?"

"No, which?"

"The house of the Countess of Glanegg."

"No, I don't know it."

"Don't you know the story of the beautiful Austrian?"

"No, Fosca, tell it me."

"Shall we go as far as the Calle Gambara? it is only a few steps."

"Let us go."

Side by side, they went towards the shut-up house. Stelio hung back a little to watch the actress, to see her walking in the dead air. His warm glance embraced her whole person, — the line of the shoulders falling with so noble a grace, the free flexible waist on the powerful limbs, the knees that moved slightly among the folds of her gown, and the pale, passionate face, the mouth full of thirst and eloquence, the forehead that was as beautiful as a beautiful manly brow, the eyes that lengthened out from among the eyelashes, hazy as if a tear were continually coming up to them and melting there unshed: the whole of the passionate face full of light and shadow, of love and sorrow: the feverish strength, the trembling life.

"I love you, I love you! You alone please me; everything in you pleases me," he said suddenly, quite low, close to her cheek, almost pressing against her as he fell in with her pace, putting his arm under her arm, unable to bear the thought of her being seized by her torment, of her suffering from the fearful admonishment.

She started, stopped, dropped her eyes, turned white.

"Sweet friend," she said in so low a voice that the words seem modulated less by her lips than by her soul's smile.

All her trouble was flowing away, was being changed into a wave of tenderness that poured its abundance over her friend. Her infinite gratitude gave her an anxious need of finding some great gift for him.

"What can I do, what can I do for you? Tell me!"

She thought of some wonderful test, some sudden strange testimony of love. "Let me serve, let me serve!" She longed to possess the world that she might offer it to him.

"What is it that you wish? Tell me, what can I do for you?"

"Love me! Love me!"

"My love is sad, my poor friend."

"It is perfect; it fills up my life."

"But you are young."

"I love you!"

"You should possess that which is strong like yourself."

"Every day you exalt my hope and my strength. The tide of my blood seems to swell when I am near you and your silence. At such times, things are conceived in me which you will marvel at in time. You are necessary to me."

"Do not say so!"

"Each day you bring me the assurance that every promise ever made to me will be kept."

"Yes, you will go on to the end of your own beautiful destiny. I have no fear for you. You are safe. No danger can frighten you. No obstacle can ever come in your way. Oh, to love without fearing! Whoever loves, fears. I do not fear for you. You seem to me invincible. For this too, I thank you."

She was showing him her profound faith which, like her passion, was lucid and unlimited. For a long time, even in the ardour of her own struggles and the vicissitudes of her wandering lot, she had kept her eyes intently fixed on his young, victorious life as on an

ideal form born of the purification of her own desire.
More than once, in the midst of the sadness of her
vain loves and the nobility of her self-imposed prohibition, she had thought: " Ah, if when the end has
come of all my courage that the storm has hardened,
if at the end of all the clear strong things that sorrow
and revolt have laid bare in the depths of my soul, if
with all that is best in me I could one day shape the
wings for your last, highest flight ! "   More than once
her melancholy had known the intoxication of an
almost heroic presentiment.   At such times, she had
subjected her soul to effort and constraint, had raised
it to the highest moral beauty she knew, had led it
towards actions that were pure and sorrowful, only
for the sake of deserving that which she hoped and
feared, only to think herself worthy of offering her
servitude to him who was so impatient of conquest.

And now a sudden violent shock of Fate had
thrown her against him with all the weight of her
trembling body like a woman full of desire.   She
had united herself to him with the sharpest of her
blood, she had watched him on the same · pillow,
sleeping the heavy sleep of love's exhaustion, she had
known at his side sudden awakenings agitated by cruel
forebodings, had known the impossibility of closing
her tired eyes again, lest he should gaze on her while
she slept, lest seeking in her face the lines of the
years that had passed he should be disgusted by them
and pant after some fresh, young, unconscious life.

" Nothing is worth what you give me," said Stelio,
pressing her arm, his fingers seeking the bare wrist
under her glove, urged by an uneasy necessity of
feeling the pulse of that devoted life and the beating

of that faithful heart in the deserted places through which they walked, under the squalid smoke that surrounded them and deadened the noise of their steps. "Nothing is worth this certainty of never again being alone until death."

"Ah, then you too feel it, you too know that this is for ever!" she cried with an impulse of joy as she saw the triumph of her love. "For ever! Whatever may happen, wherever your fate may lead you, wherever you may want me to serve you, Stelio, be it near you or from afar. . . ."

A confused monotony of sound was spreading through the air. She recognised it. It was the chorus of sparrows gathered together on the great dying tree in the garden of the Countess Glanegg. The words stopped on her lips; she made an instinctive movement, as if to turn back, as if to draw her friend away in some other direction.

"Where are we going?" he asked, shaken by his companion's brusque movement and by the unexpected interruption that was like the end of some music or enchantment.

She stopped. She smiled her slight concealing smile. "IN TIME." "I tried to escape," she said, "but I cannot, I see."

As she stood there, she was like some pale flame.

"I had forgotten that I was taking you to the closed house, Stelio."

She stood there in the ashen daylight, nerveless like one lost in a desert.

"I thought it was somewhere else we were going. But here we are. In time!"

She stood before him now as on that unforgettable

night, when she had implored him, "Do not hurt me!" She stood there clothed in her sweet tender soul, that was so easy to slay, so easy to destroy and offer up like a bloodless sacrifice.

"Let us go; let us go!" he said, trying to draw her away. "Let us go elsewhere."

"One cannot."

"Let us go home, let us go home and light a fire, the first October fire. Let me spend the evening with you, Foscarina. It is going to rain before long. It would be so sweet to linger in your room, to talk or be silent with our hands in each other's. . . . Come, let us go."

It would have pleased him to take her in his arms, to nurse her, comfort her, to feel her weeping and to drink in her tears. The very sound of his own caressing words increased his tenderness. Then, passionately, of all her loving person he loved the delicate lines that went from her eyes to her temples, and the little dark veins that made violets of her eyelids, and the undulation of her cheek, and the weary chin, and all that in her seemed touched by the disease of Autumn and all that was shadow on her passionate face.

"Foscarina, Foscarina!"

Whenever he called her by her real name, his heart would beat more rapidly, as if something more profoundly human were entering into his love, as if all of a sudden their whole past were being reknit to the figure isolated by his dream, as if innumerable threads were reconnecting all its fibres to implacable life.

"Come, let us go!"

"But why, since the house is there. Let us pass by the Calle Gambara. Don't you want to know the story of the Countess Glanegg? Look, it is like a convent!"

The narrow street was lonely; like a hermitage path it was greyish, damp, and strewn with putrid leaves. The north-east wind had brought a slow soft mist with it that deadened every noise. The monotonous twitter of the sparrows sounded now and again like the creaking of iron or wood.

"Behind those walls, a desolate soul is surviving the beauty of its own body," said la Foscarina, in a level voice. "Look, the windows are closed, the shutters are nailed, the doors are sealed. Only one is left open for the servants to pass in and out of, and through it the dead woman's food is brought to her as in an Egyptian tomb. It is an extinguished body that those servants feed and wait upon."

The almost naked tops of the trees that overtopped the cloistered enclosure seemed smoking, and the sparrows, more numerous on the branches than the diseased leaves, twittered and twittered endlessly.

"Guess what her name is. It is as rare and beautiful a name as if you had discovered it yourself."

"I don't know."

"Radiana. Radiana is the name of the prisoner."

"But whose prisoner?"

"The prisoner of Time, Stelio. Time watches at her doors, as in the old prints, with his hour-glass and his scythe. . . ."

"Is it an allegory?"

A child passed whistling. When he saw the two gazing at the closed windows, he also stopped to

look with wide, wondering, curious eyes. They
were silent. The constant twitter of the sparrows
could not overpower the silence of the walls and the
trees and the sky: its monotony sounded in their
ears like the roar in a sea-shell, and through it they
could hear the silence of surrounding things and
a few distant voices. The hoarse hoot of a siren
prolonged itself in the misty distance, becoming,
little by little, as soft as a flute note. It ceased.
The little boy grew tired of his gazing: nothing visible was happening; the windows did not open; all
remained motionless. He went off at a run.

They heard the flight of his little naked feet patter-
ing on the damp stones and the rotten leaves.

"Well?" asked Stelio, "and what about Radiana?
You have not told me yet why she has shut herself up.
Tell me! I have been thinking of Soranza Soranzo."

"She is the Countess Glanegg, a lady of the highest Viennese nobility, and perhaps the most beautiful creature that I have ever met. Franz Lenbach
has painted her in the armour of a Valkyrie, wearing
the four-winged helmet. Do you know Franz Lenbach? Have you ever been to his studio in the
Palazzo Borghese?"

"No, never."

"You must go there one day, and you must ask
him to show you that portrait. You will never
again forget the face of Radiana. You will see it
unchanged as I now see it through those walls. She
has chosen to remain such as she was in the eyes
of those who once saw her in her splendour. Once
on some too bright a morning when she noticed that
the time of withering had come for her too, she

resolved to take leave of the world in such a way that man should not stand by, watching the decay and collapse of her famous beauty. Perhaps it was her sympathy with things that fall to pieces and go to ruin which kept her in Venice. On the occasion of her leave-taking she gave a magnificent entertainment at which she appeared, still sovereignly beautiful. Then, with her servants, she retired for ever in this house which you see, in this walled garden, to await the end. She has become a legendary figure. It is said that no mirror is allowed in her house and that she has forgotten her own face. Her most devoted friends and her nearest relatives are not allowed to see her. How does she live? In the company of what thoughts? What is the art that helps her while away the time of waiting? Is her soul in a state of grace?"

Every pause in the veiled voice that questioned the mystery was filled with a melancholy so dense as to seem almost tangible; it seemed to be cadenced by the sobbing rhythm of water that is being poured into an urn.

"Does she pray? Does she contemplate? Does she weep? Perhaps she has become inert and no longer suffers, as an apple does not suffer when it shrivels up in the bottom of an old cupboard."

The woman stopped. Her lips curved downwards as if their words had withered them.

"What if she were suddenly to look out of that window?" said Stelio, his ear catching something like a real sensation, like the grinding of hinges.

Both examined the interstices of the nailed shutters.

"She might be sitting there looking at us," he added in a hushed voice.

The shudder of the one communicated itself to the other.

They were leaning against the opposite wall, unwilling to move a step. The surrounding inertia was creeping over them; the damp, greyish mist grew thicker as it swathed them; the confused monotony of the birds' twitter stunned them like certain drugs that stun fever. The sirens screeched in the distance. The screeches, dwindling little by little till they became as gentle as flute notes in the limp air, seemed to linger like the discoloured leaves that were leaving their branches one by one without a moan. How long it took for the falling leaf to drop to the earth! All was mist; all was slow heaviness, desertion, waste, ashes.

"It is inevitable! I must die, dear friend; I must die," the woman said in a heart-rending voice after a long silence, raising her face from the cushion where she had been pressing it in order to master the convulsion of pain and pleasure that his sudden, furious caresses had given her.

She saw her friend sitting apart from her on the other divan near the balcony, in the attitude of one about to go to sleep, his eyes half shut, and his head, which was thrown back, tinged with gold by the light of evening. She saw the red mark, like a small wound, just under his lip, and the disordered hair on his forehead. She felt that those were the things on which her desire fed and rekindled itself. She felt that her eyelids hurt her pupils the more she looked, that her gaze burnt her eyelashes; that the incurable evil entered through her pupils, spreading over all her withered body. Lost, lost, henceforth she was lost without remedy.

"Die?" her friend said weakly, without opening his eyes, without moving, as if speaking from the depths of his drowsiness and his melancholy.

She noticed that the little open wound moved under his lip when he spoke.

"Before you hate me."

He opened his eyes, raised himself up, held out his hand towards her as if to prevent her from saying any more.

"Ah, why do you torment yourself?"

She was almost livid; her loosened hair fell in streaks over her face; she seemed consumed by a poison that corroded her, bent as if her soul had broken through its flesh, terrible and miserable.

"What are you doing with me; what are we doing with each other?" the woman said in her anguish.

They had struggled that day: the breath of the one mingling with the other's breath, one heart against the other heart; their union had been like a scuffle; they had felt the taste of blood in the moisture of their mouths. All at once they had yielded to a sudden rush of desire as to a blind necessity of destroying each other. He had shaken her life as if to tear it up by its most hidden roots. They had felt a sharpness of teeth hiding in their cruel kisses.

"I love you!"

"Not as I would wish; this is not what I want."

"You excite me. Suddenly, the fury seizes me. . . ."

"It is like hatred."

"No, no; don't say that."

"You shake me and rend me as if you wanted to make an end of me."

"You blind me. After that I know nothing."

"What is it that agitates you? What do you see in me?"

"I don't know. I don't know what it is."

"I know it."

"Don't torment yourself. I love you! This is the love. . . ."

"That condemns me! I must die of it. Give me once more the name you used to give me."

"You are mine! I have you now and will not lose you."

"But you must lose me."

"But why? I cannot understand you. What is this madness of yours? Does my desire offend you? But you, do you perhaps not desire me too? Are you not seized by the same fury of possessing me and of being possessed? Your teeth were chattering before I even touched you. . . ."

His intolerance was burning into her more deeply, was poisoning her wound. She covered her face with her hands. Her heart had become rigid and was beating in her breast like a hammer, and the hard blows of the hammer were reverberated in her head.

"Look!"

He touched his lip where it hurt him, pressed the small wound, held out to the woman his finger tinged with the drop of blood that had oozed from it.

She rose to her feet quickly, writhing as if he had prodded her with a red-hot iron. She opened her eyes wide upon him as if to devour him with her gaze, her nostrils quivered, a fearful force heaved in her, her whole body, in vibrating, felt itself naked under her dress as if the folds no longer adhered to it. Her face, that had looked up from the hollow of her hands as from a blind mask, burnt darkly like a fire that has no rays. She was most beautiful, most terrible, and most miserable.

" Ah, Perdita, Perdita ! "

Never, never, never will that man forget that step which Lust moved towards him, the way in which it drew near him, the swift dumb wave that overthrew itself on his breast, that wrapped him round, that drank him in, that gave him for a moment the fear and the joy of suffering a divine violence, of dissolving in a kind of warm, deadly moisture, as if the whole of the woman's body had suddenly become one single aspiring mouth that drew him in and by which he was entirely absorbed.

He closed his eyes, forgetting the world and his glory. A dark sacred depth opened in him like a temple. His spirit became motionless and opaque, but all his senses aspired after the transcending of their human limits, aspired to the joy that is beyond the human impediment, became sublime, capable of penetrating the remotest mysteries, of discovering the most recondite secrets, of drawing one pleasure from another like one harmony from another harmony, became marvellous instruments, infinite virtues, realities sure as death. All was vanishing like a mist, the energies and the aspirations of the universe seemed converging in that mere union of sexes; it was consecrated by heaven, made religious by the shadow of the curtains, accompanied by the roar of death.

He opened his eyes. He saw the room, that had grown dark; through the open balcony he saw the distant sky, the trees, the cupolas, the towers, the extremity of the lagoon with the face of the twilight bending over it, and the Euganean Hills, that were quiet and blue like the folded wings of earth resting in the evening. He saw the forms of silence and the silent form of the woman adhering to him like the bark to the trunk of the tree.

The woman was lying with all her weight upon him, holding and covering him in her embrace, her forehead pressed against his shoulder, her face suffocatingly hidden; she was clasping him with a hold that did not loosen, that was indissoluble, like the grip of a corpse's stiffened arms round a living person. It seemed as if she could never loosen that clasp, as if she could never again be detached from him except by the cutting off of her arms. He felt, in that encircling clasp, the solidity and the tenacity of the bones, while on his bosom and along his legs he felt the soddenness of the body that trembled upon him now and then with a quiver as of water running over gravel. Indefinite things passed in that tremble of water, numberless continual things that rose from the depths and descended from afar; ever thicker, more impure, they passed and passed like a turbid stream of life. He acknowledged once more that his sharp desire was nourished by that very impurity, by that unknown encumbrance, by those traces of lost loves.

by all that bodily sadness and unspeakable despair. He owned once more that it was the phantoms of other gestures which spurred his gesture of longing for the wandering woman. It was because of her that he was suffering now and because of himself; and he felt her suffer, and he felt that she was his the same as fuel belongs to the fire that consumes it. And again he heard the words that had come unexpectedly after their fury had passed: "It is inevitable: I must die."

He turned his eyes to the open again, saw the gardens darkening, the houses being lit up, a star springing from the sky's mourning, the glitter of a long pale sword at the bottom of the lagoon, the mountains melting into the fragments of night, the distance stretching out towards regions rich with unknown possessions. There were actions to be accomplished in the world, conquests to be followed up, dreams to exalt, destinies to enforce, enigmas to attempt, laurels to be gathered. There were paths down there, mysterious meetings that could not be foreseen. Some veiled joy might be passing somewhere, with nobody to meet or recognise it. Was there not perhaps an equal, a brother, living somewhere in the world at that hour, or a distant enemy on whose brow the lightning-like inspiration from which the eternal work is born was about to descend after a day of troubled expectation. Some one, perhaps, at that hour had finished some great work, or had found at last some heroic reason of living; but he, — he lay there in the prison of his body under the weight of the desperate woman. Her magnificent fate, full of sorrow and of

power, had come to break against him as against a
rock. What was Donatella Arvale doing? What
was she thinking of in the evening hour on her
Tuscan hill in her solitary house, near her demented
father? Was she tempering her will for some contemplated struggle? Was she sounding her secret?
Was she pure?

He became inert under the woman's clasp, his
arms hindered by the rigid circle. Repulsion filled
his being. A melancholy as strong as pain thick-
ened round his heart; and the silence seemed
expecting a cry. The veins throbbed painfully in
his limbs, that had grown torpid under her weight.
Little by little the clasp gave way as if life were
failing it. The heart-rending words came back to
his soul. A funereal image appeared, assailing him
with a sudden frightened uneasiness. And nevertheless he did not move nor speak nor attempt to dis-
sipate the cloud of anguish that had gathered over
them both. He remained motionless. He lost the
knowledge of places and the measure of time. He
saw himself and the woman in the midst of an infinite plain, where half-scorched, scattered grasses grew
under a white sky. They were waiting, waiting for
a voice to call them, for a voice that should raise
them up. . . . A confused dream was born in his
torpor, fluctuated, changed, turned sad in the nightmare. Breathlessly he seemed to be climbing a
steep hillside with his companion; and her more
than human breathlessness increased his own. . . .

He started, re-opening his eyes at the clang of a
bell. It was the bell of San Simeone Profeta, and
it was so near that it seemed to be ringing in the

very room. The metallic sound pierced like a rapier.

"Had you, too, gone to sleep?" he asked the woman, finding her unresisting like one already dead.

And he raised one hand, passed it lightly over her hair, stroking her cheeks and chin.

She burst into sobs, as if that hand were breaking her heart. And she lay sobbing on his breast without dying there.

"I have a heart, Stelio," said the woman, looking him in the eyes with a painful effort that made her lips tremble as if she had overcome fierce shyness in order to say those words. "I suffer from a heart that is alive in me, — ah, Stelio, alive and eager and full of anguish as you will never know. . . ."

She smiled her thin, concealing smile, hesitated, held out her hand towards a bunch of violets, took it up and raised it to her nostrils; her eyelids dropped; her forehead was bare between her hair and the flowers, marvellously beautiful and sad.

"Sometimes you wound it," she said in a low voice, her breath lost in the violets. "You are cruel to it sometimes. . . ."

It seemed as if the humble, sweet-smelling flowers were helping her to confess her grief, veiling still further her timid reproach to her friend. She was silent; he bowed his head. They could hear the crackling of the wood on the fire-dogs; they could hear the even beat of the rain in the mourning garden.

"A great thirst for kindness; ah, you will never

know what a thirst it is! . . . For that kindness, dear sweet friend, that deep true kindness, knowing not how to speak, but understanding, knowing how to give all in a single look, in a little movement, strong and sure, always rising up between us and life that stains and seduces us . . . Do you know it?"

Her voice, alternately firm and vacillating, was so warm with inner light, so filled with the revelation of a soul, that the young man felt it passing through his blood, less like a sound than a spiritual essence.

"In you, in you, I know it."

He took her hands that were in her lap holding the violets, and, bending over them, submissively kissed them both. Then he remained at her feet in the same attitude of submission. The delicate perfume made his own tenderness more delicate. The rain and the fire spoke in the pause.

"Do you think I am sure of you?" the woman asked in a clear voice.

"Have you not watched me sleeping on your heart?" he answered, his tone all at once changed by a new emotion, because he had seen in that question the bare soul rise up and stand before him, had felt his secret need of believing and confiding discovered.

"Yes, but what is that? The sleep of youth is calm on any pillow. You are young. . . ."

"I love you and believe in you. I have given myself up entirely. You are my companion and your hand is strong."

He had seen the well-known anguish disturb the lines of the dear face, and his voice had trembled with love.

"Kindness!" said the woman, with a light move-ment, caressing the hair on his temples. "You know how to be kind; the necessity is in you, dear friend, of comforting. But a fault has been committed, and it must be atoned for. Once I thought that I could do the highest and the most humble things for you, and now it seems to me there is only one thing I can do, — to go away, disappear, leave you free with your fate."

He interrupted her, lifting himself up and taking the dear face in his hands.

"This thing I can do, which even love could not," she said in her low voice, turning pale and looking at him as she had never done before.

He felt himself to be holding his soul in the hollow of his hand, the image of a living spring infinitely precious and beautiful.

"Foscarina, Foscarina, my soul, my life! Yes, yes, more than love, I know that you can give me more than love; and nothing is worth to me that which you can give, and no other offer could comfort me for not having you at my side on the way. Believe, believe! I have repeated this to you so many times, don't you remember? also when you were not entirely mine, even when the prohibition still kept us apart. . . ."

Holding her closely in that same position, he bent over her and kissed her passionately on the lips.

She shivered in all her bones; the cold stream was passing over her, freezing her.

"No, no more," she begged, turning white.

She moved her friend away from her, unable to

restrain the panting in her breast. As in a dream, she bent down to pick up the violets that had fallen.

"The prohibition!" she said, after an interval of silence.

A dull roar came from a log that was struggling with the bite of the flame; the rain was pouring on the trees and stones. Now and then the sound imitated the agitation of the sea, conjuring up hostile places, inhospitable distances, beings that wandered under inclement skies.

"Why have we violated it?"

Stelio's eyes were intent on the mobile splendour of the hearth; in his flat, open hands the marvellous sensation was being continued, the vestige of the miracle still dwelt there, the trace of that human countenance across the miserable pallor of which a wave of sublime beauty had passed.

"Why?" repeated the woman, sorrowfully. "Ah, confess, confess that you, too, before the blind fury took us and carried us both away that night, — you too felt that all was about to be lost and devastated, you, too, felt that we could not yield if we wanted to save the good that was born of us, to save that strong, inebriating thing that to me had seemed the only valuable one of my life. Confess, Stelio; tell me the truth. I can almost remind you of the moment when the better voice spoke to you. Was it not on the water as we went towards my house, having Donatella with us?"

She had hesitated a moment before pronouncing that name, and afterwards she had felt an almost physical bitterness descending from her lips, as if

its syllables had become poison to her. In her
suffering she waited for her friend's answer.

"I can no longer look back, Fosca," he answered.
"Nor would I. I have lost no good thing that was
mine. I like your soul to have a mouth that is heavy,
and it pleases me to feel that your blood flies from
your face when I touch you, and you know by that
touch that I desire you. . . ."

"Be silent, be silent!" she implored. "Do not
unnerve me always. Let me speak of my trouble
to you. Why will you not help me?"

She drew back a little among her cushions, shrink-
ing as if his had been an act of brutal violence and,
in order not to look at her lover, looking fixedly
into the fire.

"More than once I have seen something in your
eyes which has filled me with horror," she at last
managed to say, with an effort that made her voice
hoarse.

He started, but dared not contradict her.

"With horror," she repeated, more clearly, implacable towards herself, having conquered her fear
and taken hold of her courage.

Both of them, with naked throbbing hearts, now
stood before the truth.

"Without weakness," the woman spoke on.

"The first time, it was that night, out there in the
garden. . . . I know what it all was that you were
seeing in me. All the mud over which I have walked,
all the infamy I have trodden under foot, all the impurity which has filled me with repugnance. . . . Ah,
you could not have confessed the visions that were
kindling your fever! Your eyes were cruel, and

your mouth was convulsed. When you felt that you were wounding me you took pity. . . . But since, but since . . ."

A blush had covered her, her voice had become impetuous and her eyes shone.

" To have nourished for years, with all that was best in me, a feeling of unlimited devotion and admiration; to have received when near you and from afar, in joy and in sadness, every consolation offered to mankind by your poetry with an act of the purest gratitude: and to have anxiously awaited other, ever greater and more consoling gifts; to have believed in the great strength of your genius from its very dawn and never to have detached my eyes from your ascension; and to have accompanied it with a wish that for years has been like my morning and evening prayer; to have silently, fervently gone on with the continual effort of imparting some beauty and some harmony to my spirit, that it might be less unworthy of approaching yours; on the stage before an ardent audience, to have so many times pronounced some immortal words, thinking of those which perhaps one day you would elect to give to the crowd through my lips; to have worked unceasingly; to have always sought after simpler and more intense art; to have aspired to perfection continually for fear of not pleasing you, of appearing too unequal to your dream; to have loved my fitful glory only because it might one day have served your own; to have hastened on the newest of your revelations with unshakable faith, that I might offer myself to you as an instrument of victory before the hour of my own decay, and to have defended this

idealism in my hidden soul against all and everything, against all and against myself: yes, more
harshly, more bravely against my own self; to have
made of you my melancholy, my unyielding hope,
my heroic test, the symbol of all things good, strong,
free, ah, Stelio, Stelio . . ."

She stopped a moment, suffocated by that memory
as by a new shame.

" . . . and to have reached that dawn, to have
seen you leaving my house in that way, in that horrible dawn."

She turned even whiter, all the blood leaving her
face.

"Do you remember?"

"I was happy, happy, happy," he cried out
to her in a choked voice, convulsed to the very
depths.

"No, no; don't you remember? You rose from
my bed as from the bed of a courtesan, replete, after
a few hours' violent pleasure. . . ."

"You are wrong; you deceive yourself!"

"Confess, tell me the truth; only through truth
can we yet hope to save ourselves."

"I was happy. My whole heart was open; I was
dreaming and hoping. I felt myself rising to new
life. . . ."

"Yes, yes; happy because you were breathing
freely again, because you found yourself still young
in the wind and the daylight. Ah, you had mingled
too many acrid things with your caresses, and there
was too much poison in your pleasure. What did
you see in her who had known agony in her renunciation so many times, — and you know it, — yes, agony,

rather than break through the prohibition necessary
to the life of the dream that she was dragging with
her in her endless wandering. Tell me, what was it
you saw in me if not a corrupt creature, a body full
of lust and remains of adventurous passions, a wandering actress who, on her bed, as on the stage,
belongs to all and to none . . ."

"Foscarina! Foscarina!"

He threw himself upon her, overcome by her words,
and closed her lips with his trembling hand.

"No, no; don't speak like that. Be silent! You
are mad; you are mad. . . ."

"The horror of it!" she murmured, falling back on
her cushions as if about to lose consciousness, wearied
by the effort, wan under the flood of bitterness that
had gurgled up from her heart's depths.

But her eyes remained open and dilated, motionless like two crystals, hard as if they had no lashes,
fixed upon him. They prevented him from speaking, from denying or diminishing the truth they had
discovered. After a few seconds he found them
becoming intolerable. He closed them with his
fingers, as one closes those of the dead. She saw
the gesture, which was one of infinite melancholy;
felt those fingers touching her lids as only love and
pity can touch. The bitterness disappeared; the
harsh knot melted away; her lashes moistened. She
held out her arms, twined them round his neck, and
supporting herself by them, raised herself slightly.
She seemed to be drawing herself together within
herself, to have become light and weak once more
and full of silent prayer.

"So I must go away," she sighed, her voice moistened by her heart's weeping. "Is there no help for it? Is there no forgiveness?"

"I love you," said her lover.

She freed one arm and held out her open hand to the fire, as if for an exorcism. Then she locked the young man again in a close embrace.

"Yes, yet for a little while, yet for a little while! Let me stay with you a little more! Then I will go away, I will go away, and die somewhere far away on a stone under some tree. Let me stay with you a little longer."

"I love you," said her lover.

It seemed as if the blind undaunted forces of life were whirling over their heads and above their embrace. Because they felt them and were terrified by them, they held each other more closely; and from the clasp of their two bodies, a good and an evil that were heart-rending, confused and intermingled and no longer separable, were born for their souls. In the silence, the voices of the elements spoke their obscure language, which was like an uncomprehended answer to their mute questioning. The fire and the rain, near them and afar, conversed, answered, narrated. Little by little these things attracted the Spirit of the Life-giver, drew it away, mastered it, dragged it into the world of innumerable myths that was born of their eternity. With a sensation that was deep and real he heard the resonance of the two melodies expressing the intimate essence of the two elementary wills: the two marvellous melodies that he had found and was going to weave into the symphonic web of his new tragedy. The stabs of pain and the vibrations of anxiety suddenly ceased as if for a happy

truce, for an interval of enchantment in the mist.
The woman's arms, too, were loosened as if obeying some mysterious liberating command.

"There is no help for it," she said to herself, as
if she were repeating the words of a condemnation
actually heard by her in the same way as Stelio had
heard the great melodies.

She leaned forward, resting her chin on her hand
and her elbow on her knee; and she remained in
that attitude staring fixedly into the fire with a frown
between her brows.

As he looked at her, he returned to his uneasiness.
The truce had passed too quickly, but in it his spirit
had been turned towards his work, and a tumult that
was like impatience had stayed behind with him. That
uneasiness now seemed useless to him, the woman's
anguish seemed importunate, since he loved her and
desired her, and his caresses were ardent, and both
were free, and the place of their dwelling was favourable to their dreams and their pleasures. He longed
to find a sudden means of snapping the iron band
that held her, of lifting her sad mists, of leading his
friend back to joy. He asked of his own spirit of
grace some delicate invention to mellow the afflicted
one and win her back to a smile. But he no longer
possessed the spontaneous melancholy, the trembling
pity that had given his fingers so soft a touch when
he closed the despairing eyes. His instinct suggested nothing more than a sensual act, the caress
that deadens the soul, the kiss that drowns thought.

He hesitated, looked at her. She was sitting in the
same bent attitude, her chin leaning on her hand, her
forehead puckered. The fire lit up her face and hair

in its glad leaping; the brow was as beautiful as a fine manly brow; there was something wild in the natural fold and the tawny lights of the thick locks where they waved back from the temples, — something fierce and rough, that reminded one of the wing of a bird of prey.

"What are you looking at?" she said, feeling his attention. "Are you discovering a white hair?"

He went down on his knees before her, flexible and caressing.

"You are beautiful in my eyes. In you I always find something that pleases me, Foscarina. I was watching the strange wave of your hair just here; it is not made by a comb, but by the storm."

He insinuated his sensual hands through her thick locks. She closed her eyes, seized by the usual chill, dominated by the terrible power; was his like a thing that can be held in the hand, like a ring on a finger, like a glove, like a garment, like a word that can be spoken or not, like a wine that can be drunk or spilt on the ground.

"You are beautiful as I see you. When you shut your eyes thus, I feel that you are mine to your last, last depths, lost in me, like the soul is confused with the body. One only life, mine and yours. . . . Ah, I cannot tell you. . . . The whole of your face turns pale within me. . . . I feel the love that is in your veins and in your very hair rising, rising. I see it overflow from under your eyelids. . . . When your eyelids beat, it seems that they must throb like my blood, and that the shadow of your eyelashes must reach to the innermost part of my heart."

She listened in the darkness where the red vibration of the flame reached her through the living tissue. And now and then it seemed that his voice came from far away and was not speaking to her, but to another; that she was listening surreptitiously to a lover's outpouring, that she was torn by jealousy, stricken by the flashes of a desire to kill, invaded by a spirit of vengeance that thirsted for blood, and that nevertheless her body remained motionless and that her hands were hanging beside her, full of heavy torpor, harmless and powerless.

"You are my joy, and you are my awakening. There is an awakening power in you of which you yourself are unconscious. The simplest of your acts is enough to reveal some truth to me that I ignored, and love is like the intellect, — shining in the measure of the truths which it discovers. Why, why do you regret? Nothing is destroyed; nothing is lost. We were meant to unite our two selves, just as we have joined them, so that together we might rise towards joy. It was necessary that I should be free and happy in the truth of your entire love in order to create the work of beauty that is expected by so many. I have need of your faith; I have need of passing through joy and of creating. . . . Your mere presence is enough to fructify my spirit incalculably. A moment ago, when you were holding me in your embrace, I suddenly felt a torrent of music, a river of melody passing through the silence. . . ."

To whom was he speaking? Of whom was he asking joy? Was not his musical necessity stretching out towards her who sang and transfigured the universe with her song? Of whom, if not of fresh youth, intact virginity, could he ask joy and creation? While she was holding him in her arms, the other woman had been singing within him. And now, now, to whom was he speaking, if not to her? Only the other could give him that which was necessary to his art and his life. The virgin was a new force, a closed beauty, a weapon not yet used, sharp and magnificent, bringing the intoxication of war. A sorrow mixed with anger tormented the woman in that vibrating broken darkness which she could not leave. She was suffering as if lying in a nightmare. It seemed to her that she was rolling to the deep with her indestructible encumbrance, with her past life and her years of misery and triumph, with her faded face and her thousand masks, with her despairing soul and the thousand souls that had inhabited her mortal shape. The passion that was to have saved her was pushing her irreparably towards ruin and death. In order to reach her and to reach his joy through her, the desire of the man she loved was obliged to force itself through the confused encumbrance, made up, as he believed, of innumerable, unknown loves; it would contaminate and corrupt itself there, become sharp and cruel; lastly, from sharpness it would pass to disgust, perhaps to hatred and contempt. The shadow of other men must ever lurk above his own caress, and that shadow must ever kindle the instinct of brutal ferocity that was hidden in the depths of his powerful sensuality. Ah, what had she done? She had armed a furious devastator and had put him there between herself and her friend. Henceforth there was no escape for her. She herself on that night of conflagration had brought him the fresh, beautiful prey on whom he had cast one of those looks that are an election and a promise. To whom was he speaking now, if not to her? Of whom was he asking joy?

" Don't be sad; don't be sad!"

She now heard the words confusedly, more faintly from minute to minute, as if her soul were sinking and the voice remaining on high, but she felt his impatient hands caressing her, tempting her. And in the blood-like darkness that was like the darkness whence folly and delirium spring, from her marrow, from her veins, from all her troubled flesh, a savage rebellion rose suddenly.

" Shall I take you to her; shall I call her to you?" she cried, beside herself, opening her eyes wide on his surprise, seizing him by the wrists and shaking him with convulsed strength. "Go, go; she is waiting for you. Why do you stay here? Go, run; she is waiting for you."

She got up, raised him as she did so, and tried to push him towards the door. She was unrecognisable, transfigured by her violence into a threatening, dangerous creature. The strength of her hands was incredible, like the energy of harm that had developed itself in all her limbs.

" Who, who is waiting for me? What are you saying? Come back to yourself, Foscarina."

He was stammering as he called her; he trembled with misgiving; he seemed to see the face of folly outlined in those convulsed features. She was like one demented and did not hear him.

" Foscarina!"

He called her with all his soul, white with terror, as if to stop with his cry the reason that was about to leave her.

She gave a great shudder, unclenched her hands, and looked round in a dazed way, as if she were awaking and did not remember. She was panting.

"Come, sit down."

He drew her back to the cushions, settled her there gently. She let herself be soothed, tended by his pained tenderness. She seemed to awake after having lost consciousness and to remember nothing. She moaned.

"Who has beaten me?"

She felt her sore arms, touched her cheeks near the joint of the jaws that hurt her. She began to shiver with cold.

"Stretch yourself out; lay your head here. . . ."

He made her lie down and rest her head, covered her feet with a cushion, softly, very gently, bending over her, as over a dear invalid, giving up to her all his heart that was beating, beating, still terrified.

"Yes, yes," she repeated, at his every movement, as if to prolong the sweetness of his care of her.

"Are you cold?"

"Yes."

"Shall I cover you up?"

"Yes."

He looked for something to cover her, found a piece of old velvet on a table. He covered her with that. She smiled up at him slightly.

"Are you comfortable like this?"

She only just signed to him with her eyelids that were closing. He picked up the violets, that were languid and warm. Then he placed the bunch on the cushion where her head was resting.

"So?"

Her lashes moved still more slightly. He kissed her on the forehead, in the midst of the perfume; then he turned to stir up the fire, added more wood, raised a great blaze.

"Does the heat reach you? Are you getting warm?" he asked in a low voice.

He drew near and bent over the poor creature. She had gone to sleep; the contractions of her face were smoothing out, and the lines of her mouth had recomposed themselves in the regular rhythm of sleep. A calm similar to that of death was diffused over her pallor. "Sleep, sleep." He was so full of love and pity that he would have liked to transfuse an infinite virtue of consolation and forgetfulness into that sleep. "Sleep on; sleep on!"

He remained there, standing on the carpet, to watch her. For a few seconds he measured her breathing. Those lips had said, "One thing I can do which even Love cannot do!" Those lips had cried out, "Shall I take you to her? Shall I call her to you?" He neither judged nor resolved, letting his thoughts disperse. Once again, he felt the blind, undaunted forces of life whirling above his head, and once again above that sleep he felt his terrible desire of life. "The bow is called *Bios*, and its work is Death."

In the silence, the fire and the water spoke. The voice of the elements, the woman sleeping in her sorrow, the nearness of fate, the immensity of the future, memory and presentiment, all those signs created a state of musical mystery in his spirit in which his unexpressed work rose up and received light. He heard his melodies developing indefinitely; he heard

a person in the fable saying: " It alone quenches
our thirst; and all the thirst that is in us reaches out
greedily towards its freshness. If it were not for it,
no one of us could live here; we should all die of
thirst." He saw a landscape, furrowed by the white
dried-up bed of an ancient river, scattered over with
lighted bonfires in the extraordinarily calm pure
evening. He saw a funereal glimmer of gold, a tomb
full of corpses all covered with gold, the body of
Cassandra crowned among the sepulchral urns. A
voice was saying: " How soft her ashes are ! They
run through the fingers like sea-sand." A voice was
saying: " She speaks of a shadow that passes over
things and of a wet sponge that wipes out all traces."
At this, night came; the stars twinkled, the myrtles
filled the air with odour, and a voice was saying:
" Ah, the statue of Niobe ! Before dying, Antigone
sees a stone statue from which issues a spring of
eternal tears." The error of time had disappeared,
the distance of centuries was abolished. The ancient
tragic soul was present in the new soul. The poet's
words and the poet's music were recomposing the
ideal unity of life.

One afternoon in November he returned on the
steamer from the Lido, accompanied by Daniele
Glauro. They had left the stormy Adriatic behind
them, and with it the roar of the green and white
waves on the desert beach, the trees of San Niccolo
despoiled by the rapacious wind, clouds of dead
leaves, heroic phantoms of leave-takings and arrivals,
the memory of the archers competing for the scarlet,

and of Lord Byron galloping, devoured by the anxiety of surpassing his own destiny.

"I too, to-day, would have given a kingdom for a horse," said Stelio, deriding himself in his irritation at the mediocrity of life "There was neither a crossbow nor a horse at San Niccolo, not even the courage of the oarsman! *Perge audacter. . . .* Here we are, on this ignoble gray carcass that smokes and grumbles like a kettle. Look at Venice dancing down there!"

The anger of the sea was spreading over the lagoon. The waters were agitated by a strong tremor, and it seemed that the agitation communicated itself to the foundations of the city, that the palaces and cupolas heaved like boats on the water. Seaweeds floated, torn up from their depths, showing all their whitish roots. Flocks of sea-gulls gyrated in the wind and at times their strange laughter could be heard hanging above the innumerable crests of the storm.

"Wagner!" said Daniele Glauro, in a low voice and with sudden emotion, pointing out an old man who was leaning against the parapet at the prow. "There with Donna Cosima and Franz Liszt. Do you see him?"

The heart of Stelio Effrena beat louder; for him too all surrounding figures disappeared; the bitter tedium ceased with the oppression of his inertia, and there remained only the sense of superhuman power conjured up by that name; the only reality above all those indistinct husks was the ideal world brought to light by that name round the little old man who was bending towards the tumult of the waters.

Victorious genius, fidelity of love, unchangeable

friendship, all the supreme apparitions of an heroic
nature were once more gathered together under
the tempest, silently. One same dazzling whiteness
crowned the three persons standing near one another;
their hair over their sad thoughts was extraordinarily
white. An uneasy sadness stood revealed in their
faces and attitudes as if one same obscure presentiment lay heavy on their communicating souls. The
woman's white face had a beautiful robust mouth,
made up of firm clear lines that betrayed a tenacious
soul; and her light steely eyes were continually
fixed on him who had chosen her for the companion
of his great warfare, continually adoring and vigilant on him who, having conquered all deadly things,
yet would not be able to conquer that other death
which so constantly menaced him. That feminine
gaze full of fear and of protection thus opposed itself
to the invisible eyes of the other Woman, and gathered a vague funereal shadow round the protected
one.

"He seems to be suffering," said Daniele Glauro.
"Don't you see? He looks as if about to collapse.
Shall we draw nearer to him?"

Stelio Effrena gazed with inexpressible emotion at
the white hairs tossed about by the harsh wind on
the aged neck under the wide brim of the soft felt
and at the almost livid ear with its swollen lobe;
that body, borne up during its warfare by so fierce
an instinct of predominance now had the appearance of a rag that the gale could sweep away and
destroy.

"Ah, Daniele, what could we do for him?" he
asked his friend, seized by a religious need of mani-

festing by some outward sign his reverence and pity for that great oppressed heart.

"What could we do?" repeated his friend, to whom that fervent desire of offering something of himself to the hero suffering from human fate had instantly communicated itself.

They were one soul in that act of fervour and gratitude, in the sudden elevation of their deep nobility; but could they give nothing except that which they gave. Nothing could stop the secret workings of his malady; and both grew more sorrowful as they gazed at the white hair, the frail half-living thing blown about on the old man's neck by the vehement breath that came from the open and brought to the shuddering lagoon the roar and the foam of the sea.

"Ah, proud sea, you must carry me still! The salvation which I seek I shall never find on earth. I will remain faithful to you, O waves of the great sea. . . ." The impetuous harmonies of the Flying Dutchman, with the despairing recall that pierces through them at intervals, awoke in Stelio Effrena's memory, and in the wind he seemed to hear the wild song of the crew again on the ship with the blood-like sails: "Iohohé! Iohohé! Come to shore, O swarthy captain: seven years have passed. . . ." And his imagination recomposed the figure of Richard Wagner as a young man, the recluse lost in the living horror of Paris, poor and undaunted, devoured by a marvellous fever, intent on his star, resolved on forcing the world to recognise it too. In the myth of the pale seaman, the exile had found an image of his own panting race, his furious struggle, his supreme hope. "But one day the pale man may be delivered if only he find in his wandering a woman who will be faithful to him unto death."

That woman was there, by the side of the hero, like an ever vigilant custodian. She, too, like Senta, knew the sovereign law of fidelity, and death was about to dissolve the sacred vow.

"Do you think that, immersed in the poetry of myths, he has dreamed of some extraordinary manner of passing away and is now praying each day to Nature to conform his end to his dream?" asked Daniele Glauro, dwelling on the mysterious will that enticed the eagle into mistaking the brow of Æschylus for a rock and brought Petrarch to expire alone over the pages of a book. "What would be a worthy end?"

"A new melody of unknown power that was only indistinct when it appeared to him in his first youth, and that he was then unable to fix, will cleave his soul in two, like a terrible sword."

"True," said Daniele Glauro.

The clouds were battling through space in phalanxes, overcoming each other, driven by the great wind; the cupolas and the towers swaying in the background also seemed deformed; the shadows of the city and the shadows of the sky, equally vast and mobile on the swollen waters, changed and merged into each other, as if made of substances equally near dissolution.

"Look at the Magyar, Daniele; his is certainly a generous spirit; he has served the hero with unlimited faith and devotion. And this servitude, more than his art, consecrates him to glory. But see, how from his strong, sincere feeling, he draws an almost histrionic performance, such as he would draw from the continual need of imposing on his spectators, to delude them, a magnificent image of himself."

The abbé half raised his thin, bony body that seemed clasped by a coat of mail. Holding himself thus erect, he uncovered his head to pray, offering his silent prayer to the God of Tempests. The wind ruffled his long thick hair, the great leonine mane whence so many flashes and quivers had started to move women and crowds. His magnetic eyes were raised to the sky, while the muttered words that sketched themselves on his long thin lips spread a mystic air over his face harsh with lines and enormous warts.

"What matters?" said Daniele Glauro. "He possesses the divine faculty of fervour and a taste for overpowering strength and dominating passion. Has not his art aspired towards Prometheus, Orpheus, Dante, Tasso? He was attracted by Richard Wagner as by the great energies of nature; perhaps he heard in him that which he tried to express in his own symphonic poem 'What is heard on the Mountainside.'"

"True," said Stelio Effrena.

Both started, however, on seeing the old bent man turn suddenly with the gesture of one about to be drowned in darkness, and clutch convulsively at his companion, who gave a cry. They ran to him. All those who were on the boat, struck by the cry of anguish, rushed and crowded about him. A look from the woman however was enough, none dared approach the seemingly lifeless body. She herself supported him, laid him on the bench, felt his pulse, bent over his heart listening. Her love and sorrow drew an inviolable circle round the motionless man. All drew back, silent, anxious, watching the livid face for signs of returning consciousness.

The face was still, abandoned on the woman's knees. Two deep furrows descended along the cheeks to the half-closed mouth, deepening near the imperious nostrils. Squalls of wind stirred the rare and very fine hair on the full brow, and the white collar of beard under the square chin where the robustness of the jawbone was apparent in spite of the soft wrinkles. A clammy sweat was dropping from his temples, and a slight tremor agitated one of the hanging feet. Every little sign in that pale face was impressed on the minds of the two young men for ever.

How long did his suffering last? Alternating shadows continued on the dark, seething water, interrupted now and then by great zones of sun-rays that seemed to cross the air and sink into the sea with the weight of arrows. They could hear the cadenced noise of the engine, the derisive laugh of the sea-gulls, and already the dull howl coming from the Grand Canal, the vast moan of the stricken city.

"Let us carry him," said Stelio, in his friend's ear, intoxicated with the sadness of things and the solemnity of his visions.

The motionless face was barely giving signs of returning to life.

"Yes, let us offer ourselves," said Daniele Glauro, turning pale.

They looked towards the woman with the face of snow, and held out their arms.

How long did that terrible removal last? The space from the boat to the shore was brief indeed, but they seemed to have gone a long way in those few steps. The water clamoured against the posts of the landing-pier, the howl broke from the Canal as if it came from the windings of a cavern, the bells of San Marco were ringing for vespers; but the confused noises had lost all immediate reality; they seemed indefinitely profound and remote, like a lament of the Ocean.

They carried the weight of the Hero on their arms; they bore the stunned body of him who had spread the power of his oceanic soul over the world, the perishable form of the Revealer who had laid the essences of the Universe, in infinite song, before men's worship. With an ineffable shiver of fear and joy, like the man who should see a river dashing itself over a rock, a volcano bursting open, a conflagration burning a forest, a dazzling meteor obscuring the starry heavens like man in the presence of a natural force that should have suddenly and irresistibly manifested itself, Stelio Effrena felt under the hand that was passed below the shoulder and sustained the bust, — he stopped a moment to grasp his strength, which was escaping him, and gazed at the white head against his breast, — he felt in his hand the renewed beating of the sacred heart.

"You were strong, Daniele, — you who cannot break a stick! That old barbarian body was heavy; it seemed built over a bronze framework of bones; solid, well-built, meant to remain standing on a shaking

deck,—the structure of a man meant for the sea.
But where did your strength come from, Daniele?
I was afraid for you. You did not even stagger!
We have carried a hero in our arms. We must mark
this day and celebrate it. His eyes opened before
mine; his heart beat once more under my own hand.
We were worthy of carrying him, Daniele, because
of our fervour."

"You are worthy not only of carrying him, but
of picking up and preserving some of the most beautiful promises offered by his art to those who still
hope."

"Ah! if only I am not overmastered by my own
abundance, and if I succeed in conquering the anxiety that suffocates me, Daniele! . . ."

On, on went the two friends, side by side, intoxicated and full of confidences, as if their friendship
had suddenly become something higher, increased by
some ideal treasure; on, on they went in the wind,
in the noise, in the evening's emotion, followed by the
fury of the sea.

"It seems as if the Adriatic had overthrown the
Murazzi this evening, and were about to scorn the
prohibition of the Senate," said Daniele Glauro, stopping before the wave that was flowing over the
Piazza and was threatening the Procuratie. "We
must go back."

"No, let us take the ferry across. Here is a skiff.
Look at San Marco on the water!"

The boatman was ferrying them to the Torre dell'
Orologio. The Piazza was inundated, like a lake in
a cloister of porticoes, reflecting the sky left uncovered by the flight of the clouds that were coloured

by the green and yellow of the twilight. The golden Basilica, more living, as if revivified like a parched forest, by contact with the water, was resplendent with wings and halos in the waning light; and the crosses of its mitres could be seen at the bottom of the dark mirror, like the spires of another submerged Basilica.

"EN VERUS FORTIS QUI FREGIT VINCULA MORTIS," read Stelio Effrena, on the curve of an arch, under the mosaic of the Resurrection. "Do you know that Richard Wagner had his first conversation with death in Venice twenty years ago now, at the time of Tristan? Consumed by a desperate passion, he came to Venice to die here in silence, and composed instead that raving second act which is a hymn to eternal night. His fate has again led him to the lagoon. It seems decreed that he is to end here, like Claudio Monteverde. Is it not indeed a musical desire immense and indefinable, this desire of which Venice is full? Here, every sound transforms itself into expressive voices. Listen!"

The city of stone and water had become sonorous like a great organ. The hiss and the howl changed into a kind of choral imploration growing and waning with a rhythmic swell.

"Does not your ear seize the line of a melody in this chorus of moans? Listen!"

They had landed from the skiff and were walking onwards in the narrow streets, crossing the little bridges, lingering by the canal footpaths, penetrating into the city at random; but even in the excitement of his speed, Stelio directed his way almost by instinct towards a distant house that now and then as in a lightning flash appeared to him animated by a deep expectation.

"Listen! I can distinguish a melodic theme that rises and falls without the power to develop itself. . . ."

Stelio stopped, listening with so acute an intensity of attention that his friend was surprised as if he were assisting at his imminent transversion into the natural phenomenon he was observing, as if he were annulling himself little by little into a vaster and more powerful will that was making him similar to itself.

"Have you heard?"

"It is not given me to hear what you hear," answered the barren ascete to the genius. "I will wait until you can repeat the words that Nature has spoken to you."

Both trembled in the intimacy of their hearts, — one most lucid, the other unconscious.

"I don't know," he said; "I don't know any more. . . . It seemed to me. . . ."

The message he had received in a passing state of unconsciousness was now slipping from his perception. The workings of his spirit began anew; his will reawakened, agitated by anxious aspirations.

"Ah, to be able to restore to melody its natural simplicity, its ingenuous perfection, its divine innocence; to draw it out all throbbing with life from its eternal sources, from the very mystery of Nature, from the very soul of universal things! Have you considered the myth referring to the early childhood of Cassandra? One night she was left in the temple of Apollo, and was found in the morning lying on the marble, held in the coils of a snake that was licking her ears. From that time she understood all the voices scattered in the air; she knew all the melodies of the world. The power of the seer was but a musical power. A part of that Apollian virtue entered into the poets who co-operated in the creation of the tragic chorus. One of those poets could boast of knowing all the different voices of birds, and another of being able to converse with the winds, and another of fully understanding the language of the sea. More than once I have dreamt that I was lying on that marble in the coils of that serpent. . . . That myth would have to renew itself, Daniele, before we could create the new art."

At every step, his speech grew more fervid; at every step he gave himself up further to the tide of his thoughts, still feeling however that an obscure part of himself was remaining in communion with the sonorous air.

" Have you ever thought what the music might be of that kind of pastoral ode sung by the Chorus in Œdipos Tyrannos when Jocaste flies away horrified, and the son of Laïus is still under the illusion of a last hope? Do you remember that? ' O Citheron, let Olympus bear witness before another full moon comes round again.' For a moment the image of the mountains interrupts the horror of the drama, the rural serenity brings a pause in the human terror. Do you remember it? Try to represent the strophes to yourself as if they were a frame within the lines of which a series of corporal movements are developed, an expressive dance-figure animated by the perfect life of melody. You would have the spirit of Earth conjured up before you in the essential plan of things; the comforting apparition of the great common Mother at the misfortune of her stricken, trembling children, a celebration, in short, of all that is divine and eternal above mankind which is dragged to madness and death by cruel Destiny. Now try by intuition to feel how much that song has helped me in my tragedy to find the means of the highest and simplest expression."

"You intend to re-establish the Chorus on the stage?"

"Oh, no! I shall not revive an antique form; I shall invent a new form, obeying my instinct and the genius of my race only, as the Greeks did when they created their drama, that marvellous inimitable edifice of beauty. For a long time the three arts of music, poetry, and dancing have separated from each other; the first two have followed their development toward greater power of expression; the third is in its decadence; therefore I think that it is no longer possible to fuse them into a single rhythmical structure without taking from one or other of them its own already acquired dominant character. If made to concur towards a common and total effect, they must renounce their supreme and particular effect and remain, in a word, diminished. Among the substances most capable of receiving rhythm, language is the foundation of every work of Art tending to perfection. Do you believe that language is given its full value in the Wagnerian drama? And does it not seem to you that the musical conception loses some of its primitive purity by often being made to depend on performances extraneous to the genius of music? Richard Wagner certainly has a sense of this weakness and confesses it when he goes up to some friend in Bayreuth and covers his eyes with his hand, that he may give himself up entirely to the pure virtue of the symphony and be therefore rapt by the greater joy into a deeper vision."

"All this which you are exposing is new to me," said Daniele Glauro; "yet it gives me a joy like that which we feel when we learn things that have been long foreseen and felt by presentiment. You will therefore superpose the three rhythmic arts, but will present them in single manifestations linked by a sovereign idea and elevated to the supreme degree by their own significant energy?"

"Ah, Daniele! How can I give you an idea of the work that is living in me?" exclaimed Stelio Effrena. "The words with which you would attempt to formulate my meaning are hard and mechanical. . . . No, no. . . . How shall I communicate to you the life and the infinitely fluid mystery that are within me?"

They were at the foot of the Rialto steps; Stelio ran up rapidly and stopped against the balustrade at the top of the arch waiting for his friend. The wind went over him like an army of flags, the ends of which were striking his face; the Canal beneath him, lost in the shade of the palaces, bent like a river running towards some cataract roaring afar; one region of sky above him was clear in the midst of the agglomerated clouds, vivid and crystalline like the serenity that spreads itself above glaciers.

"It is impossible to stay here," said Daniele Glauro, supporting himself against a shop door; "the wind will carry us away."

"Go down; I will overtake you. Only a moment," the master cried to him, leaning on the balustrade, covering his eyes with his hand concentrating all his soul into the effort of listening.

Formidable indeed was the voice of the gale in that gathering of centuries now turned to stone; it alone dominated the solitude as in the time when the marbles still slept in the bosom of the mountains, and wild grasses grew round the birds' nests in the muddy lagoon islands, long before the Doge was installed in the Rialto, long before the patriarchs had led the fugitives to their great destiny. Human life had disappeared; there was nothing under the heavens except an immense sepulchre in the hollows of which that one voice re-echoed, and that voice alone. Its unaccompanied song, its lamentation that had no hope, commemorated the multitudes that had become ashes, the dispersed pageants, the fallen greatness, the numberless days of birth and death, the things of a time without name or form. All the melancholy of the world passed with that wind over the outstretched soul.

"Ah, I have grasped you," cried out the joy of the triumphant artist.

The entire line of the melody had been revealed to him, was henceforth his, was immortal in his spirit and in the world. No living thing seemed more living to him than that one. His own life yielded to the unlimited energy of that sonorous idea, yielded to the generating force of that germ capable of infinite developments. He imagined it as steeped in the symphonic sea and unfolding itself through a thousand aspects until it reached its perfection.

"Daniele, Daniele, I have found it."

He raised his eyes, saw the first stars in the adamantine sky and intuitively felt the great silence in which they throbbed. Images of skies rounded over far-off countries crossed his spirit; agitations of sands, trees, water and dust on windy days; the Libyan Desert, the olive field on the Bay of Salona, the Nile close to Memphis, the parched Argolides. Other images overtook these. He feared lest he should lose what he had found. With an effort he closed his memory as he would have clenched his hand to hold something. Close to a pillar he noticed the shadow of a man and a glimmer at the end of a long pole, and the slight explosion of a flame that is being lit in a lantern. With anxious rapidity he marked the notes of the theme in the lamplight on a page of his notebook, fixing in the five lines the message of the elements.

"What a day of marvels!" said Daniele Glauro, watching him come down the steps as light and nimble as if he had robbed the air also of its elastic properties. "May Nature always cherish you, my brother!"

"Come, come!" said Stelio, taking him by the arm and drawing him after him with the gladness of a child. "I want to run."

He was drawing him through the narrow streets towards San Giovanni Elemosinario. He was repeating to himself the names of the three churches he would meet on his way before reaching the distant house that from time to time had appeared to him as in a lightning-flash animated by a deep expectation.

"It is quite true, Daniele, what you told me one

day; the voice of things is essentially different from
their sound," he said, stopping at the beginning of
the Ruga Vecchia close to the belfry, because he
noticed that his haste was tiring his friend. "The
sound of a wind simulates in turns the moans of a
terrified multitude, the howling of wild beasts, the
crash of cataracts, the quiver of unfurled banners,
mockery, menace, despair. The voice of the wind
is the synthesis of all these sounds; it is the voice
that sings and tells the terrible travail of time, the
cruelty of human destiny, the warfare eternally
waged for a deception that is eternally renewed."

"And have you never thought that the essence of
music is not in the sounds themselves?" asked the
mystic doctor. "That essence dwells in the silence
that precedes sound and in the silence that follows
it. Rhythm appears and lives in these intervals of
silence. Every sound wakens in the silence that goes
before and that follows it, a voice which can only
be heard by one spirit. Rhythm is the heart of
music, but its throbs are inaudible except during the
pauses of sound."

The law, metaphysical in its nature, thus announced
by the contemplator, confirmed Stelio in his belief in
the justness of his own intuition.

"Imagine," he said, "the interval between two
scenic symphonies in which all the *motifs* unite to
express the inner essence of the characters that are
struggling in the drama and to reveal the inner depths
of the action, as, for instance, in Beethoven's great
prelude in 'Leonora' or in 'Coriolanus.' That musical silence throbbing with the heart-beats of rhythm
is like the mysterious living atmosphere where alone

words of pure poetry can appear. The personages thus seem to emerge from the symphonic ocean as if from the truth itself of the hidden being that operates within them; and their spoken language will have an extraordinary resonance in that rhythmic silence, will touch the extreme limit of verbal power, because it will be animated by a continual aspiration to song that cannot be appeased except by the melody that shall again rise from the orchestra at the end of the tragic episode. Do you understand?"

"You mean that you place the episode between two symphonies, that prepare and complete it, because music is the beginning and the end of human speech."

"I thus draw the personages of the drama nearer to the spectator. Do you remember the figure used by Schiller in the ode he composed in honour of Goethe's translation of 'Mahomet,' to signify that only an ideal world can have its life on the stage? The Chariot of Thespis, like the boat of Acheron, is so frail that it can only carry shades or human images. On the ordinary stage those images are so distant that any contact with them seems as impossible as contact with mental phantoms. They are distant and strange, but by making them appear in the rhythmic silence, by making music accompany them to the threshold of the visible world, I draw them marvellously near to the spectator, because I illumine the most secret depths of the will that produces them. You understand, their intimate essence is there uncovered and placed in immediate communion with the soul of the crowd. And that crowd, under the ideas signified by voice and gesture, feels the depths of the musical motives that correspond to them in the symphonies. I show, in a word, the images painted on the veil and that which happens beyond the veil. You understand! And by means of music, of dancing, and of lyric poetry, I create round my heroes an ideal atmosphere in which the whole life of Nature vibrates, so that in each of their actions not only the powers of their preordained destinies seem to converge, but also the obscurest influences of surrounding things,— of the elementary souls living in the great tragic circle. As the creations of Æschylus bear in themselves something of the natural myths from which they sprang, I would that my creations could be felt throbbing in the torrent of savage forces, suffering from contact with the earth, drawn into communion with air, fire, water, with the mountains and with the clouds, in their pathetic struggle against a fate that must be conquered. I would that Nature could be round them as our oldest forefathers saw her: the passionate actress in an immortal drama."

They were entering the Campo di San Cassiano, that stretched out deserted on the banks of its livid stream; steps and voices echoed there as in a rocky amphitheatre, clear above the roar that came from the Grand Canal as from a great river. A purplish shadow rose from the fever-breathing water and spread in the air like a poisonous exhalation. Death seemed to have filled that place from all time. At a high window a shutter beat in the wind against the wall, grinding on its hinges like a sign of abandonment and ruin. Yet all those appearances worked extraordinary transformations in the spirit of the Life-giver. Once more he saw a wild, lonely spot by the tombs at Mycenæ in the hollow between the lower peak of Mount Eubœa and the inaccessible flank of the citadel. Myrtles grew vigorously between the harsh boulders and the Cyclopic ruins. The waters of the Fount of Perseia, springing from among the rocks, fell into a cavity like a shell, whence it ran out and was lost in the valley of stone. At its edge at the foot of a shrub lay the body of the Victim stretched out rigid, spotless. In the deadly silence he could hear the rush of the water and the intermittent breath of the wind on the nodding myrtles.

"It was in an august place," he said, "that I first had the vision of my new work : at Mycenæ, at the gate of the lions, while re-reading the ' Oresteia.' . . . Land of Fire, land of thirst and delirium, birthplace of Clytemnestra and the Hydra, soil made sterile for ever by the horror of the most tragic destiny that has ever overwhelmed a human race. . . . Have you ever thought of that barbaric explorer who, after having passed the greater part of his life among his drugs behind a counter, began digging in the ruins of Mycenæ among the graves of the Atridæ, and one day (the sixth anniversary took place not long ago) saw the greatest and the strangest vision that has ever presented itself to mortal eyes ? Have you ever considered the fat Schliemann in the act of discovering the most dazzling treasure ever accumulated by death in the obscurities of the earth for hundreds and thousands of years ? Have you ever thought that the terrible, superhuman spectacle might have appeared to another, to some youthful, fervent spirit; to a poet, a Life-giver, to you, to me, perhaps ? The frenzy of it, the fever, the madness. . . . Imagine ! "

He was flaming, vibrating, all at once carried away
by his fiction as by a storm. His seeing eyes shone
with the gleam of the funereal treasures. His creative force was flowing to his spirit like blood to the
heart. He was the actor in his own drama. His
accents, his gesture, signified transcendent passion
and beauty, overstepped the power of the spoken
word, the limit of the letter. The fraternal spirit of
his companion hung upon his lips, trembling before
the sudden splendour that was realising his divinations.

"Imagine! Imagine that the earth you are digging in is evil; it must still give out the exhalations
of monstrous deeds. The curse that weighed on the
Atridæ was so deadly that there must have remained
some vestige of it still to be dreaded in the dust that
was trodden by them. You are stricken by witchcraft,
the dead whom you seek and cannot succeed in finding have come to life in you again and breathe
within you with the tremendous breath that Æschylus
infused into them, vast and bloodthirsty as they appeared in the 'Oresteia,' thrust through ceaselessly
with the sword and brand of their destiny. Hence
all the ideal life with which you have nourished yourself must have assumed in you the form and the impress of reality. And you go on obstinately in this
land of thirst, at the foot of this naked mountain,
drawn into the fascination of the dead city, digging,
digging in the earth, with those frightful phantoms
always before your eyes, in the thirsting dust. At
every stroke of the spade you must tremble through
all your bones, longing to see really the face of one
of the Atridæ, still untouched, with the signs yet visible of the violence he endured, the cruel death. And

it appears, the gold, the gold, the bodies, great heaps of gold, the bodies all covered with gold. . . ."

The Atridæ princes were there extended on the stone, a prodigy called up in the darkness of the alley. Both the listener and he who had evoked them shuddered with the same shudder in the same flash.

" A succession of tombs; fifteen intact bodies, one beside the other, on a bed of gold, with faces covered with masks of gold, with foreheads crowned with gold, with breasts bound with gold; and over all, on their bodies, at their sides, at their feet, over all a profusion of golden things, innumerable as the leaves fallen from a fabulous forest. . . . Do you see? Do you see?"

The anxiety of rendering all that gold so that it should be palpable, of changing his hallucinating vision into a sensible reality, suffocated him.

"I see, I see!"

"For a moment, the soul of that man has leaped back hundreds and thousands of years, breathed the terrible legend, trembled in the horror of that ancient massacre. For a moment his soul has traced that ancient and violent life. They were there, the slain ones: Agamemnon, Eurymedon, Cassandra, and the royal escort lay under his eyes for a moment, motionless. And then exhaled like vapour — do you see — like melting foam, like dust that is scattered, like I know not what inexpressibly faint and fugitive thing, all vanish into their silence, swallowed up by the same fatal silence that was about their radiant immobility. A handful of dust and a heap of gold. . . ."

The miracle of Life and Death was there on the stones of the deserted alley as on the stones of the sepulchres. Inexpressibly moved, trembling, Daniele Glauro seized the hands of his friend. And in his faithful eyes the Life-giver saw the dumb flame of enthusiasm consecrated to the masterpiece.

They stopped by a doorway against the dark wall. There was a mysterious sense of distance in them both, as if their spirits were lost in the depths of time; and behind that door, antique people lived enslaved by a motionless Destiny. From the house one could hear a cradle that was being rocked to the rhythm of a low sing-song; a mother was conciliating the sleep of her child with a melody handed down from her ancestors; her protecting voice covered the menacing roar of the elements. The stars burned above the narrow strip of sky. Further down against the walls and the sand-banks the sea was lowing. Elsewhere the heart of a hero was suffering as if waiting for death, and near them the cradle rocked on, and the voice of the mother calling down happiness on the infant's wail.

"Life!" said Stelio Effrena, resuming his walk and dragging his friend after him. "Here, in one instant, all that trembles, weeps, hopes, yearns, and raves in the immensity of life, gathers itself up in one spirit, condensed there with so rapid a sublimation that it seems as if one should be able to manifest it all in a single word. What word? What word? Do you know it? Who shall ever say it?"

He was once more beginning to suffer from his anxiety and discontent that wanted to embrace all and express all.

" Have you ever seen the entire universe in a few seconds, standing out before you like a human head? I have, a thousand times. Ah, to be able to cut it off, like him who cut off the head of Medusa, at one blow, and hold it up from a scaffolding high above the crowd that it might never forget it again. Have you never thought that a great tragedy might resemble the attitude of Perseus? I tell you that I should like to take the bronze of Benvenuto away from the Loggia of Orcagna and carry it away for the vestibule of the new theatre as an admonishment. But who shall give a poet the sword of Hermes and the mirror of Athena?"

Daniele Glauro was silent. He who had received from Nature the gift of enjoying beauty, though not of creating it, well divined the torment of Stelio's fraternal spirit. Silently he walked beside his brother, bending his vast thoughtful brow, that seemed swollen by the presence of an unborn world.

"Perseus!" added the Life-giver, after a pause that had been full of the flashes of his inventions. " In the hollow, under the citadel of Mycenæ, there is a fountain called Perseia: the only living thing in that place where all is burnt up and dead. Men are attracted to it as to a spring of life in that land where the sorrowful whiteness of the dried up rivers can be seen late into the twilight. Every human thirst stretches out voraciously to its freshness. Through the whole of my work the murmur of that stream will be heard: the water, the melody of water. . . . I have found it! In it, in the pure element, the pure Act which is the aim of the new tragedy shall be accomplished. The Virgin destined

like Antigone to die 'deprived of nuptials' shall fall
asleep on its clear icy waters. Do you understand?
The pure Act marks the defeat of ancient Fate. The
new soul suddenly bursts the iron band that clasped
it with a determination born of madness, of a lucid
delirium that is like ecstasy, that is like a deeper
vision of nature. The last ode in the orchestra tells
the salvation and the freedom of man obtained by
means of pain and sacrifice. The monstrous Fate is
conquered there by the tombs into which the race of
Atreus descended, before the very bodies of the vic-
tims. Do you understand? He who has freed himself by means of the pure Act, the brother who kills
the sister to save her soul from the horror that
was about to seize her, has truly seen the face of
Agamemnon!"

The fascination of the funereal gold was again taking hold of him; the evidence of his internal vision
gave him an hallucinated appearance.

"One of the bodies exceeds all the others in stature
and in majesty: wearing a large crown of gold, with
cuirass, girdle, and shoulder-plates of gold surrounded
with swords, spears, daggers, cups, covered with innumerable discs of gold scattered over his body like
petals, more venerable than a demi-god. He bends
over him while he melts away in the light and raises
the heavy mask. . . . Ah, does he not indeed see the
face of Agamemnon? Is not this perhaps the King
of Kings? His mouth is open; his eyelids are open. . . .
Do you remember? Do you remember Homer? 'As
I lay dying I lifted my hands towards my sword; but
the woman with the dog's eyes went her way and
would not close my eyelids and my mouth, as I de-

scended to the abode of Hades.' Do you remember? Well, the mouth of the corpse is open, the eyes are open. . . . He has a large forehead bound with a round leaf of gold; his nose is long and straight; his chin oval. . . ."

The dreamer stopped a moment, his eyes fixed and dilated. It was he who was seeing; the vision was his. All about him disappeared, and his fiction remained the only reality. Daniele Glauro shuddered, for he too had seen through those eyes.

"Ah, even to the white spot on the shoulder; he has raised the armour. . . . The spot, the spot! The hereditary sign of the race of Pelops 'of the ivory shoulders!' Is he not the King of Kings?"

The rapid, interrupted words of the visionary seemed a succession of flashes by which he was himself dazzled. He himself was astonished by that sudden apparition, by that sudden discovery, that illumined in the darkness of his spirit, manifested itself and became almost tangible. How could he have discovered that spot on the shoulder of Agamemnon? From what abyss of his memory had that detail arisen, so strange and yet precise and decisive as the description necessary for the recognition of a body dead since yesterday?

"You were there," said Daniele Glauro, in his exaltation. "You yourself have raised the armour and the mask. . . . If you have really seen what you say, you are no longer a man. . . ."

"I have seen! I have seen!"

Once more he was being transformed into the actor of his own drama and with a violent palpitation was hearing from the mouth of a living person the words of his companion, those same words that were to be pronounced in the episode. "If you have really seen what you say, you are no longer a man." From that moment the explorer of tombs took on the aspect of a great hero fighting against the ancient fate that had arisen from the ashes themselves of the Atridæ to contaminate and overcome him.

"It is not with impunity," he said, "that a man uncovers tombs and gazes on the face of the dead; and of what dead! He is living alone with his sister, with the sweetest creature that has ever breathed the air of this earth, alone with her in the house full of light and silence, as in a prayer, a consecration. . . . Now imagine one who should unconsciously drink poison, a philtre, something impure, that should corrupt his blood, that should contaminate his thoughts: thus, suddenly, while his soul is in peace. . . . Imagine this terrible evil, this vengeance of the dead! He is suddenly invaded by incestuous passion; he becomes the trembling and miserable prey of a monster, fighting a desperate hidden fight, without truce, without escape, day and night, at every hour, at every moment, the more atrocious the more the unconscious pity of the poor creature stoops to his evil. . . . How can he be liberated? From the moment in which the tragedy has its beginning, from the moment in which the innocent companion begins to speak, she appears destined to die. And all that is said and accomplished in the episodes, and all that is expressed by song and by the dance and by the interludes, all serves to lead her slowly and inexorably towards death. She is the equal of Antigone.

In the brief tragic hour she passes accompanied by the light of hope and by the shadow of presentiment, she passes accompanied by song and weeping, by the great love that offers joy, by the furious love that gives birth to mourning, and never stops except to fall asleep on the clear icy water of the fountain that called her uninterruptedly with its solitary moan. As soon as he has killed her, her brother receives from her through death, the gift of his redemption. 'Every stain is gone from my soul,' he cries; 'I have become pure, quite pure. All the sanctity of my first love has returned to my mind like a torrent of light. . . . If she were to rise up now, she could walk over my soul as over immaculate snow. . . . If she were to return to life again, all my thoughts for her would be like lilies, like lilies. . . . Now she is perfect, now she can be adored like a divine being. . . . In the deepest of my sepulchres I will lay her at rest, and I will set about her all my treasures. . . .' Thus the act of death, that he has been dragged into by his lucid delirium, becomes a purifying act of liberation and marks the defeat of an ancient fate. The ode emerging from the symphonic ocean sings of the victory of man, irradiates the darkness of the catastrophe with an unusual light, raises on the summit of music the first word of the renewed drama."

"The gesture of Perseus," exclaimed Daniele Glauro, in his exaltation. "At the end of the tragedy you cut off the head of the Moira and show it to the crowd, ever young and ever new, that brings the spectacle to a close with great cries."

Both saw in their dream the marble theatre on the Janiculum, the multitude dominated by its idea of truth and of beauty, the great starry night stretching over Rome; they saw the frenzied crowd carrying in their rude hearts, as they descended the hill, the confused revelation of poetry; they heard the clamour of the immortal city prolonging itself in the shadow.

"And now good-bye, Daniele," said the master, again seized by haste, as if some one were waiting for him or calling him.

The eyes of the tragic muse gazed immovable in the background of his dream, sightless, petrified in the divine blindness of statues.

"Where are you going?"

"To the Palazzo Capello."

"Does la Foscarina know the thread of your work?"

"Vaguely!"

"And what shall be her figure?"

"She shall be blind, having already passed into another world, already half alive in something beyond life. She shall see that which others do not see. She shall have one foot in the shadow, and her forehead in eternal truth. The contrasts of the tragic hour shall reverberate in her inner darkness, multiplying themselves in it like thunder in the deep circles of solitary rocks. Like Tiresias, she shall understand all things permitted and forbidden, earthly and terrestrial, and she shall know 'how hard knowing is when knowing is useless.' Ah, I will put marvellous words in her mouth and silences that shall give birth to things of infinite beauty. . . ."

"Her power on the stage, whether she is silent or whether she speaks, is more than human. She wakens in our hearts the most hidden evils and the most secret hopes; and through her enchantment our past becomes present, and through the virtue of her aspects we recognise ourselves in the sorrows undergone by other creatures in all time, as if the soul revealed to us by her were our own soul."

They paused on the Ponte Savio. Stelio was silent under a flood of love and melancholy that suddenly invaded him. He was hearing the sad voice again: "To have loved my passing glory only that one day it might serve yours." He was hearing his own voice again: "I love you and believe in you; I give myself up entirely. You are my companion. Your hand is safe." The power and security of that alliance were swelling his pride, yet, for all that, deep in the depths of his heart there still trembled an undefined aspiration and a presentiment that grew denser at times and became as heavy as anguish.

"I am sorry to leave you to-night, Stelio," confessed the kind brother, he too falling under a veil of melancholy. "Whenever I am near you I seem to feel myself breathing more freely and living a quicker life."

Stelio was silent. The wind seemed to have grown fainter, the intermittent gusts tore away the acacia leaves and wrapped them round. The brown church and the square tower of naked brick prayed to the stars in silence.

"Do you know the green column that is in San Giacomo dall' Orio?" added Daniele, meaning to keep his friend a few moments longer, because he dreaded the farewell. "What a sublime substance it is! it seems the fossilised condensation of an immense, growing forest; as it follows its innumerable veins, the eye travels in a dream into silvern mysteries.

When I gaze at it I seem to be visiting Sila and Ercinna."

Stelio knew it. Perdita had one day remained leaning against the great precious stem for a long time, contemplating the magic golden frieze that curves out — obscuring it — above the canvas of Bassano.

"To be ever dreaming, dreaming!" he sighed, feeling a return of the bitter impatience which had suggested words of scorn to him on the boat that brought him from the Lido. "To live on relics! Think of Dandolo, who overthrew that column and an empire at the same time, and who chose to remain doge when he might have been emperor. He lived more than you do, perhaps, who wander through forests when you examine the marble he brought home as booty. Good-bye, Daniele."

"Do not diminish your lot."

"I wish I could force it."

"Thought is your weapon."

"Often my ambition burns up my thought."

"You can create; what more do you seek?"

"In other times I too might have conquered an archipelago."

"What does it matter to you? A melody is worth a province. Would you not give up a principality for a new image?"

"I would that I could live the whole of life and not be only a brain."

"A brain contains the world."

"Ah, you cannot understand! You are the ascetic; you have overcome desire."

"And you will overcome it, too."

"I don't know whether I would."

" I am certain of it."

" Good-bye, Daniele. You are the one who bears witness to me. No other is as dear to me as you are."

Their hands met in a firm clasp.

" I shall stop for news at the Palazzo Vendramin," said the kind brother. His words brought to his mind once more the great, ailing heart, the weight of the hero on their arms, the terrible removal.

" He has conquered; he can die," said Stelio Effrena.

He entered la Foscarina's house like a spirit. His intellectual excitement was changing the aspect of things. The hall, illuminated by a galley lamp, seemed immense. A *felse* upon the pavement near the door disturbed him as if he had met a coffin.

" Ah, Stelio ! " cried the actress, jumping up with a start when she saw him appear, and moving quickly towards him, impetuous with all the spring of her desire that expectation had restrained. " At last ! "

She stopped an instant before him without touching him. The impulse she had controlled vibrated visibly in her body from top to toe; it seemed to beat in her throat in a short gasp. She was as the wind is when it falls.

" Who has taken you from me ? " she thought, her heart filled with doubt; all at once she had felt something in the loved one that made him intangible to her, she had caught something in his eyes that was estranged and distant.

But she had been most beautiful in his eyes as she came forth from the shade, animated with a violence not dissimilar to that of the storm that was agitating the lagoons. The cry, the gesture, the start, the sudden stop, the vibration of her muscles under her garments, the light in her face extinguished like a flame that becomes ashes, the intensity of her look that was like a gleam of battle, the breath which parted her lips like the heat that breaks open the lips of earth, — all these aspects of the real person showed a power of pathetic life only comparable to the ferment of natural energies, to the action of cosmic forces. The artist recognised in her the Dionysian creature, the living material capable of receiving the impress of the rhythm of art, of being fashioned according to the laws of poetry. And because she was in his eyes as various as the waves of the sea, the blind mask he would put on her face seemed inert, narrow the tragic fable through which she was to pass sorrowing, too limited the order of sentiment from which she was to draw her expressions, almost subterranean the soul she must reveal. "Ah! all that trembles, weeps, hopes, yearns, raves in the immensity of life!" His mental fancies were seized with a sort of panic, with a sudden, dissolving terror. What could that single work be in the immensity of life? Æschylus had composed more than a hundred tragedies, Sophocles still more; they had formed a world with colossal fragments raised in their titanic arms. Their work was as vast as a cosmogony. The Æschylian figures seemed to be still warm with ethereal fire, shining with sidereal light, damp from the fertilising cloud. The statue of Œdipus seemed to be carved out of the same mass as the solar myth; that of Prometheus made with the same primitive tool with which the shepherd Arya had produced fire upon the Asiatic heights. The spirit of the Earth worked in the creators.

"Hide me, hide me! and do not ask me anything, and let me be silent," he implored, not knowing how to dissimulate his excitement, and failing to control the tumult of his distracted thoughts.

The heart of the woman throbbed with fear in its ignorance.

"Why? What have you done?"

"I am suffering."

"From what?"

"From anxiety, anxiety, from that malady of mine which you know."

She took him in her arms. He felt that she had trembled with doubt.

"Mine, still mine?" she asked in a suffocated voice, with her lips upon his shoulder.

"Yes, yours always."

It was a horrible tremor which shook the woman every time she saw him go away, every time she saw him come back. When he left her, was he going to the unknown wife; when he returned, had he come to take his last leave of her?

She strained him in her arms, with the love of a mistress, a sister, a mother, with all human love.

"What can I do for you, what can I do for you? Tell me!"

She was continually tormented by the need of offering, of serving, of obeying a command which should drive her towards danger and the struggle to obtain some good which she should bring him on returning to him.

" What can I give you ? "

He smiled slightly, overtaken by weariness.

" What is it you want ? Ah, I know."

He smiled, letting himself be soothed by that voice, by those adoring hands.

" Everything, is it not true ? You want everything ? "

He smiled sadly, like a sick child told by a playmate of beautiful games.

" Ah, if I could. But nobody in the world will ever be able to give you anything of any value, sweet friend. Only your poetry and your music can demand everything. Do you recollect your Ode beginning, ' I was Pan ' ? "

He bent over the faithful heart a brow that was being illumined by beautiful things.

" I was Pan ! "

The splendour of the lyrical moment went through his spirit together with the delirium of the Ode.

" Have you seen your sea to-day ? Did you see the storm ? "

He shook his head without answering.

" Was it a great storm ? You told me one day that you have many sailors among your ancestors. Have you thought of your house on the sand-hills ? Are you homesick for the sands ? Do you want to go back down there ? You have done a great deal of work down there, and strong work. That house is blessed. Your mother was there whilst you were at work. You could hear her walk gently in the neighbouring rooms. . . . Did she stop to listen sometimes ? "

He clasped her in silence. The voice was penetrating him deeply and seemed to refresh his pent-up soul.

" And was your sister with you, too? You told me her name one day. I have not forgotten it. Her name is Sophia. I know she is like you. I should like to hear her speak once, or to see her pass down the road. . . . One day you praised her hands to me. They are beautiful, are they not? You told me one day that when she is sorrowful they hurt her ' as if they were the very roots of her soul.' That was what you told me, ' the very roots of her soul.'"

He was listening to her almost in a state of beatitude. In what way had she discovered the secret of that balsam? From what hidden spring was she drawing the melodious fluidity of those memories?

" Sophia will never know the good she has done to the poor pilgrim. I know little about her, but I know that she is like you in the face, and I have pictured her to myself. . . . Even now I can see her. . . . In distant countries, far, far away in the midst of a strange, hard population, she has appeared to me more than once when I was feeling lost; she has come to keep me company. She would appear suddenly without my calling or expecting her. . . . Once at Mürren, which I had reached after a long tiring journey I had undertaken in order to see a poor sick friend who afterwards died. . . . It was at dawn; the mounains had that cold delicate colour of beryl that is only seen among glaciers, the colour of those things that will for ever remain distant and intact and, oh, so enviable, so enviable! Why did she come? We waited together. The sun touched the peaks of the hills. Then a dazzling rainbow ran along their edges, lasted a few seconds, and disappeared. . . ."

He listened to her almost in a state of beatitude Was not all the beauty and all the truth that he would have expressed contained in one of the stones or flowers of those mountains? The most tragic struggle of human passions was not worth the apparition of that rainbow on the eternal snows.

" And another time? " he asked softly.

For the pause had prolonged itself and he feared she would not continue.

She smiled, then grew sad.

"Another time, it was at Alexandria, in Egypt, one confused day of horror as if after a shipwreck. . . . The city had all the appearance of putrefaction. . . . I remember: a street full of muddy water, a whitish skeleton-like horse that was splashing in it, its mane and tail looking as if tinted with ochre; the turrets of an Arab cemetery; the distant glitter of the marsh of Mareotis. . . . Disgust, ruin ! "

" Oh, dear soul, never again, never again shall you be desperate and alone," he said in his heart, swollen with paternal kindness towards the nomad woman who was calling up the sadness of her continual wandering.

His spirit which had stretched out so violently towards the future now seemed with a slight shudder to draw back into the past the power of that voice which was being made present. He felt himself in a state of concentration sweet and full of images like that which is generated by the telling of stories round the hearth in winter. Like once before under the windows of the cloistered Radiana, he felt himself seized by the fascination of time.

" And another time? "

She smiled, then grew sad.

" Another time it was in Vienna, in a museum. . . . A great deserted hall, the cracking of rain on the glass of the windows, numberless precious shrines in crystal cases, the signs of death everywhere, of exiled things no longer prayed to, no longer worshipped. . . . Together we bent over a case containing a collection of holy arms with their metal hands fixed in a changeless gesture. . . . Martyrs' hands studded with agates, amethysts, topazes, garnets, and sickly turquoises. . . . Through certain apertures, splinters of bone could be seen in the interior. There was one that held a golden lily, another a miniature city, a third a column. One was finer than the others. It had a ring on each finger, and it held a small vase full of ointment: it contained the relics of Mary Magdalen. . . . Exiled things, become profane and no longer prayed to, no longer worshipped. . . . Is Sophia devout? Has she preserved the habit of prayer? "

He did not answer. It seemed to him that he should not speak, that he should give no visible sign of his own existence in the enchantment of that distant life.

" Sometimes she would come into your room while you were working and lay a blade of grass on the page you had commenced."

The enchantress shuddered inwardly: an image that was wrapped in veils revealed itself all of a sudden, suggesting other words which remained unuttered. " Do you know that I began loving the creature who sings, her whom you cannot have forgotten, do you know that I began to love her, thinking of your sister? In order to pour into a pure soul the tenderness which my heart would have given to your sister from whom I was separated by so many cruel things! Do you know it?" The words were living, but they remained unuttered; yet the voice trembled at their dumb presence.

"Then you would allow yourself a few moments' rest; you would go to the window and with her beside you would look out to the sea. A ploughman urged his young oxen yoked to the plough over the sand to teach them the straight furrow; you would watch them with her every day at the same time. When they were fully trained, they came and ploughed the sand no longer, but were taken up to the hill. . . . Who has told me all these things?"

He himself had told her one day, almost in the same words, but now those memories were being brought back to him like unexpected visions.

"Then the flocks passed along the seashore: they came from the mountains and went to the plains of the Puglia, from one pasture to another pasture. As they walked, the woolly sheep imitated the motion of the waves, but the sea was nearly always quiet when the flocks passed with their shepherds. All was quiet; there was a golden silence stretched over the beach. The dogs ran along beside the flock: the shepherds leaned on their staffs, and the tinkle of their collar bells was faint in the vastness. Your eyes would follow their progress as far as the promontory. Then, later, you would go with your sister and follow the marks left by their passage on the damp sand. It was here and there dotted with holes and golden like a honeycomb. . . . Who has told me all these things?"

He listened to her almost in a state of beatitude. His fever was quenched. There descended upon him a slow peace that was like slumber.

"Then the sudden squalls would come; the sea would overrun the sand-hills and the low woods, leaving its foam on the juniper and tamarisk trees, on the myrtle and the rosemary. Quantities of sea-weeds and fragments would be thrown on shore. Some boat had shipwrecked somewhere. The sea brought fire-wood for the poor and mourning who knows where! The beach would be crowded with women and children and old men vying with one another as to who should collect the largest bundle. Then your sister would bring other help: bread, wine, vegetables, linen. The blessing would rise louder than the roar of the waves. You would look on from the window; and it seemed to you that none of your beautiful images was worth the odour of the new bread. You would leave the half-written page and hasten down to help Sophia. You would speak to the women, the children, and the old men. . . . Who has told me all these things?"

From the very first Stelio had preferred going to the house of his friend through the gate of the Gradenigo garden and passing among the trees and shrubs that had grown wild again. La Foscarina had obtained leave to unite her own garden with that of the abandoned palace by means of a breach in the partition wall. But soon afterwards, Lady Myrta had

come to inhabit the immense, silent rooms that had
welcomed as their last guest the son of the Empress
Josephine, the viceroy of Italy. The rooms were
adorned with old stringless instruments, and the garden was peopled by beautiful greyhounds deprived of
their prey.

Nothing seemed to Stelio sadder and sweeter than
that walk towards the woman who awaited him,
counting the hours that were so slow and yet so swift
to fly. The canal path of San Simeone Piccolo
turned golden in the afternoon like a bank of fine ala-
baster. The reflected sun-rays played with the iron
of the prows moored in a row by the landing pier,
quivered on the steps of the church, on the columns
of the peristyle, animating the warm, disjointed
stones. A few rotten gondola cabins lay in the
shade of the pavement with their cloths spoiled and
discoloured by the rains, like biers worn by the wear
and tear of many funerals, grown old on the cemetery
road. The suffocating odour of hemp came from a
decayed palace now used as a rope factory, through
the barred windows choked with greyish down as
with accumulated cobwebs. And the garden gate
opened at the end of the Campiello della Comare,
which was grassy like the churchyard of a country
parish; it opened out between two pillars crowned
with mutilated statues, and on the limbs of these the
dried ivy branches stood out like veins. Nothing
could have seemed to the visitor sweeter or more
sad. The chimneys of the humble dwellings round
the grass plot smoked peacefully towards the green
cupola; now and then a flight of pigeons crossed
the canal, starting from the sculptures of the Scalzi;

the whistle of a train passing on the lagoon bridge could be heard, and the sing-song of a rope-maker and the roll of an organ and the chanting of the priests. The late summer was deceiving the melancholy of love.

" Helion! Sirius! Altair! Donovan! Ali-Nour! Nerissa! Piuchebella! "

Lady Myrta, seated on the bench against the wall clasped by rose-bushes, was calling her dogs. La Foscarina stood near her, dressed in a tawny garment that seemed made of the wonderful roan stuff used in ancient Venice; the sun wrapped the two women and the roses in one same fair warmth.

" You are dressed like Donovan to-day," said Lady Myrta to the actress, smiling. " Do you know that Stelio loves Donovan above all the others? "

A faint blush tinted the face of La Foscarina; her eyes sought the tawny greyhound.

" The strongest and the most beautiful," she said.

" I think he wants him," added the old lady, with her indulgent sweetness.

" What is it he does not want? "

The old woman felt the veiled melancholy; she remained silent for a few moments.

The dogs lay near them, heavy and sad, sleepy and full of dreams, far from their plains, their steppes, and their deserts, crouching on the field of clover where the marrow plants meandered with their hollow, yellow-green fruit. The trees were motionless, as if they had been fused in the same bronze that covered the three graduated cupolas of San Simeone. There was one same aspect of wildness about the garden and the great stone dwelling, darkened by the tenacious smoke of time, streaked with the rust of its irons produced by the rains of an infinite number of autumns. And the head of a tall pine resounded with the same twittering which was certainly reaching the ears of Radiana at that moment from her walled garden.

"Does he give you pain?" the old woman would have liked to ask of the woman in love, because the silence weighed upon her and the fire of that sorrowful soul was warming her like the persistent summer. But she dared not. She sighed instead of speaking. Her heart, which was ever young, could still beat at the sight of desperate passion and threatened beauty. "Ah, you are still beautiful, and your mouth still attracts, and the man who loves you can still know the intoxication of your pallor and your eyes," she said, looking at the absorbed actress, towards whom the November roses were stretching out. "But I am a shadow."

She lowered her eyes, saw her own deformed hands resting on her knees, and marvelled at their being hers, they were so dead and contorted, miserable monsters that could no longer touch anything without exciting repugnance, that henceforth had only the sleepy dogs to caress. She felt the wrinkles on her face, the artificial teeth against her gums, the false hair on her head, the entire ruin of her poor body, that at one time had obeyed the graceful dictates of her delicate spirit; and she marvelled at her own persistence in struggling against the decay of her age, in deceiving herself, in recomposing each morning the laughable illusion of essences, ointments, rouge, and dyes. But was not her youth still present in the continual spring of her dream? Had she not yesterday, only yesterday, caressed a lovable face with perfect fingers, hunted the fox and the stag in the northern counties, danced in a park with her promised bridegroom to an air of John Dowland's.

"There are no mirrors in the house of the Countess Glanegg; there are too many in the house of Lady Myrta," thought la Foscarina. "One has hidden her decadence from herself and all others; the other has seen herself growing older each morning, has counted her wrinkles one by one, has gathered up her dead hairs in her comb, has felt the first shake of her teeth in her pale gums, and has tried to repair the irreparable ruin by artifice. Poor, tender soul that would still live, smiling and fascinating! One should disappear, die, sink below the earth." She noticed the little bunch of violets fastened by a pin to the hem of Lady Myrta's dress. In every season a fresh flower was pinned there, in some fold, hardly visible, as a sign of her daily illusion of spring, of the ever-renewed incantation that she worked on herself by means of memory, music, and poetry, with all the arts of dreams against old age, ill-health, and solitude. "One should live a supreme, flaming hour, and then disappear in the earth before all fascination be lost, before the death of our last grace."

She felt the beauty of her own eyes, the hunger of her lips, the rough strength of her hair folded back by the tempest, all the power of the rhythms and the impulses that slept in her muscles and in her bones. She seemed to hear her friend's words which had praised her, to see him in the fury of his desire, in the sweetness of languor, in the moment of deepest oblivion. "For a little while longer, still for a little while, I shall please him, I shall seem beautiful to him, I will burn his blood. Still for a little while." With her feet in the grass, with her forehead lifted to the sun, in the odour of the fading roses, in the tawny dress that likened her to the magnificent beast of prey, she burned with passionate expectation, with a sudden flood of life, as if that future which she had given up by her resolution of death were flowing back into the present. "Come, come!" She called her lover inwardly, half intoxicated, sure of his coming, because she already felt him and had never yet been deceived by her presentiment. "Still for a little while!" Every moment that passed seemed an iniquitous theft. Motionless as she was, she suffered and desired bewilderingly. The whole garden, penetrated by heat to its very roots, throbbed with her own pulsation. She felt as if she were about to lose consciousness, to fall.

"Ah! here is Stelio," exclaimed Lady Myrta, seeing the young man appear among the laurels.

The woman turned quickly, blushing. The greyhounds rose, pricking their ears. The meeting of those two brought forth sparks that were like a flash of lightning. Once more, as ever, her lover had felt in the presence of the marvellous creature the divine sensation of being suddenly wrapped in inflamed ether, in a vibrating atmosphere that seemed to isolate him from the ordinary atmosphere and almost ravished him. He had one day associated that miracle of love with a physical image, remembering how on one distant evening of his childhood, in crossing a desolate plot of ground, he had suddenly found him-

self surrounded by will-o'-the-wisps and had uttered
a cry.

"You were awaited here by all that lives in this
seclusion," said Lady Myrta, with a smile that covered
the emotion which had seized the poor youthful heart
in its prison of an old ailing body, at the spectacle of
love and desire. "In coming you have obeyed a call."

"True!" said the young man, holding the collar
of Donovan, who had crept up to him, remembering
his caresses. "Indeed, I come from somewhere
very far. Where do you think I come from?
Guess!"

"From the land of Giorgione."

"No, from the cloister of Santa Apollonia. Do
you know the cloister of Santa Apollonia?"

"Is it your invention of to-day?"

"Invention? It is a cloister of stone, a real one,
with its well and its little columns."

"It may be; but all the things you have once
looked at become your inventions, Stelio."

"Ah, Lady Myrta, I should like to give you that
gem. I should like to remove it into your garden.
Imagine a small secret cloister, opening on an order
of worn columns, coupled like nuns when they
pace fasting in the sun, very delicate, neither white
nor grey nor black, but of that most mysterious
colour ever given to stone by that great master-
colourist called Time. And in the midst of these a
well, and on the margin furrowed by the rope a bot-
tomless pail. The nuns have disappeared, but I think
the shades of the Danaides frequent the place. . . ."

He interrupted himself suddenly on seeing himself surrounded by the hounds and began imi-

tating the guttural sounds made by the kennel-man
to rally them. The dogs became restless; their
melancholy eyes brightened. Two who had been at
some distance from the others bounded towards him
with long leaps, jumping over the bushes, and stopped
before him, wiry, sinuous, with strained nerves.

"Ali-Nour! Crissa! Nerissa! Clarissa! Altair!
Helion! Hardicanute! Veronese! Hierro!"

He knew them all by name; and when he called
them, they seemed to recognise him for their master.
There was the Scotch deer-hound, the native of the
highlands, with rough thick coat, rougher and thicker
round his jowls and nose and grey as new iron;
there was the reddish Irish wolf-hound, the robust
destroyer of wolves, whose brown eyes showed the
whites on moving; there was the spotted Tartary
hound, black and yellow, brought from the vast
Asiatic steppes where he guarded the tents at night
from leopards and hyenas; there was the Persian
dog, fair and small, his ears covered with long silky
hairs, with a bushy tail, his coat paler along the ribs
and down his legs, more graceful even than the ante-
lopes he had slain; there was the Spanish *galgo* who
had migrated with the Moors, the magnificent beast
held in leash by a pompous dwarf in the picture of
Diego Velasquez, trained to course and overthrow
in the naked plains of the Mancha, or in the low
woods thick with brushwood of Murcia and Ali-
cante; there was the Arabian *sloughi*, the illustrious
plunderer of the desert, with dark tongue and palate,
all his sinews visible, his framework of bones showing through the fine skin, a noble animal all pride,
courage, and elegance, accustomed to sleeping on

rich carpets and drinking pure milk in pure vessels. And gathered together in a pack they quivered round him who knew how to reawaken in their torpid blood their primitive instincts of pursuit and carnage.

"Which of you was Gog's best friend?" he said, looking from one to the other of the beautiful anxious eyes fixed on him.

"You Hierro? You Altair?"

His singular accent excited the sensitive animals, who listened with suppressed, intermittent yelps. Each movement of theirs imparted a shining wave to their various coats; and their long tails, curved at the ends like hooks, wagged lightly from side to side against their muscular haunches.

"Well, I must tell you what I have kept silent until to-day: Gog, do you hear? who could break the hare at one snap of his jowls, — Gog is crippled."

"Oh, really!" exclaimed Lady Myrta, regretfully. "How did it happen, Stelio, and how is Magog?"

"Magog is safe and sound."

They were a couple of greyhounds given by Lady Myrta to her young friend to take with him to his house on the sea.

"But how did it happen?"

"Ah, poor Gog! He had already killed thirty-seven hares. He possessed all the qualities of great breeding: swiftness, resistance, an incredible quickness at turning, and the constant desire of killing his prey, and the classical manner of running straight, and gripping from behind. Have you ever seen greyhounds course, Foscarina?"

She was so intent that she started at the unexpected sound of her name.

" Never! "

She was hanging on his lips, fascinated by their instinctive expression of cruelty in describing the work of blood.

" Never! Then you do not know one of the rarest manifestations of daring, vehemence and grace in the world."

He drew Donovan towards him, knelt on the ground and began feeling him with his expert hands.

" There is in nature no machine more precisely and powerfully adapted to its purpose. The muzzle is sharp in order to part the air in running, it is long, in order that the jaws may disable the prey at the first snap. The skull is large between the two ears in order to contain greater courage and skill. The jowls are dry and muscular, the lips short so that they barely cover the teeth."

With easy assurance, he opened the mouth of the dog, which attempted no resistance. The dazzling teeth appeared, the palate marked with large black waves, the thin rosy tongue.

" See what teeth! See how long the eye-teeth are, and a little curve at the points the better to retain his hold. No other kind of dog has a mouth constructed in so perfect a manner for the purpose of biting."

His hands lingered in the examination, and his admiration for the noble specimen seemed to have no bounds. He had knelt down on the clover, receiving in his face the breath of the animal, which was letting itself be examined with unusual docility, as if it had understood the praise of the expert and were enjoying it.

" The ears are small and placed very high, straight in moments of excitement, but falling flat and adhering to the skull when at rest. They do not prevent the collar from being taken off and put on again without undoing the buckle: so! "

He took off the collar, which exactly fitted the animal's neck, and put it on again.

" Then he has a swan's neck, long and flexible, which allows him to grasp his peculiar game at the moment of his greatest swiftness without losing his balance. Ah, I once saw Gog clutch a hare that was jumping across a ditch. . . . Now observe the more important parts: the length and depth of chest made for long runs, the oblique lines of the shoulders proportioned to the length of the limbs, the formidable muscular mass in the haunches, the short heels, the backbone saddle-backed between bands of solid muscles. . . . Look! Helion's backbone stands out plainly: Donovan's is hidden in a furrow. The paws are like those of a cat, with nails that are close, but not too much so, elastic and sure. And what elegance there is in the ribs, disposed with the symmetry of a fine ship's keel, and in that line, curving inwards towards the abdomen, which is entirely hidden. All is directed to one aim. The tail thick at its root and thin at the tip — look! almost like that of a rat — serves the animal for the purpose of a rudder and is necessary to him in order to be able to turn rapidly when the hare doubles. Let me see, Donovan, if you are perfect also in this."

He took the tip of the tail, passed it under the leg, drew it back towards his haunch-bone, where it exactly touched the projecting part.

"Perfect! I once saw an Arab of the tribe of Arbâa measuring his *sloughi* in this way. Ali-Nour! Did you tremble when you discovered the flock of gazelles? Think, Foscarina, the *sloughi* trembles when he discovers his prey, trembles like a willow, and turns two soft beseeching eyes to his master that he may be set free. I do not know why this pleases me, and moves me so much. His desire of killing is terrible in him, his whole body is ready to fly like an arrow, yet he trembles! Not with fear surely, not with uncertainty, but with desire. Ah, Foscarina, if you were to see a *sloughi* in those moments you would certainly carry away from him his manner of trembling, and you would know how to make it human, and you would give men yet another quiver with your tragic art. . . . Get up Ali-Nour! desert torrent of swiftness, do you remember? Now it is only the cold that causes your trembling. . . ."

Gay and voluble, he let Donovan go, and taking in his two hands the snakelike head of the slayer of gazelles, looked into the depths of his eyes, where lurked the homesickness of silent tropical countries, of tents unfolded after a journey that meteors had deceived, of bonfires lit for the evening meal under the wide stars that seemed to draw their life from the throb of the wind in the palm-tops. "Eyes full of dreams and of melancholy, of courage and faithfulness. Have you ever thought, Lady Myrta, that the hound of the lovely eyes is precisely the mortal enemy of the lovely-eyed animals like the gazelle and the hare?"

The woman had entered into that bodily incantation of love by which the limits of one's person seem to spread and be fused in the air, so that each word or gesture of the loved one excites a quiver sweeter than any caress. The young man had taken in his hands the head of Ali-Nour, but she felt the touch of those hands on her own temples. The young man was searching the eyes of Ali-Nour, but she could feel that glance deep in her own soul, and it seemed that his praise of those eyes flowed to her own eyes.

She was standing on the grass like the haughty animals he loved, dressed like the one he preferred of all the others, filled like them with a confused memory of a distant origin, and slightly stupefied by the glare of the sun-rays reflected by the wall covered with rose-trees, stupefied and fervent as if in a slight fever. She heard him speaking of things that were alive, of limbs apt for the chase and the capture, of vigour and dexterity, of natural power and the vigour of blood, and she saw him bending near the earth in the odour of the grass, in the warmth of the sun, pliable and strong, feeling skins and bones, measuring the energy of exposed muscles, enjoying the contact of those generous bodies, almost taking part in that delicate, cruel brutality that it had more than once pleased him to represent in the inventions of his art; and she herself, with her feet in the warm earth under the breath of the sky, in her dress that was similar in colour to the tawny plunderer, felt a strange primitive sense of bestiality rising from the roots of her being, something that was almost the illusion of a slow metamorphosis in which she was losing a part of her human consciousness and becoming a child of nature, a short-lived, ingenuous force, a savage life

Thus was he not touching the obscurest mystery of her being? was he not making her feel the animal profundity from which the unexpected revelations of her tragic genius had sprung forth, shaking and inebriating the multitude like the sights of the sea and the sky, like the dawn or the tempest? When he had told her of the quivering *sloughi*, had he not divined the natural analogies from which she drew the powers of expression that had set poets and peoples wondering?   It was because she had discovered anew the Dionysian sense of nature the naturaliser, the ancient fervour of instinctive and creative energies, the enthusiasm of the manifold god emerging from the ferment of every sap that she appeared so new and so great on the stage.   She had sometimes felt in herself something like an imminent approach of the miracle that used of old to swell with divine milk the bosom of the Mænades when they saw the young panthers draw near them craving for food.

She stood on the grass tawny and agile like the favourite hound, full of the confused memory of a distant origin, living and desirous of living without measure in the brief hour allotted to her.   The mist of tears was vain, all the stifling aspirations to goodness and renunciation fell, and all the ashen melancholies of the deserted garden.   The presence of the Life-giver seemed to widen space, to change time, to quicken the throb of blood, to multiply the faculty of enjoyment, to create once more the phantom of a magnificent festival.   She was there once more as he had wished to shape her, forgetful of fears and wretchedness, cured of her sad evil, a creature of flesh vibrating in the light, in the warmth, in the perfumes, in the play of appearances, ready to cross the suggested plains and sand-hills and deserts with him in the fury of the chase, to feel the intoxication of that ecstasy, to rejoice at the sight of courage, skill, and bleeding spoils. From second to second as he spoke and moved, he shaped her after his own likeness.

" Ah, every time I saw the hare breaking in the teeth of the hound, a flash of regret would pass over my joy for those great moist eyes that were being extinguished! Larger than yours, Ali-Nour, and larger than yours, Donovan, resplendent like pools on a summer evening, with the same circle of willows dipping into them and the same heaven mirrored and changing in them. Have you ever seen a hare in the early morning, emerge from a freshly ploughed furrow, run for a while on the silver hoarfrost, then stop in the silence, sit down on its hindlegs, prick up its ears, and watch the horizon? Its look seems to pacify the universe. The motionless hare searching the smoking field in a moment of respite from its perpetual anxiety! One could not imagine a more certain sign of perfect surrounding peace. In those moments, it is a sacred animal that we should adore. . . ."

Lady Myrta broke into the youthful laugh that revealed the whole range of her gilded elephantine teeth and shook the tortoise-like wrinkles under her chin.

" Kind Stelio," she exclaimed, laughing, " first to adore, then tear in pieces: is that your way? "

La Foscarina looked at her in some surprise, for she had forgotten her; and sitting there on the stone seat, yellow with mosses, with her contorted hands, with that glitter of gold and ivory between her thin lips, with those small blue eyes under limp eyelids, with that harsh voice and that queer laugh, she suggested the image of one of those old web-footed fairies that wander through the woods followed by an obedient toad. The words did not penetrate the oblivion in which she had lost herself, nevertheless they disturbed her as a shriek.

"It is not my fault," said Stelio, "if greyhounds are made to kill hares and not to slumber in a walled garden on the waters of a dead canal."

Again he began imitating the guttural sounds of the kennel-man.

"Crissa! Nerissa! Altair! Sirius! Piuchebella! Helion!"

The excited dogs grew agitated: their eyes lit up; the dry muscles started under the tawny, black, white, leaden, spotted, and mingled coats; the long haunches curved like bows ready to unbend and to hurl into space the carcasses drier and more slender than a bundle of arrows.

"There, there, Donovan, there!"

He was pointing to something half grey, half reddish, in the grass at the bottom of the garden, that had the appearance of a hare crouching with its ears laid flat. The imperious voice deceived the hesitating hounds, and the thin powerful bodies were beautiful to see in the sunlight, shining like living silk, quivering and vibrating at the stimulus of the human voice like the lightest flags in a pavice, answering to the breeze.

"There, Donovan!"

And the great tawny dog looked him in the eyes, gave a formidable leap, dashed towards the fancied prey with all the vehemence of his reawakened instinct. He had reached it in an instant, then stopped, disappointed, bending on his hind-legs, his neck thrust forward; then he leaped again, began playing with the pack that had followed him in great disorder, began fighting Altair, left off, and, his pointed muzzle erect, followed, barking, a flock of sparrows that had flown away from the pine top with a gay rustle in the blue.

" A marrow, a marrow," cried the deceiver, between his peals of laughter, "not even a rabbit. Poor Donovan! A bite in a pumpkin. Ah, poor Donovan, what a humiliation! Take care, Lady Myrta, lest he drown himself in the canal to hide his shame. . . ."

Seized by the contagion of his gaiety, la Foscarina laughed with him. Her roan dress and the coats of the hounds shone in the slanting sun on the green of the clover. The whiteness of her teeth and the pealing laughter filled her mouth with renewed youth. The tedium of the ancient garden seemed torn asunder like the cobwebs that are brushed away when a violent hand opens a window that has been long closed.

" Would you like to have Donovan?" said Lady Myrta, with a malicious grace in her soul that lost itself among her wrinkles like a stream in a flooded land. " I know, I know your arts. . . ."

Stelio ceased laughing, blushing like a child.

A wave of tenderness swelled the bosom of la Foscarina as she noticed the childish blush. Her whole being sparkled with love; and a mad desire to fold her lover in her arms quivered in her pulses and on her lips.

"Would you like to have him?" Lady Myrta asked again, happy at being able to give, and grateful to him who had received the gift with so much fresh, vivid pleasure. "Donovan is yours!"

Before thanking her, his eyes sought the greyhound almost anxiously, he saw him again as he was, strong, splendid, most beautiful, with the stamp of style on his limbs as if Pisanello had designed him for the reverse of a medal.

"But Gog, what has become of Gog? You have not said another word about him," said the giver. "Ah, how easily an invalid goes out of our minds!"

Stelio was watching la Foscarina, who had turned towards the group of hounds, walking on the grass with a quick undulation which was like the step called precisely by the old Venetians the greyhound step. The roan dress, gilded by the declining sun, seemed burning on her flexible figure. And it was easy to see that she was going towards the animal of her own colour, to which she likened herself strangely by her deep mimetic instinct, almost to the point of being transfigured.

"It was after a run," said Stelio. "I was in the habit of having a hare coursed along the sand-hills by the seashore nearly every day. The peasants often brought me live ones from my own grounds, dark, robust ones ready to defend themselves, most cunning, capable of scratching and biting. Ah, Lady Myrta, there is no ground for a run finer than my free seashore. You know the great plateaus of Lancashire, the dry Yorkshire soil, the hard plains of

Altcar, the low Scotch moors, the sands of southern England; but a gallop along my sand-hills, more golden and more luminous than the autumn clouds, beyond the low juniper and tamarisk clusters, beyond the small, limpid mouths of the streams, beyond the little salt pools, along a sea which is greener than a meadow, within sight of the blue and snowy mountains, would obscure your fairest memories, Lady Myrta."

"Italy! Italy!" smiled the indulgent old fairy. "The flower of the world."

"It was along that shore that I would let the hare loose. I trained a man to unleash the dogs at the right moment. and I would follow the chase on horseback. . . . Certainly Magog is an excellent courser, but I had never seen a more ready or more ardent slayer than Gog. . . ."

"He came from the Newmarket kennels," said the giver, proudly.

"One day I was returning home along the seashore. The chase had been brief. . . . Gog had overtaken the hare at the end of two or three miles. I was coming home at a slow gallop, skirting the calm water. Gog was galloping beside me, keeping up with Cambyses, jumping up now and then towards the game that hung from my saddle, and barking. Suddenly, on seeing a dead carcass before him, my horse started to one side, and his hoof wounded the dog, who began howling, holding up his left foreleg, which seemed broken at the fetlock. I reined in the frightened horse with some difficulty, and went back. But as Cambyses saw the carcass again, he shied and bolted. Then it became a furious race along the

lowns. With what emotion I cannot tell you, I heard
in a few minutes the hard breathing of Gog behind
the horse. He had followed me, you understand?
In spite of his broken leg, moved by the generosity
of his blood, forgetting his pain, he followed me, overtook me, passed me! My eyes met his sweet, beautiful eyes, and while I strove to regain my mastery
over the frightened horse, my heart broke each time
I saw his poor wounded leg graze the ground. I
worshipped him at that moment, I worshipped him.
Do you think me capable of tears?"

"Yes," said Lady Myrta, "even of tears."

"Well, when my sister Sophia began dressing the
wound with her thin hands on which the tears were
dropping, I too, I think — "

La Foscarina stood beside Donovan, holding him
by the collar, pale again, more attenuated, as if the
chill of evening were already beginning to penetrate
her; the shadow of the bronze cupola was lengthening
on the grass, on the hornbeams, on the laurels; a
violet moisture in which the last atoms of the sun's
gold were swimming spread itself among the stems
and branches that were quivering in the wind. And
once more their ears caught the twittering in the
pine tops full of empty cones.

"See, we are yours," seemed the words of the
woman, while the greyhound, seized by the first
shivers, pressed against her knees. "We are yours
for ever; we are here to serve you."

"Nothing in the world disquiets and kindles me
so much as these sudden visions of the virtue of
blood," said the young man, roused by the memory
of that hour of emotion.

They heard the prolonged whistle of a train that was crossing the bridge over the lagoon. A breath of wind stripped off all the petals of a large white rose, so that only a bud remained on the top of the stalk. The chilly dogs drew near one another, gathering together one against the other. Their slender bones shivered under the thin skin, and the melancholy eyes shone in the long heads flat as the heads of reptiles.

"Did I ever tell you, Stelio, of the way in which a lady belonging to the best blood of France died at a hunting party where I was present?" Lady Myrta asked him. The tragic image and the pitiful remembrance had been reawakened in her by the expression she had caught on the pale face of la Foscarina.

"No, never; who was she?"

"Jeanne d'Elbeuf. Through her own imprudence or inexperience, or that of the man who rode beside her, she was shot, nobody ever knew by whom, together with the hare, which passed between the legs of the horse. She was seen to fall. We all hastened to her, and found her on the grass, steeped in blood, by the side of the convulsed hare. In the silence and dismay, while we all stood there as if turned to stone, while not one of us had yet dared to speak or move, the poor creature raised one hand just a little, pointing to the wounded, suffering animal, and said (never shall I forget her voice), "*Tuez-le, tuez-le, mes amis. . . . Ça fait si mal!*"[1] Then died at once.

Heart-rending indeed was the sweetness of the late November that smiled like an invalid who believes himself to be convalescent and feels an unusual

[1] "Kill it, kill it, my friends, it hurts so!"

happiness and knows not that his agony is at hand!

"What is the matter with you to-day, Fosca? What has happened? Why are you so reserved with me? Tell me! Speak to me!"

Stelio had strolled into San Marco by chance and had seen her there, leaning against the door of the chapel that leads to the Baptistery. She was alone, motionless, her face devoured by fever and shadow, her eyes full of terror fixed on the terrible figures flaming in the yellow fire of the mosaics. A choir was practising behind the door; the chant, interrupted every now and then, began again with the same cadence.

"Leave me alone, I beg of you, I beg of you! I must be alone. I implore you!"

The sound of her words betrayed the dryness of her convulsed mouth. She turned as if to fly. He held her back.

"But tell me! Say one word at least that I may understand."

Again she moved as if to draw herself away, and her movement expressed an unspeakable suffering. She had the appearance of a creature lacerated by torture, wrenched by an executioner. She seemed more wretched than a body tied to the rack, tormented by red-hot pincers.

"I implore you. If you are sorry for me, there is only one thing you can do for me now; let me go. . . ."

She spoke very low, and the torture of her shaken soul was so evident that her not crying out, and her throat's not giving way to breathless screams, seemed inhuman.

"But one word, at least one, that I may under-stand."

A flash of fury passed over the perturbed face.

"No! I want to be let alone."

The voice was as hard as the look. She turned, taking a few steps like one overtaken by dizziness hastening to some support.

"Foscarina!"

But he dared not hold her back. He saw the desperate woman walk into the zone of sunlight that had invaded the basilica with the rush of a torrent through the door that an unknown hand had opened. The deep golden cave with its apostles, with its martyrs, with its sacred beasts, sparkled behind her as if the thousand torches of the day were pouring into it. The chant stopped, then began again.

"I am drowning in my sadness. . . . The impulse to rebel against my fate, to go away aimlessly, to search. . . . Who will save my hope? From whom will light come to me? . . . To sing, to sing! But I would sing a hymn of life at last. . . . Could you tell me where the Lord of the Flame is just now?" The words of Donatella Arvale's letter were branded on her eyes and branded on her soul with all the peculiarities of the handwriting, with all the diversity of signs as living as the hand that had penned them, as throbbing as the impatient pulse. She could see them engraved in the stones, outlined in the clouds, reflected in the waters, indelible and inevitable, like decrees of Fate.

"Where can I go? Where can I go?" The sweet-ness of things, the warmth of the golden marbles, the fragrance of the quiet air, the languor of human leisure, reached her through her agitation and despair. She looked at a woman of the people wrapped in her brown cloak and seated on the steps of the basilica, a woman who was neither old nor young, neither beautiful nor plain, who sat enjoying the sunshine, eating a large piece of bread, biting pieces out of it with her teeth and then chewing them slowly, her eyes half shut as she savoured her contentment while her fair lashes shone upon her cheeks. " Ah, if I could change myself into you, take on your destiny, be content with bread and sunshine and think no more and suffer no more." The poor woman's repose seemed infinite bliss to her.

She turned with a start, fearing, hoping, that her lover had followed her. She did not see him. She would have fled if she had seen him; but her heart failed her as if he had sent her to her death without calling her back. " All is over." She was losing all sense of measure and certainty. The thoughts that passed in her were broken and confusedly dragged on by anguish, like plants and stones by the fury of an overflowing river. In all the aspects of surrounding things, her bewildered eyes saw a confirmation of her sentence or the obscure menace of new evils, or a figuring of her state, or the signifying of occult truths about to work cruelly on her existence. At the corner of San Marco, near the Porta della Carta, she felt the four porphyry kings clasping each other as for a compact while their tough fists grasp the hilt finishing in a hawk's beak, live as if they had been made of dark blood. The numberless veins of the various marbles with which the side of the temple is encrusted, those indistinct threads of different colours, those intertwined labyrinths and meanders, seemed to make her own interior diversity visible, and the very confusion of her thoughts. In turn, she felt all things estranged, remote, unexisting, and then familiar, approaching her and participating in her intimate life. In turn she seemed to find herself in unknown places and among forms belonging to her as if her own substance had given them their material life. Like those who are dying, she was at intervals illumined by images of her distant childhood, by memories of far-away events, by the distinct and rapid apparition of a face, a gesture, a room, a whole neighbourhood. And above all these phantoms, in a background of shadow the eyes of her mother seemed gazing on her, kind and firm, no larger than human eyes while in life, yet infinite as an horizon towards which she was being called. "Shall I come to you? Are you really calling me for the last time?"

She had entered the Porta della Carta and had crossed the lobby. The intoxication of pain was leading her back to the place where on a night of glory the three Destinies had met. She sought the well which had been their meeting-place. The whole life of those few instants rose up again round its bronze rim with the evidence and the outline of reality. There she had said as she turned, smiling, to her companion, "Donatella, here is the Lord of the Flame." The immense cry of the multitude had covered her voice and a thousand fiery pigeons had lit up the sky above their heads.

She drew nearer to the well. Every detail of it impressed itself on her spirit as she stood considering it, clothing itself with a strange power of fateful life; the furrows left by the ropes in the metal, the green oxide that streaked the stone at its base, the breasts of the cariatides worn out by the knees of the women who had at one time pressed upon them in the effort of drawing water, and that deep inner mirror no longer disturbed by the shock of descending pails, that narrow subterranean circle that reflected the sky. She bent over the edge, saw her own face, saw her terror and her ruin, saw the immovable Medusa which she carried in the centre of her soul. Unconsciously she was repeating the act of him whom she loved. And she saw his face, too, and the face of Donatella, such as she had seen them shining for an instant on that night, one close to the other, lit up by the flashes from the sky as if they had been bending over a furnace or a crater. "Love, love each other! I will go away. I will disappear. Good-bye." Her eyelids dropped over the thought of death. In that darkness the kind firm eyes reappeared, infinite as an horizon of peace. "You who are in peace and who wait for me, you who lived and died of passion." She straightened herself. An extraordinary silence filled the deserted courtyard. The wealth of the high carved walls rested half in the shadow, half in the light; the five mitres of the basilica surpassed the columned cloister as light as the snowy clouds that made the sky seem more blue, the same as the jessamine flower causes the leaf to seem more green. Again through her torment she was touched by the sweetness of things. "Life might still be sweet."

She came out by the Molo, stepped into a gondola, had herself rowed to the Giudecca. The harbour,

the Salute, the Riva degli Schiavoni, all the stone and
all the water, were a miracle of gold and opal. She
looked anxiously towards the Piazzetta lest a figure
should be appearing there. The image of dead summer dressed in gold and shut in a coffin of opalescent
glass flashed on her memory. She imagined her
own self submerged in the lagoon and laid out on
a bed of seaweed, but the memory of the promise
made on that water and kept in the night's delirium,
pierced her heart like a knife, threw her once more
into a horrible convulsion. "Never more, then?
Never more?" All her senses remembered all his
caresses. The lips, the hands, the strength, the fire
of the young man, passed into her blood as if they
had melted in her. The poison burnt into her
to her furthest fibres. With him she had found at
the extreme limit of pleasure a spasm that was not
death and yet was beyond life. "And now never
more? never more?"

She was in the Rio della Croce. The foliage grew
above a red wall. The góndola stopped at a closed
door. She landed, took out a small key, opened the
door, and went into the garden.

It was her refuge, the secret place of her solitude,
preserved by her faithful melancholies as by silent cus-
todians. All came forward to meet her, the old ones
and the new ones, surrounded her, accompanied her.

With its long trellises, with its cypresses, with its
fruit-trees, with its edges of lavender, its oleanders,
its carnations, its rose-bushes crimson and crocus
coloured, marvellously soft and tired in the colours
of its dissolution, that garden seemed lost in the
extreme lagoon, on one of those islands forgotten by

man, Mazzorbo, Torcello, San Francesco Deserto. The sun embraced it and penetrated it on every side so that the shadows were so slight as to be hardly visible; so great was the stillness of the air that the dry vine leaves stayed on their tendrils. None of the leaves fell; though all were dead.

"Never more?" She walked under the trellises, went towards the water, stopped on the grassy mound, felt tired, sat down on a stone, held her temples tightly between her hands, made an effort to concentrate herself, to recover her dominion over herself, to consider, to deliberate. "He is still here; he is near me. I can see him again. Perhaps I shall find him before long at the threshold of my door. He will take me in his arms, will kiss my eyes and lips, will tell me again that he loves me, that everything in me pleases him. He does not know, does not understand. Nothing irreparable has happened. What, then, is the fact that has convulsed and broken me? I have received a letter from a woman who is far away, a prisoner in a lonely villa with her demented father, who complains of her lot and longs to change it. This is the fact. There is no more. This is the letter." She looked for it and opened it to reread it. Her fingers trembled. She felt the perfume of Donatella as if she had had her by her side there on that stone.

"Is she beautiful? Truly? What is she like?" The lines of the image were confused at first. She tried to seize them, and they vanished. One detail before any of the others fixed itself, becoming precise and evident, — the large heavy hand. "Did he see it that night? He is extremely sensitive to the beauty of hands. He always looks at them when he meets a woman. Does he not love Sophia's hands?" She gave herself up for a few seconds to childish considerations such as those, then smiled at them bitterly. And suddenly the image completed itself, grew living, shone with strength and youth, overcame her, dazzled her. "She is beautiful; and hers is the beauty which he would have her possess."

She stayed on transfixed, surrounded by the silent splendour of the waters, with the letter on her knees, nailed there by the inflexible truth. And involuntary thoughts of destruction flashed above that inert discouragement: the face of Donatella was burnt in a fire, her body deformed by a fall, her voice quenched by an illness. Horror at herself filled her, and then pity for herself and for the other woman. "Has she not also the right of living? Let her live, let her love, let her have her joy." She imagined some magnificent adventure for her, some happy love, the love of a bridegroom, prosperity, luxury, pleasure. "Is there only this one man on earth whom she can love? To-morrow could she not meet the man who is to take her heart? Could not her fate suddenly turn her elsewhere, draw her far away, lead her towards an unknown path, separate her from us for ever? Is it perhaps necessary that she should be loved by the man whom I love? They may perhaps never meet again." Thus she tried to escape her own presentiment, but a contrary spirit was telling her: "They have met once; they will seek each other; they will meet again. Hers is not the obscure soul that can be lost in a crowd or along a side-path. She carries a gift in herself resplendent as a star and that will always make her easy to recognise from afar: her song. The miracle of her voice will be her signal. She will certainly avail herself of this power in the world; she too will pass among men leaving wonder behind her. She will have glory as she has beauty, — two signal lights to which he will easily go. They have met once; they will meet again."

The woman cowered down under her pain as if under a yoke; the threads of grass at her feet seemed to withhold the rays they received, and to breathe in a green light which was coloured by their quiet transparency. She felt the tears rise to her eyes, — gazed through that veil at the lagoon which trembled with the trembling of her tears. A fair pearly light was on the waters. The islands of the Follia, San Clemente and San Servilio were wrapped in pale mist. And now and then there came from their distance faint cries, as of shipwrecked men lost in the calm, answered now by the shriek of a siren, now by the hoarse cry of the scattered sea-birds. The silence would become terrible, then it would soften again. She recovered her deep goodness, recovered her tenderness for the beautiful creature with whom she had deluded her desire of loving Sophia, the kind sister. She thought over the hours spent in the lonely villa on the hill of Settignano, where Lorenzo Arvale created his statues in the fulness of his strength and fervour, unconscious of the thunderbolt that was about to strike him. She lived in that time once more, saw those places again, — she was sitting to the famous artist who was portraying her in his clay. Donatella would sing some antique song, and the spirit of the song would animate both the model and the effigy, and her thoughts and the pure voice and the mystery of art almost composed an appearance of divine life in the great studio open to the daylight on all sides, whence Florence and its river could be seen in the spring valley.

What if not the reflection of Sophia had attracted her towards the girl who had been deprived of a mother's caresses from the time of her birth? She called her up to her memory as she had seen her standing grave and firm at her father's side, the comforter of his great work, the guardian of his sacred flame and also of a secret determination of her own that was being preserved like a sword in its sheath, bright and sharp.

"She is sure of herself and mistress of her own strength. When she shall feel herself free to do it, she will reveal herself as one made for dominion. She is made to subject men, to excite their curiosity and their dreams. Her instinct, bold and prudent as experience, is leading her already. . . . And she remembered her attitude towards the young man on that night, her almost disdainful silence, her short, dry words, and the way in which she had risen from the table, left the supper-room, and disappeared for ever, leaving her image framed in the circle of an unforgettable melody. "Ah, she knows the art of disquieting the soul of one who dreams. He cannot certainly have forgotten her. On the contrary, he certainly awaits the hour in which it shall be given him to meet her again as impatiently as she who has asked me where he is."

She took up the letter and began glancing through it, but her memory was swifter than her sight. The enigmatic question, half veiled, was at the bottom of the page like a postscript. On seeing the handwriting again, she went through the same tearing of herself asunder as on first reading it; and again all became upheaval in her heart as if the danger were imminent, as if her passion and her hope were already irreparably lost. "What is she going to do? What is her thought? Did she expect that he would seek her out without delay, and, disappointed in her expectation, does she now think of tempting him? What is she going to do?" She struggled against that uncertainty, as against a spiked door beyond which the light of her life should lie waiting to be reconquered. "Shall I answer? And if I answered in a way that would make her understand the truth, could my love lay a prohibition on hers?" A movement of repugnance, modesty, and pride uplifted her soul. "She shall never, never know of my wound from me; never, even if she should question me." And she grasped all the horror of an open rivalry between the ageing mistress and the maiden strong with the strength of her intact youth. She saw the cruelty and humiliation of the unequal struggle. "But if it were not this one," an opposing spirit urged, "would it not be another? Do you think you can keep a man of his nature to your melancholy passion? There is only one condition on which you should have loved him and offered him your love, faithful until death, and that was the prohibition which you have broken."

"True, true," she murmured, as if she were answering a distinct voice, — a clear judgment pronounced in the silence by invisible destiny.

" There is only one condition on which he will now be able to accept and recognise your love, — the condition that you leave him free, that you renounce possession, that you give up all, always, asking for nothing, always; the condition of being yourself heroic. Do you understand?"

" True, true," she repeated, raising her forehead, all her moral beauty now flashing again on the heights of her soul.

But the poison bit her. Once more all her senses remembered all his caresses, — the lips and hands, the strength and fire of the young man passed into her blood as if they were melting there. And she stayed on, motionless in her malady, dumb in her fever, consumed in her soul and in her flesh, like those red-spotted vine leaves that seemed to burn round the rims like waste paper thrown on the embers.

A distant, changeless song began vibrating on the air, trembling in the immense stupor: a song of women's voices, that seemed to come from broken bosoms, somewhat similar to the sounds awakened from the snapped wires of old spinets at a sudden touch on the worn keys, faint yet shrill, with a bright, vulgar rhythm that was sadder in that light and stillness than the saddest things of life.

" Who is singing?"

With obscure emotion she rose, drew near the shore, strained her ear to listen.

" The mad women of San Clemente!"

From the island of La Follia, from the light, desolate hospital, from the barred windows of the terrible prison, came the bright yet lugubrious chorus. It trembled, hesitated in the ecstatic immensity, became almost childlike, grew fainter, seemed about to die away; then rose up strengthened, shrieked, became almost piercing; then stopped as if all the vocal chords had snapped together; rose once more like a tortured cry, like a call from lost, shipwrecked beings who have seen a ship pass on the horizon, like a clamour of dying creatures; then it dwindled, stopped, did not rise again.

Heart-rending indeed was the sweetness of the late November! It smiled like an invalid over an interruption in his pain, who knows that it is the last, and savours of life, which is revealing its delicacies to him with an act full of new grace while on the point of forsaking him, daily slumber resembles that of a child going to sleep on the knees of death.

"Look at the Euganean hills down there, Foscarina; if the wind rises they will go wandering through the air like veils, they will pass over our heads. I have never seen them so transparent. . . . One day I should like to go with you to Arquà; the villages down there are as rosy as the shells which one finds in the earth in myriads. When we arrive, the first drops of a fine sun shower will be robbing the peach blossoms of a few petals. We will stop under one of the arches of the Palladio to keep dry. Then we will look for the Fountain of Petrarch without asking our way. We will take his Rhymes with us in Missirini's small type, — the little book you keep by your bedside and can no longer close now because

it is swollen with leaves like a doll's herbarium. . . .
Would you like to go to Arquà some spring day?"

She did not answer him, watching only the lips
that said these delicate things and hopelessly enjoying the sound and their motion and nothing else,
in a passing manner. She found the same distant
spell in those images of Spring as in a stanza of
Petrarch's, but she could place a marker near the
one and find it again, while the others were lost with
the hour. She wanted to answer, "I shall not drink
at that fountain," but remained silent that she might
not disturb the caress. "Oh, yes, give me illusions,
illusions! You must play your own game; you must
do with me what you will."

"Here we are at San Giorgio in Alga; we shall be
at Fusina before long."

The little walled island passed them with its marble
Madonna perpetually reflecting herself in the water
like a nymph.

"Why are you so sweet? I have never felt you
like this before. One is out of one's depth with you
to-day. I cannot tell you what a feeling of infinite
melody is in your presence to-day. You are here by
my side, I can take your hand; and yet you are also
diffused in the horizon, you are that horizon itself,
with the waters, with the islands, with the hills that I
would climb. When I was speaking to you a little
while ago, it seemed that each syllable was creating
in you ever widening circles, like the ones round that
leaf there which has just fallen from that golden
tree. . . . It is true? Tell me it is true. Oh, look
at me!"

He felt himself surrounded by the woman's love

by light and air; he breathed in that soul as in an element, receiving an ineffable fulness of life, as if a single stream of mysterious things were flowing from her and from the depths of the day, and pouring itself into his overflowing heart. The desire of returning the happiness which was given him raised him to an almost religious degree of gratitude, suggesting words of thanks and of praise which he would have uttered had he been bending over her in the shadow. But the splendour of sky and water had become so great all around them that he could only be silent as she was silent. It was a moment of marvellous communion in the light for both; it was a journey brief and yet immense during which both compassed the dizzy distances they had within them.

The boat touched the shore of Fusina. They gazed at each other with dazzled eyes; and when their feet touched the ground, when they saw that squalid bank where the grass grew faded and rare, a kind feeling of loss came upon them that was like a disappointment, and both moved unwillingly, feeling in those first steps that weight of their bodies which had seemed to have become lighter during the drive.

"Does he love me, then?"

Suffering and hope revived in the woman's heart. She did not believe the ecstasy of her beloved to be other than sincere; she knew that his words responded to an inward flame. She knew how entirely he abandoned himself to every passing wave that touched his sensibility, how incapable he was of dissimulation or falsehood. She had more than once heard him utter cruel truths with the same feline and flexible grace as that possessed by those men who are given to fascinating. She well knew the direct limpid gaze that sometimes became icy or cutting, that was never otherwise than straight; yet she also knew the marvellous swiftness and diversity of thought and feeling that made his an unseizable spirit. In him there was ever something voluble, fluctuating and powerful that suggested the double and diverse image of flame and of water; and she had hoped to fix him, hold him, possess him. In him there was ever an unlimited ardour of life as if every second seemed the supreme one to him, and he were about to take his leave of the joy and pain of existence, like from the caresses and the tears of a love-parting. And she would have attracted that insatiable avidity to herself as to its only nourishment!

What was she to him, if not an aspect of that "life of the thousand and thousand faces" towards which his desire, according to one of the images of his own poetry, continually shook all its thyrsi? She was a cause of visions and inventions to him, like the hills and the woods and the rain. He drank in mystery and beauty from her as he did from all the forms of the universe. Even now he was already apart from her, already intent on some new quest; his mobile ingenuous eyes were already looking round for the miracle to wonder at and adore.

She glanced at him and he did not turn his face towards her, intent on observing the damp misty country they were slowly driving through. She sat there beside him, deprived of all strength, no longer capable of living in herself and for herself, of breathing with her own breath, of following a thought that should be outside her love, hesitating even in her enjoyment of natural things that were not pointed out by him, needing to wait until he should communicate his sensations and his dreams to her before inclining her aching heart towards that landscape.

Her life seemed to be dissolving and condensing itself at intervals. When the intensity of a second had passed, she would wait for the next one, and between one and the other she would have no perception except that time was flying and the lamp was burning itself out.

"My friend, my friend," said Stelio, suddenly turning and taking one of her hands with an emotion that had risen to his throat little by little and was suffocating him, "why have we come to these places? They seem so sweet, and they are full of terror."

He was looking at her fixedly with the look that from time to time would suddenly appear in his eyes like a tear, — a look that would touch the very secret of another's existence and descend to the uttermost depths of unconsciousness, deep as that of an old man, deep as that of a child, and she trembled under it as if her soul had been one of the tears of his eyes.

"You are suffering?" he asked with a pity full of anguish that turned the woman pale. "You feel this terror?"

She looked round with the anxiety of one pursued. She seemed to see a thousand harmful phantoms rising from the fields.

"Those statues," said Stelio, with an expression in his voice that turned them in her eyes into witnesses of her own decay.

And the landscape spread silently around them as

if all its inhabitants had deserted it for centuries or were all sleeping in new graves dug only yesterday.

"Shall we go back? The boat is still there."

She did not seem to hear.

"Answer me, Foscarina!"

"Let us go on; let us go on," she answered. "Fate cannot change wherever we go."

Her body followed the motion, the slow rolling of the wheels, and she feared to interrupt it, recoiling from the slightest effort, the smallest fatigue, full of a heavy inertness. Her face was like the delicate veil of ashes that covers live coal, hiding its consumption.

"Dear, dear soul!" said her beloved, bending towards her and touching her pale cheek with his lips. "Hold on to me. Give yourself up to me. Be sure of me. I will not fail you, and you will not fail me. We shall find, we must find, the secret truth on which our love may rest for ever, unchanged. Do not shut yourself up from me. Do not suffer alone. Do not try to hide your torment from me! When your heart swells with pain, speak to me. Let me hope that I could comfort you. Let nothing be kept silent between us, and let nothing be hidden. I venture to remind you of a condition that you yourself have made. Speak to me, and I will always answer you truthfully. Suffer me to help you, since so much good comes to me from you. Tell me that you are not afraid of suffering. I believe that your soul is capable of bearing all the pain of the world. Do not let me lose my faith in this, the strength of your passion, by which you have seemed divine to me more than once. Tell me you are not afraid of suffering. . . . I don't know, perhaps I am mistaken. . . . But I have felt a shadow in you, a desperate determination as it were to go away, to draw yourself back, to find some end. . . . Why? Why? And a moment ago, looking at all this terrible desolation which is smiling at us, a great fear suddenly gripped my heart: I thought that perhaps even your love could change like all else, pass away into dissolution. 'You will lose me.' Ah, those words are yours, Foscarina. It is from your lips they fell."

She did not answer, and for the first time since she loved him his words to her seemed vain, useless sounds moving in the air quite powerless. For the first time he himself seemed a weak anxious creature, governed by unbreakable laws. She pitied him as much as herself. He was laying on her the condition of being heroic, a compact of pain and violence. While attempting to comfort and uplift her, he was predicting a difficult test, preparing her for torture. But of what use was courage, of what use was effort, what were all miserable human agitations worth; and why did they ever think of the future, of the uncertain to-morrow? The past alone reigned around them, and they were as nothing, and everything was as nothing. "We are dying; you and I are two dying creatures; let us then dream and then die."

"Be silent!" she said faintly, as if they were passing through a churchyard; and a thin slight smile appeared on the edge of her lips like the smile that was floating over the landscape, and it stopped there motionless as on the lips of a portrait.

The wheels rolled on and on in the white road along the banks of the Brenta. The river, magnified and glorified in the sonnets of gallant abbés at the

time when barges full of music and pleasure slipped
down its current, now had the humble aspect of a
canal, where the blue-green ducks splashed about in
flocks. In the low well-watered plain, the fields were
smoking, the trees rose naked, the leaves rotted in
the moisture of the earthy mounds, the slow golden
vapour floated over an immense vegetable decom-
position that seemed to touch even the walls, the
stones, the houses, and destroy them like the leaves.
From the Foscara to the Barbariga, the patrician
villas, where a life of pale veins, delicately poisoned
by cosmetics and perfumes, had flickered out in
languid games round a beauty spot or a little dog,
were falling into ruins, silent and forsaken. Some
had the appearance of a human ruin, with their
empty apertures that seemed eyeless sockets and
toothless mouths; others at first sight seemed on the
point of crumbling to bits and falling into powder
like the hair of dead women when tombs are uncovered, like moth-eaten garments when cupboards
are opened that have been too long closed; their
boundary walls were knocked down, their columns
broken, their gates contorted, their gardens overrun
with weeds, but here and there, near and far, all over
in the fruit orchards, in the vineyards, among the
silvery cabbages, among the vegetables, among the
pastures, on the heaps of manure and refuse from
the wine-press under the hay-ricks, on the threshold
of hovels and all along the river-side, rose the surviving statues. They were numberless like a dispersed
people. Some still white, some grey or yellow with
lichens or greenish with mosses, or spotted; in all attitudes, with all gestures, Goddesses, Heroes, Nymphs,

Seasons, Hours, with their bow, with their arrows, their garlands, their cornucopias, their torches, with all the emblems of their riches, power, and pleasure, exiled from fountains, grottoes, labyrinths, harbours, porticoes; friends of the evergreen box and myrtle, protectors of passing loves, witnesses of eternal vows, figures of a dream far older than the hands that had formed them and the eyes that had seen them in the ravaged gardens. And in the soft late summer sun their shadows, lengthening little by little over the landscape, were like the shadows of the irrevocable past, of all that which loves no longer, laughs and weeps no longer, will never live, will never return again. And the silent words on their lips of stone were the same as the words spoken by the immovable smile on the lips of the worn-out woman, — NOTHING!

They became acquainted with other fears that day, other shadows.

Henceforth the tragic sense of life filled them both and they strove in vain to overcome the physical sadness which made their spirits become every moment clearer and more disquieted. They held each other's hands as if they had been walking in the dark, or through perilous places. Their words were rare; but now and then they would look into each other's eyes, and the glance of the one would pour a confused wave into the other, which was only the overflowing of their love and horror; and it did not ease their hearts.

"Shall we go on?"

"Yes, let us go on."

They were holding each other's hands tightly as if making some strange experiment, as if they were determined to find out what depths could be reached by the forces of their mingled melancholy. At the Dolo their footsteps crackled on the chestnut leaves which strewed the way; and the great trees that were changing colour flamed upon their heads like crimson hangings on fire. Further off, the Villa Barbariga appeared, lonely, desolate, reddish in its bare garden, bearing traces of old paintings in the fissures of its frontage that were like remains of rouge in the wrinkles of an old woman. And at every glance the distances of the landscape became dimmer and more blue, like things that are being slowly submerged.

"Here is Strà."

They went down to the villa of the Pisani; they entered; they visited the deserted apartments accompanied by the caretaker. They heard the sound of their steps on the marble that mirrored them, the echo in the ornamented arches, the groan of the doors as they were opened and shut, the tedious voice awakening the memories of the place. The rooms were vast, hung with faded stuffs, furnished in the style of the first Empire, bearing the Napoleonic emblems. In one of the rooms the walls were covered with the portraits of the Pisani, procurators of San Marco; in another, with marble medallions of all the doges; in another, with a series of flowers painted in water-colour and mounted in delicate frames, pale as the dried flowers that are put under glass in memory of a love or a death.

In another la Foscarina said as she entered : —

"*With time!* Here too."

There, on a bracket, was a translation into marble of the figure of Francesco Torbido, made more horrible by the subtle study of the sculptor to bring out with his chisel, one by one, the wrinkles, the veins, the hollows. And at the doors of the room there seemed to appear the phantoms of the crowned women who had concealed their decay and their misery in that spacious dwelling that was like a palace and like a monastery.

"Maria Luisa of Parma, in 1817," continued the tedious voice.

And Stelio : —

"Ah, the Queen of Spain, the wife of Charles IV., the mistress of Manuel Godoï! This one attracts me above all the others. She passed by this place at the time of their exile. Do you know whether she stayed here, with the King and the favourite?"

The custodian only knew the name and date.

"Why does she attract you?" asked la Foscarina. "I know nothing about her."

"Her end, the last years of her life as an exile after so much passion and so many struggles are unusually full of poetry."

And he described to her the violent, tenacious figure, the weak, credulous King, the handsome adventurer who had enjoyed the favours of the Queen, and had been dragged through the streets by a furious crowd, the agitation of the three lives bound up by fate and driven like twigs in a whirlwind before the will of Napoleon, the tumult at Aranjuez, the abdication, the exile.

"Godoï then, the Prince of Peace, as the King had called him, faithfully followed the sovereigns into exile; was faithful to his royal mistress and she to him. And they lived together under the same roof always, and Charles never suspected the virtue of Maria Luisa, and lavished his kindness on both lovers until death. Imagine their residence in this place; imagine here such a love having come safely out of so terrible a hurricane. All was snapped, overthrown; all had crumbled to dust under the might of the destroyer. Bonaparte had passed that way and had not suffocated that love, already grey, under the ruins he left behind! The fidelity of these two violent ones touches me as much as the credulity of the gentle King. They grew old in this manner. Think! The Queen died first, then the King; and the favourite, who was younger than they, lived some few years more, a wanderer. . . ."

"This is the Emperor's room," said the custodian, solemnly, throwing open a door. The great shade seemed to be omnipresent; the sign of his power dominated from above all the pale relics collected there. But in the yellow room it occupied the vast bed and stretched itself out under the canopy, between the four posts surmounted by gilded flames. The formidable sigla between the crown of laurels shone upon the bolster; and that kind of funereal couch was prolonged in the dim mirror that hung between the two Victories supporting the candelabra.

"Did the Emperor sleep in this bed?" asked the young man of the custodian who was showing him, on the wall, the effigy of the *condottiere* mantled with ermine, and wreathed with laurel as he appeared at the coronation blessed by Pius VII. "Is it certain?"

He was astonished at not having felt the emotion produced on ambitious hearts by the traces of heroes, the deep throb which he well knew. Perhaps his spirit was stunned by the odour of the shut-up place, the stuffiness of old materials and mattresses, the dulness of the silence where the great name found no echo, whilst the buzzing of a moth persisted so distinctly that he thought he had it in his ear.

He raised the hem of the yellow coverlet and let it fall as quickly as if the pillow beneath it had been full of worms.

"Let us go; let us go out," begged la Foscarina, who had been looking through the windows at the park, where the tawny bands of the slanting sun alternated with half blue, half green zones of shadow. "One cannot breathe here."

The air was like that of a crypt.

"Now we pass into the room of Maximilian of Austria," continued the tedious voice, "who caused his bed to be put in the dressing-room of Amalia Beauharnais."

They crossed the room in a glare of crimson. The sun was beating on a crimson sofa, making rainbows in a frail chandelier with crystal drops that hung from the ceiling, kindling the perpendicular red lines on the wall. Stelio paused on the threshold, calling to life, as he looked back into the blood-like resplendence, the pensive figure of the young blue-eyed archduke, the fair flower of Hapsburg, fallen on barbaric ground one summer morning.

"Let us go," again cried la Foscarina, as she saw he was again delaying.

She was hurrying away across the immense hall which Tiepolo had decorated; behind her, the bronze gate made in shutting a clear sound like the tinkling of a bell that spread itself through the emptiness in long vibrations. She was hurrying away in distress, as if all were about to crash down upon her, and the light were about to fail, and she feared to find herself alone in the dark with those phantoms of misery and death. As he passed through the air set in motion by her flight, between those walls full of relics, behind the famous actress who had simulated the fury of deadly passions, the desperate efforts of will and desire, the violent shock of proud destinies on every stage in the world, Stelio Effrena lost the heat of his veins as if he were moving in a frozen wind; he felt his heart grow icy, his courage fainter; his reason for living lost all strength, his bonds with beings and things loosened; and the magnificent illusions which he had given his soul that it might surpass itself and his destiny trembled and disappeared.

"Are we alive still?" he said, when they found themselves in the open, in the park, far from the grim odour.

And he took the woman by the hands, shook her slightly, looked into the depths of her eyes, tried to smile; then he led her towards the sunshine on the grass of the meadow.

"How warm it is! Do you feel? How good the grass is!"

He half closed his eyes, so that he might feel the

rays upon his eyelids, once more suddenly seized by the joy of life. She imitated him, soothed by her friend's enjoyment, looking from under her eyelids at his fresh, sensual mouth. They remained thus for some time hand in hand, with their feet in the grass under the sun's caresses, feeling the blood in their veins throbbing in the silence as the streams become more rapid when the frost breaks up in spring. Her thoughts went back to the Euganean hills, to the villages rosy as fossil shells, to the first drops of rain falling upon young leaves, to the fountain of Petrarch, to all pleasant things.

"Life could still be sweet," she sighed, and her voice was the miracle of hope being born anew.

The heart of her beloved became like a fruit suddenly ripened and melted by a miraculous ray of warmth. Joy and goodness spread through his spirit and his flesh. Once again he enjoyed the moment like one about to depart. Love was exalted above destiny.

"Do you love me? Tell me."

The woman did not reply; but her eyes opened wide, and all the vastness of the universe was in the circle of her pupils. Never was immense love more powerfully signified by any earthly creature.

"Life is sweet, sweet with you, for you, yesterday as to-morrow!"

He seemed intoxicated with her, with the sun, the grass, the divine sky, as with things never seen before, never possessed. The prisoner going out at dawn from the suffocating prison, the convalescent who sees the sea for the first time after having seen death, are less intoxicated than he was.

"Do you wish to go? Shall we leave melancholy behind us? Shall we go away to countries where there is no autumn?"

"The autumn is in myself, and I must carry it with me wherever I go," she thought, but she smiled her slight, concealing smile. "It is I, I who will go away; I will disappear; I will go and die far away, my love, my love!"

She had not succeeded during that pause in overcoming her sadness, nor in renewing her hope, yet her sorrow had softened, had lost all acrimony, all rancour.

"Shall we go away?"

"To go away, to be always going away, aimlessly through the world, to go far away!" thought the wandering woman. "Never to rest, never to be at peace! The anxiety of the journey is not over, and, see, the truce has expired. You wish to comfort me, dear friend, and in order to comfort me you are proposing that we should go far away again, when I returned home only yesterday!"

Suddenly her eyes became like springs of living water.

"Leave me to my home a little longer. And you, remain if you can. After, you will be free, you will be happy. . . . You have so much time before you! You are young. You will have what is due to you. They who expect you will not lose you."

Her eyes wore two crystal masks, which glittered in the sun in her feverish face.

"Ah, always the same shadow!" exclaimed Stelio, complainingly, with an impatience which he could not control. "But what are you thinking of? What do you fear? Why do you not tell me what is troubling you? Let us talk, then. Who is it that expects me?"

She trembled with apprehension at that question, which appeared new and unforeseen, although her last words were repeated in it. She trembled at finding herself so near danger; a precipice seemed to have opened under her feet as they walked on the beautiful grass.

"Who is it that expects me?"

Suddenly, at the end of the day, in that strange place, on that beautiful meadow, after so many apparitions of spectres, sanguinary and bloodless, there rose up a wilful form alive with desire which filled her with even greater terror. Suddenly, at one stroke, above all those figures of the past there rose a figure which was the future; and the semblance of life was transformed anew, and the benefit of that brief pause was lost already, and the good grass under her feet was henceforth valueless.

"Yes, let us talk, if you wish it. . . . Not now. . . ."

Her throat contracted so that her voice could hardly pass through it, and she held her face a little raised that her eyelids might keep her tears from falling.

"Don't be sad! Don't be sad!" begged the young man, his soul suspended on her lids like those tears that would not fall. "You have my heart in your hands. I will not fail you. Do not torment yourself. I am yours."

Donatella was there for him too tall, with her curved figure, with the agile, robust body of a wingless victory, fully armed with her virginity, attractive and hostile, ready to struggle and to give herself. But his soul hung on the eyelids of this other woman, like the tears that veiled those pupils in which he had seen the immensity of love.

"Foscarina!"

The hot drops fell at last, but she did not let them flow down her cheeks. With one of those gestures that often sprang from her sorrow with the unexpected grace of a wing that is being set free, she stopped them, moistened her fingers with them, and spread them over her temples without drying them. And while she thus left her tears upon herself she tried to smile.

"Forgive me, Stelio, if I am so weak."

Then, desperately, he loved the delicate marks that went from the corners of her eyes to her moistened temples and the small dark veins that made her eyelids like violets and the undulation of her cheeks and the worn chin and all that seemed touched by the malady of autumn, all the shadow of that impassioned face.

"Ah, dear fingers! Beautiful as the fingers of Sophia! Let me kiss them as they are, still wet!"

He was drawing her over the meadow in his caress to a belt of golden green. Lightly, holding his arm under hers, he kissed her finger-tips one by one. They were more delicate than the unopened buds of flowers. She was quivering. He could feel her shudder at each touch of his lips.

"They are salt!"

"Come, Stelio, some one will see us."

"There is nobody here."

"Down there in the greenhouses."

" There is not a sound, listen! "

" How strange the silence is! It is ecstasy! "

" One could hear the falling of a leaf. "

" And that keeper? "

" He must have gone to meet some other visitor. "

" Who would come here? "

" I know that the other day Richard Wagner came with Daniela von Bülow. "

" Ah, the niece of Countess Agoult and of Daniel Stern. "

" With which of these phantoms did the great ailing heart converse? "

" Who knows? "

" Only perhaps with himself. "

" Perhaps. "

" Look at the glass of the conservatories, how it shines. It is irradiated. Time, rain, and sunshine have so painted it. Does it not seem to reflect a distant twilight? Have you ever stopped on the Fondamenta Pesaro and looked up at the beautiful petafore window of the evangelists? If you raised your eyes you could see the windows of the palace marvellously painted by atmospheric vicissitudes. "

" Do you then know all the secrets of Venice? "

" Not all yet. "

" How warm it is here! See how large those cedars are. "

" There is a swallow's nest there hanging on that beam. The swallows have gone away late this year. "

" Will you really take me in spring to the Euganean hills? "

" Yes, Fosca, I should like to. "

" How far away spring is ! "

" Life can still be sweet."

" We are dreaming."

" Orpheus with his lyre, all dressed in lichens."

" Ah, what a pathway of dreams ! Nobody passes us. Grass, grass everywhere. There is not a footstep."

" Deucalion with his stones, Ganymede with the eagle, Diana with the stag, the whole of mythology."

" How many statues ! But these at least are not in exile ; the old hornbeams still enclose them."

" Here Maria Luisa used to stroll between the King and the Favourite. She would stop at intervals, to listen to the click of the shears that were cutting the hornbeams into arches. She would let drop her pocket handkerchief, perfumed with jessamine, and Manuel Godoï would pick it up with a still graceful movement, dissimulating the pain in his hip when he bent down, that had stayed with him as a memento of the tortures suffered in the streets of Aranjuez at the hands of the mob. As the sun was warm and the snuff excellent in its enamelled box, the uncrowned king would say with a smile : ' Ah, dear Bonaparte is certainly not so well off at St. Helena.' But the demon of power, of struggle and of passion, would reawaken in the heart of the Queen. . . . Look at the red roses."

" They are flaming. They seem to have a live coal at the heart. They are flaming really."

" The sun is becoming crimson. This is the hour of the Chioggia sails on the lagoon."

" Pick me a rose ! "

" Here it is ! "

" Oh, its leaves are falling ! "

" Here is another ! "

" Its leaves are falling too."

" They are all at death's door.   Here, perhaps this one is not."

" Do not pick it."

" Look ! they become more and more red.   Bonifazio's velvet. . . . Do you remember?   It is the same strength."

" The inner flower of the flame."

" What a memory ! "

" Hark ! the doors of the conservatory are being shut."

" It is time to turn back."

" The air is already getting cooler."

" Are you cold ? "

" No, not yet."

" Have you left your cloak in the carriage ? "

" Yes."

" We will wait at the Dolo, for the passage of the train.   We will return to Venice by train."

" Yes."

" There is plenty of time still."

" What is this?   Look ! "

" I don't know."

" What a bitter smell !   A shrubbery of box and hornbeams. . . ."

" Ah, it must be the labyrinth."

A rusty iron gate shut it in between two pillars that bore two Cupids riding stone dolphins. Nothing was visible on the other side of the gate, except the beginning of the path and a kind of hard intricate thicket, dense and mysterious. A tower rose from the centre of the maze, and the statue of a warrior stood as if reconnoitring at the top of the tower.

"Have you ever been in a labyrinth?" Stelio inquired of his friend.

"No, never," she answered.

They paused a moment to watch the deceiving game composed by some ingenious gardener for the delight of the ladies and their gallants in the days of hoops and patches, but neglect and age had turned it wild and desolate, had taken from it all prettiness and regularity, had changed it into an enclosed wood brown and yellowish, full of inextricable mazes where the slanting rays of the sunset shone so red that some of the bushes here and there were like burning, smokeless bonfires.

"It is open," said Stelio, feeling the gate yield when he leaned against it. "Do you see?"

He pushed the rusty iron that creaked on the loose hinges, then took one step forward, crossing the threshold.

"What are you doing?" said his companion, with instinctive fear, stretching out her hand to hold him back.

"Shall we not go in?"

She stood perplexed. But the labyrinth attracted them with its mystery, illumined by its deep flame.

"What if we lose ourselves?"

"Don't you see? It is quite small. We shall easily find the way out."

"What if we don't find it?"

He laughed at her childish fear.

"We shall stay in it, wandering round for ever."

"There is nobody in the neighbourhood. No, no, let us go away."

She tried to draw him back. He defended himself, going backwards towards the path. Suddenly he disappeared, laughing.

"Stelio, Stelio!"

She no longer saw him, but she could hear his laugh pealing in the wild maze.

"Come back, come back!"

"Come and find me."

"Stelio, come back! You will lose yourself."

"I shall find Ariadne."

She felt her heart leap at that name, then contract, suffering confusedly. Had he not called Donatella by that name on that first evening? Had he not called her Ariadne, there on the water, while sitting at her knee? She even remembered the words: "Ariadne possesses a divine gift by which her power transcends all limits." She remembered his accent, his attitude, his look.

Tumultuous anguish convulsed her, dimmed her reason, prevented her from considering the chance spontaneity of the present occasion, from recognising her friend's unconsciousness. The terror that lay hidden at the bottom of her desperate love rebelled, mastered her, blinded her miserably. The little vain accident took on an appearance of cruelty and disdain. She could still hear that laugh pealing in the wild maze.

"Stelio!"

She cried out to him as if she had seen him in the act of being embraced by the other woman, as if she

had seen him in a frenzied hallucination, torn from
her arms for ever.

"Stelio!"

"Look for me," he answered laughing, invisible.

She darted into the labyrinth to find him and went
straight towards his voice and laugh, carried away
by her impulse. But the path deviated. A blind box
wall rose up before her, impenetrable, and stopped
her. She followed the crooked, deceiving path, and
one turning succeeded the other and all were alike,
and the circle seemed to have no end.

"Look for me!" the voice repeated from afar
across the living hedges.

"Where are you? Where are you? Do you see
me?"

She looked here and there for some thinner place
in the hedge through which she could see. All she
could perceive was the thick tissue of the branches
and the redness of evening that kindled them on
one side, while the shadows drowned them on the
other. The box bushes and the hornbeams mingled,
the evergreen leaves grew in confusion together with
the dying ones, the darker with the paler, in a
contrast of vigour and languor, with an ambiguity
that increased the bewilderment of the panting
woman.

"I am losing myself. Come and meet me!"

Again his youthful laughter pealed in the thicket.

"Ariadne, Ariadne, the thread!"

The sound now came from the opposite side,
wounding her in the spine like a blow.

"Ariadne!"

She turned, ran, wandered, tried to penetrate the

hedge, to make an opening in the foliage, broke away
a branch.

She saw nothing, except the regular ever-renewed
maze. At last she heard a step, so near her that she
thought it was behind her and started. But she was
mistaken. Again she explored the leafy prison,
whence there was no return, that was closing round
her; listened, waited; she heard her own panting and
the throb of her own pulses. The silence had become
vast. She gazed at the sky, curving immense and
pure over the two leafy walls that imprisoned her. It
seemed as if there were nothing in the world beyond
that narrowness and that immensity. And she could
not succeed in separating in her thoughts the reality
of the place from the image of her soul's torture, the
natural aspect of things from that kind of living
allegory created by her own anguish.

"Stelio! Where are you?"

No answer came. She listened. She waited in
vain. The seconds seemed hours.

"Where are you? I am frightened."

No answer came. Where had he gone? Had he
perhaps found the way out; had he left her there
alone? Was he going to continue his cruel game?

A furious longing to shriek, to sob, to throw herself on the ground, to struggle there and hurt herself
and die, seized the maddened woman. She again
raised her eyes towards the silent sky. The summit
of the great hedges were reddening like burnt vine
branches that have ceased to flare up and are about
to become ashes.

"I can see you," suddenly said the laughing voice,
in the low shadows, quite close to her.

She started violently, bent down in the shadow.

"Where are you?"

He laughed among the leaves without showing himself, like a faun in ambush. The game excited him and warmed his limbs that were stretching themselves in his exercise of dexterity; and the wild mystery, the contact with the earth, the odour of autumn, the singularity of the unforeseen adventure, the woman's bewilderment, the very presence of the stone deities, poured into his physical pleasure an illusion of antique poetry.

"Where are you? Oh, do not joke any more. Do not laugh so. It is enough now."

He had crept into the bush on his hands and knees, his head uncovered. Under his knees he felt the decaying leaves, the soft moss. And as he breathed and throbbed in the branches, letting that pleasure absorb all his senses, the communion of his own life with the life of the trees became closer, and the spell of his imagination renewed in that gathering of uncertain ways the industry of the first maker of wings, the myth of the monster which was born of Pasiphaë and the Bull, the Attic fable of Theseus in Crete. The whole of that world became real to him, he was being transfigured on that purple evening in autumn according to the instincts of his blood and the memories of his intellect, into one of those amphibious forms, half beast, half divinity, into one of those silvern genii whose throat is swollen with the same glands that hang suspended from the neck of the goat. A laughing voluptuousness suggested strange attitudes and gestures to him, surprising and whimsical, figured to him the joy of a chase, of a rapid union on the moss or against the uncultured box. Then he desired a creature that should be like him, a fresh bosom to which he might communicate his laughter, two swift legs, two arms ready for a struggle, a prey to conquer, a virginity to force, a violence to accomplish. The curved form of Donatella reappeared to him.

"Enough! I can go on no longer, Stelio. I shall let myself fall to the ground."

La Foscarina gave a scream on feeling the hem of her dress pulled by a hand that had passed through the bush. She bent down and perceived in the shadow among the branches the face of a laughing faun. That laugh flashed on her soul without moving it, without breaking the horrible suffering that had closed round her. On the contrary she suffered all the more acutely from the contrast between his merriment and her sadness, between that joy which was ever new and her perpetual anxiety, between that easy oblivion and the weight of her encumbrance. She saw her error more clearly and she saw the cruelty of life that was placing the image of the other woman there where she herself was suffering. As she bent down, as she saw his youthful face, she saw with the same clearness the face of the singer who was bending down with her imitating her gesture as the shadow repeats a gesture on an illuminated wall. All grew confused in her spirit and her thoughts were unable to place an interval between that image and reality. The other woman placed herself upon her, oppressing her, suppressing her.

"Leave me! Leave me! It is not me you are seeking. . . ."

The voice was so changed that Stelio stopped his laugh and his game, drew back his arm, rose up straight. She saw him no more, the impenetrable leafy wall was between them.

"Lead me away from this. I can hold up no longer; my strength is spent. . . . I am suffering!"

He could find no words with which to soothe her and comfort her. The simultaneous coincidence of his recent desire and her sudden divination had struck home.

"Wait, wait a moment! I will try to find the way out. I will call some one. . . ."

"Are you going away?"

"Don't be afraid! Don't be afraid! There is no danger."

And while he spoke thus to reassure her he was feeling the inanity of his words — the discord between that laughable adventure and the obscure emotion arising from a far different cause. And now he too felt the strange ambiguity by which the small event was appearing in two confused aspects: a suppressed desire of laughter persisting under his solicitude so that his suffering was new to him, like certain agitations born of extravagant dreams.

"Don't go away," she begged, a prey to her hallucination. "Perhaps we shall meet there at the next turning. Let us try. Take me by the hands."

Through one of the open spaces he took her hands and found them so cold that he started as he touched them.

"Foscarina, what is the matter? Do you really feel unwell? Wait! I will try to break through the hedge."

He tried to force through the thicket, snapped some of its branches but its robustness resisted his efforts. He wounded his hands in vain.

"It is not possible."

"Cry out. Call some one."

He called out in the silence. The summit of the high hedges had lost its colour, but in the sky above them a red light was spreading that was like the reflection of woods on fire on the horizon. A flock of wild ducks passed, arranged in a black triangle, stretching out their long necks.

"Let me go! I shall easily find the tower. And from the tower I can call. Some one will hear my cries."

"No, no!"

She heard him go away from her, followed the sound of his steps, was once more engaged in the maze, once more found herself alone and lost. She stopped, waited, listened. She looked at the sky, saw the triangular flock disappear in the distance. She lost the sense of time, the seconds seemed hours.

"Stelio! Stelio!"

She was no longer capable of an effort to dominate the disorder of her exasperated nerves. She felt the extreme access of her mania coming on as one would feel a hurricane that is drawing near.

"Stelio!"

He heard the voice full of anguish and hastened his search along the winding paths that now drew him near to the tower and now drew him away from it. His laugh had frozen in his heart. His whole soul trembled to the roots, every time his name reached him, pronounced by that invisible agony.

And the gradual lessening of the light brought up to his imagination the thought of blood that is flowing away, of life that is slowly fading.

"Here I am! Here I am!"

One of the paths brought him at last to the open space where the tower was built. He ran furiously up the winding staircase, felt a dizziness overtake him when he reached the top, closed his eyes holding on to the banisters, opened them again, saw a long zone of fire on the horizon, the disc of the rayless moon, the plain that was like a grey marsh, the labyrinth beneath him black with box bushes and spotted with hornbeam, quite narrow in its interminable folds, looking like a dismantled edifice invaded by wild vines, like a ruin and a wood, lugubrious and wild.

"Stop! Stop! Do not run like that. Some one has heard me. A man is coming. I can see him coming. Wait! Stop!"

He saw the woman running round like a mad thing along the blind uncertain paths, like a creature condemned to some vain torment, to some useless but eternal agitation, like a sister of the mythical martyrs.

"Stop!"

It seemed that she did not hear him, or that she could not stop her fatal agitation, and that he was tied down and could not rescue her, but was to remain a witness of that terrible chastisement.

"Here he is!"

One of the keepers had heard their cries, had drawn near, was coming through the gate. Stelio met him at the foot of the tower. Together they went out to seek the lost woman. The man knew the secret of the labyrinth. Stelio prevented his chatter and his display of wit by surprising him with his generosity.

"Has she lost consciousness? Has she fallen?" The shadow and silence were very sinister and filled him with dismay. When he called her she did not answer. Her steps could not be heard. Night had already descended over the place under a damp veil of mist that was slowly dropping from the purple sky. "Shall I find her stretched out, fainting, on the ground?"

He started on suddenly seeing a mysterious figure appear at a turning with a pale face that attracted all the twilight and shone like a pearl with large fixed eyes and tight stiff lips. They turned back towards the Dolo, taking the same way along the Brenta. She never spoke, never opened her mouth, never answered, as if she could not unclose her teeth, stretched out in the bottom of the carriage wrapped in her mantle up to her chin, shaken now and then by strong shudders, suffused with a livid pallor like that of malarial fever. Her friend tried to take her fingers and hold them in his own to warm them, but in vain: they were inert and seemed lifeless. And as they went the statues passed and passed on beside them.

The river flowed darkly between its banks under the violet and silver sky where the full moon was rising. A black boat was coming down stream, towed by two grey horses that trod the grass on the tow-path with a dull thud of heavy hoofs, led by a man who whistled peacefully, and the funnel smoked on the deck like a chimney-pot on the roof of a hovel, and the yellow light of a lantern flared in the hold and the odour of an evening meal spread through the air and here and there, as they went through the irrigated landscape, the statues passed and passed beside them.

It was like a Stygian plain, like a vision of Hades: a land of shadows, mist, and water. All things grew misty and vanished like spirits. The moon enchanted and attracted the plain as it enchants and attracts the sea, drinking in the vapours of earth from the horizon with insatiable, silent greed. Solitary pools shone everywhere, small silvery canals between rows of inclined willows could be seen glittering at indefinite distances. Earth seemed to be losing its solidity little by little, seemed to dissolve; the sky seemed to watch its own melancholy reflected on it in innumerable quiet mirrors. And here and there along the discoloured shore, like the shadows of a destroyed population, those statues passed and passed beside them.

" Do you often think of Donatella Arvale, Stelio?" la Foscarina asked suddenly, after a long interval in which both had heard nothing but the cadence of their own steps along the canal footpath of the Vetrai illumined by the manifold light of the frail things that filled the windows of the neighbouring shops.

Her voice was like a glass that is cracking. Stelio stopped suddenly in the attitude of one who suddenly finds himself before an unforeseen difficulty. His spirit had been wandering freely over the red and green island of Murano, begemmed with flowers in her present disconsolate poverty, in which she seemed to have lost even the memory of the joyous times in which poets had sung her praises as "a place fit for nymphs and demigods." He had been thinking of the illustrious gardens where Andrea Navagero, Bembo, Aretino, Aldo, in their learned assembly rivalled each other in the elegance of their platonic dialogues, *lauri sub umbra*. He had been thinking of convents luxurious as *gynaecus* inhabited by nuns dressed in white camelot and laces, their brows adorned with curls, their breasts uncovered after the manner of the more honoured courtesans, given to secret loves, much sought after by licentious patricians, the possessors of sweet names such as Ancilla Soranzo, Cipriana Morosini, Zanetta Balbi, Beatrice Falier, Eugenia Muschiera, pious teachers of pleasures. His fluctuating dream had been accompanied by an aria which he had heard in the museum slowly moaning in sonorous drops from a small metallic instrument set in movement by the turn of a key hidden under a garden of glass where two lovers adorned with glass beads danced round a little fountain of white agate. It was an indistinct melody, a forgotten dance tune; most of its notes were silent through dust and damage, yet so expressive that he had been unable to drive it away from his ears. And since, all around him had had the remote frailty and melancholy of those little figures dancing to sounds slower than falling drops. The faint soul of Murano has chattered in that old pastime.

At the sudden question the aria had stopped, the figures had dispersed, the spell of far-away life had vanished. His wandering spirit was called back and contracted unwillingly. By his side Stelio felt the beating of a living heart that he must inevitably wound. He turned to look at his friend. She was walking, almost calm, with no trace of agitation, along the canal between the green of the sickly water and the iridescence of the delicate vases. The only thing about her that trembled slightly was her attenuated chin just showing between the sable collar and the border of her veil.

"Yes, sometimes," he answered, after a moment's hesitation, incapable of falsehood, and feeling the necessity of raising their love above ordinary exactions and deceptions in order that it might remain a cause of strength to him and not of weakness, a free compact and not a burdensome tie.

The woman went on steadily, but she had entirely lost the sensation of her various limbs in the terrible beating of her heart that ran from neck to heels as on a single cord. She saw nothing; all she felt was the fascinating presence of the water by her side.

"Her voice cannot be forgotten," he said after a pause, gathering up his courage. "Its power is extraordinary. From the very first evening, I thought that she might be made a marvellous instrument of my work. I wish she would consent to sing the lyric parts of my tragedy, the odes that arise from the symphonies and resolve themselves into dance-figures at the end between one episode and the other. La Tanagra has consented to dance. I rely on your kind intervention, my friend, in order to obtain the consent of Donatella Arvale. The Dionysian Trinity would thus be reconstructed in a perfect manner on the new stage, for man's greater joy. . . ."

He noticed as he spoke that his words did not ring true, that his unconcerned manner contrasted too sharply with the deadly shadow on the veiled face of his mistress. Against his will he had exaggerated his frankness in considering the singer merely as an artistic instrument, as a purely ideal force to be attracted into the circle of his magnificent enterprise. Unwillingly disturbed by the suffering that walked beside him, he had stooped ever so slightly towards dissimulation. Certainly what he had said was the truth, but his mistress had asked him for another truth. He interrupted himself brusquely, unable to tolerate the sound of his own words. He felt that art in that hour had no resonance whatever between him and the actress, no living value. They were dominated by another more imperious, more turbid force. The world which intellects create seemed inert like the old stones they were treading. The only truthful and formidable power was the poison running in their human blood. The will of the one was saying: " I love you, and I want you all, body and soul, for my own." The will of the other was saying: " You shall love me and you shall serve me, but I can renounce nothing in life that excites my desire." The struggle was unequal and atrocious.

As the woman was silent, involuntarily quickening her pace, he faced the other truth.

" I quite understand that this is not what you wanted to know. . . ."

" Yes, it was not that ! Well ? "

She turned to him with a kind of spasmodic violence that reminded him of her fury one distant evening and of the mad cry: "Go! Run! She is waiting for you!" On that tranquil path between the lazy water and the frail crystals, in the quiet little island, the face of danger flashed before him.

But an importunate stranger crossed the path, offering to lead them to the neighbouring furnace.

"Let us go in! Let us go in!" said the woman, following the man and penetrating into the passage as in a refuge to avoid the shame of the open street, the profane daylight shining on her ruin.

The place was damp, spotted with sea-salt, smelling of salt like a cave. They passed through a courtyard full of firewood, passed through a decrepit door, reached the furnace, found themselves wrapped round with its fiery breath, before a great incandescent altar that imparted a painful tingling to their eyes as if the lashes had suddenly caught fire.

"To disappear, to be swallowed up, to leave no trace!" roared the woman's heart, intoxicated with a desire of destruction. "That fire could devour me in an instant like a dried stick, like a bundle of straw." And she drew near to the open mouths, whence she could watch the fluent flames, more splendid than a summer noon, surrounding the earthenware vases in which the formless mineral was being melted; the workmen disposed all round were waiting to approach with an iron tube to shape it with a breath of their lips and the instruments of their art.

"Oh, Virtue of the Flame!" thought the Life-giver, beguiled from his anxiety by the miraculous beauty of the element that had become familiar to

him as a brother from the day in which he had felt
the revealing melody. "Ah, that I might give to the
life of the creatures who love me the perfection of the
forms to which I aspire! That I might fuse all their
weaknesses in some white heat, and make of it an
obedient matter in which to impress the command-
ments of my will, which is heroic, and the images of
my poetry, which is pure. Why, why, my friend, will
you not be the divine, mobile statue of my spirit, the
work of faith and of sorrow by which our lives might
surpass our art itself? Why are we on the point of
resembling those small lovers who curse and lament?
I had truly thought that you could have given me
more than love when I heard from your lips those
admirable words: 'One thing I can do, which even
love cannot do.' You must ever be able to accomplish those things which love can, and those things
which love cannot do in order to equal my insatiable
nature."

Meanwhile, the work of the furnace was proceeding
fervently. At the end of the blowing irons, the molten
glass swelled, twisted, became silvery as a little cloud,
shone like the moon, crackled, divided into a thousand infinitely fine fragments, glittering, slighter than
the threads which we see in the forest at dawn
stretching from branch to branch. The workmen
were shaping harmonious vases, each as he operated
obeying a rhythm of his own, generated by the quality
of the matter and by the habit of movements most apt
to dominate it. The apprentices would place a small
pear-shaped mass of burning paste on the spot
pointed out by the master, and the mass would
lengthen out, twist, transform itself into a handle, a

rim, a spout, a foot, or a stem. The red heat would slowly die out under the instruments, and the half-formed chalice would again be exposed to the flame, and be drawn from it docile, ductile, sensitive to the slightest touches that adorned and refined it, conforming it to the model handed down by their fathers, or to the free invention of the new creator. The human gestures round those elegant creatures of fire, breath and iron, were extraordinarily nimble and light, like the gestures of a silent dance. The figure of la Tanagra appeared to the Life-giver like a salamander in the perpetual undulation of the flame. And the powerful melody was sung to him by the voice of Donatella.

"To-day, again, I myself have given her to you as a companion," la Foscarina was thinking. "I myself have called her up between us, have recalled her while your thoughts were perhaps elsewhere, have suddenly left her before you, as in that night's delirium."

It was true, it was true! From the instant in which the name of the singer had echoed against the armour of the man-of-war, pronounced for the first time by her friend in the shadow made by the flank of the armed giant on the twilight waters — from that instant she had unconsciously exalted the new image in his spirit, had fed it with her very jealousy, with her very fear, had strengthened and magnified it daily, had at last illumined it with certainty. More than once she had repeated to him who had perhaps forgotten: "She is waiting for you!" More than once she had presented that distant mysterious expectancy to his perhaps careless imagination. As in that Dionysian night when the conflagration of Venice had lit up the two young faces with one same reflection, it was now her passion that kindled them, and they only burned because she chose that she should burn. " Certainly," she was thinking, " he now possesses that image and is possessed by it. My very anguish excites his desire. It gives him joy to love her under the eyes of my despair. . . ." And her torture was nameless, and because it was her own love that had fed the love that was killing her, she felt her own ardour encircling it like a necessary atmosphere, without which perhaps it could not have lived.

" As soon as it is formed the vase is put in the furnace room to be tempered," one of the master glaziers answered Stelio, who had questioned him. " It would break into a thousand fragments, if it were all at once exposed to the air."

They could see the shining vases, still the slaves of the flame, still under its dominion, gathered together in a receptacle that prolonged the furnace where they had been fused.

" They have already been there for ten hours," said the glazier, pointing to his graceful family. Later the delicate, beautiful creatures would abandon their father and be separated from him for ever, would grow cold and become icy gems, would live their own new life in the world, would subject themselves to voluptuous men, would go out to meet danger, would follow the variations of light, holding the cut flower or the intoxicating wine.

" Is it our great Foscarina?" the small, red-eyed man asked of Stelio in a low voice.

He had recognised her, when, suffocating, she had raised her veil.

Trembling with ingenuous emotion, the master glazier took one step towards her and bowed humbly.

" One evening, mistress, you have made me tremble and cry like a child. Will you allow me, in memory of that evening, which I can never forget as long
as I live, to offer you a little work made by the hands
of the poor Seguso? "

" A Seguso," exclaimed Stelio Effrena, bending
quickly towards the little man to look him in the face
— " of the great family of glaziers, a pure one of the
genuine race? "

" At your service, master."

" A prince, then? "

" Yes. A harlequin shamming as prince."

" You know all the secrets, then? "

The man of Murano made a mysterious gesture
that conjured up all the deep ancestral knowledge
of which he had declared himself the last heir.

The other glaziers smiled round the furnace, interrupting their work while the glass at the end of
their irons changed colour.

" Then, mistress, you will deign to accept? "

He seemed to have stepped from a panel of
Bartolomeo Vivarini, to be the brother of one of the
faithful ones kneeling under the mantle of the Virgin
in Santa Maria Formosa: thin, bent, dried up, as if
refined by fire, frail as if his skin covered a framework of glass, with thin grey hanging curls, a thin
rigid nose, sharp chin, two thin lips from the corners
of which there started the wrinkles of wit and
attention, two flexible prudent hands, reddened by
scars where they had been burnt, expressive of
dexterity and precision, accustomed to gestures

leading beautiful lines in sensitive matter, true instruments of delicate art made perfect in the last heir by the uninterrupted practice of so many laborious generations.

"Yes, you are a Seguso," said Stelio Effrena, who had examined all this, "the proof of your nobility is in your hands."

The glazier gazed at them smiling, stretching them out flat.

"You should bequeathe them in your will to the museum of Murano, together with your blowing-pipe."

"Yes, indeed, for them to be preserved like the heart of Canova and the morello cherries of Padova."

The frank laugh of the workmen ran round the forge and the unformed vases trembled at the end of the irons, half rosy and bluish like clusters of hydrangea about to change colour.

"But the decisive proof will be in your glass. Let us see!"

La Foscarina had not spoken, fearing the unsteadiness of her voice; but all her graceful sweetness suddenly reappearing above the edge of her sadness had accepted the gift and compensated the giver.

"Let us see, Seguso."

The little man scratched his perspiring temple with an air of perplexity, divining the expert.

"Perhaps I can guess," added Stelio Effrena, drawing near the crucible chamber and throwing a glance of election on the vases gathered there. "If it be that one. . . ."

Behold with his presence he had brought an

unusual animation in the midst of a daily labour, the bright ardour of the game that he perpetually unfolded through life. All those simple souls, after having smiled, passionately awaited the test, awaited his choice with the curious anxiety with which one awaits the result of a bet, soliciting a comparison between the subtlety of the master and that of the judge. And the young unknown man who moved in their laboratory as in a familiar place, equalling himself to the men and the things around him with such rapid and spontaneous sympathy, was no longer a stranger to them.

" If it be that one. . . ."

La Foscarina was attracted by the game and almost forced to unbend, suddenly emptied of all bitterness and rancour before her friend's happiness. There too and without effort he had kindled a fugitive moment with beauty and passion, communicated to his companions the fervour of his vitality, raised the spirits he had met to a superior sphere, reawakened in those degenerate artisans the ancient pride in their art. In few moments the harmony of a pure line had become the centre of their world. And the Life-giver was bending over the grouped vases as if the fortune of the little hesitating glazier depended on his choice.

" Yes, it is quite true. You alone know how to live," she was telling him tenderly. " It is necessary that you should have all. I shall rest content with seeing you live, with seeing your pleasure. And do with me what you will."

She smiled as she annihilated herself. She belonged to him, like a thing that can be held in a

clenched hand, like the ring on a finger, like a
garment, like a word that can be spoken or held back,
like a wine that can be drunk or spilt on the ground.

"Well, Seguso?" exclaimed Stelio Effrena, growing impatient at his prolonged hesitation.

The man looked him in the face, then growing
bolder, trusted to his inborn instinct. Five vases,
among many others, had come from his own hands.
One could distinguish them, as if they had belonged
to a different species; but which of the five was the
most beautiful?

The workmen had their faces turned to him while
they exposed the vases fixed on their pipes to the
flames lest they should grow cold. And the flames,
clear as the flame from the crisp laurel leaf, swayed
in the furnace, seeming to keep those men chained
there with the irons of their art.

"Yes, yes," cried Stelio Effrena, as he saw the
master glazier pick out the chosen vase with infinite
care. "Blood cannot speak false, the gift is worthy
of the *Dogaressa* Foscarina, Seguso."

The Muranese holding the stem of the chalice
between his finger and thumb stood smiling before
the woman, illumined by the warm praise. His sharp
sagacious look put one in mind of the little golden
fox on the cock's tail in the blazon of Murano; the
eyelids, reddened by the violent glare of his furnace,
twinkled over the eyes that were turned to the frail
work still glittering in his hand before going away,
and his almost caressing fingers and his whole attitude
revealed the hereditary faculty of feeling the difficult
beauty of simple lines and extremely delicate colour-
ings. The chalice held by the bent man who had

created it was like one of those miraculous flowers that blossom on thin contorted shrubs.

It was indeed beautiful, mysterious as natural things are mysterious, holding the life of a human breath in its hollow, its transparency emulating skies and waters, similar in its purple rim to a seaweed wandering on the ocean; pure, simple, with no other ornament but that rim, no other limbs but its foot, its stem and its lip; and no man could have told why it was so beautiful, not with one word nor with a thousand. And its value was either none or incalculable, according to the quality of the eye that gazed upon it.

" It will break," said Stelio.

La Foscarina had chosen to take her gift with her without having it wrapped up, like one carries a flower.

" I will take my glove off."

She stood the goblet on the edge of the well that rose in the centre of the green. The rust of the weather-cock, the worn façade of the basilica with its Byzantine remains, the red brick of the belfry, the gold of the hayrick beyond the wall and the bronze colour of the high laurels and the faces of the women threading glass beads on the doorsteps, and the grass and the clouds and all the surrounding appearances there varied the sensibility of the luminous glass. All colours melted into its own colour. And it seemed to be living a manifold life in its frailty, like an animated rainbow in which the universe mirrors itself.

" Imagine the sum of experience which has gone to the production of this beautiful thing," said Stelio, in his wonder. " All the generations of the Seguso

contributed across the centuries with their breath
and touch to the birth of this creature, in the happy
instant in which that little unconscious glazier was
enabled to follow the remote impulse and transmit it
with precision to inert matter. The fire was equal,
the paste was rich, the air was tempered; all things
were favourable. The miracle took place."

La Foscarina held the stem of the chalice between
her naked fingers.

"If it were to break, we should raise up a mausoleum to it as Nero did to the shades of his broken
cup. Oh, the love of things. Another despot,
Xerxes, has preceded you, my friend, in adorning a
beautiful tree with necklaces."

There was on her lips below the edge of her veil a
barely visible but continual smile; and he knew that
smile through having suffered from it on the banks of
the Brenta, in the fields haunted by the statues.

"Gardens, gardens; gardens everywhere. Once
they were the most beautiful in the world, earthly
paradises as Andrea Calmo calls them, dedicated to
love, music, and poetry. Perhaps one of those old
laurels has heard Aldo Manuzio conversing in Greek
with the Navagero or Madonna Gasparina sighing
in the footsteps of the Conte di Collalto. . . ."

They were going along a road that was shut in
by the walls of desolate gardens. At the summit of
the walls, in the interstices of the blood-red bricks,
strange grasses trembled, long and stiff as fingers.
The bronze-like laurels were gilded at the tips by the
declining sun. The air seemed filled with a kind of
glittering gold-dust.

"How sweet and terrible was the fate of Gaspara

Stampa! Do you know her rhymes? I saw ther.
one day on your table. What a mixture of ice and
fire! Now and then her deadly passion, across the
petrarchism of Cardinal Bembo, gives out some fine
cry. I know a magnificent verse of hers: —

> "' Vivere ardendo e non sentire il male!'" [1]

"Do you remember, Stelio," said la Foscarina, with
that inextinguishable smile that gave her the appearance of one walking in her sleep, — "do you remember
the sonnet that begins:

> "' Signore, io so che in me non son più viva,
>   E veggo omai ch' ancor in voi son morta'?..." [2]

"I don't remember, Fosca."

"Do you remember your own beautiful image of
dead summer? Summer was lying in the funeral
boat dressed in gold like a dogaressa and the procession was leading her to the island of Murano where
a Lord of Fire was to enclose her in a veil of opalescent glass so that when submerged in the lagoon she
could at least watch the sea-weed's undulations. . . .
Do you remember?"

"It was an evening in September."

"The last of September, the evening of the Allegory. There was a great light on the water. . . .
You were a little excited: you talked on and on. . . .
How many things you said! You had just come
from solitude and you were full to overflowing. You
poured a stream of poetry over your friend. There
passed a boat laden with pomegranates. I was called
Perdita then. . . . Do you remember?"

---

[1] "To live consumed by fire and not to feel the pain!"
[2] "My lord, I know that I live no more in me,
    And I see henceforth that in you too I die."

She herself, as she walked, felt the extreme elasticity of her step, felt that something was disappearing in her as if her body were about to change into an empty chrysalis. The sensations of her own physical person seemed to depend on the glass she was carrying, seemed only to exist in the anxiety caused by its frailty and the fear of letting it fall, while her bare hand little by little became colder, and her veins changed to the colour of the violet edge running round the lip of the goblet.

"My name was still Perdita. . . . Have you in mind, Stelio, another sonnet of Gaspara's that begins:

> "'Io vorrei pur che Amor dicesse come
> Debbo seguirlo'? . . . [1]

And the madrigal that begins:

> "'Se tu credi piacere al mio signore'? . . ." [2]

"I did not know you to be so familiar with the poor Anassilla, my friend."

"Ah, I will tell you. . . . I was barely fourteen years old when I acted in an old romantic tragedy called Gaspara Stampa. I was doing the leading part. . . . It was at Dolo where we passed the other day on our way to Strà. It was in a small country theatre in a kind of tent. . . . It was a year before my mother died. . . . I remember quite well. . . . I can remember certain things as if they had happened yesterday, — and twenty years have passed. I can remember the sound of my voice, which was weak then, when I forced it in the tirades because some one in

---

[1] "I would that Love would also say
    How I should follow him."
[2] "If you think to please my lord."

the wings was whispering to me to speak louder, still
louder. . . . Gaspara was in despair, sorrowed, raved
for her cruel Count. . . . There were so many things
that I did not know, that my small, profaned soul did
not understand, and I know not what instinct of sorrow led me to find the accent and the cries that were
to shake the miserable crowd from which we expected
our daily bread. Ten starving people tortured me,
like an instrument of gain; brutal necessity was cutting and tearing away from me all the dream flowers
born of my trembling precocity. It was a time of
weeping and suffocation, of dismays, of uneasy fatigue,
of reserved horror. Those who made my martyrdom
did not know what they were doing, poor things,
blunted by poverty and weariness. God forgive
them and let them rest. Only my mother who, she
also, Stelio,

> " 'Per amar molto ed esser poco amata
> Visse e morì infelice,' [1]

only my mother took pity on me and suffered from
the same torment as myself and knew how to hold
me in her arms, how to calm my horrible trembling,
how to weep with me and comfort me. My blessed,
blessed one ! "

Her voice changed. The eyes of her mother once
more opened within her, kind and firm and infinite as
an horizon of peace. " You must tell me, you must
tell me what I should do. Guide me, teach me, you
who know." Her soul felt the clasp of those arms and
from the distance of years the pain flowed back to
her in all its fulness, but not harsh, having turned

---

[1] " For having loved too well and been too little loved,
Sorrowing lived and died "

almost sweet. The memory of her struggle and of her sufferings seemed to moisten her soul with a warm flood, upraise and comfort it. On what anvils had the iron of her will not been forged, in what waters had it not been tempered? The test had indeed been hard for her and the victory difficult, bought at the price of labour and perseverance, bought from brute forces that had been hostile. She had witnessed the darkest poverties and sombre ruin, she had known heroic efforts, pity, horror, and the threshold of death.

"I know what hunger is, Stelio, and what the approach of night is when a refuge is uncertain," she said softly, stopping between the two walls. And she raised her veil towards her forehead, looking into her friend's face with her free eyes.

He grew pale under those eyes, so sudden was his emotion, so great his dismay at the appearance of that unexpected attitude. He found himself confused as in the incoherence of a dream, incapable of connecting that extraordinary apparition with the recent traces of life, incapable of putting the meaning of those words on that same woman who was smiling to him, still holding the delicate glass in her naked fingers. Yet he had heard what she had said, and she was there before him in her great sable cape with the softness still about her of the beautiful eyes that lengthened out under the eyelashes misty as if a tear continually rose into them, and melted unshed, there before him in the solitary path between the two walls.

"And there are other things that I have known."

It did her good to speak in this way. His humility

seemed to give her heart strength like the most daring act of pride. She had never felt the consciousness of her dominion and her worldly glory exalt her before the man she loved, but now the memory of her obscure martyrdom, of her poverty and hunger, created in her a feeling of true superiority over him whom she believed invincible. As along the banks of the Brenta his words had seemed vain for the first time, thus for the first time she felt herself in her experience of life stronger than him whom all good fortune had protected from his cradle and who had not suffered except from the fury of his desires and the anxieties of his ambition. She imagined him grappling with necessity, forced to labour like the slave, oppressed by material narrownesses, subject to vile discomforts. Would he have found the energy to resist, the patience to endure? Under the sharp pinch of necessity, she pictured him weak and lost, humbled and broken. "Ah, all bright superb things are for you as long as you live, as long as you live." She could not bear the sadness of that image and rejected it with an almost maternal impulse of defence and protection. And by an involuntary movement she laid one hand on his shoulder, drew it back when he noticed, then placed it there again. She smiled like one who knows what he should never know, like one who has won victory over things that he could never have conquered. She heard within herself the words heavy with the terrible promise: "Tell me you are not afraid of suffering. . . I believe your soul to be capable of bearing all the sorrow of the world." Her eyelids, that were like violets, dropped over her secret pride, but an infinitely subtle, com-

plex beauty appeared in the lines of her face, a beauty
that was shed by a new concordance of inner forces,
by a mysterious direction of her reawakened will; in
the shadow that descended from the folds of her
veil gathered up round her eyelashes an inimitable
life animated her pallor.

"I am not afraid of suffering," she said, answering
him who had spoken on the bank of the distant river.
And lifting her hand from his shoulder, she stroked
her friend's cheek and then he understood that she
had answered his distant words.

He was silent, intoxicated as if she had given him
to drink the very essence of her heart pressed out
into that goblet. Of all the natural forms that surrounded them, in the diffused light, none seemed to
him to equal the beauty and mystery of that human
face, showing as it did beyond its features glimpses of
a sacred depth where doubtless some great thing had
been accomplished in silence. Quivering, he waited
for her to continue.

They walked on side by side between the two
walls. The path was a narrow one, dull and soft under foot, but the refulgent clouds hung above it.
They reached the cross roads where a wretched hovel
stood half ruined. La Foscarina stopped to look at
it, the gnarled, unhinged windows were held open by
a cane fixed across them. The low sun as it penetrated there beat on the smoky walls, revealed the
accessories: a table, a bench, a cradle.

"Do you remember, Stelio," she said, "that inn
where we went in at Dolo, to wait for the train —
Vampa's inn? A huge fire was burning in the grate,
the crockery shone on the walls, the slices of *polenta*

were toasting on the gridiron. Twenty years ago, they were just the same — the same fire, the same crockery, the same *polenta*. My mother and I used to go in after the performance; we used to sit down on a bench in front of a table. I had wept in the theatre, I had shrieked, raved and died of poison, or by the sword. The sound of the verses would still remain in my ears, like a voice that was not my own, and a strange will persisted in my soul which I could not drive away, like a figure trying to perform those steps and those gestures over again despite my inertness. . . . The counterfeit of life remained in the muscles of my face, and some evenings they could not rest The mask, the sense of the living mask that was already growing. . . . My eyes would remain staring. A steady chill continued at the roots of my hair. . . . I could not succeed in recovering full consciousness of myself and of what was going on around me. . . .

" The odours that came from the kitchen nauseated me; the food that was on the dishes seemed to me too coarse, heavy as stones, impossible to swallow. My repugnance rose from something unspeakably delicate and precious, which I felt at the depths of my weariness, from a confused nobility which I felt beneath my humiliation. . . . I cannot tell. . . . It was perhaps the obscure presence of that force which developed itself in me afterwards, of that election, of that difference from others by which Nature has marked me out. . . . Sometimes the feeling of that diversity became so great that it almost estranged me from my mother — may God forgive me ! — that almost separated me from her. . . . A great solitude was making its way within me; nothing that was around me seemed to touch me. . . . I used to be alone with my fate. My mother, who was beside me, was retreating into infinite distance. Ah! she was near death at the time, and was being prepared for the parting, and perhaps these were the signs. She would urge me to eat with the words she only could say. I used to answer: 'Wait! wait.' I could only drink, I had a great thirst for fresh water. Sometimes when I was still more tired and trembling I would go on smiling a long, long smile. And even my blessed one, with her deep heart, could not understand whence came my smile. . . .

"Incomparable hours, in which it seemed as if the bodily prison were being broken by the soul that went wandering to the further limits of life! What must your youth have been, Stelio? Who can imagine it? We have all felt the weight of the sleep that falls on our flesh, all of a sudden, swift and heavy like a blow from a hammer after toil or ecstasy, and seems to annihilate us. But the power of dreams, too, during our watching, sometimes takes hold of us with that same violence; it grasps us, and we are powerless to resist it, and it seems as if the whole tissue of our existence were being destroyed, as if our hopes were weaving another, brighter and more strange, with those same threads. . . . Ah, there come back to my memory some of the beautiful words you said in Venice that evening, when you pictured her marvellous hands intent on ordaining her own lights and shadows in an uninterrupted work of beauty. You alone can describe the unutterable. . . .

"On that bench there in front of the rough table,

in Vampa's inn at Dolo, where Fate led me with you again the other day, I had the most extraordinary visions that dreams have ever awakened in my soul. I saw that which cannot be forgotten; I saw the real forms that surrounded me clothe themselves with the figures that were growing from my intellect and my instinct. Under my fixed eyes, burnt by the smoky red naphtha lights of the temporary stage, the world of my expressions began to take shape. The first lines of my art developed themselves in that condition of anguish and weariness, of fever and repugnance, in which my sensibility became in a manner almost plastic, like the incandescent material we saw the glass workers holding at the end of their tubes. There was in it a natural aspiration to receive form and breath, to fill the hollow of a mould. On certain evenings, on that wall covered with copper saucepans, I could see myself as in a mirror, in an attitude of pain or rage, with a face that I did not recognise; and my eyelids would beat rapidly to escape that hallucination and to break the fixity of my look. My mother would say again and again: 'Eat, my child, eat this at least.' But what were bread, wine, meat, fruits, all those heavy things bought with hard toil, compared to what I had within me? I used to repeat: 'Wait!' and when we rose to go I used to take a piece of bread with me. I liked to eat it next morning in the country, under a tree or on the banks of the Brenta, sitting on a stone or on the grass. . . . Oh, those statues!"

La Foscarina stopped once more at the end of another path between two walls, that led to a deserted field, to the Campo-di-San-Bernardo, where the old monastery stood. The steeple of Santa-Maria-degli-Angeli rose beyond it, and a glorious cloud hung over it like a rose upon its stem; and the grass was as soft, as green, as placid as in the park of the Pisani at Strà.

"Those statues!" repeated the actress, with an intent look as if they stood there in front of her in great numbers, hindering her on her way. "They did not recognise me the other day, but I recognised them, Stelio."

The distant hours, the wet misty landscape, the leafless trees, the villas falling to ruin, the silent river, the relics of queens and empresses, the crystal masks on the feverish faces, the wild labyrinth, the vain pursuit, the terror, and the agony, the splendid, terrible pallor, the frozen body on the cushions of the carriage, the lifeless hands, all that sadness was suddenly illumined by a new light in the spirit of her beloved. And he looked at the marvellous creature, panting with surprise and dismay, as if he were seeing her for the first time, and her features, her step, her voice, her garments held manifold and extraordinary significances that were as inaccessible to him in their number and rapidity as flashes of lightning.

There she was, a creature of perishable flesh, subject to the sad laws of time; yet a vast mass of real and ideal life weighed upon her, widened round her, throbbed with the very rhythm of her breath. The wandering, despairing woman had touched the limits of human experience: she knew that which he would never know. He, the man of joy, felt the attraction of so much accumulated sorrow, of so much humility and so much pride, of so great a war and so great a victory. Willingly he would have lived that life him-self. He envied her her fate. Astonished, he watched the veins on the back of that bare hand, delicate and blue as though the skin did not cover them, and the small nails that glittered round the stem of the goblet. He thought of a drop of that blood circulating through her substance, limited by common outlines, and yet as immeasurable as the Universe. It seemed to him that there was only one temple in the world, and that temple was the human body. An anxious longing possessed him to stop the woman, to stand before her and examine her attentively, to discover all her aspects, to question her endlessly.

Strange questions rose up in his spirit. "Did you pass along the main roads when you were a young girl on the cart loaded with scenery, lying on a bundle of leaves, followed by a group of strolling players? Did you pass through the vineyards, and did some villager offer you a basket of grapes? Had the man who possessed you for the first time the figure of a satyr and did you hear the wind roaring on the plain in your terror, sweeping away that part of you which you will seek for ever but never find again? How many tears you must have drunk on the day I heard you, for the voice of Antigone to sound so pure in you? Did you win the nations one after another as battles are won to conquer an empire? Do you recognise them by their different odours as one rec-ognises wild beasts? One nation rebelled, resisted you, and in subjecting it you loved it more than those which had worshipped you at your first appearance. Another, on the other side of the ocean, to which you revealed a new unknown manner of feeling, cannot forget you, and continually sends you messages for you to return. What sudden beauties shall I see arising from your love and your sorrow?"

She appeared to him on the solitary meadow in the forgotten island, under the clear wintry sky, as she had appeared to him in the far-off Dionysian night in the midst of the praises of the poets who had sat at the supper table. The same power of imparting life, the same power of revelation, emanated from the woman who had said as she lifted her veil, "I know what hunger is. . . ."

"It was in the month of March, I remember," continued la Foscarina, softly, "I was going out in the meadows early, with my bread. I was walking at random. The statues were my destination. I went from one to the other and stopped before each, as if visiting them. Some seemed to me lovely and I would try to imitate their gestures, but as if by instinct, I remained longer with the mutilated ones, to comfort them. In the evening, on the stage during the performance I would remember some of them, with such a deep feeling of their distance and of their solitude in the quiet country under the stars, that it seemed to me as if I could not speak any more. The crowd would lose patience at these too prolonged pauses. At certain times when I had to wait for my interlocutor's first tirade to be finished, I would stand in the attitude of some one of them which was familiar to me, and remain motionless as if I too had been of stone. I was already beginning to shape my own self. . . ."

She smiled. The grace of her melancholy surpassed the grace of the declining day.

" I tenderly loved one that had lost the arms it had once used to hold a basket of fruit on its head. But the hands were fastened to the basket and moved my pity. It rose on its pedestal in a field of flax; a small canal stagnated close by, and in it the sky's reflection continued the blue of the flowers. If I shut my eyes I can still see the stony face and the sun that coloured itself in passing through the stalks of the flax, as through a green glass. Always, ever since that time, on the stage, in the most heated moments of my art, there rise visions of some landscape to my memory, especially when by the mere force of silence I succeed in communicating a great quiver to the crowd that is listening. . . ."

She had flushed a little at the cheekbones, and, as the oblique sun wrapped her round, drawing sparks from her sables and from the goblet, her animation seemed an increase of light.

"What a spring that was! In one of my wanderings I saw a great river for the first time. It appeared all of a sudden, swollen, flowing rapidly between wild banks in a plain burning like stubble under the level rays of the sun, that grazed its outskirts like a red wheel. I felt then how much divinity there is in a great river flowing through the earth. It was the Adige, coming down from Verona, from the city of Juliet. . . ."

An ambiguous emotion was taking hold of her as she recalled the poetry and poverty of her youth. She was driven to continue by a kind of fascination, nevertheless she did not know how she had arrived at these confessions, when she had meant to speak to her friend of another young life which was not past, but present. By what deception of love had she been brought from the sudden tension of her will, from her resolute decision of facing the painful truth, from the gathering up of her mislaid energy to linger in the memory of by-gone days, and to cover with her own lost virgin self that other one which was so different?

"We entered Verona one evening in the month of May through the gate of the Palio. Anxiety suffocated me. I held the copy-book, where I had copied out the part of Juliet with my own hand, tightly against my heart, and constantly repeated to myself the words of my first entrance: 'How now! Who calls? I am here. What is your will?' A strange coincidence had excited my imagination: I was fourteen years old on that very day, — the age of Juliet! The gossip of the Nurse buzzed in my ears; little by little my destiny seemed to be getting mixed up with the destiny of the Veronese maiden. At the corner of every street I thought I saw a crowd coming towards me and accompanying a coffin covered with white roses. As soon as I saw the Arche degli Scaligeri, closed with iron nails, I cried out to my mother, 'Here is the tomb of Juliet.' And I began to weep bitterly with a desperate desire of love and death. 'Oh, you, too early seen unknown, and known too late.'"

Her voice, as it repeated the immortal words, penetrated the heart of her lover like a heart-rending melody. She paused a moment and repeated, —

"Too late."

They were the very words uttered by her beloved, which she herself had repeated in the garden where the hidden stars of the jessamine blossoms had given forth their sharp perfume and the fruit had smelt as it does in the island gardens, when both had been about to yield to their cruel desire: "It is late, too late!" The ageing woman on the good grass now stood before the old image of herself, of her own virginity, panting in the garb of Juliet before her love's first dream. Having attained the limit of her experience, had she not preserved that dream intact over men and time? — but to what end? Here she was, bringing up her dead, distant youth only to tread it under foot as she led her lover to that other woman who was alive and expectant.

With the smile of her inimitable suffering she said: "I have been Juliet."

The air around them was so calm that the smoke from the furnace chimneys tarried there, contaminating it. Gold quivered everywhere. The cloud on the belfry of the Angeli was growing crimson round the edges. The water was invisible, but its sweetness was passing over the face of things.

"One Sunday in May, in the immense arena in the ancient amphitheatre under the open sky, I have been Juliet before a popular multitude that had breathed in the legend of love and death. No quiver from the most vibrating audiences, no applause, no triumph has ever meant the same to me as the fulness and the intoxication of that great hour. Truly, when I heard Romeo saying, 'Ah, she doth teach the torches to burn bright!' truly my whole being kindled; I became a flame. I had bought a great bunch of roses with my little savings, in the Piazza delle Erbe, under the fountain of Madonna Verona.

The roses were my only ornament. I mingled them with my words, with my gestures, with each attitude of mine. I let one fall at the feet of Romeo when we first met; I strewed the leaves of another on his head from the balcony; and I covered his body with the whole of them in the tomb. The air, the light, and their perfume ravished me. Words slipped from me with strange ease, almost involuntarily as in delirium, and together with them I could hear the continual accompaniment made by the dizzy throb of my veins; I could see the deep amphitheatre, half in sunshine, half in shadow, and in the illuminated part a glitter as of thousands and thousands of eyes. The day was a quiet one like to-day. There was not a breath to ruffle the folds of my dress or the hair that fluttered on my bare neck. The sky was very far, yet now and then it seemed as if my weakest words must sound in its farthest distances, like a clap of thunder, or that its blue was becoming so deep that I was coloured by it as by a sea water that was drowning me. And at intervals, my eyes would travel to the long grasses growing at the summit of the walls, and there seemed to come to me from them I know not what encouragement to what I was saying and doing; and when I saw them sway at the first breath of wind that was rising from the hills, I felt my animation increase and with it the strength of my voice. How I spoke of the lark and the nightingale! I had heard them both in the country a thousand times. I knew all their melodies of the wood, the field, and the sky; I had them wild and living in my ears. Each word before leaving my lips seemed to have passed through all the warmth of my blood. There was no fibre in me which did not give forth an harmonious sound. Ah, grace! the state of grace! Each time it is given me to touch the summit of my art I recover that unspeakable abandonment. I was Juliet. 'It is day, it is day!' I cried out in my terror. The wind was in my hair. I could feel the extraordinary silence on which my lamentation fell. The crowd seemed to have disappeared below ground. It sat silent on the curved steps that were now in shadow. Above it the top of the wall was still red. I was telling of the terror of day, but I already truly felt 'the mask of night' on my face. Romeo had descended. We were already both dead, both had already entered into darkness. Do you remember? 'Now that you are there, you appear like a corpse at the bottom of a sepulchre. Either my eyes deceive me or you are very pale.' I was icy cold as I said these things. My eyes sought the glimmer of light at the top of the wall. It had gone out. The people were clamouring in the arena, demanding the death scene; they would no longer listen to the mother or the nurse or the monk. The quiver of its impatience intolerably quickened the throbbing of my own heart. The tragedy was hurrying on. I still have the memory of a great sky white as pearls, and of a noise as of the sea that quieted down when I appeared, and of the smell of pitch that came from the torches, and of the roses that covered me being faded by my fever, and of a distant sound of bells that brought the sky nearer to us, and of that sky that was losing its light little by little as I was losing my life, and of a star, the first star, that trembled in my eyes with my tears. . . . When I fell lifeless on the body of Romeo, the

howl of the crowd in the shadow was so violent that I
was frightened.   Some one raised me up and dragged
me towards that howl.   Some one brought the torch
close to my tear-stained face; it crackled hard and
smelt of pitch and was red and black, smoke and
flame.   That too, like the star, I shall never forget.
And my face must certainly have been the colour
of death. . . . Thus, Stelio, one night in May, Juliet
came to life again and was shown to the people of
Verona."

She stopped once more, closing her eyes as if she
had suddenly turned dizzy, but her sorrowful lips still
smiled at her friend.

"Then?   The need of moving, of going anywhere,
of passing through space, of breathing in the wind. . . .
My mother followed me in silence.   We crossed a
bridge, walked along the Adige, then crossed another
bridge, entered a small street, lost ourselves in the
dark alleys, found a square with a church in it, and
so on, on, ever on.   My mother asked me now and
then, 'Where are we going?'   I wanted to find a
Franciscan convent where the tomb of Juliet was
hidden, since to my great sorrow they had not buried
her in one of those beautiful tombs closed in by fine
gates.   But I did not want to say it, and I could not
have spoken.   To open my mouth, to utter a single
word was as impossible to me as to detach a star
from the sky.   My voice had lost itself with the last
syllable of the dying Juliet.   My lips had remained
sealed by a silence necessary as death.   And all my
body seemed half alive, now icy, now burning, and
now I don't know, as if only the joints of my bones
were burning and all the rest were icy.   'Where are

we going?' that kind anguish asked of me once more. Ah, the last word of Juliet answered within me. We were again near the water on the Adige, at the head of a bridge. I think I began to run, because shortly afterwards I felt myself seized by my mother's arms and I remained there crushed against the parapet, suffocated by my sobs. 'Let us throw ourselves down! let us throw ourselves down!' I would have said, but I could not. The river was carrying in it the night with all its stars, and I felt that that desire of annihilation was not in me alone. . . . Ah, blessed one!"

She turned very pale, her whole soul feeling once more the clasp of those arms, the kiss of those lips, the tears of that tenderness, the depth of that suffering. But she glanced at her friend and suddenly a quick flood of blood spread over her cheeks and rose as far as her brow, as if brought there by a feeling of secret modesty.

"What am I telling you? Why am I speaking to you of all these things? One talks on and on without knowing why."

She lowered her eyes in her confusion. At the memory of the mysterious terror that had preceded her womanhood, at the memory of her mother's grieved love, the original instinct of her sex stirred in her barren bosom. Her feminine avidity, that rebelled against the heroic design of total abnegation, experienced a strange emotion, became willing to be deluded. From the very roots of her substance there arose an unformed aspiration that she dared not contemplate. The possibility of a divine compensation flashed on the sadness of the inevitable renunciation.

She felt the shaking of her heart, but she was like one who dares not look up to an unknown face for fear of reading there a sentence of life or death. She was afraid of suddenly seeing that thing dissolve which was not hope and yet was similar to hope, born of her soul as well as of body in so unexpected a manner. She became impatient of the great light that kindled the sky, of the places they were passing, of the steps she was taking, of the very presence of her friend. She thought of the half-waking softness, the lingering slumber of dawn when a veiled design lightly guides a happy dream. She longed for solitude, for quiet, for her distant secluded room, for the shadow of heavy curtains. Suddenly, with an impetuous anxiety that rose from that impatience as if she wanted to fix by a mental act a phantom that was about to melt away, she formed some words, and they reached as far as her lips, but did not move them: "A child, from you!"

She turned to her friend and all trembling looked him in the eyes. Her secret thought swayed in her eyes, like a thing that was both prayer and despair. She seemed to be anxiously seeking in him some unrevealed mark, some unknown aspect, almost another man. She called him gently, —

"Stelio!"

And her voice was so changed that the young man started inwardly and turned as if to help her.

"My friend, my friend!"

Fearful and surprised he watched the wide waves of life that were passing through her, the extraordinary expressions, the alternate lights and shadows, and he dared not speak and dared not interrupt the occult workings that were agitating the powers of that great, miserable soul; he could only feel confusedly beneath her words the beauty and the sadness of unexpressed things; and while he was certain that some difficult good was about to rise from so great a fever, yet he knew not the aim to which that love would be led by its necessity of becoming perfect or perishing. His spirit hung in an expectation that was full of wonder, feeling itself live with so much fervour in those forgotten places, on the lowly grass, along the silent path. He had never experienced a deeper feeling of the incalculable strength of which the human heart is capable. And it seemed to him as he listened to the throb of his own heart, as he divined the violence of the other's throbbing, that he could hear the strokes of the hammer beating on the hard anvil where human destiny is forged.

"Tell me more," he said. "Let me get still nearer to you, dear soul. No moment since I have loved you has been worth the road along which we have gone together to-day."

She was moving on with bent head, rapt in the illusion "Could it be?" She felt her barrenness about her like an iron belt. She considered the inexorable obstinacy of the maladies rooted in brute flesh. But the power of her passion, and of her desire, strengthened by an idea of justice, appeared to her in the act of accomplishing a miracle. And all that was superstitious in her nature rose to blind her lucidity and flatter a rising hope. "Have I ever loved before now? Have I not waited for years for this great love that is to save or destroy me? From which of all those who have increased my wretchedness would I have desired a child? Is it not just that a new life should come forth from my life, now that I have made the entire gift of myself to my master? Have I not brought him my girlhood's dream intact, the dream of Juliet? Has not all my life been abolished, from that spring evening to one autumn night?" She saw the whole universe transfigured by her illusion. The memory of her mother gave her a sublime image of maternal love; the kind, firm eyes opened within her again and she prayed to them. "Oh, tell me that I too shall be for a creature of my flesh and of my soul what you have been for me. Give me that assurance, you who know." Her past solitude seemed terrifying. All she could see in the future was death or that one hope of salvation. She thought she could have borne every test in order to deserve it, looked upon it as a grace to be implored, felt herself invaded by a religious ardour of sacrifice. It seemed as if the feverish throb of her distant youth which she had called up were being renewed in her emotion, and that she were being once more impelled on her way under the sky by an almost mystic force.

She was going towards the figure of Donatella Arvale, o tlined on the inflamed horizon at the end of a road that opened on the water. And her first sudden question re-echoed within her: "Do you often think of Donatella Arvale, Stelio?"

A short road led to the Fondamenta degli Angeli, to the canal encumbered with fishing-boats, whence the great lagoon was visible, calm and radiant.

She said: —

"How beautiful the light is! It is like that evening when my name was still Perdita, Stelio."

She was touching a note that she had already touched in a prelude that had been interrupted.

" It was the last evening in September," she added ; " do you remember ? "

She had lifted up her heart so high that it seemed at times as if it failed her, as if the strength of her feeling was no longer in her power, but could escape her from one moment to another, and leave her a prey to those troubled furies, to the sudden impulse to which she had already yielded more than once. She intended that her voice should not tremble in uttering the name that must needs rise in the silence between her friend and herself.

" Do you remember the man-of-war anchored in front of the gardens? — a salute greeted the flag as it slipped down the mast. The gondola grazed the ironclad as it passed."

She gave herself a moment's pause.   An inimitable life animated her pallor.

" Then in its shadow you uttered the name of Donatella."

She made a fresh effort, like a person swimming and submerged by a new wave shaking his head above the foam.

" She began to be yours."

She felt herself stiffening from head to foot, as if under the effect of a poisoned prick.   Her eyes were staring fixedly at the dazzling waters.

" She must be yours," she said, with the hardness of necessity in her voice, as if to resist with a second shock the terrible things that were struggling to rise from the depth of her fire.

Seized by violent anguish, incapable of speaking,

of interrupting with a vain word the lightning-like apparitions of her tragic soul, Stelio Effrena stopped, and laid his hand on his companion's arm to make her stop also.

"Is it not true?" she asked him with almost quiet sweetness, as if her contraction had relaxed suddenly and her passion had accepted the yoke laid upon it by her will. "Speak to me. I am not afraid of suffering. Let us sit down here. I am a little tired."

They rested against a low wall in view of the waters. The calm of the winter solstice on the lagoon was so pure that the shape of the clouds and of the objects along the shore seemed given a kind of ideal quality in their reflection there, as if they were being imitated by art. Near and distant things, the red palace of the Da Mula on the canal, and farther the fort of Tessara, had the same distinctness,— the black boats with their folded sails, with their nets hung along the masts, seemed to gather in their hulls the feeling of infinite repose that came from the horizon. Human pain seemed powerless to move any of those lines, and all seemed to teach silence, giving man a promise of peace in time.

"What can I tell you?" said the young man, in a suffocated voice, almost as if he had been speaking to himself, instead of to the woman, unable to overcome the agitation made up of the certainty of his present love and the consciousness of his desire, which was inexorable as destiny. " Perhaps what you have imagined is true, perhaps it is only a thought of your own mind. There is to-day only one certain thing which I know: that I love you, and that I recognise in you all which is noble. I also know another thing: that I have a work to accomplish and a life to live according to the disposition of nature. You, too, must remember. On that evening in September I spoke to you at great length of my life and of the genii that lead it to its aim. You know that I can give up nothing. . . ."

He trembled as if he were holding a sharpened weapon in his hands, and in moving it could not avoid hurting the unarmed.

"Nothing; and especially I cannot give up your love, which every day exalts my strength and my hope. But have you not promised me more than love? Are you not capable, for me also, of those things which love cannot do? Do you not wish to be a constant, quickening breath for my life and my work?"

She was listening, motionless, without so much as the throb of an eyelid. Like an invalid, in whom the action of voluntary motion is suddenly suspended, and who assists, like a spirit in a statue, at a sight full of horror.

"It is true," he went on, after an anxious pause, recovering his courage, dominating his compassion, feeling that on his sincerity of that moment the fate depended of that free alliance by which he intended to be upraised and not lowered, — "It is true; when I saw you come down that staircase on that night accompanied by her who had sung, I believed that some secret thought was guiding you not to come alone towards me. . . ."

She felt a subtle chill run along the roots of her hair and her eye grow dim, although they remained quite dry. Her fingers trembled round the stem of the goblet, while the colours of sky and water tinted the glass that trembled in the sorrowful hand.

"I believed that you yourself had chosen her. . . . You had the appearance of one who knows and foresees. . . . I was moved by it."

She measured by her frightful torture how sweet his falsehood would have been. She longed for him to lie, or be silent. She measured the space that divided her from the canal, from the water that swallows and deadens.

"There was in her something hostile, as if she were against me. . . . She remained obscure to me, impenetrable. . . . You remember the way she disappeared; her image grew pale, and it was only the desire of her song that remained. You who led her to me have more than once revived her image. You have seen her shadow where it was not."

She saw the face of death. No other thrust had pierced farther, had wounded her more deeply. "With my own hand! With my own hand!" And she heard once more the cry that had been her ruin: "She awaits you!" And from second to second her knees seemed to give way still more, her worn-out body seemed nearer to obeying the furious impulse that was pushing her towards the water. But there remained one lucid point in her, and she considered that that was neither the place nor the time. The sand banks left dry by the low tide were beginning to blacken on the lagoon. All of a sudden, the inner storm seemed to lose itself behind a mere appearance. She believed herself to be non-existent, marvelled at seeing the glass shining in her hand, lost all sense of her own body. All that was happening was imaginary. Her name was Perdita. The dead summer lay in the depths of the lagoon. Words were only words.

" Could I love her? "

One breath more and darkness would have come. As the flame of a candle bends under the wind as if about to separate from the wick, yet still adheres to it by a slight azure fragment, almost by a pale spark, yet will soon kindle and straighten itself again at the ceasing of the wind, the wretched woman's reason came near to being extinguished. The breath of madness passed over her. Terror whitened and convulsed her face.

He did not look at her, but stared fixedly at the stones.

" Were I to meet her again, should I long to turn her destiny towards me? "

He could see her youthful person again with its curved, powerful figure arising from the sonorous forest among the alternate motions of the violin bows that seemed to draw their occult note from the hidden music that was in her.

" Perhaps."

Again he saw the Hermes-like face, almost adamantine in its hardness, filled with some most secret thought, and the frown that made it hostile.

" And of what avail would that be? Of what avail would all the vicissitudes and all the necessities of life be against the faith which binds us? Could we two ever resemble meaner lovers who spend their days struggling to overcome each other, weeping and cursing? "

She ground her teeth; the wild instinct to defend herself, and to hurt as in a desperate struggle overpowered her. The flash of a murderous desire darted on the fluctuations of her thought.

"No, you shall not have her —"

And the cruelty of her master seemed monstrous to her. She seemed to be bleeding under the measured and repeated blows like the man she had once seen on the white road in a mining town. The horrible scene returned to her memory: the man prostrated by a blow from a mace rising and trying to throw himself against his enemy, and the mace that was hurled at him again, the blows aimed one after another by a firm, calm hand, their dull thud on the man's head, the obstinate rising, the tenaciousness of life, the flesh of his face reduced to a kind of red pulp. The images of the frightful memory mingled with the reality of her torture in her mental incoherence. She rose as if moved by a spring, impelled by the savage force that had invaded her veins. The glass broke in her convulsed hand, wounded her, fell at her feet in atoms.

The man started. Her motionless silence had deceived him, and now he looked at her and saw her; and again he saw, as on that evening when the firebrands had crackled, the features of folly outline themselves on her disordered face. He stammered as if in pain, but impatience was boiling beneath his dismay.

"Ah," said the woman, overcoming her tremor with a bitterness that contorted her mouth, "how strong I am! Another time your wounds should not be so slow, since I resist so little, my friend."

She noticed that the blood was dripping from her fingers; she wrapped them in her handkerchief; crimson stains spotted it. She glanced at the fragments of glass scattered shining on the ground.

"The goblet is broken. You had praised it too much. Shall we raise a mausoleum for it here?"

She was very bitter, almost mocking, her lips contracted by a sharp laugh that had no resonance. He was silent, disappointed, full of rancour at having seen the destruction of so beautiful an effort as that perfect vase.

"Let us imitate Nero, having already imitated Xerxes."

She felt even more acutely than her friend the harshness of her sarcasm, the dissonance of her voice, the malignity of that laugh that was like a spasm of her muscles. But she was unable to recover her hold over her soul, and she saw it slipping away from her will, irreparably, like the sailors on a ship from whose grasp the handle has slipped and who remain inert before the crane that turns fearfully backwards, unfolding, unreeling chains and cables. She felt an acrid, irresistible need of scorning, scattering, treading under foot as if invaded by some malignant demon. Every trace of goodness and tenderness had disappeared, and every hope and every illusion. She could discern in the man's glance the same shadow that passed over her own.

"Do I annoy you? Would you like to return to Venice alone? Would you like to leave dead summer behind you? The tide is getting low, but there is still enough water for one who has no intention of returning to the surface. Would you like me to try? Could I be more docile?"

She was saying these insensate things with a hiss in her voice; she had become almost livid, as if all at once consumed by some corroding poison. And he remembered having seen that very same mask on her face one distant day of pleasure, fury, and sadness. His heart contracted and then relaxed.

"Ah, if I have hurt you, forgive me," he said, trying to take one of her hands so as to quiet her with an act of gentleness.

"But had we not started together towards this point? Was it not you . . ."

She interrupted him, impatient at the gentleness of his usual balsam.

"Hurt me? And what does it matter? Have no pity, have no pity. Do not weep over the beautiful eyes of the wounded hare. . . ."

She was walking along the footpath by the side of the purplish canal, passing in front of doorsteps where the women still sat in the waning light with their baskets full of glass beads on their knees. The words broke between her teeth. The contraction of her lips changed into a frenzied convulsion of laughter that sounded like a peal of heart-rending sobs. Her companion shuddered, spoke to her under his breath in his dismay, followed by the curious gaze of those who looked on.

"Be calm! Be calm! Oh, Foscarina, I beg of you! Do not behave like this, I beg of you. Soon we will have reached the shore. We shall soon be home again. . . . I will tell you. . . . Then you

will understand. . . . We are in the street now. . . .
Are you listening to me?"

She had discerned a woman *enceinte* standing on
one of the doorsteps. She was a big woman, and
filled up the space between the door-posts; she was
eating a piece of bread with a far-off, dreamy look.

"Are you listening? Foscarina, I beg of you.
Take courage; lean on me."

He feared she would fall in her horrible convulsion,
and held himself ready to support her. But she only
quickened her pace, unable to answer, suffocating
her peals of laughter with her bound-up hand. She
seemed to feel the skin of her face cracking in her
spasm.

"What is the matter? What is it you see?

Never will that man forget the change in those eyes.
They stared sightless with a deadly stillness, in spite
of the implacable heaving as if their lids had been cut
off; and yet they saw, they saw something which was
not there; they were full of an unknown vision, occupied by a monstrous image that perhaps generated
that laughter full of anguish and madness.

"Would you like to stop? Would you like a little
water?"

They had come out again on the Fondamenta dei
Vetrai, where the shops were now shut, where their
steps re-echoed, where the bursts of atrocious merriment seemed to prolong themselves as if under a
portico. How long was it since they had passed
along that dead canal? How much of their life had
passed away meanwhile? How much shadow had
they left behind them?

In the gondola, wrapped in her mantle, paler than

she had been on the way to the Dolo, the woman tried to control her spasms, holding her jaws with both hands, but from time to time the malignant laugh would escape, hissing in the sleepy silence, breaking through the rhythm of the two oars; she would press her hands to her mouth more firmly, as if she were trying to suffocate herself. Between her veil raised above the eyebrows and the blood-stained handkerchief, her eyes remained open and staring on the immensity of the twilight.

The lagoon and the darkness swallowed up all forms and all colours; only the groups of posts, like a procession of monks on a pathway full of ashes, interrupted the grey monotony. Venice in the background was smoking like the remains of a vast pillage.

When the roll of the bells reached them her soul remembered, her tears fell, the horror was conquered.

The woman took her hands from her face, bent a little towards her friend's shoulder, recovered her voice to say. . . .

" Forgive me ! "

She humbled herself, ashamed ; each act of hers from that day silently begged for pardon and oblivion.

A new grace seemed born in her. She became lighter, she talked in a lower voice. She would move delicately about the room dressed in quiet stuffs, veiling with the shadow of her lashes her beautiful eyes, that dared not look on her friend. The fear of oppressing him, of being irksome to him, gave wings

to her instinct. Her ever waking sensibility watched
and listened round the inaccessible door of his
thoughts. She reached the point at certain hours of
feeling the rhythm of that other life beating under
her own pulse.

Her soul, intent on creating a new feeling that
should be capable of conquering the violence of instinct, revealed in her face with resplendent signs the
difficulty of her secret task. Her supreme art had
never before found expressions so singular; never
had significances so obscure come to life in the
shadow of her features. Looking at her one day, her
friend spoke of the infinite power accumulated in the
shadow produced by the helmet on the face of I
Pensieroso.

"Michael Angelo," he said, "has concentrated all
the effort of human meditation in a small hollow of
his marble. As the stream fills the hollowed palm
so the eternal mystery by which we are surrounded
fills the small space opened by the Titan's chisel in
the material that had come from the mountain, and
it has remained there and grown denser with the
centuries. I only know the changing shadow of
your own face, Fosca, that sometimes rivals it in
intensity, and even at times surpasses it."

She stretched herself out towards the Life-giver
yearning for poetry and knowledge. She became to
him the ideal figure of her who listens and under-
stands. The wild, powerful fold of her hair imitated
the impatience of wings round her pure forehead
A beautiful phrase would suddenly draw the tears
from her eyes as if it had been a drop which falls
into a vessel that is full and causes it to overflow.

She read out to him pages from the sovereign poets. The august shape of the Book seemed magnified by her attitude in holding it, by her gesture in turning the pages, by the religious gravity of her attention, by the harmony of the lips that changed the printed signs into vocal numbers. In reading the poetry of Dante she became as noble and severe as the sibyls in the dome of the Sixtine Chapel, bearing the weight of the sacred volumes with all the heroism of their bodies agitated by the breath of prophecy. The lines of her attitude, down to the slightest folds of her garment, together with her modulations, revealed the divine text.

When the last syllable had fallen she saw her friend rise impetuously, trembling with fever, wandering about the room, agitated by the god, panting in the anxiety imparted to him by the confused tumult of his creative force. She saw him coming towards her with radiant eyes transfigured by a sudden beatitude, illumined by an inner flame, as if a sovereign hope had all of a sudden been kindled in him, or an immortal truth revealed. With a shudder that abolished in the blood the memory of every caress, she saw him come to her and bend over her knees, overthrown by the terrible shock of the world he was carrying in himself, by the upheaval that accompanied some hidden metamorphosis. She knew pain and pleasure; not knowing whether his were pleasure or pain, she was filled with piety, fear, and reverence in feeling that voluptuous body labouring thus in the genesis of the idea. She was silent, she waited, she adored the unknown thoughts in the head that rested on her knees.

But she understood his great striving better when, one day after she had read to him, he spoke to her of the Exile.

" Imagine, Fosca, if you can without bewilderment, the fire and rush of the vast soul, in uniting itself to the elementary energies in order to conceive its world. Imagine an Alighieri on the road to exile, already possessed by his vision, an implacable pilgrim driven from land to land by his passion and his misery, from refuge to refuge, across fields, across mountains, along rivers, along seas, in every season, suffocated by the sweetness of spring, stricken by the harshness of winter, ever alert, attentive, his voracious eyes ever open, anxious with the inner travail that was forming the gigantic work. Imagine the fulness of that soul in the contrast between common necessities and the flaming apparitions that suddenly came to meet him at a turning of the road, on some river bank, in a rocky cave, on the slope of a hill, in the thick of a forest, in a meadow bright with the song of the lark. Manifold life poured into his spirit by means of his senses, transfiguring the abstract ideas that filled him into living images. Wherever he went unexpected sources of poetry flowed from his sorrowful step. The voice, the appearance, and the essence of the elements entered into his occult labour and increased it with sounds, with lines, with colours, with movements, with innumerable mysteries. Fire, air, earth, and water worked in collaboration at the sacred poem, pervaded the sum of its doctrine, warmed it, modified and watered it, covered it with leaves and flowers. . . . Open this Christian book and imagine the statue of a Greek god on the other side. Do you not see shadow or light break from the one as from the other, the flash or the wind of the sky? "

Then she began to feel that her own life was drifting into the all-absorbing work, that her own soul was entering drop by drop into the person of the drama, that her aspects, her attitudes, her gestures, and her accents were contributing to the formation of the figure of the heroine " living beyond life." She became the prey of those voracious eyes which she sometimes found fixed upon her with intolerable violence. She became acquainted with another manner of being possessed. It seemed to her that she was dissolving into her elements in the fire of that intellect, only to be afterwards more perfectly recomposed according to the necessities of a heroism that was to dominate destiny. Her secret task being in harmony with the virtue of the life which was being created, she was attracted by the desire of producing no discord between herself and the image which was to be like her. Art seconded the apparition of the new feeling she had prepared.

Nevertheless, she suffered from the image that threw its shadow on the reality of renunciation and sorrow. A strange ambiguity was born of the resemblance between the image and her own being. Sometimes it seemed to her that her hidden effort was preparing her for her success on the stage, and not for the conquest of her conscience over the darkness of instinct. It seemed to her sometimes that she was losing her human sincerity, and was only in the state of fictitious concentration in which she was wont to put herself while studying the character of the tragic part she was to incarnate. Thus she became acquainted with another torment. She shut and contracted her soul under his penetrating glance as if to prevent his piercing her and robbing her of her secret life. She grew to be terrified of the Seer. " He will read in my soul the silent words which he will put on the lips of his creation, and I shall only pronounce them on the stage under the mask." She felt her spontaneity being arrested. She underwent strange bewilderments and discouragements, whence she would rise at times with an impetuous need of breaking that spell, of making herself different, of separating herself from that image which was to be like her, of marring those lines of beauty that imprisoned her and forced her to a determined sacrifice. — Was there not also a virgin thirsting with love and yearning for joy in the tragedy, a virgin in whom a great spirit recognised the living apparition of his lightest dream, the Victory so often invoked that was to crown his life? And was there not also a loving woman no longer young, whose one foot was already in the shadow, and who had but a short step to take in order to disappear? — More than once she was tempted to contradict that resignation by some violent act.

Then she would tremble at the possibility of once more falling into the horror, of being once more seized by the horrible fury, grasped by the insidious beast that was not killed yet, but was living and watching in the dark for the right moment to spring upon her. Like a penitent, she increased her fervour because of the danger, hardened her discipline, sharpened her vigilance; she repeated with a kind of intoxication the act of supreme abandonment that had risen from the depths of her misery before the purifying fire. . . . "You must have all; I shall rest content with seeing you live, with seeing your joy. And do with me what you will."

Then he loved her for the unexpected visions she brought him, for the mysterious sense of inner events that she communicated to him by her vicissitudes of expression. It astonished him to find that the lines of a face, the movements of a human body could so powerfully touch and fertilise the intellect. He shuddered and turned pale one day on seeing her enter the room with her silent step, her face fixed in an extraordinarily calm sorrow, as if she were coming from the depths of wisdom whence all human agitations seem a play of the wind in the dust of an endless road.

"Ah, I have created you, I have created you!" he cried, deluded by the intensity of the hallucination, thinking he saw his heroine herself standing on a threshold of the distant room occupied by the treasures taken from the tombs of the Atrides. "Stop a moment! Do not move your eyelids! Keep your eyes motionless like two stones! You are blind. And you see all that others do not see. And nothing can be hidden from you. And here in this room the man you love has revealed his love to another, who is still trembling at the revelation. And they are still here, and their hands have not long been parted, and their love is in the air. And the room is full of funeral treasures, and on two tables are disposed the riches that covered the bodies of Agamemnon and Cassandra. There are the chests full of necklaces, and here are the vases full of ashes, and the balcony is open looking out to the plain of Argos and the distant mountains. And it is sunset, and all this terrible gold gleams in the shadow. Do you understand? You are there on the threshold, led by the Nurse. You are blind, and nothing is unknown to you. Stop a moment!"

He was speaking in the sudden fever of invention. The scene appeared and disappeared before him, submerged in a torrent of poetry.

"What will you do? What will you say?"

The actress felt a chill in the roots of her hair. Her soul vibrated with sonorous strength to the limits of her body. She became blind and prophetic. The cloud of tragedy descended and stopped above her head.

"What will you say? You will call them. You will call one and the other by name in the silence full of great royal spoils."

The actress could hear the throb of her blood, her voice was to resound in the silence of thousands of years from the distances of time. It was to reawaken the ancient sorrow of men and heroes.

"You will take their hands and you will feel their two lives stretching towards each other with all their strength and gaze fixedly at each other across your motionless sorrow, as if it were a crystal about to break."

The blindness of immortal statues was in her eyes. She saw herself sculptured in the great silence, and felt the quiver of the dumb crowd, seized at the heart by the sublime power of the attitude.

"And then, and then?"

The Life-giver rushed towards her as if he would have struck her to draw sparks from her.

"You must call Cassandra from her sleep, you must feel her ashes live once more in your hands, she must be present in your vision. Will you do it? Do you understand? Your living soul must touch the ancient soul and mingle with it into one only soul and one only misfortune, so that the error of time seems destroyed and that unity of life to which I tend by the effort of my art be made manifest. Cassandra is in you and you are in her. Have you not loved her? Do you not also love the daughter of Priam? Who that has once heard it will ever forget, who will ever forget the sound of your voice and the convulsion of your lips at the first cry of the prophetic fury. . . . 'O Earth! O Apollo!' I can see you again, deaf and dumb on your car, with that aspect on your face of a wild beast newly captured. Ah, but among so many terrible cries there were some infinitely soft, sad tones. The old men compared you to 'the tawny nightingale.' How are they? How are they? — the words when you remember your beautiful river? And when the old men question you concerning the love of the god, do you not remember them?"

The tragic actress throbbed as if the breath of the god were again invading her. She had become an ardent ductile matter subject to all the animations of the poet.

"Do you not remember them?"

"O espousals, espousals of Paris fatal to the dear ones! O you, paternal waters of Scamandros, then on your shores my youth fed upon you!"

"Ah, divine one! Your melody does not let one forget the syllables of Æschylus. I remember. The soul of the crowd, gripped by the 'lamentation of discordant sounds,' unbent and was blessed by that melodious sigh, and each of us received the vision of her distant years and her innocent bliss. You can say, 'I have been Cassandra.' In speaking of her you will remember an anterior life. . . . Her mask of gold shall be in your hands. . . ."

He seized her hands, unconsciously torturing them. She felt no pain. Both were intent on the sparks generated by their mingled forces; one same electric vibration ran along their nerves.

"You are there, close to the spoil of the enslaved princess, and you are feeling her mask. . . . What will you say?"

They seemed in the pause to be waiting for the flash to illumine them. The eyes of the actress became once more motionless; their blindness filled them once more. Her whole face became as marble. Instinctively the Life-giver left her hands free, and they sketched the gesture of feeling for the sepulchral gold. In a voice that created the tangible form she said: —

"How large her mouth is!"

He throbbed with almost fearful suspense.

"You see her, then?"

She remained silent with her intent, sightless eyes.

"I too can see her. It is large, the horrible effort of divination had dilated it; she cried out, cursed, and lamented ceaselessly. Can you imagine her mouth in silence?"

Slowly, still in the same attitude, almost in ecstasy, she said: —

"How wonderful is her silence!"

She seemed to be repeating words suggested to her by some mysterious genii; while it seemed to the poet as he heard them that he himself had been about to utter them. A deep tremor shook him as if he had been assisting at a miracle.

"And her eyes?" he asked, trembling. "What colour do you think her eyes were?"

She did not answer.

The marble lines of her face changed as if a slight wave of suffering had passed there. A furrow carved itself between her eyebrows.

"Black, perhaps," he added softly.

She spoke.

"They were not black, but they seemed so because in the prophetic ardour the pupils were so dilated that they swallowed up the iris. . . ."

She stopped as if her breath were about to fail her. A thin veil of moisture was spreading over her forehead. Stelio gazed at her, silent and very pale; and the interval was filled by the deep throbs of his heart.

"In the pauses," continued the revealer, with painful slowness, when she had wiped the foam from her livid lips, "her eyes were sweet and sad as two violets."

She stopped again, breathless, with the appearance of one who dreams and suffers in the dream. Her mouth seemed parched, her temples were wet.

"Thus they must have been before they were closed for ever."

Henceforth he was entirely carried away by the lyric whirlwind; he breathed only in the inflamed ether of his poetry. The musical sentiment that had generated the drama determined itself in the forms of the Prelude he was composing. On the sonorous fulcrum the tragedy found its perfect balance between the two forces that were to animate it, the power of the stage and the power of the orchestra. A *motive* of extraordinary vigour marked in the symphonic ocean the apparition of the ancient Fate.

"You will perform the *Agamemnon* in the new theatre, the *Antigone*, and lastly the *Victory of Man*. My tragedy is a battle: it celebrates the renovation of the Drama, with the discomfiture of the monstrous will that dragged down the races of Labdacus and Atreus. It opens with the moan of an ancient victim, and closes with a cry of light."

Revived by the melody, the Moyra lived before him again in visible shape such as she appeared before the wild eyes of the Coefore, by the mound of the slaughtered king.

"Do you remember," he said to the actress, in order to signify that violent presence, "do you remember the decapitation of Marcus Crassus in Plutarch's narration? One day I proposed drawing from it an episode for the stage. Under the royal tent the Armenian, Artavasdes, is entertaining Orodes, the king of the Parthians, at a great banquet, and the captains sit drinking round the table; and the spirit of Dionysius invades those barbarians, who are not insensible to the power of rhythm, because a performer of tragedies, called Jason Trallianus, is singing the adventures of Agave in the *Bacchantes* of Euripides.

They have not yet risen from the table when Sillaces enters, bearing the head of Crassus, and having saluted the king, throws it bleeding in their midst. A great cry of joy arises from the Parthians. Then Jason gives the garments of Pentheus to one of the chorus, while he, seizing the head of Crassus, and full of the Dionysian fury, sings these verses: —

> " ' Portiamo dai monti
> alle case un' edera tagliata di recente
> insigne preda. . . .' [1]

" And the chorus leaps with joy, and as Agave tells them how she had caught that lion cub without a net, the chorus asks, Who had wounded him first, and Agave answers, —

> " ' Mio è il vanto. . . .' [2]

" But Pomaxœthres, who had been still supping, starts to his feet and tears the head from the hands of the furious actor, crying out that it is he, rather than Jason, who should say those words, because he is the slayer of the Roman. Do you feel the portentous beauty of the scene? — the fierce face of life suddenly flashes by the side of the waxen mask of metal, the odour of human blood excites the rhythmic fury of the chorus, a death-bringing arm tears asunder the veils of the tragic fiction. This unusual, astonishing epilogue closing the expedition of Crassus fills me with enthusiasm. Well, the eruption of the ancient Moyra in my modern tragedy is like the sudden arrival of Sillaces at the banquet of the Armenian. At

[1] " Let us take home from the hills the
newly cut ivy as an illustrious
spoil. . . ."

[2] " Mine is the boast. . . ."

the beginning, on the loggia that guards the Cyclopic walls and the gate of the lions, the virgin has in her hands the book of the Tragedians, and is reading the lamentation of Antigone. The fatal divinity is enclosed in the book, dominating the images of pain and crime. But those images are called up by the living words; and close to the pure peplum of the Theban martyr glows the insidious crimson stretched out by Clytemnestra, and the Heroes of the Orestidæ seem to recommence a new life while a man explores their tombs in the Agora. They seem to move at the back of the stage like shadows, impelled by obscure agitation; they seem to bend down listening to the dialogues, to poison the air with their breath. Suddenly a cry is heard announcing the great event. Here comes the man who has uncovered the tombs and has seen the face of the Atridæ. Here he comes irradiated by the wonders of death and of that gold. He stands there, like one delirious. Their souls are trembling. Is the fable rising from the soil to delude men once more? Their souls are anxious and trembling. Suddenly the power of the curse and ruin rushes upon them and seizes them to drag them towards infamous crimes; the desperate struggle begins. The tragedy no longer wears its motionless mask, but shows its naked face; and the book that the unconscious virgin was reading can no longer be re-opened without a shudder, because their souls have felt that that distant horror has become living and present, and that they are breathing and raving in it, as in an inevitable reality. The Past is in action. The illusion of Time has fallen. Life is one."

The very greatness of his conception filled him

with dismay. At times he would look anxiously about him, examine the horizon, question dumb things as if he were calling for help or hoping for a message. He would lie in silence for a long time, his eyes shut, waiting.

"I must raise this enormous mass at one stroke before the eyes of the multitude. In this, you see, lies the difficulty of my prelude. This first effort is the greatest that my work will demand of me. At the same time I must call my world forth from nothing and place the manifold soul in the musical state most apt to receive the unusual revelation. The orchestra must produce this miracle. 'Art, like magic, is practical metaphysics,' Daniele Glauro says. And he is right."

He would sometimes come to the house of his friend panting and agitated as if pursued by Erinnys. She never asked him questions, but her whole person would soothe the unquiet one.

"I was afraid," he said one day, smiling, — "afraid of being suffocated. . . . You believe I am a little mad, do you not? Do you remember that stormy evening when I returned from the Lido? How sweet you were, Fosca! Not long before on the Bridge of Rialto I had found a *Motive*. I had translated the words of the element into notes. . . . Do you know what a *Motive* is? It is a small spring that may give birth to a flock of streams, a small seed that may give birth to a wreath of forests, a small spark that may give birth to an endless chain of conflagrations: a nucleus producing infinite strength. There is no more powerful thing in the world of ideal origins, nor more virtuous organ of generation; and there is no greater joy for an active mind than that which may be given him by the developments of that energy. . . . Joy, yes, but also terror sometimes, my friend."

He laughed his ingenuous laugh. The manner in which he spoke of these things was a symptom of the extraordinary faculty which likened his spirit to that of the primitive transfigurations of nature. There was a deep analogy between the spontaneous formation of myths and his instinctive necessity of animating all that fell under his senses.

"A little while ago I had begun developing the *Motive* of that stormy evening, which I shall call the Wind-bags of Æolus. Here it is. It is this."

He went to the keyboard and struck a few notes with one hand.

"No more than this, but you cannot imagine the generating force of these few notes. A storm of music has arisen from them, and I have not been able to master it. . . . I have been overcome, suffocated, forced to fly."

He laughed again, but his soul was swaying like the sea.

"The Wind-bags of Prince Æolus, opened by the companions of Ulysses. Do you remember it? The imprisoned winds break forth and push the ship back. Man trembled with fear."

But his soul could find no rest, and nothing could free it of its agitated workings. And he kissed the hands of his friend, and walked away from her and wandered about the room, stopping before the instrument that Donatella had touched in singing Claudio's melody; restlessly he went to the window, saw the leafless garden, the beautiful solitary clouds, the sacred towers. His aspiration went out to the musical creature who was to sing his hymns at the summit of the tragic symphonies.

In a low limpid voice the woman said: —

"If only Donatella were here with us!"

He turned, took a few steps towards her, and looked at her fixedly, silently. She smiled her slight concealing smile on seeing him so near to her and yet so far away. She felt that he loved no one at that moment: not her and not Donatella; but that he considered them both as pure instruments of his art, as forces to be used, "bows to be drawn." He was burning in his own poetry, and she was there with her poor wounded heart, with her secret torture and her silent prayer, intent on nothing but the preparation of her sacrifice, ready to pass away beyond love and life as the heroine of the future drama.

"Ah, what is it that could draw you near me, that could throw you on my faithful heart, quivering with another anguish?" she thought, seeing him estranged and lost in his dream. "A great sorrow perhaps, a sudden blow, a cruel disappointment, an irreparable evil."

There returned to her memory the verse of Gaspara Stama which he had praised: —

> "Vivere ardendo e non sentire il male!"

And she remembered his sudden pallor when she had stopped in the path between the two walls, and had declared her first titles of nobility in the struggle to live.

"Ah, if only one day you could be brought to feel the value of a devotion such as mine, of a servitude such as the one I offer you, if you were truly to need me one day, and, discouraged, you should draw a new faith from me, and weary, you should draw your strength from me!"

She was reduced to invoking sorrow to strengthen her hope an᷄ while saying to herself " if only one day!" . . . tne sense occupied her, the sense of time that flies, the sense of the flame that is consuming itself, of the body that is fading, of the infinite things that wear out and perish. Henceforth each day must dig its mark in her face, discolour her lips, destroy her hair; henceforth each day was in the service of old age, would hasten the work of destruction in her miserable flesh. "What then?"

Once more she recognised that it was desire, unconquerable desire, that forged all the illusions and all the hopes which seemed to help her in accomplishing "what even love cannot do."

She recognised that every effort to root it out would be vain, and, discouraged, she saw the artifice into which her soul had been forced by her will drop away in an instant. With secret shame she felt how miserably she resembled at that moment the actress who lays aside her mask on coming away from the stage. In pronouncing those words that had interrupted the silence and expressed an unreal regret with the accents of sincerity, had she not been like one reciting a part? But she had suffered, but she had wrung her heart, but she had extracted that sweetness from the bitterness of her blood. What then?

She recognised that the torturing constraint of those days had not succeeded in creating in her even a symptom of the new feeling by which love was to be made sublime. She was like those gardeners who with their shears have given an artificial shape to tenacious plants which still preserve their powerful trunk and all their roots intact, and outrun the design with rapid expansion, if the work of the shears round their branches be not assiduous. Her effort was therefore as useless as it was painful, since it only had an outward efficacy, leaving her depths unchanged; on the contrary even increasing there the intensity of her evil by compressing it. Her secret task, therefore, was reduced to a constant dissimulation. Was it worth while living for this?

She could not and would not go on living except on condition of at last finding her harmony. But the experience of those days had done nothing beyond making the discord greater between her goodness and her desire, had only succeeded in sharpening her restlessness and her sadness, or in losing itself entirely in the whirl of the creative soul that was attracting her to mould her like a plastic substance. She was indeed so far removed from the harmony she sought that she had at one moment felt her spontaneity ceasing and her sincerity clouding itself; a dull ferment of rebellion swelling her heart and a threatened return of the feared madness.

Was it not the same woman sitting in shadow among the cushions of the divan who had said to her friend one evening in October burnt up by the poison, " It is necessary; I must die "? Was it not the same woman, — was it not the same woman who had risen thence when he had prodded her and had sprung upon him as if to devour him?

If the young man's turbid desire had then caused her to suffer cruelly, she now suffered still more cruelly in observing that his ardour had quieted itself and that a kind of reserve had taken its place in her friend, — a kind of reserve that was sometimes impatient of the gentlest caress. She was ashamed of her regret, seeing that he was possessed by his idea and intent on concentrating all his energies on his mental effort alone. But a dark rancour would master her of an evening when he took his leave of her, and blind suspicions at night tormented her sleepless soul.

She yielded to the nightly evil. Throbbing and feverish in the darkness of a gondola cabin, she wandered along the canal, hesitated before giving the oarsman the name of a distant Rio, tried to turn back, sobbed, suffocated over her wound, felt her pain becoming intolerable, inclined herself towards the lethal fascination of the water, conversed with death, then gave herself up to her misery. She watched the house of her friend. She remained there during long hours in fearful and useless expectation.

They were her worst agonies those which she endured in that melancholy Rio della Panada that ends in a bridge under which the mortuary island of San Michele was visible in the open lagoon. The old Gothic palace at the corner of San Canciano was like a suspended ruin that must all at once crash down upon her and bury her. The black *peate* went to pieces along the corroded walls, uncovered by the low tide, exhaling the odour of dissolution; and once she heard the little birds awakening at dawn in the garden of the Poor Clares.

"To go away!" The necessity of the act came

upon her, suddenly urgent. She had already told her
friend on one memorable day: " Now it seems to me
that there is only one thing I can do: go away, disappear, and leave you free with your fate. This
thing I can do which even love could not do."
Henceforth delay was no longer possible; she must
break through every hesitation; she must emerge at
last from that kind of fatal immobility of events, in
which she had been agitated for so long between life
and death, as if she had fallen into the dumb troubled
water, close to the sepulchral island, and were struggling there in anguish, feeling the soft sand give way
beneath her feet, ever believing herself to be swallowed up, ever having before her eyes the level
stretch of that great calm, and never drowning. . . .

Nothing indeed had happened, nothing was happening. Since that October dawn their outward life
had continued unchanged. No word had been pronounced that might have established an end, that
could point to an interruption. It almost seemed as
if the sweet promise of the visit to the Euganean hills
were about to be kept, as the time for the blossoming
of the peach-trees drew nearer. Nevertheless, she
felt at that moment the absolute impossibility of going
on living as she was then living by the side of her
beloved. It was a definite and unquestionable feeling,
like the sensation of one who finds himself in a burning house, of one who is stopped on a mountain-side
by a chasm, or of one who in the desert has drunk of
the last drop from his gourd. There was in her
something that was fully accomplished as in the tree
that has given forth all its fruit, as in the field where
the harvest has been reaped, as in the current that has

reached the sea. Her inner necessity was as the necessity of natural facts, of tides, seasons, and celestial vicissitudes; she accepted it without examination.

And her courage revived, her soul grew stronger, her activity reawakened, the virile qualities of the leader rose up in her once more. In a very short time she settled her tour, reassembled her people, fixed the date of her departure. "You must go and work down there among the barbarians beyond the ocean," she told herself harshly. "You must still go on wandering from town to town, from hotel to hotel, from theatre to theatre, and every night you will raise a howl in the crowd that pays you; you will earn much money, you will come back laden with gold and with wisdom unless it so happens that you remain crushed by chance under a wheel at a crossing of the roads some foggy day.

"Who knows!" she added. "From whom have you received the order to go away? From some one who is within you, deep, deep within you, and who sees that which you cannot see, like the blind woman in the tragedy. Who knows whether down there on one of those great peaceful rivers your soul will not find its harmony, and your lips will not learn that smile which they have so often attempted in vain! Perhaps you will discover a few white hairs and that smile in your mirror at the same time. Go in peace."

And she began preparing her *viaticum* for her journey.

From time to time the breath of the premature season seemed to be passing in the February sky.

"Don't you feel the spring?" said Stelio to his friend, and his nostrils quivered.

She threw herself back a little, feeling that her heart was melting, and offered her face to the sky, which was full of scattered vapours like slight feathers. The hoot of a siren prolonged itself in the pale estuary, becoming little by little as sweet as a flute-note. It seemed to the woman that something had escaped from her inmost heart and faded away in the distance with that sound like a pain that little by little is changing into a memory.

She replied:

"It has arrived at the Tre Porti."

Once more they wandered at random along the lagoon on the water which was as familiar to their dream as the web to the weaver.

"Did you say 'to the Tre Porti'?" exclaimed the young man, quickly, as if some spirit were awaking in him. "Precisely there in the neighbourhood of the low beach, when the moon goes down, the sailors take the wind prisoner and bring it in chains to Dardi Seguso. One day I will tell you the story of the Archorgan."

She smiled at the mysterious way in which he had alluded to the mariners' act.

"Which story?" she said, yielding to the enchantment; "and how does Seguso come into it? Is it the master glazier?"

"Yes; but an ancient one, who knew Greek and Latin, music and architecture; who was admitted to the Academy of the Pellegrini; who had his gardens in Murano, and was often invited to supper by Vecellio in his house on the Contrada dei Biri; who

was the friend of Bernado Capello, of Jacopo Zan
and other Petrarchian patricians. It was in the house
of Caterino Zeno that he saw the famous organ
built for Matthias Corvinus King of the Hunga-
rians, and it was there that his fine idea came to
him, in the course of a dispute with that Agostino
Amadi who had succeeded in picking up for his
collection of instruments a real Greek lyre, a great
Lesbian heptachord adorned with gold and ivory. . . .
Ah, do you imagine that relic of the school of Mitylene brought to Venice by a galley that in passing
through the waters of Santa Maura, caught and
dragged the dead body of Sappho as far as Malamocco like a bundle of dead grass? But this is
another story."

Once more the wandering woman seemed to
recover her youth, and to smile with the surprise of a
child who is being shown a picture-book. What
marvellous stories, what delightful inventions, had not
the Image-maker found for her on the water in the
slowness of that hour! How many enchantments he
had composed for her to the rhythm of the oar with
those words of his that made everything visible!
How many times, sitting by his side in the light boat,
she had tasted of that kind of lucid slumber in which
all agitations were interrupted, and only the visions
of poetry were allowed to live on!

"Tell it me," she begged; and she would have
added, "It will be the last," but refrained because
she had as yet concealed her resolution from her
friend.

He laughed.

"Ah, you are as greedy for stories as Sophia."

At that name, as at the name of spring, she felt her whole heart melting and the cruelty of her lot passing through her soul, and her whole being turning to the things she had lost.

"Look," he said, pointing to the silent level of the lagoon, creased here and there by the passage of a breeze. "Do not those infinite lines of silence aspire to become music?"

The islands stood lightly on the afternoon illusion of the estuary as the lightest clouds hung from the sky. The long thin streaks of land seemed as vain as the black gatherings of refuse that sometimes float in zones on the calm waves. In the distance Torcello, Burano, Mazzorbo, San Francesco del Deserto did not seem like real landing-places, but more like submerged regions, the summits of which pierced the level of the water like the protruding parts of vessels that have gone to the bottom. The traces of man were faint indeed in that level solitude, like letters corroded by time in ancient inscriptions.

"Well, then, the master glazier, hearing the famous organ of Matthias Corvinus praised in the house of Zeno, cried: '*Corpo di Baco!* They shall see what organ I can make with my tube, my liquid Muse of song. I will make the god of organs. *Dant sonitum glaucæ per stagna loquacia cannæ.* . . . The water of the lagoon shall give forth its sound and the posts and the stones shall sing too. *Multisonum silentium.* . . . They shall see! *Corpo di Diana!*' All who were present laughed, except Giulia da Ponte, who did not laugh because her teeth were dark. And Sansovino straightway began a dissertation on hydraulic organs. But the boaster

before taking his leave invited the company to hear
his new music on the day of the Sensa and promised
that the Doge and his Bucintoro would stop to listen
in the middle of the lagoon.   That night a rumour
spread through Venice that Dardi Seguso had lost
his reason.   And the Council, which was extremely
careful of its glaziers, sent a messenger for news to
Murano.   The messenger found the artist with his
mistress Perdilanza del Mido, who was caressing him
anxiously and in dismay because it had seemed to
her that he was raving.   The master, after having
looked at him with flaming eyes, burst into a mighty
laugh that reassured him more than any words, and
calmly ordered him to refer to the Council that by
the day of the Sensa Venice, besides San Marco, the
Canalazzo and the Palace of the Doges would possess
another wonder;   and the day after he applied for
leave to take possession of one of the five little
islands round Murano like the satellites of a planet,
that have disappeared to-day, or are changed into
sand-banks.   After having explored the waters about
Temòdia, Trencòre, Galbaia, Mortesina, and la Fo-
lèga, he chose Tremòdia as one chooses a bride, and
Perdilanza del Mido entered into great affliction. . . .
Look, Fosca, we are perhaps passing now upon the
memory of Tremòdia.   The pipes of the organ are
buried in the mud, but they cannot know decay.
They were seven thousand.   We are passing over
the ruins of a singing forest of glass.   How delicate
the seaweeds are here ! "

He was bending over the beautiful waters, and she
was bending over them too on the other side.   The
ribbons, the feathers, the velvet, the other delicate

substances that made up the head-gear of la Foscarina mingled with sober art, her eyes and the blue
shadows that encircled them, the very smile with
which she made an enchanting grace of her waning
beauty, the bunch of jonquils that was fixed in the
prow in place of the lantern, the rare imaginings of the
Life-giver, the dream-names of the vanished islands,
the blue appearing and disappearing in the snowy mist,
the faint cries coming now and then from a flock of
invisible birds, — all the most delicate things seemed
conquered by the play of those transient apparitions,
by the colour of the salt locks that lived in the
vicissitudes of the tide, coiling and turning as if at an
alternating caress. Two mingled miracles seemed
to colour them. Green as the grain fresh growing in
the furrow, tawny as the leaf dying on the young oak,
and green and tawny in their innumerable variations
as of plants that both live and die, they gave the
impression of an ambiguous season reigning exclu-
sively in the bed of the lagoon. The light which
illumined them through the clear water lost none of
its strength; while its mystery was increased so that
there lurked in their languor a memory of their obe-
dience to the moon's attraction.

"Why, then, did Perdilanza enter into great affliction?" asked the woman, still bending on the beautiful waters.

"Because her name had been conquered in the
mouth and in the soul of her lover by the name of
Tremòdia, which he uttered passionately, and because
the island was the only place to which she might not
follow him. There he had constructed his new works,
and he would remain there a great part of the day

and nearly the whole night, assisted by his workmen, whom he had bound by an oath of silence sworn at the altar. The Council, having given orders that the master should be provided with all that might be needful for his terrible work, condemned him to decapitation, in case the same work should turn out inferior to his pride. Then Dardi tied a scarlet thread round his bare neck."

La Foscarina straightened herself to arrange herself more comfortably. She was in a dream. She was losing herself as in the labyrinth, between the apparitions at the bottom of the lagoon and those of the story, and she was beginning to feel the same anxiety as reality mingled with the phantoms in her spirit. He seemed to be speaking of himself in those strange images, as when in the last hour of the September twilight he had declared to her the myth of the pomegranate; and the name of the imaginary woman began precisely with the first two syllables of the name he used to give her then! Did he wish to signify something under the veil of his story? And what then? And why did it please him, in the neighbourhood of the place where she had been seized by that horrible laughter to call up by that phantasy the memory of the broken cup?— The enchantment was broken, oblivion vanished. By trying to understand, she herself fashioned with that dream-matter an instrument of torture. She seemed to forget that her friend was unconscious of her coming farewell. She looked at him, recognised in his face the intellectual joy that always shone in him like something sharp and adamantine. Instinctively she said to herself, "I am going; do not wound me!"

"Zorzi, what is that white thing floating there under that wall?" he asked the boatman behind him.

They were coasting by Murano. The garden walls appeared and the tops of the laurel shrubs; the black smoke of the furnaces floated like mourning raiments hanging in the silvery air.

Then, with sudden horror, the actress saw the distant port where the great throbbing ship was waiting for her, saw the perpetual cloud on the brutal city of the thousand and thousand roads, with its mountains of coal, its forests of masts, its monstrous arms. She heard the thud of sledge-hammers, the creaking of the cranes, the panting of the engines, the vast moan of the iron under the burning darkness.

"It is a dead dog," said the oarsman.

A swollen, yellowish carcass was floating under the red brick wall in the cracks of which grasses and flowers trembled that were children of ruin and wind.

"Row," cried Stelio, full of disgust.

The woman closed her eyes. The boat leaped under the effort of the oars, gliding swiftly on the milky water; the sky had become quite white; an equally diffused splendour reigned on the estuary. Fishermen's voices came from a barge laden with green stuff. A twittering of sparrows came from San Giacomo di Palude. A siren screeched in the distance.

"And then the man with the scarlet thread? . . ." la Foscarina asked, anxious to hear the remainder because she wanted to understand.

"Often he felt his head shaking on his shoulders," Stelio continued, laughing. "He was obliged to blow tubes that were as thick as the trunks of trees, and

he had to do it with the art of a living mouth, not
with the strength of a bellows, and at a single breath,
and without interruptions. Imagine! The lungs of
a Cyclops would not have been sufficient. Ah, one
day I shall tell the ardour of that life placed between
the executioner's axe and the necessity of a miracle,
in communion with the elements. He had fire, earth,
and water, but air was missing, the motion of air.
Meanwhile the Ten sent him a red-haired man to bid
him good-day every morning: you know? that red-
haired man with his cap on his eyes, who stands embracing the column in the Adoration of the Magi by
the second Bonifazio. After infinite attempts a
good idea came to Dardi. That day he conversed
with the Priscianese, under the laurels of the palace,
of Æolus and his twelve sons and of the landing of
the Laertian on the western island. He re-read
Homer, Virgil, and Ovid in Aldo's beautiful types.
Then he went and sought a wizard who had the
fame of being able to cast a spell on the winds
in favour of long navigations. ' Mi gavaria bisogno
de un venteselo ne tropo forte ne tropo fiapo docile
da podermelo manipolar come che vogio mi, un
venteselo che me serva per supiar certi veri che go
in testa. . . . *Lenius aspirans aura secunda venit.* . . .
M' astu capìo, vechio?' " [1]

The story-teller burst into a ringing laugh, because
he could see the scene with all its details in a house
in the Calle de la Testa at San Zanepolo, where the

---

[1] " I am in need of a little wind, neither too strong nor too feeble,
and quite docile, that I could manage as I please; a little wind with
which to blow some glass which I have in my head. . . . *Lenius
aspirans aura secunda venit.* . . . Have you understood me, old man ? "

Schiavone lived with his daughter Cornelia Schivo
netta, honorata cortegiana (piezo so pare scudi 2).[1]

"What is the matter with him? Is he going mad?"
thought the two boatmen, on hearing him speak their
dialect, mingled with obscure words.

La Foscarina tried to second his gaiety, but she
was suffering from his youthful laughter as once
before in the mazes of the labyrinth.

"The story is long," he added; "one day I shall
do something with it, but I am keeping it for some
idle time. . . . Imagine! the Schiavone works the
spell. Every night Dardi sends his boatman to the
Tre Porti to lay the trap for the Little Wind. At
last one night not long before dawn, while the moon
is setting they surprise it sleeping on a sand-bank in
the midst of a flock of tired swallows brought hither
by it. . . . It is lying there prostrate, sleeping as
lightly as a child in the aroma of the sea-salt, almost
entirely covered by the numberless forked tails.
The rising tide favours its sleep; the black and white
travellers flutter all over it, wearied by their long
flight. . . ."

"How pretty!" exclaimed the woman at the fresh
picture. "Where have you seen it?"

"And here begins the grace of the fable: they
seize it, bind it with willows, take it on board, and
sail towards Tremòdia. The boat is invaded by the
swallows that will not abandon their leader."

Stelio stopped, because the details of the adventure were thronging to his imagination in such numbers that he did not know which of them to choose.
But he listened to a song that was in the air coming

[1] An honourable courtesan (at the house of her father, two crowns)

from the direction of San Francesco del Deserto. They could discern the slightly inclined belfry of Burano, and behind the island of thread the belfry of Torcello in its solitary splendour.

"And then," urged his companion.

"I can say no more, Fosca; I know too many things. . . . Imagine that Dardi falls in love with his prisoner. . . . Its name is Ornitio because it is the leader of migrating birds. A continual twitter of swallows is about Tremòdia; the nests hang from the posts and the shafts of the scaffolding that surrounds the work! Sometimes a wing is burnt by the flame of the furnace when Ornitio blows into the iron, making a light luminous column with the incandescent paste. Ah, but what trouble had to be gone through before it could be tamed and taught its work! The Lord of the Flame began by talking Latin to it and reciting to it some of Virgil's poetry, thinking to be understood. But the blue-haired Ornitio spoke Greek, of course, with a slightly hissing accent. . . . It knew two of Sapho's odes by heart unknown to classical scholars that it had brought one spring day from Mitylene to Chio; and in breathing through the unequal tubes, it remembered the pipe of Pan . . . One day I will tell you all these things."

"And what did it live on?"

"On pollen and salt."

"And who brought it this food?"

"No one. It was sufficient for it to breathe the pollen and the salt that are diffused in the air."

"And did it not try to escape?"

"Always. But Dardi used infinite precautions, like the lover he was."

"And did Ornitio return his love?"

"Yes, it began to return his love because it liked the scarlet thread that the master always wore round his bare neck."

"And Perdilanza?"

"She languished in her sorrow, forsaken. Some day I will tell you. . . . I will go one summer on the seashore of Palestrina to compose this fable for you by the golden sand."

"But how does it end?"

"The miracle takes place; the arch-organ is built in Tremòdia with its seven thousand glass pipes, like one of those congealed forests that Ornitio, inclined to magnify its journeys, declared it had seen in the country of the Iporborrei. And on the day of the Sensa, the *Serenissimo*, between the Patriarch and the Archbishop of Spalatro goes forth upon the harbour of San Marco in the Bucintoro. Ornitio believes it must be the Cronide returning in triumph, so great is the pomp. The cataracts are let loose round Tremòdia, and animated by the eternal silence of the lagoon, the gigantic instrument, at the magic touch of the new musician, spreads a wave of harmonies, so vast that it reaches the mainland and travels down the Adriatic. The Bucintoro stops because its forty oars have suddenly dropped along its sides like wounded wings, abandoned on their rowlocks by the bewildered crew. But suddenly the wave breaks, dwindles to a few discordant sounds, hesitates, and melts away. Dardi suddenly feels the instrument growing dumb under his hands as if its soul had failed it,— as if some strange force working in its depths had ravaged the prodigious instrument. What has happened?

All he hears is the great clamour of scorn that passes between the silenced pipes, with the noise of artillery and the tumult of the populace. A canoe leaves the Bucintoro bearing the red-haired man with his block and his axe. The blow aims at the scarlet thread. The head falls, and is thrown on the water, where it floats like the head of Orpheus. . . . "

" What had happened ? "

" Perdilanza had thrown herself in the cataract ! The water had dragged her into the depths of the organ. The body with all its famous hair thus placed itself across the great delicate instrument stifling its musical heart. . . ."

" But Ornitio ? "

" Ornitio picks up the bleeding head on the water and flies away towards the sea. The swallows hear of its flight and follow it. In a few seconds a black and white cloud of swallows thickens round the fugitive. All the nests remain empty at this sudden departure, in Venice and in the islands. The summer has no more flights. September no longer knows the farewells that once made it both sad and joyful. . . ."

" And Dardi's head ? "

" Where it can be, no one knows ! " the story-teller concluded, laughing.

And again he fell to listening to the song that was in the air, in which he was beginning to distinguish a rhythm.

" Do you hear ? " he said.

And he signed to the oarsmen to stop. The oars rested on the rowlocks.

The silence was so intense that one could hear

both the song in the distance and the dripping of the water from the posts.

"That is the wood-lark," Zorzi informed them in a subdued voice; "it still sings, poor thing, to the memory of Saint Francis."

"Row!"

The gondola glided on the milky quiet of the water.

"Would you like to row on to San Francesco, Fosca?"

The woman's head was bent in thought.

"Perhaps there is a hidden meaning in your story," she said after a pause. "Perhaps I have understood."

"Alas, yes, if there were any similarity between my daring and that of the man of Murano. I think that I too should wear as a warning a scarlet thread round my neck."

"You will have your great destiny. I have no fear for you."

His laugh ceased.

"Yes, my friend, I must win, and you shall help me. Every morning I too receive my threatening visitor, — the expectation of those who love me and of those who hate me, of my friends and of my enemies. Expectation should wear the executioner's dress because nothing on earth is more pitiless."

"But it is the measure of your power."

He felt the vulture's beak at his heart. Instinctively he drew himself up, seized by a blind impatience that made the slowness of their progress a suffering. Why was he lying idle? At every hour, at every moment, he should be feeling, struggling, increasing and asserting himself against destruction, diminution, violation and contagion. At every hour, at every moment, his eyes should be fixed on his aim, all his energies should be made to converge to it without fail and without respite. — Thus the need of glory seemed ever awakening within him a warlike instinct, the madness of struggle and retaliation.

" Do you know this maxim of the great Heraclitus,' ' the name of the bow is BIOS and its work is death ' ? This is a maxim that excites our spirit even before communicating to it its precise meaning. I heard it continually repeated within me while sitting at your table that autumn night at the Epiphany of the Flame. I went through an hour of truly Dionysian life, an hour of delirium restrained but as terrible as if I were holding in myself the burning mountain where the Thyades howl and writhe. Now and then I actually seemed to hear songs and clamours and the cries of a distant massacre. And it surprised me that I could remain motionless, and the sense of my bodily stillness seemed to increase my deep frenzy, and I could see nothing else but your face, which had suddenly become most beautiful ; and in your whole person I could see the might of all your soul, and behind it I could also see other countries and multitudes. Ah, if I could only tell you how I saw you in the tumult while the marvellous images passed accompanied by gusts of music ! I spoke to you as if across a battle-field. I threw out a rallying cry that you perhaps heard, not for love only, but for glory, not for one thirst, but for two thirsts, and I knew not which was the most ardent. And the face of my work appeared to me then the same as your face. I saw it ! Do you hear ? With incredible rapidity my work shaped itself into words and song and gesture and symphony. It was so living that if only I succeeded in breathing a small part of it into the forms I wish to express I could truly inflame the world."

He spoke, controlling his voice; and the smothered impulse of his words seemed to have a strange reflection in the calm water, in the white glare that prolonged the even cadence of the two oars.

"Expression, that is the necessity. The greatest vision has no value unless it be manifested and condensed in living forms. And I have everything to create. I am not pouring my substance into hereditary forms. My whole work is an invention; I cannot and will not obey other than my own instinct and the genius of my race. And, nevertheless, like Dardi, who saw the famous organ in the house of Caterino Zeno, I too have another work before my spirit, a work accomplished by a formidable creator that stands gigantic in the midst of men."

The image of the barbaric creator reappeared to him; the blue eyes shone under the vast forehead; the lips tightened above the robust chin armed with sensuality and pride and disdain. Then he saw once more the white hair blown about by the sharp wind on the aged neck, under the wide brim of the felt hat and the almost livid ear with the swollen lobe. Then he saw the motionless body lying unconscious on the knees of the woman with the face of snow, and the slight tremor in one of the hanging feet. He thought of his own ineffable quiver of fear and joy when he had suddenly felt that sacred heart beating again beneath his hand.

"Ah! not before but round my spirit, I should

say. Sometimes it is like the sea in a tempest, trying to drag me down and swallow me. My Temodia is a rock of granite in the open sea, and I am like an artisan intent on building up on it a pure Doric temple, having to defend the order of his columns from the violence of the waves, his spirit incessantly strained that he may never cease through all that noise to hear the secret rhythm which alone must regulate the intervals between his lines and his spaces. In this sense, too, my Tragedy is a battle."

Once more he saw the patrician palace as it had appeared to him in the early October dawn with its eagles, its horses, its pitchers, and its roses, closed and dumb like a great sepulchre, while above it the breath of the day was kindling the sky.

" In that dawn," he added, " passing through the Canal after the night's delirium, I gathered from a garden wall some violet flowers that grew in the interstices of the brick, and I made the gondola stop by the Palazzo Vendramin and threw them before the door. The offering was too small; I thought of laurels and myrtles and cypresses. But the spontaneous act served to express my gratitude towards Him who was to impose on my spirit the necessity of being heroic in its liberating and creating effort."

Bursting into sudden laughter, he turned to the oarsman at the poop: —

" Do you remember, Zorzi, our regatta one morning to reach the *braghozzo* ? "

" Indeed I remember ! What a row it was ! My arms are still stiff ! And that rascally hunger, master, where do you put it? Every time I see the master of the boat, he asks after the stranger who ate up that loaf of bread with that basket of figs and raisins. He says that he will never forget that day, because he drew the heaviest net of his life. He caught such mackerel as is never to be seen. . . ."

The oarsman went on chattering until he noticed that his master was no longer listening to him and that he was expected to keep quiet, even to hold his breath.

" Do you hear the song? " said Stelio to his friend, gently taking one of her hands because it distressed him to have awakened a memory which gave her pain.

Raising her face she said : —

"Where is it? Is it in Heaven? Is it on earth?"

An endless melody was flowing over the peaceful whiteness.

She said : —

" How it rises ! "

She felt a quiver pass through her friend's hand.

"When Alessandro enters the illuminated room where the virgin has been reading the lamentation of Antigone," he said, gathering from his consciousness some sign of the obscure process which was going on in the depths of his mystery, " he tells how he has come on horseback through the plain of Argos, crossing the Inachus, a river of burnt up flint; the whole country is covered with little wild flowers that are dying, and the song of the larks fills the sky . . . thousands of skylarks, a multitude without number. . . . He tells how one fell all of a sudden at the feet of his horse, heavy as a stone, and remained there silent, struck down by its own frenzy, by having sung with too much joy. He picked it up. 'Here it is.' You then hold out your hand towards him; you take it and murmur: 'Ah, it is still warm.' . . . While you are speaking the virgin trembles. You can feel her trembling." . . .

Again the tragic actress felt the chill at the roots of her hair as if the soul of the blind woman were re-entering her own soul.

"At the end of the Prelude the impetus of the chromatic progressions expresses this growing joy, the anxiety of delight. . . . Listen, listen! . . . Ah, what a marvel! This morning, Fosca, only this morning I was at my work. . . . My own melody now develops itself in the heavens. . . . Is not grace upon us?"

A spirit of life was running through the solitude; a vehement aspiration filled the silence with emotion. It seemed as if a natural desire of ascension were passing like an awakening, or the announcement of some great return, over the motionless lines, the empty horizon, the flat waters, and the outstretched shores. The woman gave up her whole soul to it as a leaf gives itself up to the whirlwind, ravished to the heights of love and faith. But a feverish impatience to act, a desire of work, a need of hastening the accomplishment, seized the young man. His capacity for work seemed multiplied. He considered the fulness of the hours to come. He saw the concrete aspects of his work, the mass of pages, the volume of scores, the variety of the task, the wealth of the substances capable of receiving rhythm. In the same way he saw the Roman hill, the rising building, the harmony of cut stones, the workmen busy with their masonry, the architect watching them, severe and vigilant, the Vatican standing before the Theatre of

Apollo, and the Holy City beneath it. Smiling, he called up the image of the little man who was supporting the work with truly papal magnificence, saluting the bloodless, large-nosed figure of the Roman prince who had not degenerated from the traditions of his name, and who, with the gold accumulated in centuries of plunder and nepotism, was building up an harmonious temple for the Renaissance of the Arts that had thrown a ray of beauty on the mighty lives of his fathers.

"In a week's time, Fosca, if grace assist me, my prelude will be finished. I should like to try it with an orchestra immediately. I shall perhaps go to Rome for this. Antimo della Bella is more anxious even than I am. I get a letter from him nearly every morning. I think my presence in Rome for a few days is necessary also in order to avoid some error in the construction of the Theatre. Antimo writes concerning the possibility of pulling down the old stone steps leading from the Corsini Garden to the Janiculum. I don't know whether you remember the aspect of the place? The road that will lead to the Theatre passes under the Arch of Septimus, turns along the side of the Palazzo Corsini, crosses the garden, and reaches the foot of the hill. The hill — do you remember? — is all green, covered with little fields, canes, cypresses, plane-trees, laurels, and olm-oaks; it has a wooded and sacred look, with its crown of tall Italian pines. There is quite a forest of holm-oaks on its slope watered by subterranean streams. All the hill is steeped in a wealth of living waters. The fountain Paulina towers on the left. The Parrasio wood, the ancient seat of the

Arcadi, blackens below it. A flight of stone steps in two branches, passing along a succession of wide, overflowing basins, leads to a raised plain from which open two paths flanked by truly Apollo-like laurels, indeed worthy of leading men towards poetry. Who could imagine a more noble entrance? Centuries have shrouded it in mystery; the stone of the steps, of the balustrades, of the basins, of the statues, vies in roughness with the bark of the venerable plane-trees that old age has made hollow. No sound is heard but the song of birds, the splash of the fountains, and the murmur of leaves. Ah! and I believe that poets and simple souls can even hear the throb of the Hamadryads and the breath of Pan. . . ."

The aerial chorus was rising, rising untiringly, filling every space with itself like the immense desert, like the infinite light. The impetuous melody created in the sleep of the lagoon, the illusion of a unanimous anxiety that rose from the waters, from the sands, from the grasses, from the vapours, from all natural things to follow the ascension. All those things which had seemed inert, now seemed to be breathing deeply, to be gifted with a soul that was full of emotion, possessed by a desire of expression.

" Listen! Listen!"

And the images of life created by the Life-giver, and the ancient names of those immortal energies circulating in the Universe, and the aspirations of men to transcend the circle of their daily torment, to appease themselves in the splendour of an Idea, and all wishes, and hopes, and daring, and effort in that place of hope and oblivion, before that humble island where the Spouse of Poverty had left the traces

of himself, seemed delivered from the shadow of
Death by the mere virtue of that song.

"Does it not seem like the frenzied joy of an
assault?"

The squalid shores, the crumbling stones, the
putrefying roots, the traces of destroyed works,
the odours of dissolution, the funereal cypresses, the
black crosses, in vain reminded him of the same
words that the statues along the river had spoken
with their lips of stone. Only that song of victory
and liberty, stronger than all other signs, touched
the heart of him who was to create with joy. "On!
on! Higher! ever higher!"

And the heart of Perdita, purified from all cowardice, ready for every test, seconding the hymn's ascension, betrothed itself to life again. As in the distant
hour of that night's delirium the woman repeated:
"Let me serve! Let me serve!"

The boat entered a canal closed between two green
banks, which reached the line of the eye so precisely
that one could see the numberless reeds and point
out the new ones by their lighter colour.

> " Laudato si, mi signore, per sora nostra matre terra,
>   la quale ne sustenta et governa
>   et produce diversi fructi con coloriti flori et herba."

From the fulness of her soul the woman measured
the love of the Poor Man of Assisi for all created
things. Such was her abundance that she sought for
living things to worship everywhere; and her look

[1] "Be praised, my Lord, for our Lady the Mother Earth who feeds
and governs us and brings forth divers fruits with coloured flowers
and grass."

became childlike again, and all those things were reflected in it as in the peace of the water, and some seemed to return from the far past and reappear like unexpected apparitions.

When the ship touched the shore, she was astonished at having arrived already.

"Would you like to land or would you prefer to go back?" Stelio asked her, pulling himself together.

She hesitated a moment, because her hand was in his, and the separation would have been a lessening of the sweetness.

"Yes," she answered, smiling. "Let us walk a little on this grass too."

They landed on the island of San Francesco. A few young cypress-trees greeted them shyly. No human face appeared. The invisible myriads filled the desert with their praise. The mist was rising, massing into clouds, obscuring the sun.

"How much grass we have walked on, have we not, Stelio?"

He said, —

"But now comes the steep boulder to climb."

She said, —

"Let the boulder come and let the ascent be steep."

He wondered at the unusual joy in her tone. He looked at her and saw intoxication in her beautiful eyes.

"Why," said he, "do we feel so free and happy in this lonely island?"

"Do you know why?"

"This is a sad pilgrimage for other people. Those who come to this place leave it with the taste of death in their mouths."

She said: —

" We are in a state of grace."

He said : —

" They who hope most, live most."

She said : —

" They who love most, hope most."

The rhythm of the aerial song went on, attracting their ideal essences.

He said : —

" How beautiful you are ! "

A sudden blush covered the impassioned face. She paused for a moment, quivering. She half closed her eyes. In a suppressed voice she said : —

" A warm current is passing. Did you not feel a rush of warmth on the water from time to time ? "

She drank the air in.

" There is something like a smell of new-mown hay. Do you notice it ? "

" It is the smell of the banks full of seaweeds that are being uncovered."

" Look what a beautiful landscape."

" Le Vignole. And that is the Lido. And that is the island of Sant' Erasmo."

The sun had cast its veils and was now embracing the estuary. The moisture of the emerging sand-banks suggested the brightness of flowers. The shadows of the small cypress-trees were beginning to lengthen and becoming of a deeper blue.

" I am sure," she said, " that almond-trees are blossoming in the neighbourhood. Let us go on the dyke."

She threw her head back with one of those movements that were natural to her, that seemed to break a bond or rid her of an impediment.

" Wait ! "

And drawing out the two pins that fastened her hat, she quickly uncovered her head. She went back to the steps of the landing and threw the shining thing into the gondola. Then she returned to her friend nimbly, running her fingers through the mass of her hair, and the air passed through it and the sun shone on it. She seemed to feel relieved, as if her breathing were easier.

" Did the wings hurt? " said Stelio, laughing.

And he looked at the rough furrow, not ploughed by the comb, but by the storm.

" Yes, the smallest weight worries me. If it did not seem strange, I should always go bareheaded. But when I see the trees, I cannot hold out any more. My hair remembers its wild birth, and longs to breathe in its own way, in the desert at least."

She spoke frankly and vivaciously, walking on the grass with her quick swinging movement. And Stelio remembered the day when, in the Gradenigo garden, she had seemed to him very like the beautiful tawny greyhound.

" Oh, here is a Capuchin friar ! "

The friar was coming towards them and greeted them affably. He offered to show the visitors round the monastery, but informed them that the cloister was closed to his companion.

" Shall I go in? " said Stelio, looking at his companion, who was smiling.

" Yes, go ! "

" And you will remain alone? "

" I will remain alone."

" I will bring you a piece of the sacred pine-tree."

He followed the Franciscan under the portico where the empty swallows' nests hung from the raftered ceiling. Before crossing the threshold he turned once more to say good-bye to his companion. The door closed upon him

"O BEATA SOLITUDO!
O SOLA BEATITUDO!"

Then, as a sudden change in one of the stops at once changes all the notes in an organ, all the woman's thoughts were transfigured. The horror of absence, the worst of all evils, stood before her loving soul. Her friend was no longer there: she no longer heard his voice, no longer felt him breathing; she no longer grasped his kind, firm hand. She no longer saw him live, no longer felt the air, the light, the shadows, the whole life of the world, harmonise with his life. "What if he should not come back, if that door were not to reopen?" It could not be. He would certainly cross that threshold again in a few minutes, and she would receive him again into her eyes and her very being. But it was thus, thus, that he would disappear in a few days; and first the plain, then the mountain, and then plains and mountains and rivers, and then the strait and the ocean, the infinite spaces that cries and tears cannot overcome, would step between her and that forehead, those eyes, those lips. The image of the brutal city to which she was going, blackened by coal and bristling with weapons, filled the quiet island. The crash of sledge-hammers, the shriek of cranes, the panting of engines, the immense groan of iron, drowned the melody of spring. And in contrast to each of those simple things, to the grass, the sands, the water, the seaweed, the soft feather dropping perhaps from the throat of a song-bird, there appeared streets, invaded by the human stream, houses with their thousand deformed eyes, full of fevers that make sleep unknown, theatres filled with the breath or the stupor of a crowd that has relaxed for an hour the tension of its will and fiercely outstretched in the war of lucre. And she saw her name and her portrait on walls defiled by advertisements, on boards carried about by stupefied porters, on great factory bridges, on the doors of swift vehicles, high and low and everywhere.

"Here! look! The branch of an almond-tree. The almond-tree is blossoming in the convent garden, in the second cloister, near the grotto with the sacred pine-tree. And you knew it!"

Her friend was hastening to her, joyful as a child, followed by the Capuchin friar, who was holding a little bunch of thyme.

"Take it! See what a marvel!"

Tremblingly she took the branch, and tears dimmed her eyes.

"You knew it!"

He noticed the sudden brightness between her eyelashes, something tender and silvery, — a shining and trembling moisture which made the white of her eyes like the petals of a flower. Of all her beloved person, he passionately loved the delicate marks that went from the corners of the eyes to the temples, and the small dark veins which made the eyelids like violets, and the undulation of the cheeks, and the weary chin, and all that could not flower again, all the shadows on the impassioned face.

"Ah, Father," she said with a merry look, restraining her sorrow, "will not Christ's Poor Man weep in heaven for this torn off branch?"

The Father smiled with sprightly indulgence.

"This good gentleman," he answered, "did not give me time to say a word when he saw the tree. He already had the branch in his hand, and all I could say was 'Amen.' But the almond-tree is rich."

He was placid and affable, with a crown of hair nearly all black still round the tonsure, with a refined, olive face, with two large tawny eyes, shining as clear as topazes.

"Here is the savoury thyme," he said, offering the herbs.

They heard a choir of young voices singing a Response.

"They are the novices; we have fifteen of them."

And he accompanied the visitors to the field behind the convent. Standing on the bank, at the foot of a cypress-tree that had been destroyed by lightning, the Franciscan pointed to the fertile islands, praised their fruitfulness, enumerated their kinds of fruit, extolled the most luscious according to the various seasons, pointed out the boats sailing to the Rialto with the new crops.

"Be praised to Thee, O Master, for our Mother Earth," said the woman with the blossoming branch.

The friar, sensitive to the tenderness of that feminine voice, was silent.

Tall cypress-trees surrounded the pious meadow; and four of them,—the oldest,—leafless, sapless, bore signs of lightning. Their tops were motionless,—the only emerging things in that level posture of the fields and waters that stretched on a line with the horizon. Not even the faintest breeze ruffled the infinite mirror. The depths full of seaweeds were transparent and seemed like bright treasures; the marsh reeds shone like rods of amber; the freshly uncovered sands had the changing colours of mother-of-pearl; the very mud imitated the opaline tenderness of the medusæ. A profound enchantment that was like rapture filled the desert with joy. The melody of winged creatures still continued from invisible places; but it, too, seemed to be quieting down at last into the holy silence.

"At this time, on the hills of Umbria," said he who had robbed the almond-tree in the cloister, "every olive-tree has at its feet, like a cast-off slough, a bunch of its cut branches; and it seems tenderer because the bunch hides the roughness of the crooked roots. Saint Francis passes in mid-air healing with his finger the pain of the wounds made by the pruning knife."

The friar crossed himself and took his leave.

"Praise be to Jesus Christ!"

The guests saw him moving away among the shadows cast by the cypress-trees on the meadow.

"He is in peace," said the woman. "Does it not seem to you, Stelio? A great peace was on his face and in his voice. Look at his step, too."

First a ray of sunshine, then a ray of shadow, touched his tonsure and his tunic.

"He gave me a splinter of the pine-tree," said Stelio. "I will send it to Sophia, who has a great devotion for the Seraphic Saint. Here it is. It no longer smells of resin. Smell it."

For Sophia's sake she kissed the relic. The lips of the good sister would be laid on the same place where hers had rested.

"Send it."

They walked in silence a while with lowered heads, in the footsteps of the man who was at peace, going towards the quay between the rows of cypress-trees laden with berries.

"Do you not want to see her again?" la Foscarina asked her friend with a tremor of shyness.

"Yes, very much."

"And your mother?"

"Yes; my heart goes out to her who daily expects me."

"And you would not like to go back?"

"Yes, I will go back, perhaps."

"When?"

"I do not know yet, but I long to see my mother and Sophia. I desire it indeed greatly, Foscarina."

"And why do you not go? What keeps you here?"

He took the hand that was hanging loosely at her side, and they continued their walk. As the oblique rays of the sun lighted up their right cheeks, they saw their united shadows preceding them at one level on the grass.

"When you pictured to yourself the hills of Umbria a moment ago," said the woman, "perhaps you were thinking of the hills of your own country. That figure of the pruned olive-trees was not a new one to me. I remember your talking to me one day of the pruning. . . . In no other labour can the peasant acquire a deeper sense of the dumb life that is in the tree.

When he stands in front of the apple or pear or peach
tree with the pruning knife and scissors that should
increase their strength and could at the same time
cause their death, the spirit of divination rises in him
from all the wisdom acquired in his communings with
earth and sky. The tree is then at its most delicate
moment, when its sensibility re-awakens, flowing to
the buds which are swollen and about to open. Man
with his cruel knife must regulate the mysterious
movements of the sap. The tree is still intact,
ignorant of Hesiod and Virgil, labouring with its
blossom and its fruit, and every branch in the air is
as much alive as an artery in the arm of the pruner.
Which is the one to be lopped off? Will the sap
heal the wound? . . . Thus, one day you spoke to
me of your orchard. I remember. You told me
that all the cuts should be turned to the north that
the sun should not see them."

She was speaking as on that distant November
evening when the young man had come to her
through the violent wind, panting after having carried
the hero.

He smiled. He let the dear hand lead him. And
he drank in the fragrance of the blossoming branch,
very like the smell of some bitter milk.

"It is true," he said. "And Laimo would prepare the ointment of Saint Fiacre, mixing it in the
mortar, and Sophia would bring him the strong
linen to bind the larger wounds, after they had been
dressed. . . ."

He could see the peasant on his knees mixing cow-
dung, clay, and barley husks in the stone mortar,
according to the rules of antique wisdom.

"But in ten days," he added, "the whole hill seen from the sea will be like a fresh, rosy cloud. Sophia has written to remind me of it. . . . Has she appeared to you any more?"

"She is with us now."

"She is looking out of the window at the sea, which has become purple, and my mother is with her at the window, and she is saying, 'Who knows if Stelio may not be in that sailing boat waiting at the mouth of the river for the coming of the wind? He promised me he would return unexpectedly by sea, in a brig.' And her heart aches."

"Ah, why do you disappoint her?"

"Yes, it is true, Fosca; I can be away for months and months, and feel that my life is full. But then, an hour comes when nothing in the world seems to me sweeter than those eyes; and there is a part of myself that remains inconsolable. I have heard the sailors of the Tyrrhenean Sea call the Adriatic the Gulf of Venice. To-night I am thinking that my home is on the Gulf, and that seems to bring it nearer."

They were at the landing. They turned to look once more at the island of Prayer with its beseeching cypresses.

"Yonder is the canal of the Tre Porti that leads to the open sea," he said, homesick. He saw himself on the deck of the brig in sight of his tamarisks and myrtle-trees.

They went on board. They were silent for a long time. Quietly, meanwhile, the melody descended on the archipelago. As the light from the sky penetrated the waters, so the song from the sky came and rested on the fields. But Burano and Torcello appeared like two broken galleons against the dazzling west, and the clouds were ranging themselves in phalanxes, down towards the Dolomites.

"Now that the scheme of the work is finished, all you want is peace for your work," said the woman, softly continuing her persuasion, while her soul trembled in her breast. "Have you not always worked best in your own home? In no other place will you be able to appease the anxiety which oppresses you. I know it."

He said: —

"It is true. When the craving for glory seizes us, we believe that the conquest of art resembles the siege of a stronghold, and that noise and sound accompany the bravery of the assault. But it is only the work which has grown in the austerity of silence that is of any value; only the work done with slow and indomitable perseverance; work done in hard, pure solitude. Nothing is of any value but the complete surrender of spirit and flesh to the Idea which we long to establish among men as a commanding force for ever."

"Ah, you know it."

The woman's eyes filled with tears on hearing his smooth words, in which she felt all the depth of his manly passion, the heroic need of spiritual dominion, the firm determination to surpass himself and to force his destiny.

"You know it!"

And she felt a shudder like that which is caused by cruel sights; and in the face of that living will everything else seemed vain, and the other tears that had blinded her when he had offered her the blossoms seemed mean and effeminate compared with those that were now rushing to her eyes, and were alone worthy to be drunk in by her friend.

"Well, then, go back to your sea, to your own lands, to your house. Re-light your lamp with the oil of your own olives."

His lips were closed, and there was a furrow between his eyelids.

"The kind sister will come again to lay a blade of grass on the difficult page."

He bent his brow which a thought was oppressing.

"You will rest by talking to Sophia at the window, and perhaps you will see the flocks passing again on their way from the plains to the mountains."

The sun was nearing the gigantic acropolis of the Dolomites. The immense phalanx of clouds was disordered as if by a battle, shot through by numberless beaming arrows, and bathed in a marvellous blood-like crimson. The waters extended the great battle fought round the impregnable towers. The melody had melted into the shadow of the already distant islands. The whole estuary seemed mantled in gloomy warlike magnificence as if myriads of flags were bending over it, a silence that seemed only waiting for a flourish of imperial trumpets.

Softly, after a long pause, he said: —

"And if she were to question me about the fate of the virgin who reads the lamentation of Antigone?"

The woman started.

"And if she were to question me about the love of the brother who searches the tombs?"

The phantom filled the woman with fear.

"And if the page on which she lays the blade of

grass were the one where the trembling soul tells its desperate hidden fight against the horrible evil?"

The woman could find no words in her sudden dismay. Both remained silent, gazing at the sharp peaks of the mountains in the distance, which shone as if they had only just emerged from primordial fire. The sight of that solitary, eternal grandeur brought a sense of strange fatality to their two souls and almost an uncertain terror, which they could neither conquer nor scrutinise. Venice was darkened by the masses of burning porphyries; she lay on the waters all wrapped in a violet veil; from it the marble pillars emerged, carved by man to guard the bells that give the signal for customary prayer. But the customary work and prayer of man, the old city tired with having lived too long, its mutilated marbles and its worn-out bells, — all those things oppressed by the weight of memories, and all perishable, become lowly in comparison with the tremendous inflamed Alps that lacerated the sky with their thousand inflexible points, themselves an enormous, solitary city, waiting perhaps for a young nation of Titans.

Abruptly, after the long silence, Stelio Effrena asked the woman: —

"And you?"

She did not answer.

The bells of San Marco gave the signal for the Angelus, and the powerful roll dilated in long waves over the still crimsoned lagoon which they were leaving in the hands of shadow and death. From San Giorgio Maggiore, from San Giorgio dei Greci, from San Giorgio degli Schiavoni, from San Giovanni in

Bragora, from San Moise, from the Salute, from the Redentore, and on through the whole domain of the Evangelists, from the far towers of the Madonna dell' Orto, of San Giobbe, of Sant' Andrea, the bronze voices answered, mingled in one great chorus spreading on the quiet gathering of stones and waters one great invisible dome of metal which seemed to communicate by its vibrations with the twinkling of the first stars.

Both shivered when the gondola entered the damp of the dark Rio, passing under the bridge that looked towards the island of San Michele, passing near the black *peate* putrefying along the corroded walls. From the nearest belfries, from San Lazzaro, from San Canciano, from San Giovanni e Paolo, from Santa Maria dei Miracoli, from Santo Maria del Pianto, other voices answered. And the roll above their heads was so strong that they seemed to feel its vibration in the very roots of their hair like a quiver of their own flesh.

" Is it you, Daniele? "

It seemed to Stelio that he had recognised the figure of Daniele Glauro on the Fondamenta Sanudo, near the door of his house.

" Oh, Stelio, I was waiting for you ! " cried the agitated voice, in the storm of sound. " Richard Wagner is dead."

The world seemed to have lost value.

The wandering woman armed herself with her courage and went on preparing her viaticum. From the hero lying on his bier a great inspiration rose to all noble hearts. She knew how to receive it and convert it into living thoughts and actions.

It happened that her friend came upon her while she was collecting her familiar books, the small things that were never parted from her, the pictures that had over her a power of enchantment or of consolation.

"What are you doing?" he asked.

"I am preparing to start."

She saw his face change, but did not hesitate.

"Where are you going?"

"Far away. I am crossing the Atlantic."

He became a shade paler. And at once he doubted; thought that perhaps she was not speaking the truth; that perhaps she was only sounding him; that the resolve was not a fixed one, and that she was only expecting to be urged to stay.

His unexpected disappointment on the shores of Murano had left its traces on his heart.

"Have you decided on it, then, all of a sudden?"

She was simple, sure, and ready.

"Not all of a sudden," she answered. "My idleness has been lasting too long, and I have the burden of all my people upon me. While I wait for the Theatre of Apollo to be opened and for 'The Victory of Man' to be ready, I shall go and take my leave of the Barbarians. I will work for the great undertaking. We will need a great deal of gold to build up again the treasures of Mycene! And everything connected with your work should have the aspect of an unusual magnificence. I do not want the mask of Cassandra to be of some base metal. . . . And what I especially want, is to satisfy your desire: that the people shall have free access to the Theatre for the first three days, and always after that, on one day in the week. This faith helps me to leave you. Time flies. Every one must be at his place, in full possession of all his powers, when the time comes. I will not fail you. I hope you will be satisfied with your friend. I am going to work; and certainly I find it more difficult this once than at other times. But you, but you, my poor child, what a burden you have to bear! What an effort we are asking of you! What great things we expect from you! Ah, you know it! . . ."

She had begun bravely, in a tone that at times had seemed almost cheerful, trying to appear what she was meant to be above all, — a good and faithful instrument at the service of genius; a virile, willing companion. But some wave of repressed emotion, escaping, would come into her throat and choke her voice. Her pauses became longer, and her hand became uncertain in its wandering among her books and relics.

"May all things be ever propitious to your work! This only matters; all the rest is nothing. Let us keep our hearts on high!"

She shook back her head with its two wild wings, and held out her two hands to her friend. He pressed them, pale and serious. In her dear eyes that were like living springs of water he caught a gleam of the same flash of beauty that had dazzled him one night in the room where the logs roared, and he had heard the unfolding of the two splendid melodies.

"I love you and believe in you," he said; "I will not fail you, and you will not fail me. Something proceeds from us that will be stronger than life."

She said : —

" A melancholy."

The familiar books lay on the table before he
with their dogs' ears and marked margins, with some
leaves, a flower, a blade of grass between page and
page, with their landmarks of the sorrows which
had asked and obtained from them consolations of
enlightenment or oblivion. All the small beloved
objects were scattered before her, strange, various
and nearly all valueless things, — a doll's foot, a votive
offering in the shape of a silver heart, a small ivory
compass, a dialless watch, a little iron lantern, an odd
earring, a flint, a key, a seal, other refuse ; but all
were consecrated by some memory, animated by
some superstitious belief, touched by the finger of
love or death, relics that could only speak to one soul
and that spoke to it of tenderness and cruelty, of war
and peace, of hope and dejection. Before her, too,
were images suggesting thought, and disposing for
reflection, — figures to which artists had intrusted a
secret confession, mazes of signs in which they had
enclosed an enigma, simple lines that imparted peace
like a glimpse of the horizon, profound allegories
veiling some truth that, like the sun, could not be
gazed on by mortal eyes.

" Look," she said, to her friend, pointing to an old
engraving, " you know it well."

They both knew it well, yet together they bent
down to examine it again, and it seemed to them as
new as music which, whenever questioned, gives
some different answer. It came from the hand of
Albert Dürer.

The great Angel of Earth with the eagle's wings

the sleepless spirit crowned with patience, sat on the bare stone with his elbow on his knee, his cheek supported on his hand, a book on his other knee, and a compass in his other hand. At his feet, coiled round like a serpent, lay the faithful greyhound, the dog which has hunted side by side with man from the very dawn of time. By his side, almost crouching on the edge of a millstone, like a bird, slept a child, sad already, holding the style and the tablet with which to write down the first word of his science. All round him were scattered the instruments of the works of man, and on his watchful head, near the summit of a wing, the silent sands of time ran through their hourglass; and in the background there was the sea with its gulfs and its ports and its lighthouses, the calm, unconquerable sea over which, when the sun had set in its rainbow glory, the twilight bat would fly with the revealing word written on its membrane. And those ports and those lighthouses and those cities were the work of the sleepless spirit crowned with patience. He had broken the stone for the towers, cut down the pine-tree for the ships, tempered the iron for every struggle. He himself had laid on Time the instrument that measures it. Seated not to rest, but to meditate on some new work to be accomplished, he fixed on life the powerful eyes shining with the free light of the sun. Silence rose up to him from every surrounding form but one. And that only voice was the voice of the roaring fire in the furnace, under the crucible where sublimated matter would presently generate some new force that would serve to cure some evil, or to teach some law. And this was the answer of the great Angel of

Earth with the eagle's wings from whose steel-bound flank hung the keys that open and shut, to those who were questioning him: "The sun sets. The light that is born in the heavens dies in the heavens, and each day is ignorant of the light of another day. But the night is one, and its shadow is on every countenance, and its blindness is in every eye except on the countenance and in the eyes of him who feeds his fire in order to illumine his strength. I know that the living are as the dead, the waking as the sleeping, the young as the old, because the change of the one brings forth the other, and each change has pain and joy for equal companions. I know that the harmony of the Universe is made of discords as in the lyre and in the bow. I know that I am and that I am not, and that one alone is the way, high or low. I know the putrid odour and the numberless infections that go hand in hand with human nature. And yet, beyond my knowledge, I continue the accomplishment of my manifest or secret works. I see some perish while I still last, I see others that seem as if they must last eternally beautiful and exempt from all miseries, no longer mine, although born from my deepest evils. I see all things changing before fire as fortunes do before gold. Only one thing is constant and that thing is my courage. I can never sit down except to rise again."

The young man passed his arm round his friend's waist; and together, speechless, they went to the window.

They saw the far, far distant sky, the trees, the cupolas, the towers, the end of the lagoon over which the face of twilight was bending, and the Euganean hills as quiet and blue as if they were the wings of earth folded in the repose of evening.

They turned, facing each other, looking into the depths of each other's eyes.

Then they kissed each other, as if sealing an unspoken compact.

The world seemed to have lost value.

Stelio Effrena had asked the widow of Richard Wagner for the two young Italians who had carried the unconscious hero from the boat to the shore one November night, and four of their companions, to be granted the honour of carrying the bier from the death-chamber to the boat and from the boat to the carriage. She had granted it.

It was the sixteenth of February. It was one o'clock in the afternoon. Stelio Effrena, Daniele Glauro, Francesco de Lizo, Baldassare Stampa, Fabio Molza, and Antimo della Bella were waiting in the hall of the palace. The latter had arrived from Rome after having obtained permission to bring with him two artisans engaged in the construction of the Theatre of Apollo, that they might carry at the funeral bunches of laurels gathered on the Janiculum.

Speechless, without even looking at each other, they waited, each overcome by the beating of his own heart. Nothing was heard except the feeble splash of the water on the steps of the great door where on the candelabra at the doorposts two words were engraved, *Domus Pacis*.

The boatman, who had been dear to the hero, came

down and called them. His eyes, in his faithful manly face, were burnt by tears.

Stelio Effrena went first; his companions followed him. When they had ascended the staircase, they entered a low half-dark room, full of a sad odour of flowers and perfume. They waited a few seconds. The other door opened. One by one they entered the adjoining room; one by one they turned pale.

The body was there, shut in its crystal coffin, and standing beside it was the woman with the face of snow. The second coffin of burnished metal shone open on the pavement.

The six bearers stood before the body waiting for the signal. The silence was very great, and none stirred; but an impetuous sorrow had forced itself into their souls like a gust of wind, and was shaking them to their deepest roots.

All were gazing fixedly at the chosen one of Life and Death; an infinite smile illumined the face of the prostrate hero — a smile as distant and infinite as the rainbow of a glacier, as the gleam of the sea, as the halo of a star. They could not bear to see it, but their hearts, with a wondering fear that made them religious, felt as if they were receiving the revelation of a divine secret.

The woman with the face of snow moved slightly, yet remained in the same attitude, rigid as a monument.

Then the six companions moved towards the bier, held out their arms, gathered up their strength. Stelio Effrena had his place at the head and Daniele Glauro at the foot, as on that other day. They raised their burden at one effort, at a low command from their leader. A glamour struck their eyes as if a belt of sun had crossed the glass. Baldassare Stampa broke into sobs. One same knot gripped all their throats. The coffin wavered, then was lowered again, entered its metal wrapper as in an armour.

The six companions remained prostrate all round, hesitating before closing the cover, fascinated by that infinite smile. On hearing a slight rustle, Stelio Effrena looked up. He saw the face of snow bending over the body, like a superhuman apparition of love and sorrow. That second was like all eternity. The woman disappeared.

When the coffin was closed, they lifted up its increased weight; they bore it slowly out of the room and down the staircase. Wrapped in a kind of sublime anguish, they could see their fraternal faces reflected in the metal case.

The funeral boat awaited them at the door. The pall was drawn over the coffin. The six companions waited with bared heads for the family to come down. It came, gathered close together. The widow passed veiled. But the splendour of her countenance was in their memories for ever.

The procession was brief: the funeral boat went first; the widow followed with her dear ones, then the group of young men. The sky was encumbered with clouds, above the wide pathway of stone and water. The great silence was worthy of Him who had transformed the forces of the Universe for man's worship into infinite song.

A flock of pigeons, starting from the marbles of the Scalsi, flew with a quivering flash over the bier and across the canal, wreathing the cupola of San Simeone.

At the landing a silent group of devoted friends was waiting. The large wreaths perfumed the grey air; they could hear the water beating under the curved prows. The six companions lifted the coffin from the boat and carried it on their shoulders to the compartment that was waiting for it in the station. The friends drew near and laid their wreaths on the pall. No word was spoken.

The two artisans drew near with their bunches of laurels gathered on the Janiculum.

They were vigorous, powerful men, chosen among the strongest and finest, and they seemed to be shaped in the ancient mould of the Roman race. They were quiet and grave, with all the wild liberty of the Agro in their bloodshot eyes. Their strong outlines, narrow forehead, low crisp hair, firm jaws and bull-like neck, recalled the profile of some of the Consuls of old. Their attitude, exempt from any servile obsequiousness, made them worthy of their mission.

The six companions in turn, equal now in their fervour, strewed branches from the bunches of laurel over the hero's coffin.

Noble indeed were those Latin laurels, cut from the shrubs of the hill where, in the days of remote antiquity, the eagles descended with their prophecies, where in recent though still fabulous times a stream of blood has been shed for the beauty of Italy by the soldiers of the Liberator. They were straight, dark robust branches; the leaves were hard, strongly veined, with sharp margins, green as the bronze of fountains, rich with the aroma of triumph.

And they travelled towards the Bavarian hill still slumbering under its frost, while their noble trunks were already budding in the light of Rome to the murmur of hidden springs.

SETTIGNANO DI DESIDERIO:
XIII DI FEBRUARY, MDCCC.

HORACE BRODZKY · 10